DON'T MISS ANY OF
CHRISTOPHER ROWE'S ADVENTURES

THE BLACKTHORN KEY

MARK OF THE PLAGUE

THE ASSASSIN'S CURSE

A
BLACKTHORN KEY
ADVENTURE

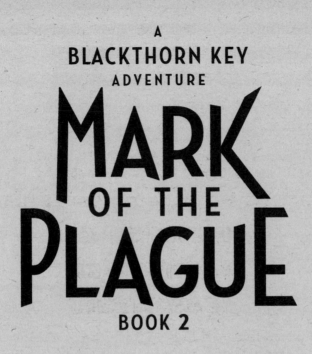

MARK
OF THE
PLAGUE

BOOK 2

KEVIN SANDS

ALADDIN
NEW YORK   LONDON   TORONTO   SYDNEY   NEW DELHI

The author and publisher would like to thank the Wellcome Trust and Wellcome Library for the digital images of the Bills of Mortality on pages 304 and 508.

ALADDIN
An imprint of Simon & Schuster Children's Publishing Division
1230 Avenue of the Americas, New York, New York 10020
This Aladdin paperback edition May 2017
Text copyright © 2016 by Kevin Sands
Cover illustration designed by James Fraser copyright © 2016 by Puffin Books
Type design by Laura Lyn DiSiena and Greg Stadnyk
Also available in an Aladdin hardcover edition.
All rights reserved, including the right of reproduction in whole or in part in any form.
ALADDIN and related logo are registered trademarks of Simon & Schuster, Inc.
For information about special discounts for bulk purchases, please contact
Simon & Schuster Special Sales at 1-866-506-1949 or business@simonandschuster.com.
The Simon & Schuster Speakers Bureau can bring authors to your live event.
For more information or to book an event contact the Simon & Schuster Speakers Bureau at
1-866-248-3049 or visit our website at www.simonspeakers.com.
Interior design by Karin Paprocki
The text of this book was set in Adobe Garamond Pro.
Manufactured in the United States of America 1117 OFF
2 4 6 8 10 9 7 5 3
The Library of Congress has cataloged the hardcover edition as follows:
Names: Sands, Kevin, author.
Title: Mark of the plague / Kevin Sands.
Description: First Aladdin hardcover edition. | New York : Aladdin, 2016. |
Series: Blackthorn key ; 2 | Summary: As the plague decimates London
in 1665 and an assassin threatens the apothecary's life, apprentice Christopher Rowe and
his faithful friend Tom, following a trail of puzzles, riddles, and secrets, risk their lives to
untangle the heart of a dark conspiracy.
Identifiers: LCCN 2016001356 (print) | LCCN 2016027348 (eBook) |
ISBN 9781481446747 (hc) | ISBN 9781481446761 (eBook) | ISBN 9781481446754 (pbk)
Subjects: | CYAC: Apprentices—Fiction. | Supernatural—Fiction. |
Pharmacists—Fiction. | Friendship—Fiction. | Secret societies—Fiction. |
Plague—Fiction. | Conspiracies—Fiction. | London—History—17th century—Fiction. |
Great Britain—History—Charles II, 1660-1685—Fiction. | BISAC: JUVENILE
FICTION / Fantasy & Magic. | JUVENILE FICTION / Mysteries & Detective Stories. |
JUVENILE FICTION / Action & Adventure / General.
Classification: LCC PZ7.1.S26 Mar 2016 (print) | LCC PZ7.1.S26 (eBook) | DDC [Fic]—dc23
LC record available at https://lccn.loc.gov/2016001356

MARK
OF THE
PLAGUE

MONDAY, AUGUST 31, 1665

Yesterday's plague deaths: 1,143

Total dead: 30,551

I'LL SAY THIS: HEDGEHOG FUR *really* burns.

Discovering that curious fact was not the point of my most recent experiment. Nonetheless, as Master Benedict always said, one never knows what will prompt a breakthrough. Though the way Tom's eyes widened at the flames spreading across the head of the stuffed hedgehog on the windowsill made me think this was less of a "breakthrough" and more of a "setback."

In my defense, I hadn't *meant* to set fire to Harry. This argument, of course, would carry no weight with Tom. *You never mean to set fire to anything,* he'd say, crossing his giant arms and glaring down at me. *Still happens a lot.*

It began, as it always did, with an idea. And with me ignoring that voice that said: This is a *bad* idea.

CHAPTER

"THIS IS A BAD IDEA," TOM SAID.

He stared sidelong at the device at the end of the work-bench, as though, if he looked at it directly, it might poke out his eyes.

"You don't even know what it does yet," I said.

He bit his lip. "I'm pretty sure I don't want to."

The contraption did look rather . . . well, odd. It was five inches tall, with a bulging top balanced over a narrow upright cylinder, wrapped tightly in folded paper. The upper part of the device balanced on three wooden prongs sticking out of the bottom. A wick of cannon fuse trailed from its end.

"It's like a mushroom," Tom said. "With a tail." He edged away from the workbench. "A *flammable* tail."

I couldn't help feeling slightly wounded. Odd or not, this device was the most important thing I'd ever made. All of the other equipment in the apothecary workshop—the ceramic jars, the molded glassware, the spoons and cups and pots and cauldrons—lay crammed on the side benches, cold and quiet. Only the faint scent of ingredients and concoctions lingered in the room. Even the giant onion-shaped oven in the corner was still. Because *this* was the creation that would save my shop.

I held it up with pride. "Blackthorn's Smoke-Your-Home! Guaranteed to . . . uh . . . smoke your home. Well, that advertisement needs work."

"Your brain needs work," Tom muttered.

Now that was going too far. "My inventions do exactly what they're supposed to."

"I know," Tom said. "That's the problem."

"But—look." I put my Smoke-Your-Home back down—gently—and showed him my design, sketched on an unrolled sheet of vellum.

"It's like a firework," I said, which in retrospect was probably not the best way to start.

Blackthorn's Smoke-Your-Home

Invented by Christopher Rowe, Apothecary's Apprentice

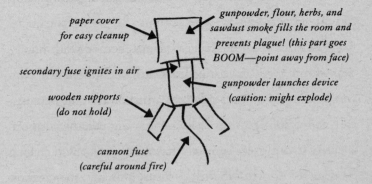

paper cover
for easy cleanup

gunpowder, flour, herbs, and
sawdust smoke fills the room and
prevents plague! (this part goes
BOOM—point away from face)

secondary fuse ignites in air

wooden supports
(do not hold)

gunpowder launches device
(caution: might explode)

cannon fuse
(careful around fire)

"You light the fuse at the bottom. The gunpowder in the lower part pops the top into the air. Then the second fuse makes that burst." I swept my arm over it like I was hawking silks at the Royal Exchange. "Fills any room with smoke to keep your family safe! Designed to help drive off the plague!"

"Uh-huh," Tom said. I think my theatrics made him less impressed. "Why is it full of flour?"

"That's the best part. Watch."

I went to the side of the workshop, where I'd stored the two sacks of flour I had left. I grabbed a handful of it and picked up the taper burning on the workbench. When I puffed the flour into it, it burst with a bright flash of flame.

"See?" I said. "It explodes. That's what blew up Campden's mill last summer. There was too much flour in the air."

Tom pressed his fingers to his forehead. "You based an invention on an exploding mill?"

"Well . . . it's less dangerous than gunpowder, right?" Tom didn't seem to think that was a selling point. "Anyway, when the flour explodes, it incinerates the sawdust and herbs, filling the room with smoke. And that smoke is the best thing we know of that will prevent you getting the plague. We can even make them to order, put whatever wood inside the customer wants."

"Why couldn't they just make a fire?" Tom said.

"You can't just light random fires around your house," I said.

"Yes, this seems *much* safer."

"It is," I insisted. "You just have to keep it away from curtains. And oil lamps. And pets. And—look, I'll show you."

Tom backed away. "Wait. You're not really going to set that off?"

"What else would I do with it?"

"I thought you were just playing a joke on me."

From high up on the ingredient shelves, a plump salt-

and-pepper-speckled pigeon fluttered down to where I stood. She cooed.

"That's right, Bridget," Tom said. "Talk some sense into him."

Bridget pecked at the cannon fuse. She recoiled with a grunt and took off, wings flapping her up the stairs.

"See?" Tom ducked behind the workbench. "Even the bird thinks you're mad."

"You're going to regret this when I'm knee-deep in gold," I said.

Tom's voice called from behind the wood. "I'll take my chances."

I lit the fuse. I watched it crackle and spark, then joined Tom behind the bench. Not because I was worried, of course. It just seemed . . . prudent.

The fuse reached the bottom. For a moment, there was nothing.

Then the gunpowder ignited. There was a hissing, and sparks shot from the bottom. The cylinder popped into the air.

I pulled on Tom's sleeve. "It works! It *works*!"

Then the second charge began to burn. A thin, smoking flame rushed out of the bottom. Slowly, it tipped sideways. Then it rocketed through the door into the shop.

"Was that supposed to happen?" Tom said.

"Well . . . ," I said, but the correct answer was: no.

From the doorway to the shop came a flash. Then a BOOM. The boom was expected. The voice that followed it was not.

"AAHHHH!" it said.

CHAPTER

WE SCRAMBLED INTO THE SHOP.
There, I found myself somewhat conflicted.

On the one hand, my invention had worked! My Smoke-Your-Home had indeed filled the shop with a thick, sweet-smelling haze. On the other hand, there was a big black scorch mark on the wall between the front door and the window. Also on that hand, Harry, the stuffed hedgehog on the windowsill, was on fire.

Waving his arms and coughing, Tom rushed forward and threw the front door open. He grabbed the hedgehog's tail—the only part of it that hadn't yet begun to blaze—and hurled it down the street. Harry tumbled end over end in a flaming arc, bouncing twice on the cobblestones before he came to rest, burning lazily in the lane.

Tom turned to glare at me. I flushed. "Now, wait a minute—" I began. Then I noticed: The shop was empty. "Didn't we just hear someone scream?"

Tom's eyes went wide. "You blew up a customer."

"Just missed, actually," a warbling voice said.

The top of a man's head peeked out from behind the display table near the fireplace. I saw the familiar shock of wispy white hair, the slightly clouded eyes. And my heart leaped.

"Master Isaac!" I said.

"Nice to see you boys are keeping busy." Isaac crawled out from under the table and pushed himself to his feet with the creaking slowness of the elderly.

I rushed forward, stopping just short of touching him. "Are you all right?"

"Better than the hedgehog." Isaac brushed off his breeches. "Might I inquire as to the purpose of this? Did the beast anger you in some way?"

"That was my invention. It's supposed to stop the plague."

He nodded. "I imagine turning someone to cinders would indeed prevent the sickness."

My face burned. "I'm really sorry."

"No harm done." He spotted a scorch mark on the shoulder of his doublet. "Well, some harm done, then. Oh, don't worry about it."

As embarrassed as I was, I was so happy to see him again. Isaac Chandler, the bookseller, had been one of Master Benedict's few friends—and mine, too, it turned out, in helping me and Tom stop the Cult of the Archangel, which had murdered a dozen men last spring, including my master. Isaac owned a shop tucked away in a block of warehouses north of the Thames. More importantly, in a vault deep below that shop, he kept a secret alchemical library, filled with ancient works that spanned centuries of arcane knowledge. I'd been there twice: once to collect a key that helped me find a secret of Master Benedict's, and the last time, four weeks afterward, to hide that same secret my master had sent me to find: the recipe for a terrible, explosive weapon called the Archangel's Fire.

I wished I'd been there more. Isaac's warm, cozy shop had quickly become one of my favorite places. But right now, I was just glad Isaac was here. He'd been out of town for two months.

"Are you back in London for good?" I said.

"Yes. And no." Isaac dragged a large leather satchel from under the display table. "May I sit? The journey home was tiring."

"Of course." I took the satchel and began to lead him to the comfortable chair by the fireplace.

He nodded toward the workshop. "Privacy would be better, I think."

Surprised, I escorted him into the back. Tom stayed behind and picked up a brush, giving me a long-suffering look as he began scrubbing the scorch mark from the wall. Isaac hobbled over to a stool at one of the benches and motioned for me to join him.

I did, placing the satchel between us. Now that we were out of the haze in the shop, I could see Isaac much clearer. He didn't look well.

A knot twisted in my gut. "Is something wrong?"

"I don't have the plague, if that's what you mean," he said. "I do, however, appear to have grown very old."

He slumped on the stool, eyes sunken, face dirty with dust from the road. I brought him a mug of stale beer from the one remaining barrel in my pantry, along with the last breakfast bun Tom had baked this morning. Isaac drained the mug in four gulps.

"Thank you. It's been many years since I've been on a horse." He shifted on the stool. "My backside wishes it had been longer."

"Did you just get in?" I said.

He nodded. "An hour ago. Arrived with an old friend of yours."

I frowned. Did I even *have* an old friend?

"Lord Ashcombe," Isaac said.

Lord Richard Ashcombe was the King's Warden, personal protector to His Majesty, Charles II. Along with Isaac, Lord Ashcombe had been instrumental in helping stop the Cult.

"I thought he was in Wiltshire with the king," I said.

"He's only returned to London for the day. But I needed to meet him, as he'd collected something for me."

Isaac opened his satchel and pulled out two packages. The first was wrapped in a linen cloth. Isaac patted the second. It was covered with a greased-leather sheath and tightly bound with rope. The knots were sealed with wax.

"What is it?" I said.

"A book," he said. "A very special book. One I've waited thirty years to acquire."

I stared at the package, as though if I tried hard enough, I could see through the leather. "What's it about?"

Isaac ran his fingertips along the rope. "That's not important at the moment. Perhaps one day I'll show it to you. But not today."

Master Benedict used to say the same thing. It drove me mad. But I didn't imagine I could cajole Isaac into telling me, so I tamped down my disappointment and said, "What's in the other package?"

"Nothing quite so valuable, but precious to me nonetheless." He pulled away the linen. Underneath was a freshly baked honey cake, icing frosted on top.

"My favorite," he said. "Have some."

I cut a piece, my mouth watering, still studying the mysterious package on the counter. "Where did it come from?"

"The bakery on Fleet Street."

"I meant the book."

"Did you?"

"Master Isaac," I said, exasperated.

"Egypt. It came from Egypt. And that's all I'm telling you," he said good-naturedly. He stuffed the book back in the satchel. "I'm glad to see the plague hasn't dampened your curiosity. Or your appetite."

I'd already finished the first piece of cake. I guess he'd seen me eying the rest of it. "Sorry."

He cut me another slice. "I'm happy to share it. I've been worried about you. News from London has been particularly bad."

Whatever he'd heard couldn't possibly convey the darkness that shrouded the city. When the Cult of the Archangel had murdered my master, I'd thought they were the worst thing that could happen to our city. I was wrong.

The plague, quiet in London for almost thirty years, had returned with a vengeance. What began as a few scattered cases outside the city walls spread quickly, finally exploding with the heat of the summer. The Bills of Mortality, published every Thursday, kept the grim official tally—6,102 deaths last week alone—but everyone knew that number was low. The true count was probably double that. The total was thirty thousand dead now, and rising every day.

A child was the first on our street to go: Jonathan Hartwell, the silversmith's son, only ten years old. In the beginning, his parents held out hope the boy had a different illness, as the plague started like many others: chills, cramps, the sweats. But then things turned. The vomiting started, uncontrollable. Seizures racked his body. Delirium took him; his mind leaped from angels to demons, seeing rapture and torment in turns, praying with one breath, cursing the next. Still the Hartwells denied it was the sickness, until the proof finally marked the boy's skin.

Unique to the plague were "the tokens": horrible black swellings on the neck, under the arms, at the groin—or in rarer cases, rashes and red, blotchy skin. Like most, little Jon had the swellings. He screamed so badly I could hear him four houses down, through locked doors, shuttered windows, my hands clamped over my ears.

There wasn't really anything I could do. I took his father some poppy to try to alleviate the poor boy's agony, but that was little comfort against the sickness. Even then, his mother held out hope, as some did actually survive the plague. But the ultimate quiet finally took him, replaced by his mother's wailing, and all I could do was listen; helpless, useless. Like now.

"Things just keep getting worse," I said to Isaac. "I'm really scared."

"The sickness makes us all the same," he said. "Have you been following that prophet, then?"

"Who?"

"The report I heard," Isaac said, "is there's a prophet in the city who can predict the course of the plague. Have you seen him?"

I'd never even heard of him. "Tom and I pretty much just stay in the shop. We don't get news from outside. Except for the Bills of Mortality, I guess."

Which was more than either of us wanted to know. Like everyone else, Tom and I tried to keep safe by staying indoors, as no one really knew how the sickness spread. Everyone believed smoke would keep it away—hence my not-quite-successful invention—but you could never be sure whether someone was infected until the tokens came.

There wasn't much reason to go out now, anyway. The plague had ground London to a halt. Most shops had closed, jobs disappearing with them. Anyone who could afford to leave had already gone; all summer, London's streets had been clogged with carriages, the wealthy fleeing in panic to the safety of the countryside. The only regulars on the road these days were the keepers of the dead-cart, hauling away token-marked corpses every night with a ringing bell and that terrible cry. *Bring out your dead.*

Isaac shook his head. "There have been three plagues in London during my lifetime: 1603, 1625, and 1636. And I tell you, Christopher, this one is worse than all of those together. If there really is a prophet out there, it's a dreadful sign that the worlds beyond have taken an interest in our city once again. And I don't have to explain to *you* how dangerous that is."

I shuddered, thinking of the Archangel's Fire. "When the plague struck, I thought you might not come back at all."

"I hadn't planned to. But the news of this prophet—and the reports of looting in the city—made up my mind. That's why I stopped here on the way back. I wanted to let you know I'm closing my shop."

His announcement felt like a punch in the gut. Though I'd only been to Isaac's twice, his connection to my master made me feel like I was losing a second home. "But . . . why? And what's going to happen to the library in the vault?"

"Nothing. That library is precisely why I'm shutting the store down." Isaac sighed. "I love my shop, almost as much as your master loved this place. But the library . . . that is my *purpose*. Everything I've ever done has been to serve it, grow it, protect it. Nonetheless, I've been foolish." He motioned to the book inside his satchel. "I've been purchasing works for the future. What I should have done was *prepare* for it.

"I have no apprentice," he said. "If I die, there will be no one to take my place. And that library *must* survive. So, I must survive along with it. At least for a little while longer."

Isaac stared into his mug. "I'd have preferred not to return at all. But if my shop gets looted, and thieves find the secret passage to the library . . . I can't let that happen. If I must be in London, then there's only one sure way to avoid the sickness: No contact—with *anyone*—until it's over.

"So that's what I shall do," he said. "I'm going to shut the shop and seal myself away in the vault. It's clear now that the plague will last for several months more. I've just arranged for enough food to be delivered to last me through it."

I tried to imagine spending months underground. Never breathing fresh air, never seeing the sun. It sounded awful. "Won't you be lonely?"

"My books will keep me company. Unless you'd like to stay."

I blinked. "Me?"

He nodded. "That's why I stopped by. With your master gone, I wanted to offer you the chance to join me in the library. There's plenty of space for both of us, and even with my books, it would be considerably more pleasant with someone to talk to. It would put my mind at ease, as well. I wouldn't have to worry about you catching the sickness."

I wasn't sure what to say. I didn't really want to live

underground. Then again, I didn't really want to live through this plague, either. I'd also get the chance to know Isaac better, to hear his stories about Master Benedict. And that library! All those books. And all the time in the world to read them.

"What about Tom?" I said. "Could he come, too?"

Isaac pursed his lips. "Tom's family. Are they still alive?"

"Yes."

"And would they want to know where he's gone?"

Now I understood why Isaac had asked for privacy. "Yes," I said, downcast.

"Tom himself would be welcome," Isaac said. "I trusted him earlier with our secret, and your friend's loyalty proved him worthy of that. But, as you've already learned, the knowledge in that library would be dangerous in the wrong hands. His family cannot be told. So I'm afraid the answer must be no."

I was disappointed, but I didn't blame Isaac. Tom's mother was a decent person, but a terrible gossip. Tom's sisters were good girls, as well, but far too young to be trusted with this kind of responsibility. As for Tom's father, the less said about him, the better. Clearly, Tom couldn't come.

That gave me my answer, too. What if Tom got sick

while I was safe underground? I couldn't abandon him. Nor could I abandon what my master had left me.

"I'd really like to come," I said to Isaac. "But Tom might need my help. And . . . I don't know. I've been hoping that maybe I could find something to do to help the city."

I felt kind of stupid saying that. But Isaac just smiled and placed a hand on my shoulder.

"I made the same offer to Benedict, back in 'thirty-six," he said. "And he told me the exact same thing. Very well. On to practical matters. Before I seal myself away, is there anything you need?"

I was embarrassed. "Well . . . now that you mention it . . . I was wondering, maybe . . . I mean, if you had any . . ."

Isaac raised an eyebrow. "I'd like to return home *before* I catch the plague, Christopher."

"Right. Um . . . could I maybe . . . um . . . borrow some money?"

"Money?"

"I'll pay you back, I promise," I said quickly. "It's just . . . I'm sort of . . . out of it."

Isaac regarded me sternly. "The Apothecaries' Guild gave you ten pounds after Benedict's death. Surely you haven't squandered all of it?"

"I haven't squandered *any* of it," I said. "I never got it."

Realization dawned. "Let me guess," Isaac said. "You went to collect it every week. They always had some excuse as to why it wasn't ready. And now, with the plague, they've closed their doors, and you *can't* collect."

"They were always very polite about it."

"I'm sure. What have you been living on all this time?"

"I've been selling off some of the shop's stock to other apothecaries," I said. "But no one will buy them anymore."

"Because they're worried they're tainted by the sickness?" Isaac said.

I nodded, feeling miserable. The murder of my master hadn't just left a hole in my heart. It had left me with no way to support myself. After the business with the Cult of the Archangel, the Apothecaries' Guild was supposed to assign me a new master. But when the plague swelled, the Guild Council had closed Apothecaries' Hall and fled alongside the rest of the wealthy. With Guild business shut down, any chance of me getting a master disappeared—along with my promised ten pounds.

As an apprentice, it was illegal for me to sell remedies on my own; hence the Smoke-Your-Home. Since smoke only prevented you catching the plague instead of curing it, technically, smoke wasn't a remedy, so selling it wouldn't be illegal. But that big black scorch mark beside the door—and the charred hedgehog in the street—made it pretty clear my invention wasn't quite ready to market. And with the few remaining apothecaries no longer willing to buy my stock, my strongbox was finally empty.

"Oh, Christopher," Isaac said. "I shouldn't have left you alone. Here." He pulled five silver shillings from his doublet and placed them on the table. "I'd give you more, but I spent the rest of my savings provisioning for the plague. Tell you what, take the honey cake, too. No, no, don't argue." He patted his stomach. "I may love it, but it doesn't love me."

If it weren't for the sickness, I'd have hugged him. "This will be a *huge* help."

"But not enough," Isaac muttered.

It wouldn't last the whole outbreak, to be sure. But those silver shillings would keep me fed for a few weeks yet. Tom, in particular, would be thrilled—and not just to see the honey cake. His family's bakery had shut down, since all their regular customers had fled, and with flour so cheap, most people left now baked their own bread.

His father, being a considerable miser, had money stashed at home to last a while, so neither Tom nor his five sisters would starve. But his father wouldn't spend a farthing on me. In fact, he'd gone so far as to actually *encourage* Tom to spend the days with me, so Tom would eat from my stores instead of his. What he didn't realize was that Tom had been sneaking food from home and bringing it to me the whole time. But he couldn't take too much, just a bun or two, small enough to hide under his shirt. So Isaac's money would make a huge difference, at least for a while.

I jumped from my stool to go tell Tom.

"Wait," Isaac said.

I stopped in the doorway. In the front, Tom had finished scrubbing away the scorch mark and was putting the curios back in their places. Through the window, I could see a pair of men walking toward my shop.

"I gave Benedict my word that I wouldn't say anything," Isaac said. "But I suppose, under the circumstances, he wouldn't mind my breaking that promise."

He sat up on his stool. "I guess you haven't found your master's treasure."

CHAPTER

I BLINKED.

"Treasure?" I said. "What treasure?"

The front door opened, and the two men I'd seen cross-ing the street walked in. Isaac cocked his head, listened. Then he put a finger to his lips.

Tom looked back at me questioningly. I motioned to him to take care of the visitors, then closed the door to the workshop and ran back to Isaac. "Treasure?"

He nodded. "When Benedict saw the Cult of the Archangel was getting close to discovering him, he wrote a new will, leaving everything to you. Even so, your master remained concerned about what would happen to you after he was gone. In particular, there was something he wanted you to have, but he didn't want to name it. In case the will fell into the wrong hands, you see."

"Treasure?" I appeared to have turned into a parrot. "What is it?"

Isaac frowned. "I'm not certain. I know he had money—a *lot* of money—but Benedict hinted he'd left you something special. Something he wanted only you to have. He wouldn't tell me what it was; he wanted you to find it on your own. Yet he was worried you wouldn't. So he left one last thing with me, just in case." Isaac motioned to the satchel on the workbench. "There's a bundle of letters in there. One is for you. Go ahead."

I found seven of them, tied together with twine. I didn't recognize the first five names. The sixth, I did: Lord Richard Ashcombe.

I lingered on it for a moment, curious as to what business Isaac had with the King's Warden. But it was the last name I really wanted to see. It was written in my master's smooth hand. I traced my finger over the letters.

Christopher Rowe
Blackthorn Apothecary, London

"Benedict made me promise not to give that to you until at least a year had passed," Isaac said. "He really did want you to find what he left for you on your own. But given the sickness . . ."

I turned the letter over. On the seal, my master had inked a single symbol: a circle, with a dot in the center.

I recognized it. As a secret alchemist, my master had searched for the truths of the universe beyond the mortal world. To keep their research hidden, alchemists used special symbols to represent materials, celestial bodies, instructions, and the like. The circle with the dot in the center represented the Sun: light, life, warmth. Like all celestial bodies, the Sun was linked to an earthly metal. Mars was iron. Mercury was quicksilver. The Sun?

The Sun was gold.

Voices came through the door from the shop. I ignored them. I broke the seal and read my master's message.

Christopher:

Somewhere in our home is a prize, hidden for you: Treasure.

Understanding your nature, you probably haven't found it yet. Doubtlessly, you'd like to get it sooner rather than later. Yet you won't find it until you realize something incredibly important.

Our home is now yours. Use everything you've been given. Recognize exactly what that is.

But if I say more right now, you won't listen, so you'll have to figure this one out on your own. Read this message closely. Decipher its meaning. Solve this one last riddle, and you'll not only find your treasure, you'll learn one last thing—and that is the most important thing i'll ever want you to know.

My eyes stung. My heart ached as much as it had since he'd been taken from me. But still his letter made me smile. Because—of course—he'd left me a puzzle.

My master had had an absolute passion for puzzles: secrets under secrets, codes inside codes. Among other things, he'd passed that love on to me. I wiped my eyes and scanned the letter for clues.

Isaac cleared his throat. "I can see you won't pay any attention to me anymore."

I looked up. "Sorry."

He waved my apology away. "Benedict was exactly the same." He stood. "I wish I could help you find whatever's hidden in that message, but I wouldn't know where to begin. In the meantime, I'm sure you'd like to start looking. And it's time for me to return home." He frowned. "Besides, I think Tom might need your assistance."

I'd been so focused on my master's letter that I hadn't noticed what was happening out front. Now I heard them: sharply raised voices. An argument.

I opened the door to the shop. Tom stood at the counter, trying to placate two different groups. A pair of men were right in front of me, the two I'd seen before. A third man stood on the opposite side of Tom, hunched over. He must have come in after I'd shut the workshop door.

This man had clearly fallen on hard times. His clothes were stained and worn, with home-sewn patches covering the tears. His skin was just as filthy, as was his unwigged, unwashed hair. His hands were scabbed, and he had a giant wart near the tip of his bulbous nose. Worst of all, he smelled like he'd just stepped in something decidedly unpleasant. The first two men seemed to object to his presence as much as to what he was doing: He was begging.

"Please, master," he said to Tom. "Anything."

"I'm sorry," Tom said. "But I told you, it's not my shop—"

"We were here first," one of the other two men complained.

Tom looked relieved I'd finally come out. The beggar spotted Isaac in the doorway behind me. He went straight for him, hunched over and limping. "Good sir—"

Before he could continue, Isaac motioned to me. The beggar looked a bit surprised, but he pled his case to me nonetheless. "Please, young master. My name is Miles Gaspar. I was a tanner, down by the docks, before the sickness came. Now the tannery's closed down. I've been out of work for two months. Do you have a job for me? I'll do anything, anything."

"I'm sorry," I said. "I don't—"

"Oh, please, sir, I'm not proud. Anything, no matter how small. I can't feed my family." Miles wrung his hands together. "My wife and I have two little ones. We've lost our lodging, because we can't pay the rent. We give the children what little we can find. I haven't eaten for three days. Please. *Anything.*"

I felt terrible. Seeing this shop, he must have thought I was swimming in gold. How could I tell him I'd had to beg Isaac for money myself?

"I . . . I don't have anything I can afford to give," I said. "I'm really sorry."

He bowed his head. "I understand. I'm sorry to trouble you." He turned away.

Watching him limp out reminded me of my own life, a few short months ago. I'd been out on the streets, too. And even with Isaac's shillings, if I didn't find Master Benedict's treasure, I might be on the streets once again, and soon.

There wasn't much I could do for the man; I really did have next to nothing. But I remembered that back in June, someone who *also* had next to nothing had kept me safe—and had passed over a fortune in reward money to do it.

"Wait," I said.

Halfway through the door, Miles turned back, hopeful. I went through the workshop to the pantry. It was nearly empty, just half a sack of oats, a barrel of stale beer, and a wedge of salted cheese. I took the cheese, wrapped it in the linen cloth from Isaac's honey cake, then went back to the shop.

I held it out to him. "For your children."

Miles took the food with trembling hands. He blinked away tears. "The Lord bless you, kind master. God's blessing be upon you."

"That's all I have," I said.

"I understand, master, I do. I won't trouble you again, I promise. God save you."

God save us all, I thought as Miles left. Tom looked pleased that I'd been able to help the man. The other two in the shop seemed more pleased the beggar was no longer fouling the air.

"Do you have time for paying customers now?" said the man who'd spoken before.

A lack of time wasn't my problem. "I'm sorry, but I can't—"

"Our master sent us to buy your Venice treacle." This had become a popular request. Many believed Venice treacle, an antidote for certain poisons, could also fight the plague. "We'll take everything you have, and any more you can make."

I'd placed a sign in the window two months ago: TEMPORARILY CLOSED—OPENING SOON! That didn't always help, as plenty of people couldn't read. "I'm sorry, sir," I said, "but the shop isn't open yet. I'm waiting on a new master."

"Will he be here this morning?"

"Uh . . . no." I didn't want to tell him Blackthorn was closed indefinitely. If word got out before I was appointed a new master, I might lose all our former customers for good. "He . . . won't be here for some time."

The man held out a coin purse, already open. "Well, we don't have time to wait. Give us whatever this will pay for."

I stared at the purse. The coins inside were gold. Guineas, worth a pound and a shilling each. I could see at least eight of them.

My throat tightened. "I . . . I can't sell it to you."

"Don't you have any?"

I had plenty, right up there on the shelf behind the counter. "I'm . . . not allowed to sell remedies without a master." I swallowed. "There's another apothecary down on—"

"We don't want another apothecary," the man said. "Our master ordered us to buy it here. He said Blackthorn's treacle was the best."

Every word this man spoke made me feel even worse. Our treacle *was* the best. And the money in that purse could keep me fed for *years*.

Tom gaped at the coins. *Just take them,* a small voice said in my head.

I looked the men over. They'd mentioned their master, but I didn't know who that was. As for the men themselves, I didn't recognize them. They both wore fairly plain clothes, wool and linen. Servants, I'd have guessed, except for two things.

First, both were carrying weapons. One had a war club slung over his back, an iron spike at the end; the other had a short sword in his belt. And second, both had a small bronze medallion sewn onto the breast of their doublets, right over their hearts. Each bore the same design: a circle with a triangle in the center, and inside that, what looked like a cross. Engraved around the edge were letters of some kind. I couldn't see what they were.

The man thrust the purse toward me. The coins jingled. If I took them, we'd be fine until the plague ran its course.

And if their master told anyone where they got the treacle?

I felt Tom's eyes on me as I searched for something to say. But I knew what my answer had to be. "I . . . I can't. I'm sorry."

The man held the purse out for a second more. Then he drew it closed. "Our master won't be pleased with you."

He said it like a threat. It didn't make any difference. If I got caught selling remedies, I'd lose everything: my shop, my future, all Master Benedict had left me. I wouldn't throw that away. Not for all the gold guineas in the world.

"I really am sorry," I said.

The man opened his mouth to retort, but Isaac stepped forward. "The boy's made his decision."

The man glared at all of us. Then he spun on his heel and left, taking his companion with him. It took every bit of will not to run after them.

Isaac put his hand on my shoulder. "You did the right thing. You'll feel better when you buy new food from the market. And even better once you find Benedict's treasure."

I nodded miserably. Tom just looked confused.

"Treasure?" he said. "And *food*?"

Tom almost cried when he saw the honey cake. I showed him my master's message as he munched on it.

"Amazing," he said, spraying crumbs everywhere. Tom looked around the workshop, as if wondering which of the hundreds of apothecary jars that lined the shelves hid Master Benedict's treasure.

I didn't think it was in any of them. "He wanted me to figure out this puzzle to get it. He wouldn't hide it somewhere I might stumble upon out of luck."

Tom took another piece of cake. "Why did Master Benedict think you *wouldn't* find it?"

To me, that was the biggest puzzle of all. He'd mentioned it twice in the letter.

Understanding your nature, you probably haven't found it yet.

You won't find it until you realize something incredibly important. . . . Recognize exactly what that is.

Yet it obviously mattered a great deal to him. And to me. Not just for the money, either. *You'll learn one last thing,* the letter said. *And that is the most important thing i'll ever want you to know.*

Even Isaac had noted it. *Benedict hinted he'd left you something special. Something he wanted only you to have.*

What could my master have believed was so important, yet he felt I'd never realize it on my own? I didn't understand what he was getting at. But I *had* found something in his message.

Tom noticed it, too. He pointed to the last line. "Shouldn't this *i* be a capital letter?"

"Yes," I said. "That's not a mistake Master Benedict would have made. It has to be a clue."

"A clue to what?"

I didn't know. Master Benedict had taught me so many different ciphers during the last three years that I couldn't begin to remember them all. And, of course, there were plenty of codes he'd never taught me: ones he'd planned to explain but never had the chance, or that he'd wanted me to figure out on my own.

I wondered if I should try searching through his notes. The problem with that was my master's notes were, to put it kindly, a mess. He'd kept the store and workshop in perfect condition, but upstairs was a different matter. Most of the rooms, including my master's bedroom and the hall leading to it, were so stuffed with books and papers he could have started his own library. And my master had never kept his notes organized—at least not in a way other people could understand.

He'd often sent me upstairs for a work. "Get me Culpeper's herbal," he'd say. "It's in the storage room on the third floor."

In an ordinary house, the "storage room" would have been someone's bedroom. Here, it was filled with stacks of papers and books, just like everywhere else. In fact, the only space my master *didn't* store his books was in the crawl space underneath the house where we kept our ice vault, which he'd always meant to turn into a proper cellar but never got around to it. And the only reason that crawl space wasn't filled with notes was because he was worried about the damp.

So up I'd go, knowing I'd stand there helplessly. "Master . . . ?"

"Twelfth stack from the northwest corner, widder-shins," he'd call up the stairs. "Fourth from the bottom. The cover is patterned leather." And I'd come back down, holding that exact book and shaking my head.

But my master was no longer around to tell me where to look. So Tom and I sat there, eating honey cake and staring fruitlessly at an uncapitalized *i*.

It was later that morning that I figured it out.

We made plans to go spend Isaac's money at the mar-ket after lunch, since I wanted to keep working on Master Benedict's message. Bridget kept us company, marching around the workbench and pecking at whatever she could find as Tom made today's bread. He was taking the freshly baked buns out of the oven with a wooden peel when I jumped from my stool with a whoop, sending Bridget scurrying for cover. "That's it!" I shouted.

"Aaahh!" Tom started, and the steaming bread went flying.

"Sorry," I said.

Bridget flapped her wings at me, annoyed. Tom looked

forlornly into the cauldron, in which a pair of golden-brown lumps were slowly sinking. "You made me lose my buns."

"Never mind those. Come look." I smoothed my master's message out on the workbench. "I've got the answer. That *i* at the end isn't uncapitalized because it's important. It's uncapitalized because it *isn't*."

"I don't understand," Tom said.

"I thought not capitalizing it meant Master Benedict had made it part of the message. But he did that so it *wouldn't* be part of the message. You see? He hid the secret in the capitals."

I took an inkpot and used a quill to circle every capital letter in my master's message.

Ⓢomewhere in our home is a prize, hidden for you.Ⓣreasure.Ⓤnderstanding your nature, you probably haven't found it yet.Ⓓoubtlessly, you'd like to get it sooner rather than later.Ⓨet you won't find it until you realize something incredibly important.

Ⓞur home is now yours.Ⓤse everything you've been given.Ⓡecognize exactly what that is.

Ⓑut if Ⓘ say more right now, you won't listen, so you'll have to figure this one out on your own.Ⓡead this message closely.Ⓓecipher its

meaning.Solve this one last riddle, and you'll not only find your trea-
sure, you'll learn one last thing—and that is the most important thing
i'll ever want you to know.

The message popped out, one word per paragraph, clear and
easy to read.

STUDY OUR BIRDS

Tom looked impressed. "Clever," he said. Then he saw
the horror dawning on my face. "What's the matter?"

"Tom," I said. "Our birds are *gone*."

CHAPTER
4

WE LOOKED OVER AT BRIDGET.
She'd gone back to pecking at the specks of flour that had
spilled onto the counter. She noticed us staring at her and
looked up with an inquisitive coo.

Before the Cult of the Archangel had murdered my
master, we'd kept a few dozen pigeons in a wood-and-wire
coop on the flat roof of the house. When the Cult ransacked
our home, most of the birds had been scared away. Only
Bridget had stayed.

Master Benedict had written this message to me
months before he'd died, well before our pigeons had
fled. He couldn't have imagined they'd disappear. "How

am I supposed to study our birds if they're gone?"

"Maybe you're not reading his message right," Tom said.

"How else could you read this?"

"I don't know. I just don't see how your birds could help us find your master's treasure. Where's it supposed to be, under their feathers?"

"Maybe they were supposed to lead me to it. They're really smart." When she'd been out of her coop, Bridget had followed me all around the city as I'd fled from the Cult.

"But Master Benedict says whatever you're supposed to find is *inside* your home."

That was a good point. Plus, while my master was alive, he rarely let the pigeons out of the coop. It wouldn't make sense that they'd lead me to it. Would it?

Bridget returned to the flour. I watched her. *Somewhere in our home is a prize.*

In our home?

"Do you think the roof counts?" I said.

We stared at each other for a second. Then I grabbed a startled Bridget and bolted up the stairs, through the hatch, and onto the roof.

The pigeonholes in the coop had been cracked when my house was ransacked. At the time, I'd been bitterly disappointed to lose our birds, but with the coming of the sickness I found myself glad they'd gone. City plague ordinances ordered every householder to kill their pets, to try to slow the spread of the infection. I was already supposed to have killed Bridget—as if I'd ever even *consider* that.

Still, it meant I had to keep her inside all the time, so no one could hear her coos. For that reason, I'd never bothered to repair the coop. I'd just left the remains of it open, in case any surviving pigeons needed somewhere safe to spend the night. Today, a single bird was there, a robin, searching for food among the abandoned nests. It flapped away when we went inside.

I put Bridget on the ground. "Go on, then."

"What are you doing?" Tom said.

"Studying our birds." Bridget poked at my boot. I nudged her away. "Come on, Bridget. Find Master Benedict's treasure."

Tom looked at me as if I'd lost my mind. Bridget, for her part, did what a pigeon does. Which was mostly nothing.

Tom shifted uncomfortably as my face grew warm. This had not been one of my better ideas. "Maybe we should just look ourselves?" Tom said.

So we did. We searched the abandoned coop from top

to bottom. We overturned the nests in the broken pigeon-holes, pulled away loose boards, peeked behind the pinewood planks that had held it all together.

"There's nothing here," I said, disappointed.

"At least we know the treasure's inside your home," Tom said. "Why don't we go to the market and look again when we get back? Maybe you'll think of something while we're out."

I was pretty sure he just wanted to go buy food. But he was right; I wouldn't think of anything standing here. Tom was pleased when I agreed.

As for me, I wasn't looking forward to the trip.

The Royal Exchange was depressing.

The market had once been one of my favorite places. When I came here with my master, I'd gawk at all the goods on display: flashing rainbow silks from China, floral perfumes from Arabia, the sweet scent of roasting coffee beans from the New World. The merchants' cries would echo in the galleries as they hawked their wares while customers browsed the shops, haggling with the sellers, lounging over wine and freshly baked pastries and chatting with friends well met.

Not anymore. Most of the stalls had closed, shut down by fleeing merchants and the lack of trade coming into the city. The crowds were smaller, too, the atmosphere muted and fearful. Shoppers darted from stall to stall, silent, buying only what they needed, exchanging coins by dropping them in bowls of vinegar in the hope the acid might burn away the sickness.

Tom and I made our way carefully through the stalls, trying to avoid the other customers as much as we could. We bought only the cheapest food, piling it in the handcart I'd brought from the workshop, all the while trying to breathe as little as possible—and not only because of the miasmic air of the plague.

The stink of the crowd was *appalling*. It wasn't just the usual body odor, waste, and manure stench of the city, either. Since smells were believed to fend off the sickness, people wore, chewed, or bathed in anything aromatic they could get their hands on. One man was drenched in vinegar, apparently reasoning if it was good enough for the coins, it was good enough for him. Another man wore a garland of rotting onions around his neck. He was accompanied by a woman who'd stuffed her cheeks so full with garlic and rue that she looked like a squirrel.

Tom covered his nose with his sleeve. "If I wanted to throw up, I'd dunk my head in the Thames. Would you look at that?" He nodded toward a man who'd wrapped a cloth around his head. In a nest made on top, a brazier of wood coals was burning, surrounding him with smoke. "Now there's a customer for your Smoke-Your-Home."

I bit back a retort as we edged away to a less rancid spot where the hot breeze blew into the open market. We ended up smelling something that was, in its own way, much more painful.

A woman in a butcher's apron called from her stall. "Pork!" she hollered. "Roast pork, fresh from the countryside!"

Tom grabbed my arm and moaned. "Meat! I can't even remember the last time I *saw* meat."

My stomach grumbled like an angry lion as I clutched the remainder of Isaac's coins. Best not even to look. We couldn't afford to waste money on luxuries.

But that *smell*. Tom stared dolefully at the butcher woman's stock as we pushed our cart past it. "Oh . . . just think, Christopher. Fresh crackling . . . marinated ribs . . . chops in sauce . . ."

I stopped at a miller's stall to buy more flour. Tom

went on like that until he ran out of things to do to a pig. Then he turned to different animals. "Roast beef . . . glazed pheasant . . . lamb stew, with those little carrots in . . ."

"All right, Tom," I said.

"Mutton sausage . . . chops in sauce . . ."

"You said that already."

Tom's lower lip trembled. "I bet the king has chops in sauce anytime he wants."

I pressed my fingers against my temples. "I can't listen to this."

Tom's mournful memories of meat were bringing my spirits even lower. We'd kept our purchases simple: mostly flour, plentiful and cheap; some oats and grains; hard, salty cheese; eggs and butter; a new cask of ale; a block of ice to replenish our vault; and six dozen carrots, which I'd somehow found for a penny the bunch. Each sale reminded me these humble groceries were all that stood between me and starvation.

And as I pushed my cart along, I began to wonder if I was being watched.

I caught a movement out of the corner of my eye. There, behind the wheat farmer's stall. I whirled.

The figure darted away. I spotted a green dress and a

shock of auburn curls before it pulled back, slipping deeper into the Exchange.

"Did you see that?" I said.

"See what?" Tom said.

"I think some girl is following us."

Tom scanned the crowd. "A pickpocket?"

I wasn't sure. But I could have sworn I'd seen her earlier. "She was shadowing us on our way here, on the streets."

Tom kept one hand on the cart as I pushed forward, watching for little-girl thieves. But those weren't the only kind in the market. In the fear that gripped the city, a new breed of merchant had carved out a space in the Exchange's double galleries, selling their own unique product: plague cures.

The markets had become notorious for these quack-salvers. The fact that none of their cures ever worked had no effect on the brazenness of their guarantees—nor, sadly, on the hopes of their desperate customers.

One quack seemed to have drawn a bigger crowd than his competitors. He stood atop a crate, gripping a copper box. "In here," he shouted, "is the secret! The secret that will save you, your family, your children. Yes, sir, very smart, thank you; your family will thank you."

The merchant broke his patter to let a burly man in the front drop a silver crown—five shillings' worth—into a jar of vinegar. He wrapped some of the herbs from the box in paper and passed them down before turning back to the crowd.

"That's Saint Stephen's Breath, that is. Contains a special blend of herbs, with none of that heathen poison from foreign lands those apothecaries peddle. The goodness in Saint Stephen's Breath comes only from the rolling hills of England, blessed by the grace of the Lord."

"Liar."

"What—?" The quack stopped, surprised, as a man pushed through the crowd. He was tall and broad, with long blond hair—real hair, not a wig—that swept over his shoulders in waves. He wore a jacket and breeches of silk, marred by multicolored stains.

I recognized those stains. My master and I had sported more than a few of them ourselves over the years: black charcoal smudges on his collar; drops of dried blood on his cuff; sticky, honey-colored treacle smeared across his thigh.

This man was an apothecary. And he was staring at the quack with disdain.

The merchant smiled. "Liar, you say? But, sir, I have

proof. Look upon the magic of Saint Stephen's Breath!"

He held out his hand. A small boy stepped from behind him up onto the crate.

"Just three days ago," the quack said, "this boy was afflicted, delirious, standing before Peter at the Pearly Gates. Then I gave him Saint Stephen's Breath. Now look! Not a trace of plague!"

The apothecary snorted. "Nonsense."

"Do you not have eyes, sir? Here he is! Fully healed—"

The apothecary turned to the crowd. "Did anyone see this boy with the rash? The swellings? Did anyone even see him sick?"

The quack flushed. Some of the crowd began to grumble. Others took up the man's defense. "I suppose you've got your own cure, then?" the burly man said to the apothecary, still holding his package of the quacksalver's remedy.

"I do."

The quack grinned. "Aha! Finally, we see the truth of the matter. He's selling his own cure—and like all apothecaries, no doubt he'll charge you a dozen pounds a bottle! Good people, for only *a single crown*, you can have Saint Stephen's—"

"Nothing."

The crowd looked back at the apothecary.

"My cure costs nothing," he said.

The quack's face turned red. "You're giving it away?" he said incredulously. "What's your game?"

"I'm not the one playing tricks." The apothecary turned to the crowd once again. "I tell you truly: My cure will cost you nothing. I won't take a single coin from you or your families. The rich get their remedies; the poor die in pain. But everyone, rich and poor alike, deserves to be saved.

"I'm offering my cure to the Lord Mayor and the magistrates of London," he said. "And I won't let them charge you a thing. Just go to the government offices at Guildhall and ask them to approve Galen Widdowson's cure."

Tom looked over at me, surprised. "Do you know that man?"

I didn't. I'd heard the name Galen from my master, of course—Galen of Pergamon, from ancient Greece, was the greatest physician in history—but I couldn't remember my master ever mentioning an apothecary with that same name. Still, I watched him, impressed. His quiet confidence—and his contempt for those who would cheat the desperate—reminded me a lot of Master Benedict.

Galen's objections seemed to have found their mark.

The crowd's grumbling grew louder; calls of "fraud" rang out. The quack's defenders took up his cause, and arguments began to boil over. One man got shoved; he shoved back.

Tom didn't like the way the mood was shifting. He grabbed my sleeve. "We should go."

The quack looked furious. He slipped a club from a loop on his belt and pointed it at Galen. "You clear off."

"And leave you to steal from these people?" the apothecary said. "I'd rather take the stick." He turned back to the burly man. "His cure is a fraud, and I can prove it. Because I know what it really is."

Galen snatched the pouch from the man's fingers.

"Hey!" the man said. But Galen had already torn the paper open. The dried herbs spilled into his palm.

The man grabbed Galen by the collar. He drew back his fist.

Galen thrust his palm under the man's nose. "Tea."

The man looked down at the herbs.

"From the rolling hills of England?" Galen said. "Blessed by God's grace? This is tea, from the Orient, tuppence-ha'penny the ounce."

Everyone stared up at the quack. He'd gone pale, sweat

beading on his forehead. His eyes darted from face to face. "It's . . . it's not . . . you . . ."

Suddenly, he lashed out at Galen. The club cracked the apothecary on his temple, and he went down, lost among the crowd.

Too late. "You'd cheat my family?" the burly man bellowed, and took a swing at the quack. The merchant stumbled back, flinging the copper box at his assailant. The herbs inside—tea, from the Orient, tuppence-ha'penny the ounce—scattered over the crowd.

Some, desperate as they were, grabbed for it, unwilling to believe it wasn't a cure. Others reached for the quack to hold him. The rest went for his stock, tied in burlap beside the crate. The sack tore open; the tea scattered everywhere.

Then the riot began.

CHAPTER
5

CHAOS.

The mob snatched up the fallen tea, shouting, punching, fighting for their share. Each swing brought in a new combatant, and the brawl began to spill further into the Exchange. Frantically, merchants pulled their wares behind their stalls. As some people fought, others fled—many stealing from the displays as they ran.

We stood in the middle of it all. Tom backed into me, frightened. I only had a moment to gape in horror before I felt my handcart shake.

I turned. A woman had pulled a sack of flour from the back.

"Hey!" I reached for her, but she dodged my out-stretched fingers, bumping my cart. A basket of eggs slid to the side and tipped. Two of them fell, shattering into goop on the stone.

I grabbed at the rest of my precious eggs, smashing another shell against my wrist. The yolk burst, staining my sleeve. "Tom! Help!"

Tom, flustered, turned at my cry. He threw his arms around our supplies, shielding them. He nodded toward a narrow hall in the west gallery, leading out between two shuttered shops. "There!"

I pushed the cart, trying not to lose any more eggs. Tom jogged beside it, scanning the mob for threats. Just before we reached the pathway, the wheel on the cart twisted in a crack in the stone. A sack—my oats!—tumbled over the side.

People dived for it, hands grasping. Tom jumped over the cart and barreled into the would-be thieves. He grabbed the sack, tearing it away. The burlap ripped, sending a third of the oats flying. Tom clutched the remainder of the sack and backed away as fingers scooped grains from the stone.

I wanted to help him, but I couldn't. If I turned away

from the cart, they'd take it all. I just kept pushing until I was safe inside the sheltered pathway.

Or so I thought.

I skidded the cart to a halt. Halfway down the path, a pair of men loomed over a small figure lying on the ground. A girl with auburn curls in a green woolen dress.

One of them kicked her in the ribs. She curled up, trying to protect herself. The man booted her again. His companion crouched over her, pulling at her dress, patting her down.

She clawed at his cheeks. The man swatted her hands away, then quieted her with a hook to the jaw. He turned her over, groping her still form for money.

"She's got nothing," he said.

The man who was standing spat on her, kicked her once more out of spite.

Then he saw me.

He grabbed his friend by the collar, pulled him up. They stared at me, my cart, the food.

The man who'd patted the girl down pulled out a knife.

My heart sank. I had a knife of my own, but I wouldn't win any fights with it. *I'm going to lose everything,* I thought in despair.

Then I felt a presence loom behind me. The men looked over my shoulder. They stopped, wavered, and then bolted, running for the afternoon light.

Tom put a hand on my shoulder before placing the oats back in the cart. His shirt was torn, his cheek scratched. Fortunately, the thieves had been more concerned about Tom's size than the fear in his eyes.

I wanted to hug him. First, we needed to figure out what to do. The men had left the girl behind. She lay on the ground, facedown, moaning.

Tom and I glanced at each other. For the briefest moment, we almost decided to run. From the look on Tom's face, he felt just as ashamed as I did about it.

Still, we needed to be careful. Tom and I pushed the cart forward, stopping six feet from the girl. We didn't dare step any closer until we'd seen her skin.

I recognized the dress, the curly hair. This was the girl who'd been following us. "Are you all right?" I said.

She tried to push herself up, but she couldn't stand. She crawled to the side of the passage and leaned against the wall, her curls covering her face.

I scanned her neck. I couldn't see any swellings or red splotches, and she didn't seem to have the sweats. She was having trouble breathing, and her stomach clearly hurt, but all of that could be explained by the beating the thieves had given her.

I was pretty sure she didn't have the sickness. Feeling more secure, I crouched beside her. The girl tried to pull herself upright before giving up and slumping back against the stone. As she slipped down, her hair fell away from her face.

I'd assumed she was young because of her size, but up close I could see she was older than I'd originally thought, maybe twelve or thirteen. She had big green eyes, and a slightly upturned nose with a light dusting of freckles across its bridge. Seeing her more clearly gave me a surprise.

I knew her.

CHAPTER

"SALLY?" I SAID.

Sally was from Cripplegate, the same orphanage in which I'd grown up before Master Benedict had given me a home. Since the masters at Cripplegate housed the girls separately from the boys, I'd never got to know her well. But I'd helped the nurses care for her one winter when she'd had the flux, and then met her again a few months ago on the street during Oak Apple Day, when she'd helped me play a prank on an enemy of my master's.

She gave me a pained smile. Her teeth were bloody. "Hello, Christopher," she said.

Tom stepped back, alarmed. But bleeding in the mouth

wasn't a symptom of the sickness, just of the beating. "Let's take her home," I said.

After a glance to see if I was sure, Tom leaned in to pick her up.

She spat out blood. "I can walk."

Sally tried to stand once more. She almost made it to her feet before her eyes lost focus. Her knees buckled, and she went down, smacking her cheek against the wall.

"Ow," she said.

This time, she didn't protest when Tom scooped her up. He lifted her as easily as that sack of oats he'd rescued—and since she was about half a foot shorter than me, and half as thin again, she probably didn't weigh much more than it had.

We hurried home as fast as we could. Sally winced and grunted with every step Tom took, but right then, there wasn't anything we could do about her pain. From the sound of the riot, we needed to put the Royal Exchange as far behind as possible.

Tom carried Sally into the shop. Inside, I pulled my palliasse, the straw mattress that served as my bed, from under the shop's counter. I dragged it over to the smoking fireplace. Tom laid her down, then went out to the back and hauled in our supplies.

I held a cotton rag to her mouth to catch the blood. In the light of the fire, I could see a growing splotch on her cheek where the thieves had punched her. Despite the smoke from the fire, she wasn't coughing, so her lungs were probably all right. But the way she flinched as she twisted made me worry the blood was coming from her stomach.

I needed to examine her. First, she'd need something for the pain. "Can you bring me the poppy?" I said to Tom.

He scanned the shelves. "Uh . . ."

"In the corner, second shelf from the top. Next to the big brown jug of alcohol."

I dipped a copper pot into our water barrel and placed it on the fire to boil. When it was ready, I took the apothecary jar Tom brought me and—

"This is the wrong one," I said. The jar should have contained poppy straw: chopped, dried seed heads and stems. Instead, it was filled was a thick, goopy syrup, smelling of honeyed herbs. "This is Venice treacle."

"Sorry." Tom took the jar back. "I thought you said it was next to the alcohol."

"It is. It's right—" But when I turned to show him, I

saw I was wrong. The poppy was two jars down.

"It's that one." I pointed, frowning.

Tom brought me the right jar. I stared at the shelf, confused, until Sally moaned and I remembered what I was supposed to be doing. I threw a generous spoonful of the mixture into the steaming water and stirred it with honey to sweeten it. When I handed Sally a mugful, she gulped it down hot.

I let the infusion work for a few minutes before kneeling next to her. "Why were you following us?" I said.

"I saw you in the street," she said.

"But why didn't you just come say hello?"

"I wanted to wait until you came back, when you were with your master."

I supposed she'd had no reason to know Master Benedict had been killed. I was about to ask her why she wanted to meet him when she flinched and grimaced.

"I'm going to have to check your ribs," I said.

Sally breathed for a moment, steeling herself, then drained the last of the poppy infusion and undid the buttons on the front of her dress. Covering her chest, she slipped the woolen bodice down and turned away on the palliasse, spitting blood into the rag.

When Tom saw her, he drew in a breath. Pressed into Sally's pale skin was a boot print, treads and all, where one of the thieves had kicked her. The stamp was so deep it was hard to believe he hadn't broken her in two.

Tom looked upset. "This city's getting worse every day."

I couldn't argue. As disheartening as the riot at the Exchange had been, such things were all too common now. One of the worst aspects of the plague was the way the sickness had turned us against ourselves. The trust of the community had been shattered. We might as well have been living beside strangers.

Of course, Sally had come from Cripplegate, where trust had never had much to do with anything. "What were you doing over here?" I said. "I figured with the plague, the masters would lock you in."

"Cripplegate's shuttered," she said. "The Bird Man told us we were all going to die."

"Who?"

"The prophet." The poppy infusion had turned her eyes a bit glassy. "He came to see us."

I looked at her in surprise. "I've heard about him." When Tom looked at me quizzically, I said, "Isaac told me.

He said there was a prophet in London who could predict the course of the plague."

"He can," Sally said, and Tom's eyes widened. "He warned us that we were going to get sick. The masters gave us all medicine, but the Bird Man said medicine couldn't stop what was coming. And it didn't. That day, three of the little ones caught the sickness."

"What happened to them?"

"They were sent to the pest house north of Bishopsgate." The pest house was a ramshackle, timbered shed where some of the sick had been isolated. I shuddered to think of the children sent to die there.

Sally's eyelids drooped. "The masters wanted to lock us up inside, but the Bird Man said more would get sick if we stayed. So they closed the orphanage and moved the healthy ones to Saint Mark's in Wembley."

"You didn't go?"

"They wouldn't let me. I'm too old." The mug I'd given her, now empty, dangled from her finger. "That's why I followed you. I remembered you said you were apprenticed to Master Apothecary Benedict Blackthorn. I thought maybe he might need a maid." She gazed up at Tom. "You're really big."

Tom looked at me bemusedly.

"That's the poppy working," I said quietly. "It addles the brain." I turned back to Sally. "I'm going to have to examine your stomach now."

"Awright."

She hummed some unknown tune to herself as I pressed on her stomach and back. When I got to her ribs, she yelped.

"Sorry." I pressed again, and she scrunched her face into the straw with a squeak. Luckily, nothing moved where it shouldn't.

"It doesn't look like they broke anything," I said, which was a miracle in itself. "But your ribs are badly bruised."

"Don't want that." Her words slurred together. "Can I sell 'em?" She giggled.

"Hold her for me," I said to Tom.

He propped Sally up. She stared at Tom with unfocused eyes and returned to her humming. I wrapped her tightly, binding her chest and abdomen with a linen wrap over a plaster of comfrey, which would help mend her bones and insides. She'd got scraped up a bit, too, so I smeared some honey and garlic over the abrasions.

She looked down at the amber goo glistening on her skin. "I've turned into a sticky bun." Her humming faded as she lolled her head forward into Tom's shoulder. "G'night, Mr. Giant," she said, and drifted away.

Tom laid her back on the palliasse. "What's going to happen to her now?" he said.

I wondered the same thing. Her injuries, though painful, didn't appear as serious as I'd feared; she'd probably be all right in a week or so. But she had a bigger problem. Being dismissed from Cripplegate meant she'd be on the streets unless she could get a job, and that was next to impossible. The few wealthy folk who'd remained in the city weren't taking on new servants. And even if a job did open, she'd have to compete against the tens of thousands of other unemployed girls in the city.

"She can stay here for a few days," I said. "She should rest a bit, anyway." After that, I honestly didn't know what to do. I hated the thought of turning her out, but the food we'd brought back from the Exchange wouldn't last nearly as long with an extra mouth to feed. I was beginning to think I should have taken Isaac's offer to stay in the vault.

If only I could find Master Benedict's treasure! I needed to get back to trying to decipher his message. I went to put away the jars Tom had brought me, and as I climbed up the low step to return them, seeing the shelves made me frown again.

"Have you been playing around up here?" I said to Tom.

"No," he said.

"Then why are these jars all moved?"

I could see now that it wasn't just the poppy that had been in the wrong place. Several of the jars were out of place. Master Benedict's books and notes may have been a mess, but he'd always kept the shop in perfect order for our customers. Or, more accurately, he'd had *me* keep the shop in perfect order. Though both he and our customers were gone, I still wanted everything the same way.

But the jars here were all wrong. Even the labels weren't aligned properly. "It's fine if you were looking in them," I said.

"I wouldn't touch your things without asking you," Tom said. "Besides, I don't even know what they are."

Of course I believed him. But then why were these jars out of place?

I hopped down from the step and looked around the shop.

"What's the matter?" Tom said.

I walked into the workshop. I didn't tend to keep this

room quite as tidy, and with the various experiments I'd been working on, things got moved around, especially on the workbenches. But everything on the shelves still had its place. I examined these jars, too. As I stared at them, my heart began to thump.

Tom watched me from the doorway, looking nervous. "What's wrong?"

"My ingredients are not the way I left them," I said.

"What does that mean?"

"It means someone else has been in here." My heart was pounding. "Someone broke into my shop."

CHAPTER

TOM SWALLOWED. "ARE YOU . . .
are you sure?"

I *really* didn't want to be. But why else would my things
have moved?

"You could have done it," Tom said. "By accident."

"I dusted the shop this morning," I said. "Everything
was exactly where it was supposed to be."

Whoever broke in must have done it while we were at
the market. The idea worried Tom as much as me. "What
did they steal?" he said.

That was the strange part. I looked in all my jars, but
as far as I could tell, whoever had been in my home had

taken nothing. They'd left a small fortune in remedies on the shelves. The books, also valuable, were still there, too. Even the strongbox was where I'd left it under the counter.

"But if they didn't want to steal anything," Tom said, "why would anyone break in?"

I thought of the Cult of the Archangel, who'd ransacked the place three months ago. They hadn't been looking to steal money or ingredients, either. They'd been looking for something specific, something hidden—

My throat tightened. "Oh no."

"What?" Tom said.

"The treasure. Master Benedict's treasure." If someone had stolen it—

"Wait a minute," Tom said. "How could anyone steal Master Benedict's treasure? You don't know where it's hidden. *Isaac* doesn't know where it's hidden. Until he came here, you didn't even know there *was* a treasure."

I gasped. "The letter!" Master Benedict's letter. I went over to it, my head in my hands. It was open, sitting as I'd left it on the bench in the workshop. "I even circled the secret message for them!" I said in despair.

Tom found it hard to believe that some thief had

successfully deciphered a puzzle that I couldn't. He wasn't even convinced I was right about the break-in.

"My jars were moved," I insisted.

Tom made a face. "Right after you learn about Master Benedict's treasure, someone comes to steal it? How would they even know it was here?"

I stiffened. "Those men," I said.

"What men?"

"Today. In the shop. That beggar, Miles Gaspar. Or—the other two!"

"What about them?"

I went to the front and pointed to the end of the counter. "They were standing by the door to the workshop, while I was in the back with Isaac. Those two men were standing right here *the whole time.*"

"The door was closed," Tom said.

"So? I could hear you. Were you paying attention to them?"

"Yes. Well . . . sort of. When Miles came in, I was talking to him."

I recalled the argument. Venice treacle. Those two men had said they'd come for their master, who wanted the Venice treacle.

And that was one of the jars that had been moved.

I pulled it from the shelf. But inspecting it a second time just confirmed what I'd seen: There was the exact amount of treacle as there should have been. None of it had been stolen.

"There. You see?" Tom said. "If it was them, they'd have taken it."

"Then it must have been Miles Gaspar," I said. And I'd given him our *food*.

Tom shook his head. "There's no way he could have heard what you were saying. He was never even near the door."

"Then we have to figure out who was in here."

"Who's going to tell you that? Bridget?"

My pigeon looked over from the mantel and cooed.

"No." I jerked a thumb toward the window. "We'll ask the one person who's always watching the shop."

Across the street, in one of the windows of the Missing Finger tavern, sat a tall girl of seventeen. Dorothy, the publican's daughter, was leaning back in her chair and knitting, feet up on the windowsill. She saw me pointing and waved with a smile.

Tom flushed a little. "Oh. All right. Um . . . I'll wait here."

"What for?"

"Well . . . uh . . . Sally!" he said suddenly. She was sleeping on my palliasse, her chest rising and falling with hushed breaths. "Someone should look after her."

"I gave her a lot of poppy. She'll be out for hours."

"Still. I'd better stay." He shuffled from foot to foot. "Just to be safe."

I frowned. "What's going on?"

Tom's cheeks flushed a darker shade of red. "I don't want to go to the Missing Finger."

"Whyever not?"

Tom nudged his head toward the tavern, where Dorothy was half watching through the window. "I don't like the way that girl looks at me."

"How does she look at you?"

"Like she's a butcher," Tom said, "and I'm a prize-winning cow."

I had to smother a laugh. "I promise you'll be safe. Dorothy's harmless."

"She wants me to introduce her to my *family*."

"Oh, come on," I said. I still had to drag him across the cobbles.

• • •

The Missing Finger, like everything else in the city, had lost almost all its business. Before the sickness came, the tavern had bustled as busily—and as noisily—as the streets once had. I'd always liked the warmth of the place, so sometimes, for a special treat, Master Benedict brought me here for supper. Dorothy had worked for her father as a serving girl, always bringing a friendly word with a hot bowl of stew. But with the arrival of the plague, there wasn't much for her to do anymore. So she spent her time knitting in the window instead.

Today—as with most days now—the serving room was nearly empty. The only patron was a solitary drunk, half sleeping, half slurring vulgar songs in the chair by the fire.

Dorothy looked pleased we'd come in. "Hello, Christopher," she said. Her eyes flicked to Tom. She sat up in her chair and smoothed her apron over her turquoise linen dress.

Tom tried to hide behind me. Being twice my size, he didn't do a very good job of it. Dorothy gave him the most winning smile I'd ever seen. "It's so nice to see you again, Thomas."

Tom flushed. "H'lo," he said.

"I was really hoping you'd come and visit," she said.

Tom turned so red I thought he might catch on fire. He

mumbled something back. It could have been "Too busy," although it sounded a lot like "Please help me." It appeared Tom was right after all; the publican's daughter was indeed looking for a future husband. Anger swelled within me toward the thieves, because this was all very funny, but I was far too upset to enjoy it.

Dorothy turned to me, still smiling. "Who was that girl you brought home?"

I told her quickly about Sally, then got to the point. "Someone broke into my shop."

Dorothy stopped in the middle of a stitch, jaw open. "When?"

"When I was at the market. Did you see me leave this morning?"

"Sure."

"Did anyone go inside afterward?"

"Yes."

I gaped at her. "Who?"

"Some man." She shrugged. "Never seen him before."

"Why didn't you come tell me someone had broken in?" I said, flabbergasted.

She looked confused. "But he didn't break in. He walked in."

"What do you mean?"

"Just that. You left. A few minutes later this man walked into your shop."

"But . . . the door was locked."

Dorothy pursed her lips. "You know, that was kind of strange. I thought I saw you lock it before you left. But then that man went in, so I figured Thomas was still in the shop."

Of course. While I'd locked up, Tom had brought the handcart from around the back. Since Dorothy hadn't seen him leave, she wouldn't have thought anything was wrong. But that still left a question.

How did the man get in?

I ran back across the street. Tom followed. Dorothy watched from the window as the two of us stood in front of my shop.

"I *know* I locked up," I said.

"Maybe something's wrong with your key," Tom said.

There was nothing to do but try it. I turned it in the lock. It felt stiff, but I heard the bolt slide. Tom pushed on the door. It stayed closed.

"See?" I said. "It's fine."

Tom jiggled the handle. "Then how could—"

Creak.

The door popped open.

We stared at it, swinging on its hinges. "What . . . ?"

Then I spotted the bolt on the side. It hadn't come all the way out. When Tom had jiggled the handle, he'd moved the bolt just enough to free it from the frame.

With the door open, I turned the key again. This time, there wasn't any stiffness; the bolt clacked out like it was supposed to.

"Christopher." Tom knelt beside the doorjamb and peered inside the bolt hole. "Look."

I saw what he'd spotted. Inside was a piece of wood, preventing the bolt from sliding all the way.

Tom pulled his knife and tried to pry out the wood. It wouldn't come. "This was no accident," he said. "Someone jammed this block in here good."

I couldn't believe what I was seeing. Someone had tampered with my door.

I ran back to the Missing Finger. "The man you saw go into my shop. How long was he in there?"

Dorothy was standing now, watching. "A while. An hour, maybe? I'm not sure."

An *hour.* "Did he take anything with him when he left?"

She closed her eyes, trying to remember. "I didn't see anything. He stopped in the doorway on the way out, poked at the frame for a moment."

"The frame?"

"Where Thomas is." She motioned to where Tom was trying to pry the wood from the lock.

"There were three men who came into my shop," I said, "earlier this morning."

She shook her head. "It wasn't them, if that's what you're asking. This man was taller. And he was dressed all in blue. Blue doublet, blue breeches, blue leather shoes."

I tried to think back. I couldn't remember anyone dressed like that coming into the shop. Of course, it was his face I really wanted to know about.

"I couldn't see it," she said apologetically. "He had a black wig, but he wore a scarf. Blue, like the rest of his clothes. He held it in front of his face the whole time, for the sickness."

A lot of people kept perfumed handkerchiefs over their noses to protect themselves from the plague. But I doubted that was why this thief had pressed his scarf to his face.

A man, slightly taller than average, dressed in blue. That wouldn't be any help at all. Disappointed, I turned to go.

"Wait."

I stopped.

"There was one thing," she said. "When the man left your shop, he'd covered his face so much that I could see there was something below his scarf, on his chest. A little brass button."

"On his doublet?"

"Yes. But it was here, on the side." She tapped her chest, above her heart. "I only saw it for a moment. He covered it quickly when he realized it was showing."

A little brass button.

My heart quickened. "This button," I said. "Could it have been bronze?"

"Maybe."

Bronze. A little bronze button . . . or medallion.

Like the one the two men had been wearing.

I rushed back across the street. Tom was kneeling in the doorway, sucking blood from the side of his thumb. He'd managed to pry the wood out, nicking himself in the process. I told him what Dorothy had seen. "It *was* them. The thief had the same medallion. One of them must have tampered with the door when he came in."

"I didn't see that," Tom said, crestfallen. "I'm sorry."

I didn't blame him. But I was fuming. "I'm not letting anyone steal from me."

"I thought Dorothy said he didn't leave with anything."

"He could have easily tucked a bag of coins or something into his doublet. With the scarf over him, she wouldn't notice."

Tom looked skeptical. "Coins? You mean from Master Benedict's treasure? You really think he could have found it?"

"I don't know," I said, frustrated. "But whoever it was searched through my things for an hour. He didn't steal any remedies, ingredients, equipment, or books. Except for the treasure, I don't *have* anything else. So if he didn't come for that, why break in at all? What could he possibly have wanted?"

Tom didn't have an answer for that. He did have another point, though. "Even if that's the case, we don't know who this man was. What can *we* do about it?"

"The men in the shop said they served some master," I said. "And they wore the same bronze medallion as the thief. If we find out what that medallion is, maybe we can find out who was in here."

And I knew the one person who just might be able to help.

CHAPTER

TOM STAGGERED, THEN SLOWED TO
a stop. He leaned over, hands on his knees, panting. "Did
we really . . . have to run . . . all the way here?"

"I didn't . . . want . . . to miss him," I said, just as
breathless. By the looks of things, we'd made it just in time.

The stone walls of the Tower of London rose high above
us, its square towers standing guard over the city. Flags and
banners with the king's coat of arms flapped from the turrets, beacons of color in a world turned gray by the sickness.
At the gate, four horses waited. Three of the King's Men,
tabards sporting the royal crest, hauled bundles onto the
animals' backs, loading them up.

We dragged ourselves over to the gate. A man waited nearby, watching the soldiers work. He was dressed in black satin, with a battle-worn broadsword and pearl-handled pistol at his belt. He wore a patch over his left eye. That side of his face, scarred and twisted from nose to neck, was marked by a fresher scar, still red from healing. The wound ran from the middle of his brow, under his eye patch, all the way to the corner of his mouth, twisting his lip in a permanent half scowl. It had come from a strike that would have killed an ordinary man. I knew that because I'd witnessed the ax blow that had caused it.

This was Lord Richard Ashcombe, the King's Warden. His fearsome appearance—and equally fearsome reputation—belied a gentle heart, unswervingly loyal to our king. After the business with the Cult of the Archangel, he'd proven to be an equally helpful friend to me. Though I had to admit, he still made me nervous.

He spotted us as we approached. He spoke a few words to the soldier closest to him, then walked over, a sheaf of papers curled in his hands. He didn't step too close.

"Boys." His voice grated, made harsher by the scar that disfigured his face. "Glad to see you're not dead."

I couldn't disagree with that. "Is . . . uh . . . is the king well, my lord?"

"He is, though he worries about his people. How did you know I was in London?"

"Master Isaac told me."

Lord Ashcombe grunted. "I came to collect some reports on the war with the Dutch"—he held up the papers he was carrying—"and I need to hurry back to His Majesty straight-away." His men brought his horse over. "Did you come down here just to say hello, or was there something you needed?"

I told him about the break-in at Blackthorn. He listened, one hand on his saddle. He raised an eyebrow when he heard about the wood in the bolt hole.

"That's bold," he said.

I thought it was cowardly, and I said so. But Lord Ashcombe shook his head. "Whichever of those two men tampered with your door risked being spotted while he was doing it. Then there's the chance of their accomplice getting caught during the theft—or being remembered, if their plan was discovered. Would've been much easier to break a window at night." His eye narrowed. "Of course, then he'd have left a trail."

"My lord?"

"Think about it. This thief wouldn't have been noticed if he hadn't made a mistake with your apothecary jars. And you only confirmed he'd been there because he couldn't get the wooden block out of the door with that tavern girl watching. There's more going on here than a simple break-in. As far as this thief was concerned, it was just as important that no one knew he was there at all."

I realized he was right. If Master Benedict hadn't been so particular about how he kept things, I wouldn't even have known the thief had been in my shop. Especially because he hadn't taken anything I'd been able to see.

"That's what's most curious." Lord Ashcombe gave me a pointed look. "Why go to all this trouble and then take nothing?"

My cheeks flushed. The King's Warden had always had this way of telling when I was lying. Obviously, I didn't want to tell just anybody about Master Benedict's treasure, but in this case, there wasn't much reason to hide it. I knew Lord Ashcombe could be trusted. And I needed his help.

I said it in a low voice so the King's Men nearby wouldn't hear. "Master Benedict left me something in secret. I think that might be what the thief was looking for."

Now Lord Ashcombe was *really* interested. And I knew why. He'd never found where I'd hidden the recipe for the Archangel's Fire. And he wanted it.

"It's not *that*," I said quickly. "Master Benedict would never have kept that recipe in the house."

"But this 'treasure' could be something like it," Lord Ashcombe pressed. "The serving girl said she couldn't see if the man was carrying anything; if it was a parchment—a recipe—that could easily slip inside his doublet."

That hadn't even occurred to me. But now I thought back to what Isaac had said.

He hinted he'd left you something special. Something he wanted only you to have.

Master Benedict had always hidden his best recipes behind secret codes, to keep them safe from other apothecaries who would do anything to steal his work. That was why he'd taught me how to decipher them. To Master Benedict, a secret recipe *was* a treasure.

He'd kept his most valuable recipe—the Archangel's Fire—just for me. And if this new treasure was anything like the Archangel's Fire, it could be just as wondrous . . . or just as dangerous.

And worth much more than gold.

Lord Ashcombe's black eye seemed to burn into me. "Tell me everything you can about these thieves."

I described what I could, including the thief's blue clothes and the medallions. "They had a symbol on them. A circle, with a triangle inside, and a cross."

Lord Ashcombe shook his head. "Nothing I know matches that insignia. They mentioned their master. Was there anything else on the medallions? A motto? A badge or a crest?"

There had been words around the edges, but I hadn't been able to read them. I was about to say so when one of his soldiers spoke. "Did you say they was bronze?"

We turned. The King's Man held the reins of his horse, frowning. "Them medallions. They was bronze? Wore 'em over their hearts? Oh, sorry, General," he said, realizing he'd spoken out of turn.

Lord Ashcombe waved the apology away. "Say what you know."

"Well, I can't swear it's the same," the soldier said, "but me wife works at Guildhall, in the kitchens, right? And she's been saying everyone's jabbering about some prophet."

I looked over at Tom. That prophet again. The one

Sally had called the Bird Man. This was the third time today I'd heard about him.

For Lord Ashcombe, it appeared to be the first. "Prophet?"

The soldier nodded. "Knows where the plague's going to strike next and everything. Anyway, me wife says he's got these followers, right? And they wear these protection amulets. Little bronze medallions, right over the heart." He tapped his leather tabard.

"What's this prophet's name?"

The soldier made a face. "Sorry, General, I wasn't listening that hard. I love our Agnes, but she do go on a bit."

I remembered what Isaac had told me earlier. *If there really is a prophet out there, it's a dreadful sign that the worlds beyond have taken an interest in our city once again. And I don't have to explain to you how dangerous that is.*

That man in the shop had warned me his master wouldn't be pleased with me. Was he this Bird Man? Had I annoyed a prophet?

Lord Ashcombe ordered us to follow up on it. I don't think Tom liked that idea, and in spite of wanting to catch these thieves, I wasn't sure I did, either. But I couldn't think of anything else to do.

"Go to the city's offices at Guildhall," Lord Ashcombe said to us. "Talk to Will Gonson. He's an alderman for the parish of Crooked Lane."

The soldier cleared his throat. "Er . . . begging the general's pardon once more, but Gonson's dead, sir. Three weeks now, of the sickness."

The King's Warden cursed. "He fought with us at Edge Hill. Who's in his place?"

"Maycott, I think."

"Fetch me something to write with."

"Er . . . ," the soldier said again, looking about.

"I have these, my lord," I said.

I lifted my shirt. Underneath, wrapped around my waist, I wore my master's apothecary sash. It was stitched with narrow pockets, most holding stoppered glass vials containing ingredients and remedies. But they also held several useful tools. From one of them, I pulled a short quill and an ink vial.

Lord Ashcombe's expression shifted for a moment. If I didn't know better, I'd swear the King's Warden was amused. He tore a strip from one of the papers he carried and scribbled on it before handing it to me.

"Take that to Magistrate Maycott at Guildhall. Ask him about any break-ins, and find out what you can about this prophet. Maycott's not one of mine, so I can't promise he'll help you, but he's a decent enough man, and even without my seal, he should recognize my hand. Just make sure you stay away from his clerk, Shingleton. That man's a weasel if there ever was one."

Tom and I read the note.

Maycott,
Give the boy what he wants.
Ashcombe

"That's to the point," Tom whispered.

Lord Ashcombe swung himself onto his horse. The King's Men climbed onto their own mounts and rode in behind him.

"Should I tell you what happens?" I said.

"Your shop is your business," Lord Ashcombe said, "and I need to return to the king, so you'll have to solve this mystery yourself. Unless you find your master's left you something interesting. Then I want to know. Immediately."

He leaned toward me. "And, Christopher—if it *is* a recipe, I'll expect to see it. So there'd better not be any convenient explosions this time. Understand?"

"Y-yes, my lord," I stammered. "But . . . how will I get in touch with you? Aren't you going back to Salisbury?"

"Just for a day." He lowered his voice. "Don't spread the word, but the plague is growing in Wiltshire now. The Court will move to Oxford soon. So after tomorrow, that's where I'll be, securing a place for His Majesty's arrival."

"Should I leave messages for you at the Tower, then?"

"No. Don't tell this to anyone, either, but the Tower's closed. I'm leaving a guard at the gate, to make it look otherwise, but no one else is in there. If you need to send me a message, just tell Maycott. He'll get it done."

"Oh. Uh . . . all right."

"What's the problem now?"

"It's nothing. Just . . ." I told him about Sally. "I was hoping maybe there'd be work for her at the Tower."

"Tell you what," Lord Ashcombe said. "If you let me go, maybe I can ask at Court whether someone needs a servant. After I deliver these papers. To the king. Who is waiting for me."

I flushed. "Sorry."

He snapped his reins, and his horse began to move. Lord Ashcombe's expression softened—if only slightly—as he raised a hand to us in salute.

"I really am glad to see you well, boys. We've lost too many good men to this sickness already. So keep yourselves safe." He shifted his pistol in his belt. "Consider that an order."

CHAPTER
9

GUILDHALL WAS PACKED.

The government offices were nestled in a complex behind Blackwell Market, near the northwest part of London Wall. The two entrances off Cat Street and Basinghall had so many people streaming through them that the lines wrapped around the market, winding all the way down to Cheapside.

Like Tom and me, everyone was clamoring to see the magistrates. Some wanted a certificate of health, which would declare them free of the sickness and give them permission to travel England's roads. Others came to plead for a job, or for charity for relief for the poor. Many had shown up fuming about some proposed fire tax that would see the government lighting bonfires around the city to slow the plague.

The crowd must have numbered in the thousands, some of whom had been waiting to see the magistrates for weeks. Tempers were short as the people pressed and jostled and shouted and threatened, and after our adventure at the Royal Exchange—never mind the risk of catching the sickness—I had no interest whatsoever in waiting in that line.

"I have an idea," I said.

"Oh no," Tom said.

"It's a good idea."

"Oh *no*."

"Would you just . . . come on." We squeezed over to the Cat Street gate. There I started shouting. "Message for Magistrate Maycott! Message for Maycott! King's business! Make way!"

I prodded Tom forward. The crowd grumbled, but they parted, if only halfheartedly. Tom's bulk pushed us past them until we reached a side entrance. We slipped through and found ourselves in a blissfully empty hall.

There were office doors everywhere. Finely carved and polished wood paneling lined the walls. A corridor led off in both directions, forking at several intersections along the way.

Tom looked around. "Where do we go now?"

I had no idea. I'd never been here before; Master Benedict had always kept as far as possible from politics. "I guess we could ask somebody," I said.

"But we're not supposed to be here."

"Actually, we sort of are." I chose a direction randomly, pulling Lord Ashcombe's note from my sash. "With Ashcombe's signature, this *is* the king's business. If we just explain—oof!"

I bumped into someone as I turned the corner, bowling him over in a tangle of wig and linen. The man I'd knocked down was rather tall, with squinty eyes. With his backside gracing the floor, those eyes did not look happy.

"Sorry, sir. Sorry," I said.

"Get off me." He pulled away. "Who are you? How did you get in here?"

"We're . . . uh . . . couriers," I said. "We have a message from Lord Ashcombe for Magistrate Maycott."

He held out his hand. "Let me see it."

I hesitated.

"I am Maycott's clerk, Geoffrey Shingleton," he said. "All the magistrate's messages go through me."

I remembered Lord Ashcombe's warning. "But—"

That's as far as I got. Shingleton snatched the scrap of paper out of my hand.

He peered at it. Then he snorted. "Is this some childish jest?"

"What? No."

"There is no seal," Shingleton said, squinting his eyes so much I wasn't sure how he could see anymore. "There is barely a signature. It's not even on a proper piece of paper. This is the worst attempt at a forgery I've ever seen."

"It's not a forgery," I said indignantly. "Lord Ashcombe ordered us to come here. He said Magistrate Maycott would recognize his handwriting."

"That would be a neat trick." Shingleton lifted the glass cover of the wall lamp beside us and held the paper with Lord Ashcombe's signature in the flame. I stared in horror as it crisped, curling into ash and smoke.

A man walked around the corner. His black jacket and crest marked him as an officer of the court.

"Perfect timing, Mr. Reed," Shingleton said. "Put these two in the street."

"In the street" is exactly where I landed. Mr. Reed dragged us down the hall by our collars and rammed us out of a side door at the opposite end of Guildhall, away from the queues.

The guard shoved me hard, sending me sprawling into the dirt. He looked like he might do the same to Tom, but the boy's bulk made him think better of it. Instead, he patted the blade by his side.

"Ply your trade elsewhere," he said, before slamming the door shut behind us.

Tom helped me up. I grumbled as I climbed to my feet. "No one ever throws *you* in the mud."

"What are we going to do now?" Tom said.

I felt like kicking the door. "We have to get back inside."

The problem was I didn't have any idea how to do that. Shingleton having burned the message I'd brought, I couldn't go to Magistrate Maycott with nothing. But I couldn't go back to Lord Ashcombe, either, as he'd already left the city. And the one man who could put me in contact with the King's Warden was—of course—Magistrate Maycott. I'd officially run out of places to go.

I decided to kick the door after all. It trembled with a mighty *thump*. That wasn't nearly as satisfying as it sounded. And now my foot hurt.

"Maybe that guard at the Tower could help us," Tom said. "We could ask his wife what she knows."

I pulled my boot off and rubbed my toes. "He left with

Lord Ashcombe. I wouldn't even know how to find his wife. I don't suppose your father had any customers who worked at Guildhall?"

As it turned out, both of us knew someone who worked for the city—though neither of us expected it in the slightest. The door we'd been tossed out of opened. In the doorway stood a man dressed in finery.

"Tom!" he said. "I thought that was you!"

Tom blinked, confused. Then he said, "Dr. *Parrett*?"

The man standing before us had once been one of the most respected physicians in all of London. Then last summer, his wife and his son James had died in a fire. Driven mad with grief, he'd abandoned his practice and wandered the streets aimlessly, sleeping in the burned-out shell of his home, believing James was still alive and living there with him.

When the Cult of the Archangel had been chasing me, Dr. Parrett had welcomed me into what was left of his home, giving me somewhere to hide for the night. Afterward, Tom and I had checked in on him to see if he was all right—at least, as all right as he could be—but neither of us had seen him since the summer started, since his madness kept him mostly to himself, and with the plague running rampant, we'd stopped roaming the streets entirely.

To find him at Guildhall was unexpected, but that wasn't what surprised us the most. After the death of his family, Dr. Parrett had lived—and dressed—like a pauper. Yet today he was wearing a fine silk doublet and breeches, and a brand-new wig as well. He still had that slightly wild look in his eyes, but he looked so much better than the last time I'd seen him. A bit of hope swelled inside. Perhaps his madness had finally cleared.

Dr. Parrett spotted me. "And Christopher, too! Well, of course, who else would be with Tom?"

"What are you doing here?" I said. Suddenly, I realized how that sounded. "I mean . . . it's good to see you, sir."

He smiled. "And you as well. I'm sorry I haven't stopped by Blackthorn for a visit, but I've been rather busy. To answer your question, I've taken employment as a plague doctor."

That explained everything. Plague doctors were paid by the city to minister to the sick—especially the poor, who couldn't afford to pay for treatment. It was a job most doctors wouldn't touch, as it put them in constant contact with the sickest of the plague victims. It also left one basically ostracized, as no one wanted to spend time with a man who spent his days going in and out of plague-infested houses. But being a plague doctor paid very well. And for

Dr. Parrett, ostracism wasn't an issue. All his friends had already abandoned him.

As for me, I was pleased. Working as a plague doctor was incredibly dangerous, but it appeared it had been very good for Dr. Parrett, and I told him so.

"Yes," he said. "I feel a renewed sense of purpose. And, of course, the money is welcome. I've been starting to worry about how I was going to take care of James."

My heart fell.

"So what brings you boys to Guildhall?" he said. "And why on Earth did Mr. Reed throw you out?"

"Lord Ashcombe sent us here with a message for Magistrate Maycott," I said. "His clerk thought we were thieves."

Dr. Parrett shook his head. "I tell you, I've never met a more sour man than that Shingleton."

"Could you get us in to see his master?" I asked hopefully.

Dr. Parrett scratched under his wig. "I've never met Maycott." Then he brightened. "But I do know Magistrate Aldebourne. He's in charge of disbursing the charity collected through the churches around the country, to help feed London's poor during this plague. Perhaps he could provide an introduction."

I wasn't sure if that would do. With Lord Ashcombe's note destroyed, I'd have to hope that Dr. Parrett's word would be good enough for Aldebourne to pass us along. Despite Dr. Parrett's improved appearance, his madness clearly hadn't left him; he still seemed to think his son was alive.

Even so, it was the only chance we had. Dr. Parrett held the door open for us, smiling. Tom went inside. I brushed myself off and followed him in. The same guard who'd tossed us out was still in the hallway. He started forward when he saw us.

Dr. Parrett held up his hand. "They're with me, Mr. Reed."

I brought up my own hand, intending to show Mr. Reed something, too. Tom quickly swatted it down.

Dr. Parrett led us to a set of offices connected to the main hall where the petitioners waited. "So why did Ashcombe send you to Guildhall?"

I wasn't sure how much to tell him. "I don't suppose you've seen anyone come through here wearing a bronze medallion over his heart?"

"I've seen several. Were you looking for someone in particular?"

"Anyone dressed all in blue?" I said eagerly.

"Blue?" Dr. Parrett cocked his head. "I don't think so."

"Those medallions they wear," Tom said. "Do you know what they're for?"

"They're protection against the angel of death."

"But only some people are wearing them," I said.

"Yes," Dr. Parrett said. "Those are Melchior's men."

Melchior. Finally, I had a proper name for the man I'd been hearing about all day. "Someone I know called him the Bird Man."

Dr. Parrett laughed. "Ha! That's rather a good description. Though not as respectful as he deserves, I think."

"People are saying he's a prophet."

"He *is* a prophet."

Tom looked nervous. "Truly?"

"Oh, yes." Dr. Parrett nodded. "Officially, he's a plague doctor, like me. But he has the gift. He knows things only someone with foresight could possibly know."

Tom's eyes went wide. "Like what?"

Dr. Parrett stopped in front of one of the heavy wooden doors that lined the corridor. "Melchior understands the course of this plague like no other. I don't mean from a physician's perspective, though he's clearly practiced in that area as well. No, he can predict the path of the sickness itself. Melchior knows who will be the next to die."

My blood grew cold. Sally had said the same thing, but she'd been addled by poppy at the time. I wasn't really sure I'd believed her. "How is that possible?"

"I don't know. But I've seen it happen. Our paths have crossed on occasion. Four of those times, he's had these . . . visions, I suppose, of who will fall ill. Without fail, that poor soul became afflicted with the sickness. His talent is unquestionably real." Dr. Parrett lowered his voice. "Though perhaps I shouldn't say that so loudly in these halls."

"Why not?"

"Well . . . Melchior recently made some predictions about certain magistrates. It has some people around here rather nervous." Dr. Parrett knocked on the door in front of us.

"Enter," said a voice from inside.

The office behind the door was narrow and cramped, with barely enough space for the door to open without hitting the desk in the middle of the chamber. The room itself, however, was impeccably tidy, the desk and shelf piled neatly with papers and leather-bound ledgers.

A very small man sat at that desk, hunched over and scribbling in one of those books. He looked to be about fifty years old. He'd placed his wig on top of one of the stacks, exposing the bald spot growing at the center of his crown.

"Good day, Henry," Dr. Parrett said.

"Hmm?" Henry scribbled a little more, then peeked up at us from over a pair of silver, round-rimmed spectacles perched precariously on the tip of his nose. "Oh, hello, John," he said pleasantly. "Just place your report there, please." He motioned absently with his quill to a towering stack of papers on the corner of his desk.

"Actually, I'm here on behalf of these boys," Dr. Parrett said. "I'd like you to meet Christopher Rowe, apothecary's apprentice, and Thomas Bailey, baker's son. They need Aldebourne's help."

"Oh?" Henry looked us over with friendly curiosity. "What can the magistrate do for you?"

Dr. Parrett turned to us. "This is Henry Cole, Magistrate Aldebourne's clerk. Tell him what happened with Shingleton."

I recounted how Shingleton had burned Lord Ashcombe's note. Before I'd even finished, Henry was rolling his eyes. "I'd like to see him do that in front of the King's Warden— oh, fiddlesticks."

A spot of ink from the end of Henry's quill had dropped

onto the page he'd been working on. He stood and pulled a rag from a nearby drawer, dabbing at the ink. He didn't stand much taller than he'd been in his chair. I think Sally could have looked him straight in the eyes.

"I've ruined it." Henry tossed aside the rag with a sigh and turned his attention back to us. "Christopher, was it? I'm happy to ask Magistrate Aldebourne to speak to Maycott directly, though I'm not sure when he'll be back at Guildhall. I've been delivering him work at his home. He's not feeling well."

Tom glanced over at me. I knew exactly what he was thinking. So, apparently, did Dr. Parrett. "Has anyone examined him?" he said, alarmed.

"It's just a mild cold," Henry said quickly.

"But has anyone *examined* him?"

Henry straightened his spectacles. "Er . . ."

"Henry!" Dr. Parrett said.

"He wouldn't let me call a physician," Henry said defensively. "But look, he can't possibly have the sickness. If he hadn't told me, I wouldn't even have known he was ill."

Dr. Parrett frowned. "Aldebourne's staying home because he's unwell . . . but he doesn't appear ill? Is the magistrate the type to shirk his duties?"

"Of course not."

"When you were at Aldebourne's house," Dr. Parrett said, "did you see his family?"

"No, we met alone."

That didn't sound good at all. Tom had already begun backing away. As for Henry, he just looked puzzled.

"Melchior made a prediction," Dr. Parrett reminded the clerk.

"Melchior? No, no, no. I assure you, John, the magistrate is—" Henry's hand flew to his mouth. "Wait . . . you don't think—Aldebourne's *family*—?"

A woman screamed.

It came from outside, from the direction of the main hall. For a moment, no one moved.

Then came more shouts and screams.

"What the devil . . . ?" Henry said.

He grabbed his wig from the desk as he hurried past us into the corridor. We ran after him. The shouting intensified. It sounded like another riot had broken out. Then the noise began to ebb.

Henry was first through the door. The people who'd jammed the queues had mostly fled. Some of those remaining were lying on the ground, moaning, having been trampled by the fleeing crowd. A score of petitioners were pressed against the walls, trapped on the wrong side of the hall by the figure in the center of the chamber.

It was a man. He was dressed well, though his clothes were rumpled, his chin unshaven. In his arms, he carried a young girl of about nine years old, her emerald dress frilled with lace. Her head lolled back against the crook of his arm.

Henry shrank back. "M-Magistrate Aldebourne!" he said.

Aldebourne turned toward us. Now we could see the girl's face. From her mouth, a trail of bloody saliva trickled down her cheek and into her ear. She stared sightlessly at the ceiling.

The girl he was holding was dead.

CHAPTER
10

TOM BACKED INTO ME SO QUICKLY
he almost knocked me over. Henry stood frozen in the
doorway, his spectacles slipping down his nose, face as pale
as the dead girl's.

Magistrate Aldebourne didn't appear to notice. "Will
someone help me? My daughter." He shook her gently. "She
won't wake up."

Calmly, Dr. Parrett stepped forward. "Why don't we let
her rest, sir?" he said softly.

Magistrate Aldebourne blinked. "Oh. Yes. Of course."
He knelt on the stone and laid the girl's body down. He
brushed the hair from her face, pulling strawberry-blond

strands from the bloody froth on her cheek.

The door we'd come through was close to the main entrance to the hall. Unlike those trapped at the back, all we had between us and the open air were a few injured people on the ground. I felt a swelling desire to flee with the rest of the crowd. So did Tom; his hand inched toward my arm as if he planned to drag me with him.

A man at the back looked over at us as if he wished he could swap places. "The fool's doomed us all," he groaned.

Dr. Parrett held out his hand. "Calm, please. No diagnosis has been made."

"It's the sickness; of course it is!" a woman said.

That seemed pretty clear to me, too. But someone stepped in to disagree.

The voice carried from the other end of the hall. It boomed through the chamber, echoed from the walls.

"Do you presume to speak for us, then?"

Everyone turned. Between the open doors, a shadowed figure stood silhouetted against the brightness of the summer sky. Then the man—or whatever he was—stepped forward.

He wore a cherry-red, ankle-length overcoat of heavy leather. His gloves were leather, too, dark brown, the fingers so long that the tips curled forward like talons. On his head was a wide-brimmed black hat. But what was most startling was what covered his face.

The man wore a leather mask. In the center was a long, slightly curved beak. From the end of that beak, a thin curl of smoke rose, like his breath itself was fire.

The Bird Man, I thought.

The mask wrapped around his head, covering it completely. A pair of thick glass lenses was sewn into the leather, like giant spectacles. Through them were the only parts of the man I could see: his eyes. They burned with an intensity I'd only ever seen once before, in Lord Ashcombe.

The man stepped forward. In his hand, he held a three-foot silver staff, one inch thick, capped by a miniature gargoyle, its head and body soot black. A pair of silver wings spread out from its shoulders. He raised the staff like a totem.

The crowd went still. When Tom spoke, his voice was so quiet, that even in the silence, I barely heard him. "What is *that?*"

"That," Dr. Parrett said, "is Melchior."

From behind this other plague doctor—*or prophet,* I thought—eight men stepped into view. They were stone-faced, all dressed in the plain wool and linen of the commoner. They all wore one other thing: On their chests, sewn onto their doublets right over their hearts, were bronze medallions.

These were the men I'd wanted to find. Yet I barely glanced at them. Like Tom, I just stared openmouthed at the man in the bird mask.

He came forward, leather heels clopping on the stone. His men followed. They flanked him like a personal guard, weapons slung from their belts: swords, axes, clubs, and flintlocks, just like the men in my shop.

Melchior himself carried no weapon. He didn't wear a medallion, either. Instead, he had a symbol on his leather overcoat, painted black, right above his heart.

It was the same as the symbol on the talismans: a circle, with a triangle in the center, pointing up. But Melchior's was large enough that I could see I'd made a mistake; the glyph inside the triangle was a downturned sword, not a cross. I could finally read the writing around its edge, too.

It was Latin: *Contra malignitatem protege nos.* Protect us against malice.

He nodded to Dr. Parrett. The smoke from his mask swirled around him. "I greet you, sir."

Dr. Parrett bowed respectfully. "An honor, Melchior, as always."

Melchior stared at the girl's body through the lenses in his mask. "Another?"

"I haven't yet examined her," Dr. Parrett said.

"Then let us begin."

Melchior reached down with his silver staff. The gargoyle's head tipped the girl's chin from side to side, exposing her neck. Finding no black swellings, Melchior hooked a silver wing under her dress and pulled open the laces, exposing the skin below her collarbone.

He stopped.

The girl's skin had turned a bright red.

The crowd moaned. Quietly, Dr. Parrett confirmed it. "She has a token. It is the plague."

Henry made the sign of the cross so quickly he nearly knocked his spectacles off. Tom crossed his fingers on both hands and pressed into me. I pressed right back.

"We must remove the body from the hall," Dr. Parrett

said, his voice still low. "I need you, please, Tom."

Tom pressed so hard I thought he'd squash me against the wall. *"Me?"*

Dr. Parrett motioned to the people who still lay on the ground. "Just help the injured outside, will you? I'll take the girl."

Tom looked as if he might pass out from relief. He backed away from the body and half ran to the closest person who'd been trampled, an elderly woman. She held her wounded ankle, but she didn't appear to be feeling the pain. Instead—like most of the others, I noticed—she was staring at Melchior in awe.

I moved to help Tom, but Dr. Parrett stopped me. "Stay with the magistrate," he said under his breath. "But don't touch him."

I didn't need to be told *that* twice. Dr. Parrett gathered the girl in his arms and carried her out. Magistrate Aldebourne remained where he was, staring at the floor.

"It is as ordained," Melchior said, seemingly to no one. I remembered what Dr. Parrett had told us. *Melchior recently made some predictions about certain magistrates.* Another prophecy come true.

Henry stepped forward cautiously. "Er . . . excuse me? Sir?"

Melchior's men shifted as Henry approached. They watched him carefully, hands sliding almost imperceptibly toward the weapons in their belts.

Henry stopped and glanced nervously from Melchior's men to the prophet himself, who towered over him. Melchior didn't notice. He was scanning the ceiling, as if looking for something.

Henry cleared his throat and tried again. "Sir?"

Melchior finally looked down. He stared through the lenses in his mask. "Who are you?"

The little man shrank back. "H-Henry Cole, sir. I'm Magistrate Aldebourne's clerk. I help administer the charity."

Melchior said nothing.

Henry pulled at his collar. "John Parrett told me you . . . er . . . made more predictions recently."

Melchior tilted his head sideways. The smoke from his beak glinted in the sunlight.

Now I worried Henry might pass out. "He said . . . I heard one of them . . . was Magistrate Dench? That he would become ill. Has . . . has anyone checked in on him?"

The crowd waited, silent. Melchior continued to stare down at Henry. Then, finally, he spoke.

"I visited the house of Dench this morning. He is afflicted."

The people moaned.

Melchior's gaze drifted back toward the ceiling. "I have sealed his house in quarantine."

The strain of Melchior's presence finally became too much for Henry. He backed toward me and slumped against the wall, pulling off his wig. He dragged its curls across his face, mopping the sweat that dripped from his brow. "Magistrate Aldebourne's house should have been sealed, too," he whispered to me. "The people will be furious. And I was *there*. How could I have missed this?"

Actually, it was easy to understand how he'd missed it. Though the law required a household to send for an examiner within two hours of any symptoms showing, many tried to keep them hidden. Plague ordinances required all infected houses to be sealed—with every member of the house inside to be quarantined as well, whether they had the sickness or not.

For those trapped inside, it may as well have been a death sentence. Some families bribed the examiners to claim their loved ones' illness was something other than the plague. Others simply never told anyone—which, it appeared, was what Magistrate Aldebourne had done.

Henry's worry was well placed. The twenty souls trapped at the back of the main hall glared murderously at the grieving magistrate. It wasn't just that he'd put them in danger by bringing his daughter's body here. They didn't like officials not following the rules everyone else was expected to obey. Certainly, any one of *them* who'd done the same would be punished. If they could have, they'd have strung him up in the streets.

I looked back at Melchior and his men. My guts fluttered when I saw Melchior was already staring at me.

"I see you," he said. "I see you now."

He swayed back and forth, like an invisible breeze pushed him. His head tilted, as if he were listening to something.

I couldn't hear anything except the thumping of my heart. Henry, beside me, took a step back.

"Is something wrong?" he said.

"He is here," Melchior said.

My voice came out as a croak. "Who is?"

Melchior stepped closer. "Where are you?"

The people's grumbling had stopped. Even Magistrate Aldebourne stared up at Melchior, transfixed.

Melchior lifted his staff. His followers dropped to their

knees. Slowly, Melchior turned his head and stared at the gargoyle on the end of the rod in his hand.

"You have been touched," he said.

He was still staring at the gargoyle. But that wasn't who he was talking to.

"T-touched by w-what?" I stammered.

"By an angel," Melchior said.

Slowly, the staff lowered. The gargoyle's blackened head came toward me. I pressed backward. I'd have melted into the stone if I could.

"You walked with an angel," he said.

My jaw dropped. "How . . . how did you—"

"Now an angel walks with you. He calls to you. You and yours belong to him now. You belong to the angel of death."

Melchior's eyes burned into me. "Someone you love is going to die."

CHAPTER
11

I COULDN'T MOVE.

The hall was completely silent. All I could see was the gargoyle at the end of Melchior's staff, grinning at me with blackened teeth.

Then Melchior collapsed.

He fell to his knees. The staff clanged off the floor, sagging from fingers gone limp. His men rushed forward, grabbing him as he slumped. He lolled in their arms, shaking his head, lost in the grip of a nightmare.

I suddenly realized no one was near me. The rest of the crowd was still pressed against the back of the hall, staring at me in horror. Henry had stepped even farther away. He stood in the doorway through which we'd entered, his body half hidden by the frame.

The silence ended with the return of Dr. Parrett and Tom. As they passed Melchior, Tom shuffled to the other side, keeping Dr. Parrett between him and the masked prophet.

Dr. Parrett knelt beside Magistrate Aldebourne. "Your daughter is resting outside, on the grass," he said.

Aldebourne bowed his head. Dr. Parrett stayed beside him, talking quietly. I wasn't listening. I kept my eyes on the beaked plague doctor, hanging in the arms of his men. My ears buzzed, Melchior's voice bouncing inside my skull. *You walked with an angel.*

"Christopher."

I turned.

Tom, next to me, looked scared. "Why didn't you answer me? I asked if you were all right."

Someone you love is going to die. "You . . . you didn't touch the girl, did you?" I said.

"Of course not." Tom looked at Dr. Parrett. The doctor's hand rested softly on Magistrate Aldebourne's arm. "I don't understand how he can do that."

"He's a good man." *Besides,* I thought, *it's not like he has anything left to lose.*

Dr. Parrett called Henry over. "There's nothing else to be done here," he said quietly. "We should clear the hall, take the magistrate to his office."

"Right. Yes. Of course." Having something to do seemed to steady the little man. "Good people," he called to the remaining crowd. "Our offices will be closed for the afternoon. Please return tomorrow and we will help you then."

"Help them with what?" a man said.

We all turned. The man who'd spoken stood between the open doors at the entrance to the hall, where Melchior had been just moments before. Tall; broad shoulders; long blond hair.

I looked at Tom in surprise. It was Galen, the apothecary we'd seen at the market. Apparently, Henry recognized him, too, because he sighed and muttered, "Again?"

Galen hadn't survived the riot unscathed. There was a lump on his temple where the quacksalver had hit him, an angry red welt, already growing purple. His eyelid was swollen, the eye beneath bloodshot, the skin starting to blacken. His ingredient-stained clothes were rumpled, with a new tear in the seam of his doublet's collar.

The apothecary entered the hall. He slowed as he passed

Melchior and his men, inspecting the Bird Man with mild curiosity, before stopping in front of us.

"Please, Mr. Cole, tell them," he said. "How is it, exactly, that you can help these people?"

"Mr. Widdowson," Henry said. "This is not the time."

"Oh? When would be the time?" Galen motioned to the remaining crowd. "After they catch the sickness, too?"

The crowd gasped. Henry looked flustered. "No one here will catch the sickness." He whirled on Galen. "Will you go away!"

"I'd very much like to," Galen said. "But the city insists I deal with you."

"And I've given you my decision. We're not interested."

"How can you not be interested in a cure for the plague?"

A murmur ran through the crowd. Dr. Parrett, I noticed, actually *didn't* seem interested; he barely glanced at the man. Melchior, still recovering from his spell in his men's arms, didn't appear particularly impressed, either.

"He doesn't have a cure," Henry assured everyone.

Galen arched an eyebrow. "You are as wise," he said dryly, "as you are tall."

Henry turned bright red. "How dare you!"

The scene had pulled Magistrate Aldebourne from his

grief. He looked up from the floor. "What's going on? Who are you?"

"Ah. Forgive me, Magistrate." Galen gave a deep bow. "My name is Galen Widdowson; I'm an apothecary. I've been studying abroad, searching for anything that might act as a remedy against the plague. After many years, I've returned home. For I've finally found that cure."

Henry stepped between Galen and his master. "The man has just lost his daughter," he said to Galen. "Have you no decency?"

Galen's eyes flashed. "Decency, Cole, would have allowed me a chance to save the girl. Not sent me to treat the children you don't care about."

"I care about every child in this city," Henry sputtered.

"Is that so? Then this should please you." Galen turned toward the entrance to Guildhall and called out. "Come!"

A woman in ragged clothes peeked nervously through the open doors. She entered slowly, pushing a young girl in front of her, her hands on the girl's shoulders.

"It's all right," Galen said, his voice softening. "Don't be afraid." He guided the woman to stand before him. "Now, love, tell us. Which of these gentlemen was treating your daughter?"

She pointed to Dr. Parrett.

"Show him," Galen said.

With gentle prodding, the woman curtsied to Dr. Parrett. "Please, your worship," she said. "Do you remember Beatrice? You've been tending to her in the pest house?"

She brought the girl forward. Dr. Parrett peered at her. "Hm? Oh, yes, of course. I . . . Good Lord."

He stared.

We all watched as Dr. Parrett examined the girl. Melchior, recovered from his spell, observed from the ranks of his men. Dr. Parrett looked into the girl's eyes, down her throat, felt under her arms. He pulled aside her dress.

Then he stepped back, stunned.

"How is this possible?" he whispered.

The woman held the girl to her breast. "Good Master Galen gave our Beatrice some medicine, your worship. And she got better."

The crowd was buzzing now. Aldebourne was staring at the girl like she'd returned from the dead. "Is this true?" he said.

Dr. Parrett examined the girl more closely, turning her this way and that. "She had the sickness but a day ago," he said to Melchior, amazed. "She was certain of death."

Slowly, Melchior looked over at Galen. "A miracle," he murmured.

"A coincidence," Henry said, looking a little thrown.

Galen shook his head, as if disappointed at a poor student. Henry, meanwhile, seemed oblivious to the fact that the crowd was glowering at him with the same unfriendly eyes that had stared daggers at Magistrate Aldebourne.

"With respect, John," Henry said to Dr. Parrett, "there is no cure. The girl must have been misdiagnosed."

Dr. Parrett shook his head. "I assure you, she was not. Beatrice had headaches, the sweats, vomiting, pain in the joints. She was delirious, and the seizures had begun. And her chest showed one of the tokens: a skin of reddish hue, just like—" He caught his words with a glance at Aldebourne. "Like many others," he finished.

Melchior's eyes were still on Galen. "Remarkable." There was something in the man's tone I found unsettling: a bite, a sting. Muffled by the bird mask, I couldn't quite tell what it was.

For the first time, the crowd trapped in the hall came forward. "We're saved!" one of them cried, and others took up the call.

"Now, wait—" Henry began.

Magistrate Aldebourne stood. He grabbed Galen's arm. "Can you really stop this plague?"

Galen clasped his hand over the magistrate's. Since the plague had started, it was the first time I'd seen strangers willingly touch skin.

"I can," he said. "I swear it on my life."

Aldebourne stared at him, as if he wasn't sure the apothecary was real. "My other daughter, Annabelle. She has the sickness, too."

"Then take me to her," Galen said. "And I'll show you what I can do."

CHAPTER
12

EVERYONE WENT WITH HIM. GALEN led the crowd, marching at the front with the magistrate. Tom and I followed, walking with Dr. Parrett. Behind us stomped a red-faced Henry, muttering under his breath.

My mind was such a jumble I didn't know where to put my thoughts. *A cure for the plague.*

A *real* cure?

Back at the Exchange, I'd admired the way Galen had stood up to that fraud. His contempt for the quacksalvers reminded me of the way my master had scorned them. Yet when the apothecary had claimed he had his own cure, I hadn't really given it any weight. Since Dr. Parrett had diagnosed that girl free of plague, I was so stunned—and hopeful—that I found it hard to concentrate on what I'd gone to Guildhall for in the first place. Or what I'd just heard when I was there.

Melchior. He was here, too, his men guarding him as he walked alongside the crowd. The plague doctor had recovered fully from his spell. He strode in his long leather coat, the smoking beak surrounding his head in a gray haze.

His prediction made, he no longer seemed to have any interest in me. His focus was fully on Galen. With the mask covering his face, I couldn't tell what he was thinking. Frankly, I was just grateful he was no longer looking my way.

His men weren't paying any attention to me, either. I studied them as we walked, looking for anyone familiar. None of them matched Dorothy's description of the thief— all dressed in blue—though of course, clothes could be changed. I didn't recognize any of them as the men who'd come to my shop, either.

That meant these eight weren't all of them. There were at least two more—the ones from my shop—plus the thief himself, who, since I'd never seen his face, could have been anyone at all. I wondered how many more followers Melchior had gathered. It almost took my mind off Melchior's prophecy, still bouncing around my head.

Someone you love is going to die.

"Remarkable, isn't he?"

Dr. Parrett nodded toward Melchior and his men. He'd spotted me looking across the way.

I spoke in a low voice, so only Dr. Parrett, Tom, and Henry could hear me. "Why does he look like that?"

"The costume?" Dr. Parrett said. "That's from the Continent. Plague doctors wear them there. It's supposed to shield them from infection. The leather protects the skin, and aromatic herbs in the beak clean the air. Though Melchior's mask is unusual." He studied the plague doctor, curious. "I've never seen one give off smoke before."

"How come you don't wear one?" Tom said.

Dr. Parrett shrugged. "I'm not certain it works. Plague doctors still contract the disease, and in high numbers. Either way, I can't imagine trying to treat someone in that outfit. The appearance alone may frighten the patient and further imbalance the body's humors. My son is terrified of him."

Henry paused from his grumbling to agree. "Gives me the chills."

Tom nodded, too, though whether he was chilled by Melchior's appearance or by Dr. Parrett's reference to his dead son, I couldn't tell.

"Still, Melchior's ministrations have been most welcome," Henry added.

"Yes," Dr. Parrett said. "But it is his gift that truly sets him apart."

Now *I* felt a chill, right down my spine. "Did he really predict the death of Magistrate Aldebourne's daughter?"

"Not specifically," Dr. Parrett said. "He just said the plague would strike close to Aldebourne."

"His prediction about Magistrate Dench has come true, as well," Henry said.

Dr. Parrett shook his head. "Make no mistake, boys. When Melchior speaks, you'd be wise to listen."

My stomach fluttered as Henry's eyes flicked toward me. I'd already noticed he was walking an extra pace away.

"Isn't it possible this is all coincidence?" I said hopefully. "I mean, so many people are dying now. If you made a bunch of predictions, you'd be bound to get some right. Wouldn't you?"

Dr. Parrett smiled. "You sound like Benedict. Normally, I'd agree with you: During an outbreak this severe, it wouldn't be hard to predict some deaths accurately, even if other predictions went wrong. But that's what sets Melchior apart, you see. He hasn't been wrong. Not once."

I felt sick.

Dr. Parrett motioned to the men surrounding Melchior. "His success has gathered him quite a following. He's even taken to preaching in one of the abandoned churches."

"Preaching?" Tom said. "I thought he was a plague doctor."

"He is. But the flight of the clergy with the sickness has left a spiritual thirst in the city. Many are taking the pulpit back for the people. Personally, I think Melchior's gift makes him the perfect man to fill that need. I hear his sermons are packed."

"What does he say in them?"

"I don't know. I've been meaning to go, but my duties have kept me too busy." Dr. Parrett stared into the sky with a faraway look. "I've heard of such individuals, blessed by God with this kind of foreknowledge. Plagues always bring out the doomsayers, but Melchior . . . he is truly touched by something beyond the mortal realm. I've only ever seen his like once before, during the outbreak in Paris, back in 1652." His eyes cleared as he turned to me with interest. "I first met your master there, you know."

I blinked. "You did?"

"Indeed. There was a swelling of plague in the French capital that year, and many believed it would spread to London next. I went abroad because I'd had no experience treating it, and I wanted to see the latest techniques. Anyway, I was invited to a dinner party, and Benedict was there. Funny, isn't it? We lived but a few blocks away from each other, yet we had to travel to another country to meet."

"Why was he in Paris?" I said, fascinated.

"Your master traveled all the time, in those days. The sickness was rather an obsession of Benedict's back then, as I recall. He was determined to find a cure. The host of that dinner had been your master's friend for years, said it was something to do with Benedict's past. An old apprentice of his, I think. Ah, here we are."

I frowned. Master Benedict, obsessed with the plague? Since when? I wanted to ask Dr. Parrett more, but Magistrate Aldebourne was already unlocking the front door to his house.

Melchior followed him inside. Dr. Parrett did, too. "You boys stay here," he said.

"As if we needed to be told," Tom said, incredulous.

Galen stayed outside, too, waiting for the diagnosis from the plague doctors. The apothecary hadn't said anything since we'd left Guildhall. Now he stood with folded arms, staring quietly at the ground, oblivious to the whispers from the crowd.

Henry seemed angrier than ever. With the doctors gone, he'd gone back to glaring daggers at the man.

"Mr. Cole?" I said.

"Yes?" Henry said, still staring.

"How come you're so skeptical of Galen's cure?"

"I thought John said you were apprenticed to an apothecary. Doesn't your master have to deal with these quacks?"

"My master died, sir." I scuffed the dirt. "A few months ago."

"Oh." Henry turned to me, embarrassed. "I'm sorry, lad; I didn't realize. The sickness, was it?"

Tom said it, so I didn't have to. "He was murdered by the Cult of the Archangel."

Henry looked surprised. "The Cult of . . . Wait. John said your master's name was Benedict. He didn't mean Benedict Blackthorn?"

"You knew him?" I said.

"Only by reputation. Such a loss for the city! Especially now. Did he teach you what he knew about it?"

"About what?"

"The plague, of course."

Now I was confused. Again. "We never talked about it."

"But Benedict Blackthorn was a plague specialist," Henry protested. "Surely he must have discussed it with you. His investigations into potential remedies? Similar diseases and cures? Herbs and the like that provoke or relieve plague symptoms?"

I shook my head. Henry frowned. "I could have sworn Blackthorn was an expert in such matters," he said. "Well, perhaps I'm out of touch. I wasn't here for that Cult business. I actually haven't lived in London proper since the last time the plague hit the city. I only returned to work for Magistrate Aldebourne two months ago, when his previous clerk fell to the sickness."

"You came *to* the city?" Tom said. *"Now?"*

"Absolutely," Henry said proudly. "In my own way, I'm a plague specialist myself. I know I'm not in the vanguard with the doctors, like Melchior or John, but it is our duty to offer according to our talents, and I am blessed with a skill for numbers. So I help manage towns in times of crisis.

Because when a sickness breaks out, a well-run town saves lives—especially the lives of those most in need. Take the charity away from the poor, and they'll die.

"*That* is my problem with Galen. Plagues attract frauds like the harvest brings locusts. They sweep in to prey on the most desperate with 'remedies' that couldn't even burst a blister. I've seen this time and time again—and you'll see the same here, I promise you."

"But Galen was *fighting* the quacksalvers in the market," I said. "And he isn't charging anyone for his cures."

Henry scratched his head. "I admit, that is different. When he came to my office, he didn't really want anything for himself. All he asked was for the city to buy the ingredients, and then provide the cure to the people for free."

"So if he's not trying to cheat anyone—" I began, excited.

"He has an actual cure? Impossible."

"Why?"

"Because there's no such thing," Henry said simply. "I've seen enough of the sickness to know it's the handiwork of forces beyond our realm. The best we can do is try to alleviate the suffering."

Magistrate Aldebourne's door opened. Melchior stepped out and went to stand among his men. He handed something to two of them, something small. I couldn't see what it was. The men looked down at it for a moment, then marched away.

Dr. Parrett came to us. "It's as Aldebourne said. His daughter is infected. We have to seal the house immediately."

Henry looked downcast. "Dear God," he said. Then he nodded to a group of men who'd followed us to the house.

They'd already brought the supplies they needed. They nailed wooden planks over the ground-floor windows. The door was left unboarded, but one man painted a big red cross, three feet high, on its front. Above it he wrote the same message that adorned so many houses in the city.

LORD HAVE MERCY ON US

Dr. Parrett handed the house keys to Henry. The clerk arranged with his men for a pair of guards to stand watch. One would work the day shift, the other one the night. They'd be responsible for keeping the family inside; from this point only physicians, nurses, or apothecaries were allowed to leave the house. Anyone else who went in would be quarantined with the rest of Aldebourne's family.

The magistrate himself watched these sad proceedings from the entryway. Galen spoke to him. "Don't be afraid. I'll cure Annabelle. You have my word." And with that, he strode inside.

Melchior turned to Dr. Parrett. "I wish to observe this," he said, and both he and Dr. Parrett followed the apothecary through the door.

"I want to see, too," I said to Tom.

Tom placed a hand on my shoulder. "If you try to go in there, I will put you on the ground and sit on you."

"I meant let's look through the window. Come on."

It was easy enough to find a ladder. Four houses nearby were already boarded up, the same cross and sorrowful plea painted on their doors. Wherever this happened, the guards arranged for ladders, since the safest way to pass food or supplies to the infected without going inside was through the upper windows.

Dealing with the quarantine guards could be tricky. They weren't well liked. Although everyone was afraid of plague carriers, people hated seeing their neighbors sealed up to face an almost certain death. It didn't help that the guards had a reputation—not entirely undeserved—for drunkenness, irresponsibility, and sloth. Even the decent ones had to stay wary, as guards were often attacked in attempted escapes. Tom and I had witnessed a terrible assault ourselves; on my own street, a lawyer and his wife broke out of their quarantine by burning their guard with gunpowder. The poor man had lain on the cobbles, crying piteously, too hurt to save. All we could do was ease his pain by giving him enough poppy tea so he could pass on in peace.

The guard nearest the Aldebourne house eyed us warily when we asked to borrow his ladder. He was reluctant to let it go—he was, after all, responsible for it—but we promised to return it, and seeing who we were with, he could hardly refuse. Back at the magistrate's place, I climbed up and peeked in the third-floor window.

Magistrate Aldebourne was in the corner, pressed

against the cupboards, as if he wished he could climb inside. He held a sobbing woman in his arms; his wife, I guessed. They both stared at the bed where his daughter lay.

The girl looked terrible. Her long dark hair was damp, stuck to her face with sweat. Her cheeks were pale, her eyes haunted. Clutching her stomach, she leaned over and vomited into a chamber pot.

Dr. Parrett held her close. Annabelle jabbered at him, delirious, and though her words were nonsense, Dr. Parrett nodded and spoke to her soothingly.

Galen was at the fireplace, his back to me. Melchior stood alone in the corner opposite the magistrate, watching. The way the firelight reflected off the lenses of his mask made him look like he was burning inside.

Tom climbed up behind me, one rung down but tall enough to look over my shoulder. He made a choking sound. "That's . . . that's . . ."

For a moment, I thought he was looking at Melchior. Then I realized what had shaken him. The Aldebourne girl looked a lot like his oldest sister, Cecily. Long, dark hair, round face, pale skin, pretty eyes. Even the nightgown she was wearing was nearly identical to Cecily's.

"I don't want to see this," Tom said, and he climbed

back down. I was about to go with him—he really looked like he needed a friend right now, and I didn't want him to stand there alone—but then Galen shifted, and I could see what he was doing.

He'd placed a pot of water on the fire; it was boiling. He poured that water into a heavy mug. Then, from underneath his belt, he pulled out a small black leather pouch.

Melchior turned to Galen as well. We both watched as Galen stirred the water, cooling it. Then, from the pouch, he poured a large quantity of a grayish powder into the mug. He continued to stir all the while.

After a minute, Galen handed the mug to Dr. Parrett. The words came through the window, muffled by the glass. "Give her this. She must drink it all."

Dr. Parrett coaxed Annabelle to sip the concoction. "How long will this take?" he asked.

"Less than a day," Galen said. "She'll start to improve before nightfall. You'll see."

Dr. Parrett spotted me at the window. He came toward me, but left it closed. "I'm going to stay and watch over Annabelle," he called through the glass. "You'd best go on home. I'll stop by Blackthorn if anything happens."

I said goodbye and climbed back down. Tom was standing by himself, hunched over by the corner of Aldebourne's house, hands clasped in prayer. As I went to him, Henry stopped me.

"So? What happened?" he said.

I told him what I'd seen.

"That's it?" Henry said. "A 'grayish powder'? That's what's going to stop the plague?" He threw his arms up and walked away.

I understood his reaction. But Henry wasn't an apothecary. He didn't realize that nothing we made ever *looked* impressive. Yet from the sash hidden under my shirt, I could pull a vial filled with a simple yellow liquid that could eat through iron, or a half dozen little black beans that could kill in minutes. We couldn't dazzle you with magic. The blessings in our remedies were hidden within.

If this cure actually worked, the girl upstairs was just the beginning. Tens of thousands—more—would be saved.

A world without plague.

I thought of Master Benedict, and wished he were here to see it.

CHAPTER
13

WE RETURNED TO THE SHOP TO
hear something I'd never heard in my home before.

Tom cocked his head. "Is that . . . singing?"

It was coming from over by the fireplace. From behind
the display table, a pair of buckled shoes stuck over the top,
bobbing in time with the song. "My dame has a lame, tame
craaane . . . my dame has a crane that is laaaaaaame . . ."

"Sally?" I said.

Her head poked around the leg of the table. "Hello,"
she said brightly, her big green eyes shining. She was lying
on her back on my palliasse, her legs up in the air, propped
against the table. Bridget was sitting on her chest.

Sally returned to her song, humming this time. "I like your bird," she said. Bridget certainly seemed like she was enjoying the music, her eyes half-closed in contentment.

"Is she like that because of the poppy?" Tom whispered, puzzled.

"I think that's just her," I whispered back. I went around the table. "Why are you lying that way?"

"My chest doesn't hurt as much if I stick my legs up," she said.

Of course, with the tea's effect faded, the pain had returned. Giving her poppy repeatedly would be dangerous, so I got Tom to help me prepare an infusion of willow bark instead. As Sally drank it down, Tom said, "I'm starving," and began attacking the remainder of the honey cake. I was hungry, too; with all the running around we'd been doing, we'd missed lunch. I sat on the counter next to Tom and started slicing the wheel of Cheshire cheese I'd bought at the market. Sally remained on the palliasse.

"Don't you want any?" I said.

"I'm all right," she said. Her growling stomach said otherwise.

I rescued the last piece of honey cake from Tom's

clutches and gave it to Sally on a plate with some of the Cheshire. "Take more if you want."

She shook her head. "This is enough, thanks." But she cleared her plate even more quickly than Tom. When I dropped another slice of cheese on it, she hesitated.

"This isn't Cripplegate," I said. "You're allowed to have seconds. Look at him."

Tom grunted in protest, even though his knife was already halfway through the cheese again. Sally looked from me to Tom, then back again.

"I'm paying you back," she said.

"Sure."

I soon discovered she'd started paying me back for letting her stay before I'd even got home. After polishing off the rest of her plate, she picked up a needle and a pair of woolen breeches from beside the palliasse and began threading the needle along the hem, humming.

Those breeches were mine. "What are you doing?"

"Your clothes are too short for you," she said. "I'm letting them down."

I flushed. Having Tom around meant I never felt tall. But I'd grown an inch and a half over the summer, and I was starting to outgrow what I owned. If Master Benedict had still been around, he'd have bought me new things—all the while despairing theatrically that Cripplegate didn't teach its boys to sew. If I'd had any money, I'd have bought new outfits myself. Especially breeches. Mine were getting uncomfortably tight in places I'd much prefer were loose.

"And all your things have holes in them," Sally said disapprovingly.

I really did need to take better care of my clothes. "Thank you," I said, embarrassed.

"Told you I could help," she said cheerfully. "Besides, you're an apprentice for a very important shop. You shouldn't walk around with holes in your breeches." She stuck her hand inside and wiggled her fingers through a huge rip in the backside.

"But . . ." I turned to Tom, who was stuffing cheese in his mouth. "I wore those yesterday."

"I know," he said.

"Didn't you see the hole?"

"Of course I did."

"Why didn't you say something?"

"I thought it was funny."

Sally giggled.

I sputtered. "You . . ."

"After that Smoke-Your-Home," Tom said indignantly, "I'd say we're even."

"Not yet. But we will be." I pulled a vial from my apothecary's sash and held it up.

Tom looked suspicious. "What's that?"

"Castor oil."

His eyes went wide. "You wouldn't."

"Oh?" I went into the workshop and stomped upstairs. "Hope you enjoy tonight's dinner," I said in farewell.

I decided I'd let Tom stew over whether or not I'd really give him a bad case of the trots. But that wasn't why I went upstairs. I didn't want them to notice how little I'd eaten.

In all the excitement of a possible cure for the plague, we'd forgotten a terribly important fact: I still had no money. If I was going to be feeding Sally now, too, we'd have to start rationing food.

I should have said so right away, but I'd felt awkward about it. Tom always looked forward to eating. And I wanted Sally to understand that this really *wasn't* Cripplegate. Three years ago, Master Benedict had given me a home, made me feel safe and wanted. I could do the same for Sally, even if it was just for a few days.

I sighed. I was probably being foolish. Tom already understood the situation, and I was sure Sally would, too, if I explained it. Yet I didn't want to have that conversation, in large part because I was feeling like such a failure. Tom and I had gone to Guildhall to find the man who'd broken into my home. Not only had we come back empty-handed, I didn't even know what to do next.

And, possible plague cure aside, I was really worried. About Melchior, his predictions, his prophecy to me. And the thieves, who we now knew were among the plague doctor's followers.

My thoughts had me running around in circles. If I knew exactly what those men had stolen, then I might be able to make sense of all this. Tom still thought it unlikely that they'd taken my master's treasure, but he couldn't think of another good reason why anyone would have snuck into the shop. Even if they hadn't overheard what Isaac had told me, they'd certainly have seen the letter on the workbench with the secret message circled. And as Lord Ashcombe had pointed out, this crime had been well planned. They obviously wanted *something* of my master's.

But what? Gold, as I'd originally thought? A recipe, like the King's Warden had suggested?

Or was it something else?

I thought of the clue my master had left me: *Study our birds.*

I still didn't have any idea what that meant. I wandered about the upper floors, poking around the book stacks, hoping something would jump out at me. Something did: a *really* big spider, crawling on a tome of Italian plague remedies.

After a brief bout of running away in panic, I cooled my thumping heart, grabbed a nearby glass, and plonked it over the spider, trapping it. I didn't like the ugly things, but that spider's legs, hair, and extract were valuable ingredients.

I watched it scrabble against its prison. As I did, my gaze slipped toward the book below it. I held the glass down to keep the spider inside as I slid the volume out from underneath.

Italian plague remedies.

The book made me think of what Henry had said. *Benedict Blackthorn was a plague specialist.*

Dr. Parrett had said the same thing. *The sickness was rather an obsession of Benedict's, as I recall. Something to do with his past. An old apprentice of his, I think.*

I realized I might actually be able to find out more about this reported obsession. Master Benedict hadn't just made notes on his studies and experiments. As it turned out, he'd also kept journals of his daily life, diaries of his thoughts and happenings. I'd discovered them after his death, tucked away under books he hadn't touched in years.

The journals went all the way back to when he'd joined his first master, a man named Allan Wade, who'd studied under the great John Parkinson, apothecary to King James I and founder of our Guild. The first volume I'd discovered was dated 1624, when my master had been my age. It was so strange to think of him being an apprentice, just like me.

The pages, old and yellowed, had come alive with my master's words. His handwriting was different, that of a young man, not as smooth and stylized as it would become. When I'd first found that journal, I'd devoured those pages, fascinated— fourteen-year-old Benedict Blackthorn, complaining about always scrubbing floors!—but the taste soon turned to ashes in my mouth. Reading his words made me miss him so much that I'd had to put the journal down and walk away. I'd returned to it once, one sleepless night, reading by candlelight. I'd only got a few pages in before that same sadness drove me away again. After that, I'd given them up for good.

But now I had a purpose. *An old apprentice of his.*

I thought back to what Isaac had told me. There had

been three plagues this century: 1603, 1625, and 1636. Master Benedict had been born in 1610, so in 1625, he'd have been fifteen years old, still an apprentice. But in 1636, he'd have been a young master.

With an apprentice of his own?

I squeezed between the stacks to where he'd kept his journals. I rooted through them, looking for entries dated 1636. I found three bound tomes for that year, filled with daily entries.

Plague swelled in warm weather, so I skipped forward to the summer months. Master Benedict noted the sickness started growing significantly in June, though from his own records, that year's plague was nothing compared to this one; not even a tenth as deadly. But in spite of the lower mortality, my master's household had been unlucky: a death in his own home.

George.

George Staple. I remembered now. I'd once asked Master Benedict about his previous apprentices. He'd had three before me. One I knew: Hugh Coggshall, who later became his friend and died in the search for the Archangel's Fire. The other two were George Staple, his first apprentice, and Peter Hyde, his third. He'd only ever told me their names; when I'd tried to get more information about them, he'd always changed the subject.

The first relevant entry was dated July 2, 1636. It was just a single line.

My apprentice has the sickness.

There were no entries for the next three days. Then, on July 6, his recordings returned.

George has died. I tried every remedy I could find. None of them had any effect.

This morning, I heard word of a remedy from Newcastle that many claim is a cure. I didn't inquire further; there was no point. George was too far gone to help.

The poor boy was in such pain. In his delirium, he called out for his father. I didn't have the heart to remind him his father was gone. Instead, I said, "I am here," and held his hand as if he were my own.

I know I shouldn't have touched him. I didn't care. George was a sweet and gentle boy. He didn't deserve this. None of them do.

This suffering must end. I swear to you, O Lord: I will find a cure for this terrible affliction.

Tomorrow I travel to Newcastle.

I already knew that trip wasn't successful. Among his books and his journals, I'd also discovered notes on plague remedies. My gaze immediately fell on one bound sheaf of parchment I'd read two months ago.

I picked it up again. As I flipped through the pages, I heard the stairs creak, then a heavy footfall behind me.

"I'm not really going to poison you," I said.

"I know." Tom squeezed through the stacks and sat on the floor beside me. "I just thought you might want some company."

I did. "Look at this," I said, and turned the book around so Tom could see it.

At some point, Master Benedict had compiled a list of all known plague remedies and proposed cures. Everything I'd ever heard of was there, from the familiar and common (Venice treacle, blistering plasters) to the head-shakingly odd (plucking chickens and tying them to the soles of the patient's feet). Page after page of remedies was inked over with a black slash. At the end, at the bottom of the final page were two words, written in capitals.

ALL WORTHLESS

"That's all he ever writes," I said. "None of the supposed remedies actually work, which is why I've been experimenting with preventatives instead, like my Smoke-Your-Home. Yet, when I read these notes before, it never occurred to me: for my master to make all these remedies, test them, realize they don't do anything . . . this is *years* of research. So Dr. Parrett and Henry must have been right. Master Benedict *was* obsessed with finding a plague cure. And I've found out why."

I showed Tom the journal entry my master had made about the death of his apprentice. "That's awful," Tom said. "But why is this so important to you?"

"Because if Master Benedict was a plague specialist, how come he never said anything to me about it?"

We'd discussed everything. It was one of the things I missed most about him. Yet in three years, there was only one time I remembered the plague coming up: last December, when a comet had appeared in the sky.

Everyone agreed the comet was a portent of terrible things to come. Some specifically predicted a plague. Worried, I'd asked my master about it as I'd served us that night's soup.

He'd sat quietly, watching the steam rise from the bowl. "We can never be precisely sure what a comet portends."

"But *could* it mean a plague is coming?" I'd said.

Master Benedict had taken so long to answer that I wasn't sure he was going to. Finally, he'd said, "Let us pray that it does not." And he'd never spoken another word about it.

Tom returned the book to me. "Dr. Parrett met your master in 1652. His apprentice died in 1636. Things change. Maybe your master moved on. Started working on"—he lowered his voice—"the Archangel's Fire instead."

"Maybe." The whole thing still seemed very strange.

"Anyway, are you going to tell me what happened when I was outside Guildhall or not?"

I looked up from my master's notes. "What do you mean?"

"I saw you when I came back. Something was wrong."

I wasn't sure exactly how much I should tell him. I searched through the piles for another set of notes, one I remembered reading long ago. I found them in a sheaf of parchment, tied together with twine loops. When I showed it to Tom, he groaned.

On the Other Worlds and Their Inhabitants:

Angels, Devils, and Other Miscellaneous Creatures

"Not *again*," he said.

"Listen," I said. I flipped through to a passage and read it.

The Archangel Michael serves God above all. As His general, Michael leads the Lord's armies into battle against the forces of hell. His powers are a gift from God; his Holy Fire burns the wicked and the evil. If only we could harness this gift! What wonders could we create?

"Master Benedict wrote this almost forty years ago," I said. "He was still an apprentice, but even then he'd wanted to find something greater than anyone had ever discovered before."

"What does this have to do with Guildhall?" Tom said.

"Melchior knew," I said. "He knew about the Archangel's Fire."

Tom's jaw dropped. "He said that?"

"Sort of. I don't think he knew about the Fire specifically. But he knew I'd done something. He told me I'd walked with an angel, so now an angel was hovering over me." I traced a finger along the floorboards, thinking about Melchior's prophecy. "He said it was the angel of death."

Tom crossed his fingers and pressed them to his chest. "What else did he say?"

Someone you love is going to die.

"Nothing," I said. "But listen to this." I read more from Master Benedict's notes.

In addition to his place as God's general, Michael is more broadly a figure of healing and protection.

"That doesn't sound so bad," Tom said.

He also serves as the angel of death.

"Oh," Tom said.
"It gets worse," I said.

According to Roman Catholic teaching, Michael carries the souls of the deceased to heaven. At their hour of death, he descends and gives each soul the chance to redeem itself before passing. However, Michael is not the only angel of death in theistic lore.

His opposition is Samael, the destroyer. Samael is Michael's counterpart and enemy. Some sources place him with Lucifer at the head of all devils, and as a leader of the rebel armies of heaven. As the archangel of death, he drips poison into the mouths of men. This poison corrodes them from within, and they die.

Tom crossed his fingers so hard that they turned white. "That's the plague. He's talking about the plague."

That was what alarmed me the most. According to Dr. Parrett, Melchior *predicted* the course of the plague. He knew about angels. He knew I'd walked with one a few months ago.

And his men had broken into my home.

Why? Was this passage the answer? Was it something to do with the Archangel's Fire?

Or was it because of the plague? My master was apparently known as a plague expert. So were the thieves looking for a recipe, like Lord Ashcombe thought? Or something special my master knew about how to fight the plague?

And if he knew something like that, why was it not in his notes? And why had he never mentioned it to me?

Melchior had seen the angel of death at Guildhall. He'd said I was marked. I wondered: What if this was my fault? What if using the Archangel's Fire attracted Michael's attention? Worse, what if it attracted Samael's? What if *Samael* was the angel Melchior saw hovering over me?

Someone you love is going to die. With Master Benedict gone, there was only one person left that could mean. He sat across from me, scanning the pages with an increasing look of dread. Inside, I felt the same.

What if I'd killed my best friend?

We pored over Master Benedict's notes for a couple more hours, reading anything to do with angels of death. When I went to check on Sally, she had, despite being in pain, repaired all my clothes. She showed me her handiwork, looking pleased.

Tom found her puzzling. "She's pretty cheery for an unemployed homeless girl who's just taken a beating."

But I understood her. I'd come from Cripplegate, too. "This morning," I said, "she was on the street, not sure where she could go or what might happen to her. This afternoon, she has a roof over her head and a full stomach. Beating or no, her life's a lot better than she'd thought it would be."

If it wasn't for Master Benedict, I'd have ended up the same. I was still worried about what was going to happen to Sally, as I couldn't afford to keep her here much longer. Nonetheless, I was glad she'd come to me for help.

I kept reading, working into the evening, moving downstairs to keep Tom company as he baked buns for us with our new flour. They filled the house with that wonderful scent of fresh bread. I'd never want to be anything but an apothecary, but there was no denying his trade smelled much better than mine.

For dinner, we ate that bread, dipped in oil. Sally, curious about the way Tom and I were living, asked where my master was. I told her what had happened with the Cult—minus a fact here or there—and she listened, wide-eyed. She seemed most amazed at the notion that a boy three years out of Cripplegate—*anyone* out of Cripplegate, really—could make something of his life. Her eyes gleamed as they looked around the shop. I wondered what she was imagining for herself.

Our dinner was cut short by the sound of the front door banging open. It was Dr. Parrett. He stood in the doorway, staring through us as if we weren't there.

We sprang to our feet. "Dr. Parrett?" I said. "What's wrong?"

He blinked, as if my voice had woken him. "Wrong? Nothing. Nothing's wrong." He pulled his wig off, eyes shining.

"The cure," he said. "Galen's cure. It works."

CHAPTER
14

I WAS THE FIRST TO BREAK THE
silence.

"Are . . . are you sure?" I said. "There's no chance . . . I
mean . . . it's not just a coincidence?"

Dr. Parrett leaned against the door, mopping his brow
with his handkerchief. "You saw Aldebourne's girl. The
delirium, the tokens on the skin. When they're that far
gone . . . But Annabelle's stopped vomiting. The sweats
are gone. Her sense has returned. And she's hungry. She's
actually hungry." He shook his head. "It's a miracle,
Christopher. A true miracle."

We heard a noise, coming from outside. "They're passing this way," Dr. Parrett said. He leaned out of the door and waved. "Here!" he shouted. "In here!"

In here? I went to see to whom he was calling.

It was Galen. He was hurrying down the street, in the direction of Guildhall, at the head of what could only be termed a horde. They were shouting, praying, clutching at his clothes as they begged him to help them, too. Galen looked flustered; their attention was growing rougher by the second. Henry, beside him, had to run to keep in front of them. He kept looking back, even more worried than Galen about the horde that followed.

I was worried, too. Hordes *broke* things.

"Close the shutters!" I said to Tom and Sally. We did, hooking them shut just as the crowd arrived.

Galen nearly fell into the shop, the collar on his doublet torn away, buttons missing from his shirt. Henry *did* fall, toppling to the ground and crawling, panicked, across the floorboards.

I tried to slam the door. The press of people slowly pushed me backward. Tom shoved the door closed, then lent his shoulder to the wood long enough for me to throw the bolt. The door—the *wall*—shook as they hammered on it, cheering for Galen. I prayed they didn't try that on the windows.

Dr. Parrett helped Henry to stand. Sally bent over to pick up the clerk's spectacles, wincing and holding her ribs. Tom and I stood near Galen. He leaned on the counter, breathing heavily.

Dr. Parrett grabbed his hand and shook it. "You are a gift from God, sir," he said.

Galen flushed, embarrassed. Henry looked like he wanted a second opinion. "Where's Melchior? I thought he was returning to Guildhall with us."

My stomach fluttered. *Melchior? Coming here, to my home?*

"Melchior left with his men," Dr. Parrett said. "But he saw what I saw. Ask him; he'll tell you. The cure works."

Henry began to respond. He was silenced by the *thwap* of a small black leather pouch hitting his chest.

Galen had finally lost his patience. "Your Magistrate Dench has the sickness, doesn't he? Give him that. And watch him recover in your arms."

"I will," Henry said. I think he meant it to sound like a threat. It came out more like a pout. "And I'll need your recipe, as well."

I cringed. Had Henry really asked an apothecary for his secret recipe? For a moment, Galen just stared at him, mouth open. Then he drew himself up.

"Mr. Cole," he said. "I have spent the last twenty years searching the world for this cure. I have laid my head to sleep in cesspools. I have eaten meals made of nothing but worms. And I have faced dangers so beyond your comprehension that if I told you about them, you would say I was making up stories to frighten the children."

He pointed to the pouch in Henry's hands. "That recipe is the culmination of decades of work. I have devoted my entire life to its discovery. And I will not give it up. Not to you. Not to the magistrates. Not even to the king himself, if he promised me all of England. Do you understand?"

Henry's face reddened. "We'll see about that," he muttered, and he turned to go. Then he glanced nervously at the door, which still shook with the crowd's blows. "Er . . . Christopher? I don't suppose your shop has a back exit?"

"A moment, Henry," Dr. Parrett said. "We have to make arrangements to distribute the cure to the city. Galen, how much more do you have with you?"

Galen seemed surprised at the question. "None."

We all stared at him, jaws open.

"None?" Tom said, horrified.

"Sir!" Dr. Parrett protested.

Galen looked flustered. "How much did you think I

could have? The cure's ingredients are rare—and expensive. I only arrived in England on Saturday, and I had to give the ship's captain most of what I'd already made just to get him to drop me off anywhere *near* London. What little I had left went to treat Beatrice at the pest house, and Aldebourne's girl. The last of it you hold in your hand." He nodded at Henry.

"What will you need to make more?"

"Ingredients. Tools. A workshop. A warehouse, really, if I'm to make enough for a whole city."

My heart leaped. A *workshop*? "Use Blackthorn," I said.

"Yes!" Dr. Parrett's eyes shone. "Good lad!"

Galen blinked. "What's Blackthorn?"

"This is, Master," I said. "Here. This shop."

I tried to stay calm, but inside, I was jumping up and down. This was *perfect*. With funds from the city, the shop would be out of danger. And more important, *far* more important, my master's workshop could help save the entire city!

"We have everything you need," I said. I rushed into the workshop to show him. "Look."

But Galen wasn't as impressed as I'd hoped. "No, lad. This won't do," he said, and my heart sank. "It's a fine workshop, to be sure. But I will need much larger amounts of the ingredients. And this room is hardly big enough to serve the whole of London."

"But it's a start, is it not?" Dr. Parrett said. "Until the magistrates find you a proper establishment. Sir, please. People are dying. You must begin your work immediately!"

"John is correct," Henry said. "It seems to me that this is a perfect place for you to begin. As approval for any funds for supplies will come from Magistrate Aldebourne, *I'll* be signing off on all transactions."

Galen seemed taken aback by Henry's sudden change in tone. "I told you, this isn't big enough to—"

"Nonetheless. It's where you'll work, until larger quarters are found."

Galen eyed Henry suspiciously. "Nothing will happen if you don't provide what I need."

"I'll speak to Magistrate Aldebourne about it personally," Dr. Parrett said. "In the meantime, Christopher can help you get started."

I could barely believe what I was hearing. I was going to help make the plague cure! "Let me show you where everything is, Master—"

"Wait." Galen placed a finger against my breastbone.

He looked from me to Henry. "Weren't you at Guildhall with him?"

"No," I said. Galen's eyes narrowed. "Well—yes. Sort of. I mean, I was with him, but not—"

"And we just *happened* to end up here. How curious." Galen looked me up and down. "Yet I still don't know who you are."

"Oh, sorry, Master," I said. "I'm Christopher Rowe. I'm the apprentice here. Or, I was. I mean, I still am, but—"

"Ah." Galen looked around the workshop. "So you know what all this equipment does, then? What all these ingredients are for?"

"Yes."

"Then no."

"I—Master?"

"You are not acceptable."

"But . . . why?"

"Because *you*"—Galen prodded me in the chest—"were at Guildhall with *him*." He pointed at Henry.

"Christopher was only there to petition the magistrate," Dr. Parrett said.

"And Henry *only* wants me to work here." Galen turned

back to me. "Tell me: your former master, this Blackthorn. Did he share his recipes with the world?"

I flushed. "Well . . . no." Exactly the opposite, really. "But—"

"There you are, then."

"Sir," Dr. Parrett said patiently. "You must produce enough cure for the city. That will require many men: assistants, apprentices. You cannot work alone."

"I don't plan to work alone. But my assistants, *I* will choose."

Galen looked around the room. Sally was standing at the back. She'd kept her eyes on everything, watching intently, but she'd been so quiet and stayed so far out of the way that I'd forgotten she was even there. Galen didn't appear to give her any thought at all. His gaze skimmed over her as if she were one of the shop's stuffed animals and came to rest on Tom.

"You." He scanned my friend up and down. "Do you work here, too?"

Tom was startled to be addressed. "Me? No, sir. I'm a baker's apprentice."

"Ah." Galen nodded as he pulled a ceramic jar from the

shelves and placed it in front of Tom, the label hidden. He opened the lid and pushed it toward my friend. "What is this?"

Even from a distance, I could see it was cinnabar. Tom looked at me, puzzled, before answering. "I don't know."

"And this?" He placed a clear glass jar in front of Tom. The smell wafted over; an alcoholic tang, with the scent of unwashed socks. I tried to will the answer to Tom. Tincture of valerian. *Tincture of valerian.*

"I don't know," Tom said again, even more confused. "Like I said, sir, I'm just a baker's apprentice. Christopher is the apothecary—"

"Perfect." Galen placed a hand on Tom's shoulder. "I choose him."

Tom blinked. "But I—"

"Don't know anything," Galen said. "Exactly. And since you won't know what you're working with, you can't possibly steal my recipe."

My jaw dropped. "Master Galen," I said. "I'd never steal your recipe!"

Galen raised an eyebrow. "I should certainly hope not," he said. Then he put his hand on my chest, walked me backward, and shut me out of my own workshop.

TUESDAY, SEPTEMBER 1, 1665

Yesterday's plague deaths: 1,198

Total dead: 31,749

CHAPTER 15

AGAIN.

I'd been kicked out of my own home *again*. Not literally, at least; this time, I didn't have to find somewhere else to live. But Galen had not only barred me from the workshop while he was working, he'd banned me from the room entirely. "Neither prying eyes nor curious minds are welcome," he said.

Henry and Dr. Parrett weren't any help. Dr. Parrett was sympathetic, but he was also adamant that the man who'd discovered the plague cure should be allowed to make certain demands.

"I know it seems unfair," Dr. Parrett said. "But your

shop will be this city's salvation. Lending it to Galen for a few days is a small price to pay, isn't it? And you must admit, Christopher, your master was rather the same when it came to protecting his work."

That didn't make it any less frustrating. It also didn't make my case easy to argue. Especially because I didn't really have an actual argument. Though Master Benedict had left me Blackthorn in his will, according to law it wouldn't officially be mine until I grew up and became a freeman of the city. I'd hoped Henry would have been more of an ally, as he clearly didn't trust Galen. As it turned out, that's why he'd wanted Galen to work at Blackthorn.

"I'll need to coordinate with Magistrate Aldebourne regarding the city's funds," he said when Dr. Parrett wasn't listening. "If the cure really works, then the quarantine on the magistrate's house will be lifted. For now, Galen being here will make it easier for me to keep an eye on him. Tell me if you see anything strange, won't you?"

I said I would, though I wasn't sure what I was supposed to see through a closed door. Still, trading conspiracies with Henry reminded me why I'd come to Guildhall in the first place. I asked about an introduction to Magistrate Maycott.

"Oh . . . right," Henry said, as he and Dr. Parrett were

leaving. "I'll ask. But honestly, Christopher, that's going to be a very low priority for Magistrate Aldebourne right now. You may have to wait a few weeks."

A few weeks! Whichever one of Melchior's men had broken in could be halfway across Europe by then! But I was just a masterless apprentice. As always, I had no standing to argue.

"Doesn't stop them using my stuff, though, does it?" I grumbled after they left.

"Pardon?" Sally said.

"Nothing." I threw myself into the chair by the fireplace and . . . well, I'd say "brooded," but it was probably closer to "sulked." Sally tried to talk to me, but after I threw a few grunts her way, she gave up and spent the rest of the time playing with Bridget before drifting off to sleep. I stayed up so I could talk to Tom when Galen was through with him.

Even that plan was foiled. Galen kept him locked in the workshop until midnight before shooing him home. Then he confiscated my key and locked the workshop so I couldn't enter even after he'd gone. The fact that passing through the workshop was the only way to get upstairs didn't seem to trouble him in the slightest.

Galen didn't realize that wouldn't stop me. Master Benedict had always kept a spare key hidden outside, behind a marked brick in the back corner of the house. As soon as Galen was gone, I went inside the workshop, looking everywhere. I'd told him the truth; I would never have stolen his recipe. That didn't mean I didn't want to know what it was.

Carefully, I walked through the room, scanning the benches, the tools, the shelves. Unfortunately, Galen had made Tom clean the workshop from top to bottom before they left. Some of my jars had been moved around, and the apparatus I'd piled together at the ends of the benches had been spread out again. But without any clue as to what they'd been doing with my ingredients, I had no idea what went into the actual cure. If I wanted to know anything about it, I'd have to wait for Tom to return.

There were too many things swirling around in my head for me to fall asleep. To make things worse, I'd let Sally keep my palliasse to ease the pain of her bruised ribs. For myself, I gathered up a pile of blankets and laid them out on the wood under the counter, next to a snoozing Bridget. Better than nothing, I supposed.

Not much better, it turned out. All I got for my trouble

was an ache in my back and a pounding head. After tossing around for a few restless hours, I gave up sleep for good and went upstairs. With Galen keeping me from my workshop, I wanted to collect Master Benedict's notes on plague remedies—and angels of death—while I had the chance.

Bridget woke and came with me, but even an affectionate pigeon cooing from atop my shoulder didn't sweeten my mood. Neither did the sound of small footsteps from behind.

"Good morning," Sally said brightly.

"Morning," I grumbled.

"What are you doing? Can I help?"

How could she possibly be so happy at this ungodly hour? "Tom was right," I said. "You *are* too cheerful."

"Would you prefer it if I moped?" she said.

"Yes."

She put on a sad face.

"Much better," I said. "Thank you."

I went back to searching. Then I heard another sound behind me.

"Sally," I said.

"Yes?"

"Mopey people don't hum."

There was a pause. "What if I give you a sad song? Then you can cry."

I whirled on her. She'd contorted her features into something so ridiculously tragic she looked like a lost puppy in a thunderstorm. I tried not to, but it made me laugh.

"All right," I said. "I'm sorry. A little music would be nice for once, actually."

"Oh?" She brightened. "Well, if you have a lute, I could play for you."

"A lute?"

She nodded. "They taught us girls to play instruments at Cripplegate, so when we got jobs we could entertain our masters."

"No instruments here," I said. "I don't think Master Benedict cared for music."

"Really? I couldn't live without it. It's my favorite thing."

I waved my arm at the stacks of tomes and papers that filled the room. "This was our favorite thing."

"I like books, too." Sally picked one of them up and began leafing through the pages. "My father taught me to read before he died. And to do sums."

Sally had been a late arrival at Cripplegate. I'd come to the orphanage as a baby, but Sally's parents hadn't died until she was eight, lost on a merchant ship bound for the Continent. From the depths of my memory, I finally recalled her family name: *Deschamps.* "Your father was French, wasn't he?"

She nodded, pleased that I'd remembered. "But my mother was English, so when they fell in love, he moved all the way to London to marry her." She traced a finger along the cover of the book she was holding. "I don't think he ever felt at home in England. He really missed Paris."

Her mention of Paris made me think of what Dr. Parrett had told me yesterday, and the journal entry I'd found. I thought again about Master Benedict's dead apprentice, and wondered, disappointed, why he'd never talked about the sickness with me.

Bridget nuzzled against my ear. She'd always been able to tell when my mood was low. I think Sally could see it, too, because she changed the subject. "Which ones should I carry?"

"None of them," I said. "Your ribs are bruised. You're supposed to be resting."

A flicker of worry crossed her face. "I don't want to sit around doing nothing while everyone else is working."

Living with Master Benedict's kindness sometimes made me forget where I'd come from. Sally, a Cripplegate girl, understood her future all too well. Nothing would be discarded more quickly than an orphan without any use.

"All right," I said. "But you shouldn't be lifting things. How about making breakfast instead?" Though sunrise was still a couple of hours away, I was already hungry. "We need to move the food from the pantry before Galen comes, anyway. Otherwise we'll starve all day."

She clapped her hands together. "Do you have eggs? I make good eggs."

I did have eggs, thanks to Isaac. "Use whatever herbs you want from my stock."

I swear I'd never seen someone so happy about eggs. Downstairs, she helped transfer the food—small loads, I had to keep reminding her—from the pantry to one of the display tables, then sang softly to herself as she cooked over the fireplace in the shop. In the meantime, I gave up on sorting my master's papers and just lugged whole stacks down to one corner of the shop behind the counter. As I moved them it occurred to me that I *did* have a way to the upper floors, even if the workshop stayed locked: the hatch in the roof. It wouldn't be ideal—I'd need to steal a ladder to get up there—but I left it unbolted just in case.

I was collecting one last load from Master Benedict's

bedroom when Sally appeared in the doorway, holding her side and wincing.

"Breakfast's ready," she said, her voice tight.

"I warned you," I said.

"It's not that bad," she said, but her grimace told a different story. Slowly, she lowered herself to the edge of Master Benedict's bed. With the weight off, she sighed, then lay all the way back on the mattress. "This is really nice. It's so soft."

"It's goose down."

Sally propped herself on her elbows. "Then why do you sleep in the shop?"

"What do you mean?"

"You have a proper room and a goose down bed," she said. "Why do you still sleep on a sack of straw under a shop counter?"

"Well . . . that's where my bed is," I said. "This is Master Benedict's room."

"I thought he left the house to you," she said.

"He did. But these are *his* things."

I held out my hand. She stared up at me for a moment before taking it.

I lifted her off the bed. I smoothed out its covers. Then

I picked up the pile of papers and carried them down. Sally followed, watching me all the while.

Tom arrived early, three soft cinnamon buns hidden under his jerkin. He nearly choked on his when he learned I'd unlocked the workshop.

"Galen's not going to be happy if he finds out," he said.

I was really starting to lose my temper. "This is *my* home!" I pounded my fist into my palm. "My. Home."

"And if you cross Galen, he'll get you thrown out of it. He's already got his eye on you."

"What does that mean?"

"Last night," Tom said, "Galen kept asking questions about you and Master Benedict. Who your master was, what he knew about treating the plague, your remedies and cures. He's convinced you're looking to steal his recipe. He thinks that's why Henry wants you to help him."

I flushed. That *was* why Henry wanted me to help him. But that wasn't my fault. "I don't want to steal any-one's recipe!"

"I know that," Tom said patiently, "but Galen doesn't. If he complains about you to Magistrate Aldebourne, you'll be out on the street. So don't push him." Tom gave me a mournful look. "Besides, I don't think you even *want* to work for him."

"Why? What's he got you doing?"

"Chopping and grinding what's left of your ingredients. And cleaning. But that's not the problem. He's paranoid. He won't let me anywhere near him while he's working. Half the time, he thinks *I'm* going to steal his secrets, too."

I hadn't really given Galen's worries any thought. I just wanted to help make the plague cure. And despite the fact that he didn't trust me, I wanted to see if I could learn from the man. Though not nearly as kind, he reminded me in many ways of my master: his dedication, his obvious concern for his patients, his contempt for cheats. Keeping secrets was just like Master Benedict, too. The similarities struck me even more now that I'd learned about my master's past. They'd both traveled to foreign lands, searching for a cure for the sickness.

And it occurred to me: I still needed a new master. I sat up on my stool, thinking. I was going about this the wrong way. I should be trying to *impress* the man. If I showed him how much Master Benedict had taught me, how useful I could be, maybe he'd let me help.

I'd have to think about how to convince him. In the

meantime, my curiosity still raged. Somewhere in my workshop were the ingredients that cured the plague. "At least show me what you're mixing," I said.

"Christopher."

"Just one thing. That's all. Then I'll leave."

"Christopher."

"Please? Pleeeease? Pleeeeeeeease? Pleeeeeeeeeeeeeeee—"

"All *right*." Tom glanced nervously at the door. "But you can't tell *anyone*."

"Who would I tell?" I said. "I only talk to you and Bridget. And she knows how to keep a secret."

Bridget cooed in agreement. Tom looked at Sally.

"I won't tell, either." She smiled brightly. "I haven't even *got* any friends."

CHAPTER
16

WE PILED INTO THE WORKSHOP, waiting. Tom bit his lip.

"The truth is," he said, "I don't really know what I'm mixing."

He took us to the workbench opposite the oven in the corner. A set of large jars cluttered the space underneath, with a host of smaller ingredient jars stacked on the shelves above it. "I mean, I know the charcoal and the sugar, obviously. But I don't have any idea what these other things are."

I could hardly blame him. I counted twenty-eight jars above the bench alone. Apart from a few common ingredients, like parsley and black pepper, the rest of the jars were exotics:

turpentine from Cyprus, *bolus armenus* clay from Armenia, *delphinium staphisagria* from the African continent. Galen was so serious about keeping his secret that he'd blacked out the labels on the jars; I only recognized them because I'd used them so often.

Tom said he'd spent most of last night grinding powders, especially charcoal, which Galen had ordered him to pound into a fine black dust. *Grayish powder,* I remembered. *So the cure contains charcoal.*

I heard Master Benedict's voice, as if he were back in the workshop, standing over my shoulder. *Many ingredients could give a gray color. Examine everything before you draw conclusions.*

He was right. It was possible there was very little charcoal. In fact, considering how secretive Galen was, it wouldn't surprise me if he'd ordered Tom to grind charcoal as a ruse, and another ingredient entirely was what turned the mixture gray. But which one? And which ingredients were special? Was it one in particular, or the way they all combined?

I heard Master Benedict again. *Look carefully, Christopher. Do any of these ingredients seem familiar?*

And I realized: They did.

Venice treacle. Most of the ingredients Galen had set Tom to work with were constituents of Venice treacle. But Galen's cure was a grayish powder, while Venice treacle looked like, well, a treacle: gooey and sticky.

"What was Galen doing while you were putting this together?" I said.

Tom shrugged. "I don't know. He won't let me near him." He pointed to the far corner of the room. "Galen sits over there. He yells at me if I get too close."

Sally, watching silently, raised her eyebrows. I suspected we were thinking the same thing.

I hurried to the corner. Tom protested. "You said show you *one* thing."

There was nothing to see here, anyway. Whatever equipment Galen had used had been put away. And he'd cleaned the area so thoroughly he hadn't left a single speck of dust. Even the broom, brush, and rags next to his bench were spotless.

"Did Galen take any of the ingredients he gave you for himself?" I said.

"I don't think so," Tom said. "But he was definitely working on something."

Even more interesting. He hadn't taken any of my

ingredients, but he still had something to work with.

Because he already had it with him?

A secret ingredient, I thought. *Which he mixed with something used in the Venice treacle?*

I stood in my workshop and stared at the empty workbench.

Tom didn't let me stay much longer. After a marvelous bout of complaining—"How long can you stare at an empty bench, anyway?"—he finally just grabbed me by the collar, dragged me from the workshop, and made me lock the door. It was a lucky thing, too, because it was only a few minutes later that Galen strode into the shop.

His eye had blackened completely from the blow he'd taken yesterday. Despite that, he was in good cheer. "Good morning, all," he said.

After what I'd seen in the workshop, I had an idea. "Master Galen?" I said. "May I show you something?"

He hesitated, but he nodded. I jumped up from my stool, collected my jar of Venice treacle, and spooned some into a bowl. "This is the recipe my master taught me."

He accepted the bowl indifferently, barely humoring

me. But when he saw what was inside, he began to inspect its contents with interest. "Good consistency. Strong fragrance. Where do you get your laurel?"

"Spain," I said.

He dipped a finger in and tasted it. His eyebrows shot up. "That's extraordinary." He took another taste. "Blackthorn made this?"

"I did, sir."

He regarded me curiously for a moment. "I confess, Mr. Rowe, I am impressed. You have a skill I wouldn't have expected from an apprentice."

"I had a wonderful master," I said.

"So Tom was telling me."

"Master Benedict taught me all kinds of ways to keep secrets, too." I needed to tread carefully here. "All sorts of codes and things. I was thinking—"

Galen clapped a hand on my shoulder. "Thinking is good. But let's not get ahead of ourselves, all right? Come, Tom."

He prodded my friend into the workshop. Tom gave me an apologetic look before he shut the door. Face burning, I put the jar back and sat quietly on my stool.

Sally had watched it all perched on the windowsill at the front. She had the good grace to ignore my embarrassment. "So what do we do now?" she said.

It was clear my remedies weren't going to impress Galen enough to let me help him. Maybe I should have made another Smoke-Your-Home instead. I could only imagine Tom's horror. *Setting Galen on fire won't change his mind, Christopher.*

The real problem was this: He simply didn't trust me. If I wanted to work for him, I'd have to figure out how to prove I was reliable. I resolved to think about it some more. In the meantime, I had something else to do. After seeing the ingredients Tom had been mixing for Galen, I wanted to read my master's notes on the plague again.

I indicated the stacks behind the counter. "I need to go through these."

Sally slid down from the sill. "Can I look, too?"

"Sure."

We started on the books, Sally turning the pages with curiosity. I'd already seen my master's views on plague cures in his reference guide—*ALL WORTHLESS*—so I tried to follow the trail of his plague-cure experiments throughout the years instead. Even from just his notes, I could see his skill and understanding as an apothecary grow. Yet his success in treating the sickness did not.

> Tried the Bournemouth remedy. No effect.
>
> Tried the Newcastle cure. No effect.
>
> Tried all radix angelicae variations. No effect.
>
> No effect.
>
> No effect.
>
> No. Bloody. Effect.

By the end of the notes from 1636, his frustration bled from the scratches on the page.

> The greatest result is noted with the consumption of the Venice treacle, with similar effectiveness witnessed through the application of the Paris and London treacles. Many believe that there are ingredients in these that, with the correct balance and counterbalance of substances, could emphasize their healing powers and stop the plague. I am not certain of this. The most beneficial effect of these remedies appears to be the relaxation of the afflicted, so helpful to the body, and I suspect that it is the poppy alone that causes this. Certainly, I have not noticed any difference in mortality between using the treacles or a straight infusion of essence of poppy.

All other proposed cures do nothing. I have spent nearly every penny I possess trying to acquire any cure that crossed my path. I have even tried the quacks touting their remedies at the Exchange. In this way, I am like the poor and desperate folk these mountebanks prey upon. In hoping their own lives, or the lives of those they love, may be saved, these innocents throw all manner of money at the cater-wauling cranks who promise deliverance, no matter how preposterous or outlandish their claims.

I thought of Galen fighting the man in the market. I read on.

Some of the quacks are simple zealots, who genuinely believe they've discovered a cure. I buy freely from these, as who can say what truths a man may stumble upon, even by accident? Others are pure cheats. Some are so brazen that they prey repeatedly on the same town, plague after plague. There was one devil whose tongue was so smooth, and who presented two such plausible recently "cured" brothers, I nearly bought his remedy. Then I recalled I had seen his face before: The same man had stood in the exact same spot, touting a different cure with two young children, back in 1625. The supposed recently saved brothers were the same little children who'd grown up to become so horribly afflicted again!

Yet, what else can I do? Still I *buy their quackish remedies, and I test. Because, like the Israelites of old, who can tell the difference between the madman and the prophet?*

I stared at the passage.

"What's wrong?" Sally said.

"That prophet," I said, "who came to Cripplegate."

"The Bird Man?"

"His real name's Melchior. Did you hear him make his predictions? I mean, hear him yourself?"

She nodded. "The masters lined us all up to be examined when he came. He said the angel of death had come to the school, and that three of the children would get the sickness."

"He actually *told* you that?"

"Well . . . sort of. The Bird Ma—Melchior was talking to Reverend Talbot. I snuck close so I could listen. I wasn't supposed to."

"But his prophecy came true."

"Yes. Melchior even named them. Though they weren't sick, the masters separated them right away, and they asked Melchior to give all of us medicine, just in case."

"What did he give you?" I said.

"I think it was that." She pointed to the bowl on the table, where I'd poured the remedy to show Galen.

Venice treacle, again. That's what Melchior's followers had come looking for, yesterday. *Our master said Blackthorn made the best.*

An entire orphanage would use up a lot of Venice treacle. "Did you all take it?" I said.

Sally nodded. "Melchior agreed to give it to everyone, but he warned the masters that medicine couldn't stop what God had already decreed. And it didn't." She wrapped her arms around her knees, holding them to her chest. "After that, more caught the sickness. Reverend Talbot sent the sick to the pest house and sealed the orphanage. That's when I came here."

My blood had frozen. I told Sally what Melchior had predicted at Guildhall. She listened, her hand over her mouth.

"Please don't tell Tom," I said. "It'll scare him." As if I wasn't already frightened myself.

"Are you sure that's who Melchior was talking about?" she said.

"I can't see who else he could have meant." I cared about Isaac and Dr. Parrett and Lord Ashcombe, too. But Tom . . .

except for Master Benedict, he'd been my only real family. Even thinking about him getting sick made my guts twist. I didn't know what I'd do without him.

"Do you think Melchior really sees the angel of death, then?" Sally said.

"I don't know. I mean . . ." I told her what I'd read about the Archangels Michael and Samael. "And *I've* seen things, too. Their power." I shook my head. "I wish I knew what Melchior was doing. If he can't save anyone, what's the point of his predictions? Why even *be* a plague doctor? What's he doing preaching in a church? And then there are his men."

"They were there, too," Sally said. "They came with him to the orphanage, kept him surrounded as he examined the children. It's like he's gathered a small army of his own."

That was it. "It *is* an army." I sat up. "They're just like soldiers. They follow *his* orders."

"So?"

"One of them broke in here yesterday."

"Really? What for?"

"I'm not exactly sure. The point is they do whatever Melchior says. So if one of them broke in here—"

Sally's eyes went wide. "Then they did it on Melchior's

command. But . . . what would a prophet want from here?"

His men had claimed they'd come for my master's Venice treacle. Yet none of that was stolen. "I don't know what he wants," I said. "That's what worries me. I need to find out more about him."

Sally brightened. "Well, if you want that," she said, "I know exactly where to go."

CHAPTER
17

THERE WAS AT LEAST ONE GOOD
thing about Melchior's appearance: People tend to notice
when you walk around in a smoking bird mask. I thought
we might find him by checking the usual places to hear
city gossip: taverns, coffeehouses, markets, and the like.
Sally, however, had some inside information.

"He's living at Saint Andrew's," she said.

"The church beside Cripplegate?" I said. "What happened to Reverend Glennon?"

"Ran away when the plague came. Melchior moved in
right after. That was the day before he came and made his
prediction."

Melchior and Cripplegate. Two of my least favorite things, together. "He's living in the rectory, then?"

She shook her head. "The sexton's quarters, underneath the chapel."

That was odd. The rectory would be much nicer than some dank basement. Why not stay there? "I wonder where he came from."

"Reverend Talbot said it was the Continent."

I frowned. Even through the mask, Melchior's accent was clear. "He sounds English."

Sally shrugged. "Talbot said plague doctors move from city to city, going where they're needed."

We walked on toward the church, but we didn't make it. As we crossed Cheapside, I held up a hand. "Wait."

From the south came the sounds of a crowd. In these times, other than another riot—and it didn't sound like a riot—that could mean only one thing. So we hurried down, following the noise, and found him.

Melchior walked at the head of a mass three hundred strong. Just like yesterday, he had eight men with him. They ringed their leader, shoving back against the jostling crowd. The people called out to him. Some begged for his aid. Some just wailed; a raw keening that assaulted the ears.

Melchior himself said nothing. He simply walked, holding that silver staff with the gargoyle head in front of him, the too-long fingers of his leather gloves clutching the rod.

Joining the crowd was like running into a herd of cattle; we were carried with the flow of people. I tried to get close to Melchior, but I couldn't squeeze through the press of bodies. Sally, smaller and nimbler, slipped away into the melee, and I lost sight of her.

The path we walked seemed to be chosen at random. At intersections and alleyways, Melchior would change direction abruptly, plague doctor staff raised high, eyes staring up through the lenses in the beaked mask, as if following heavenly signposts through the maze of London streets. Whatever guided his path eventually brought us to a wide, four-story house at the corner of Budge Row and Walbrook Street.

Melchior stopped. The house had been sealed; the red cross and plea for the Lord's mercy were already painted on the door. A few paces in front, a bonfire burned, snapping embers sparking in the heat. The smell of turpentine wafted with the thick smoke that drifted across the intersection.

The guard at the door eyed the crowd nervously. Melchior approached. This time, everyone else stayed where they were. All went silent.

"I am here to tend to Magistrate Eastwood," Melchior said, his voice muffled by his mask.

Another infected magistrate, I thought. At the rate they were catching the sickness, it was a miracle anyone took the job. As for the guard, he just looked relieved the plague doctor wasn't coming for him. He unlocked the door, and Melchior disappeared inside.

Everyone milled about, waiting. I scanned the crowd for Sally, but I couldn't see her. I was about to go look for her more seriously when the door burst open. The people hushed.

Melchior stared at the guard. The man shrank from the bird mask, its curls of smoke blowing away in the breeze.

"Where is he?" Melchior said.

"Eastwood?" The guard's eyes widened. "No one's left the house, your worship; I swear."

"Magistrate Eastwood is dead," Melchior said. "I was speaking of the angel of death. He is no longer in this place."

The guard shook so hard he dropped his halberd. It tumbled off the step, clattering on the cobbles. "I . . . I . . . I . . ."

Melchior strode over to the bonfire. The rising heat made his mask waver, like he was melting in the flames. He reached into a pocket in his leather overcoat. His crooked fingers came out clasped together, holding something trapped inside.

The street was silent, the only sound the crackling of the fire. Then came a low murmur.

It was Melchior. He bent over, one gloved hand wrapped over the other. He was saying something I couldn't hear.

Then, suddenly, he cast his arm up. From his hand flew a hundred white feathers. They caught the draft from the flames and rose, like an earthly snow falling toward heaven. They wavered and spun, hovering in the air. Slowly, slowly, then ever more quickly, they spiraled into a twister.

Thirty feet above, the feathers sheared from their spinning path. They flew on wings of their own along the street.

Then, as if guided by an invisible hand, they turned. The feathers fluttered down, landing at the doorstep of another house.

"There," Melchior said. "The angel of death is there."

The crowd erupted. Some fled, shrieking. I just stood there, trembling, and stared at the feathers twitching in the mud.

The morning sun hovered over the house Melchior's

prophecy had marked. The roof glowed in the haze, a reddish tint. Melchior hurried toward the house. His guards rushed to follow him, as did most of the remaining crowd, scrambling from their knees in the dirt.

A hand tugged at my sleeve.

I turned. It was Sally. Her fingers were in her mouth.

I couldn't think. "What happened to you?"

"Uh brrnd muhslph."

"What?"

She pulled her fingers from between her lips. "I burned myself."

The oddness of what she'd said nearly made me forget what I'd just witnessed. "Let me see."

Her fingers were red. Two of them had already begun to blister. "How did this happen?" I asked.

"I stuck my hand in the bonfire," she said.

"Why on Earth would you do that?"

"To get these."

She put her burnt fingers back in her mouth and held out her other hand. In her palm were two charred, curled strips of parchment. They were long and narrow, barely more than a quarter inch wide. On one side of each, written in a thin ink, were letters.

SDOIEEETH

OPRRUORHSTTSNAAIOHEN

"Where did these come from?" I said.

Sally took her fingers out of her mouth again to answer. "From Melchior. I saw him take it out of his hand while he was mumbling to himself. Then, when he threw the feathers into the air, he dropped it in the fire."

I hadn't noticed that at all. "I was watching the feathers."

"Everyone was," she said. "I think that was the point. I don't think he wanted anyone to see him throw this away."

CHAPTER
18

I HUNCHED OVER THE COUNTER, staring at the parchment. "Tell me again what you saw," I said.

We'd returned home to treat Sally's hand. In the shop, I'd slathered her blistered fingers with Blackthorn's Soothing Burn Cream and wrapped them in cotton. Then I'd taken the two fragments Sally had recovered and spread them out on the countertop.

Sally sat opposite me. She'd grabbed one of the downy feathers that Melchior had thrown in the air and brought it back with her. Now she shifted on her stool, twirling it between her unburnt fingers. I wished she'd stop. For some reason, that feather made me nervous.

"I was up at the front," Sally said, "right beside Melchior, next to the bonfire. While he was chanting, he pulled the feathers out of his pocket. Then, when he was hunched over, he stopped right in the middle of what he was doing, like he'd been surprised. He stuck his fingers into the hand with the feathers and pulled that out." She pointed to the fragments on the counter. "Then, when he threw the feathers into the air, he let that drop from his other hand into the fire. Everyone else was looking up, and . . . I don't know. I just thought it was strange. Like back in Cripplegate, I guess. How people acted when they had something they didn't want the masters to see." Sally craned her neck to read the letters on the parchment. "What do you think they mean?"

I had no idea. I was only sure of one thing: This message was in code. And codes were for hiding secrets.

What secrets would a prophet need to keep?

Nothing about this man seemed to make any sense. First he'd sent his men to break into my home. Now we'd found him with a code—just like my master used to use to hide secrets of his own.

I shook my head. Mulling over possibilities was a waste of time. What I needed to do was decipher Melchior's message. Unfortunately, that brought up an entirely different problem.

The fragments Sally had found would be nearly impossible to crack. Deciphering *any* secret message was hard, as you'd first need to know what kind of code they'd used to encipher it. Simple letter shifts weren't so bad; for example, where E represented F, and F represented G, and so on. But some ciphers were mind-bogglingly complicated, with letter shifts and swaps so sophisticated you'd need a specific key to unlock them.

Sometimes, if you were lucky, you'd be able to work it out anyway. I wasn't feeling very lucky. Worst of all, we didn't even have the whole message. I didn't know how long the original scroll was, but it was clear that some of the letters had burned away in the fire. With letters missing, I wasn't sure that figuring out what kind of cipher this was would be possible.

Still, I sat with those fragments and studied them. Melchior hadn't wanted anyone to see this message. That meant I wanted to know what it said.

. . .

The voice in my ear made me jump. "What are those?"

I turned. Tom hovered over my shoulder, looking at the notes I'd been making. His face was dusted with white powder.

"Where did you come from?" I said.

"Galen sent me out of the workshop," he said.

"What did you do?"

"Nothing. He's working on something secret now. I'm supposed to guard the door." He looked at the books I'd laid out in front of me, the notes I'd been scribbling. "More codes?"

I told Tom what had happened with Melchior outside the magistrate's house. "Another prediction," he said, wide-eyed.

"Well . . . yes," I said, shivering at the memory. "But look at what Sally found—where'd she go?"

She'd left Melchior's feather resting on top of a volume of bound notes. Bridget sat next to it, right at the edge of the counter. But Sally was nowhere to be seen.

Now I was thoroughly confused. "How long have I . . . what time is it?"

"Two o'clock." Tom looked longingly at our makeshift pantry in the corner. "Can I please have some food? Galen won't let me eat while I'm working. I've been sneaking powdered sugar for an hour."

Judging from the streaks on his face, "sneaking" might not have been the right word. But his mention of food made me realize how hungry I was, too. Trying to decipher Melchior's code, I'd completely lost track of time.

Tom cut us both a big hunk of Cheshire. We didn't have bread today; with Galen taking over the workshop, we didn't have access to the oven anymore.

"We'll have to bake it at night, when he's gone," I said. Tom looked deflated. "I'll do it," I said. "You don't have to stay."

He sighed. "No, I can—"

The front door opened, and Sally came in, humming some unknown tune.

"Where'd you go?" I said.

"The tavern across the street," she said. "I was talking to that girl, Dorothy."

I looked through the window at the Missing Finger. "She have anything to say?"

"Not about Melchior."

She smiled at Tom. He flushed and stuffed more cheese in his mouth. I smothered a laugh as Sally eased herself onto a stool between us and motioned to the book I was reading. "Did you find something?" she said.

I shook my head. "You?"

"I'm not sure." She picked up Melchior's feather and slid the book on which it had rested over to me. It was a collection of Master Benedict's bound notes. He'd inked the title on the leather.

Observations on the Behavior of Birds

"I found this among your books," she said. "I wondered if Melchior had used these feathers for a reason, so I tried to figure out what bird it came from." She held the feather out to Tom. "I think it's from a dove."

Tom looked as if he didn't know what to do with that information. I wasn't sure, either. Melchior had used those feathers to find where the angel of death had gone. Was the way he did the divination important?

I started to flip through Master Benedict's notes. Bridget, seemingly aware that we were talking about birds, stood with a grand flapping of wings and marched across the counter to where I was sitting. She stepped onto the book, cooing at me. I picked her up and stroked her feathers.

Thinking of birds reminded me of something my master had taught me during one of our discussions about the ancient Romans. They'd had priests called augurs who predicted the future by studying the flight patterns of birds. The type of bird you watched mattered. Maybe this was the same. If a divination were like a recipe, then the ingredients you used would be important. If we found out the reason Melchior used this feather, then, we might uncover something about the way he'd learned—

I stopped, halfway through turning a page.

Sally was watching me. "What's the matter?"

I held Bridget up, staring at her. My pulse was racing.

"Birds," I said.

Bridget cooed.

"Is this a private conversation?" Tom said.

I handed Bridget to him and picked up the book. I ran my hands over the title on the cover. *Observations on the Behavior of Birds*.

"You found it," I breathed.

Tom looked at Bridget. "I did? Found what?"

"Not you. Her." I pointed at Sally.

I flipped through the pages, faster now. I found what I was looking for in the last section—the biggest section, for these were the birds Master Benedict knew best.

Pigeons

I flipped the pages again, faster and faster, barely able to see the words. When I got to the penultimate page, a folded piece of parchment flew out. It skittered across the wood and fell to the floor.

Sally picked it up, opened it. Then she held it out. "It's for you."

The handwriting was Master Benedict's. My heart thumped as I read it.

Christopher:
The young bird finds its treasure when it settles in its place,
Hidden deep, beneath its feet; don't let it go to waste.

I remembered my master's secret message. *Study our birds.*

He hadn't told me to watch them. He'd told me to *study* them. And here were his notes.

"This is it," I said. "This is the clue."

"I don't understand," Tom said.

"It's from Master Benedict." I held up my master's message. "This says how to find his treasure."

CHAPTER
19

TOM GRABBED THE MESSAGE, excited. Sally leaned over the counter to look at it again. As for me, the thrill of the discovery quickly turned to disappointment.

"A lot of good that'll do," I said, "if Melchior's men already stole it."

"You don't know what they took," Tom said patiently.

Sally looked at me, not comprehending. I hesitated, not sure how much I should say. Then I sighed. She'd already read the message and heard us talk about treasure; there wasn't much point in hiding the rest. Besides, if she'd planned to steal from me, she would have taken my stock and fled yesterday, after she'd woken up here all alone. I'd have to assume she was as decent as she seemed.

I explained what had happened and showed her Master Benedict's letter with the capitals circled. She frowned.

"So why do you think they might have found the treasure?" she said.

"I left this letter out when we went to the market," I said. "The thief would have seen it."

"But that letter doesn't tell you where the treasure is. It just—"

I sat up with a jolt. "—tells me where to find the next *clue*."

My mind raced. Sally was right; the letter didn't lead to the treasure itself, only another message. So even if the thief saw the code hidden in the capitals, he couldn't possibly know where the treasure was located from that alone.

That would mean . . . I tried to piece together the possibilities.

The thief figured out the letter's riddle, found this message, and found the treasure. Extremely unlikely.

The thief hunted for the treasure and found it by accident. Possible, but also unlikely.

The thief found nothing and left empty-handed. Also

possible, but also unlikely. If they'd come just to steal, there was no reason to leave without taking something valuable from my stock.

Or the treasure was never the point of the break-in . . . and the thief came for something else entirely.

I still had no clue as to what that could be. Nor did anyone else. But Tom had a good idea. "Why don't we search for the treasure regardless? If we find where Master Benedict hid it, then either it'll be gone, and you'll know the thief took it, or it'll be there, and you'll have it after all. Right?"

Absolutely right. Excited once more, I smoothed the note out on the counter. *The young bird finds its treasure*, it said. Birds, again.

That was interesting. Master Benedict had always paid attention to our pigeons, and not just as sources of saltpeter. After I'd joined him, caring for our birds had become one of my duties. Sometimes, however, my master would look after them. He'd claim it was so I could spend more time on my studies, but secretly I always thought it was just because he liked them.

"Don't you have an old pigeon coop on the roof?" Sally said.

"We already looked there." I grabbed Tom's sleeve. "But we didn't look *underneath* it. That's it. Tom, that's *it*!"

Tom frowned. "What's underneath the coop?"

"The dirt, on the floor. And what's on *top* of it."

"What's on top of it?"

"Pigeon poop!" I said, triumphant.

Tom and Sally exchanged a glance. "All . . . right," Tom said.

"I'm serious. Look at the clue." I pointed to the second line of the message. "'Hidden deep, beneath its feet; don't let it go to waste.' Well, if the coop is the pigeons' place, what's beneath their feet? *Pigeon waste*. Even better: it's a *double* meaning. Because Master Benedict and I *didn't* let it go to waste. We used it to make saltpeter. It's why he started keeping pigeons in the first place."

Tom considered it. "That's pretty clever," he said finally. "But is there enough room to hide a treasure under the coop? There isn't much dirt there."

I thought about it. *Hidden deep*, the clue said. Tom had a good point; the layer of dirt under the birds was shallow. When we collected their waste, we'd scrape most of the dirt off, then scatter another layer on—

"The tiles!" I said. "The roof tiles, underneath. If Master

Benedict pried one up, he could hide the treasure beneath it. Then, when it's covered with dirt, no one would ever know it's there. It's brilliant!" I shook Tom's arm. "Who would ever think to look for treasure under a layer of pigeon droppings?"

"Only you," he said.

I ignored that. "Let's go."

"Go where?" Tom said.

"The roof, of course."

"Galen won't let us through the workshop."

"We'll borrow a ladder from one of the quarantine guards."

"Where are we going to get a ladder tall enough to reach your roof?"

"We won't," I said. "We'll go up as far as we can and then climb the last bit on the half timbers."

Tom stared at me in horror. "The half . . . wha . . ."

"What's the matter?" I said.

"I'm not crawling up the side of your house!"

"Why not?"

"I should think that answer's fairly obvious."

"We go up to the roof all the time."

"Through the hatch, not climbing the walls! Can't we just wait until Galen's finished?"

"I don't want to wait," I said, my voice rising.

Tom shushed me, glancing back at the door to the workshop.

I didn't care. "What's he doing in there, anyway?" I said. "If he has you grinding the ingredients, then how does he spend his time all day?"

Tom thought about it. "He's always reading. There are books all over the place. Oh, and once I saw him handling this little pouch. Like the one he threw at Henry yesterday."

Another black pouch? "I don't suppose you saw what's in it."

"No. He almost never uses the equipment when I'm around." Tom jerked a thumb toward the workshop. "I think that's why he kicked me out. He's doing something he doesn't want anyone to see."

Well, now *I* wanted to see it. The trouble was I didn't know how. There were no windows in the back; Master Benedict had bricked them up when he'd first bought the shop, to prevent people doing precisely that. He'd even installed plates to slide over the keyholes to the workshop doors for the same reason. I really had no way of seeing what Galen was doing—

Wait a minute. I *did*.

"No," Tom said.

"No to what?" I said.

"Whatever you're thinking."

"I haven't even said anything yet."

"And I'm happier that way."

"I know how we can spy on Galen," I said.

"You're not opening that door," Tom said.

"I don't have to. We go up to the roof, like I said. But we get inside the house from there. Then we creep downstairs and peek into the workshop—"

"How would you get inside? The hatch is bolted."

"No, it isn't," I said. "I unbolted it this morning."

Tom turned to Sally. "See? I was happier not knowing."

"It's a perfect plan," I said.

Tom folded his arms. "First of all, if Galen sees you, he'll think you're trying to steal his recipe. He won't just have you thrown out of this house; he'll have you clapped in irons. And second, your plan can't work, because you'll never get down the stairs. They creak too much. Galen will hear you the moment you take your first step."

That, I couldn't deny. I slumped down onto the stool. "I want my home back."

Then I had a thought.

"No!" Tom said.

"I haven't even said anything yet!" I said.

"And I'm happier that way!"

"If we slide down the bannister—"

The front door opening spared me from Tom's retort. Dr. Parrett stepped inside. Henry came with him, holding a ledger.

"Wonderful news," Dr. Parrett said. His shirt and jacket were rumpled, like he'd slept in his clothes—or hadn't slept at all. But his eyes were shining. "Aldebourne's daughter has recovered completely! And Magistrate Dench, after getting the cure . . . well, you tell them, Henry, you administered it!"

Henry seemed in a bit of a daze himself. "It worked. The magistrate is recovering as well. I . . . I was wrong. Galen truly has found the cure."

I felt like an enormous weight had been lifted from my shoulders. After the horror we'd been living, it was almost impossible to believe, but for the first time in months, I was no longer filled with fear. Neither Tom nor Sally spoke, but I could see the same joy on their faces—and the same relief.

Dr. Parrett and Henry looked just as relieved, though, after his earlier protests, Henry was feeling rather sheepish.

He sighed. "No doubt Galen will make me eat my words. No less than I deserve, I suppose."

"We've come to see him," Dr. Parrett said. "Is he in the workshop?"

Tom stopped him from going further. "I'm sorry, Doctor. Master Galen asked me not to let anyone in."

Dr. Parrett took it with good humor. "Then I shall remain out here."

Henry wasn't quite as phlegmatic. "No, no," he said. "We must speak with Galen right away. There is a serious problem with his requests." He held up the ledger he was carrying.

"What's wrong with them?" I said.

"The amount is what's wrong. Look at this."

Henry opened the ledger and showed us a list Galen had given him. I saw the problem immediately. Galen had ordered ingredients by the cartload. Like the jars Tom had shown me in the workshop, some of the ingredients were common enough—cloves, charcoal, lavender, sugar—but many were much harder to get, especially in large amounts. What Galen had given Henry was a manifest for a dozen apothecaries. I couldn't begin to imagine the cost.

Henry could. "A thousand pounds. And that's just to

secure the initial shipment and the warehouse. The final sum will be ten times that, at least."

"Money well spent," Dr. Parrett said.

"Spent from where?"

Dr. Parrett answered impatiently, like he'd already heard this complaint. "Aldebourne ordered you to use the charity."

"But then there won't be anything left," Henry said. "How am I supposed to pay the doctors, the nurses, the quarantine guards? And the poor, how will we support them? I can't manage a city on pennies."

"We'll have no need to manage anything if the plague is cured." Though Dr. Parrett said it calmly, an edge had crept into his voice.

"Yes, but it'll take *weeks* to manufacture enough cure. What are we supposed to do until then?"

"Cut back. Sacrifice. Here, man, I'll forfeit my salary."

Henry was taken aback. "I . . . well. A most gracious gesture, John. But that won't feed two hundred thousand poor. Surely Galen can find at least a few cheaper alternatives among these ingredients." He stepped past Tom and knocked on the door to the workshop. "Galen! Could you open the door for a moment? I must speak with you."

Dr. Parrett wouldn't let the argument go. "Others will

make the same sacrifices, Henry. How can they not, when people are dying?"

Henry looked incredulous. "Very easily, sir; you'd be surprised. That's not the point. Without these funds, people will starve before anyone even gets the cure."

"Then we can bring them back!" Dr. Parrett shouted.

Henry looked puzzled. "What on Earth are you—"

Thunk.

The sound came from the workshop. Like an ax hitting wood.

Then we heard the scream.

"Help!"

That was Galen's voice.

"Help! Heeeellp! Heeeeeeeeeeeeeeeeeellllllp!"

Henry grabbed the handle on the door. He tried to turn it.

It was stuck.

Galen continued to scream.

"What the devil—is this locked?" Henry said.

Tom, frightened, shook his head.

"Then why won't it—!"

The door popped open. The five of us nearly fell over each other into the workshop.

The back door swung open in the breeze. My eyes tracked from the brightness to the far corner of the workshop. Galen was there. He huddled against the wall, screaming.

"Help! Assassins! Help me!"

For a moment, I thought the man had gone mad. There was no one else here.

Then I saw the gash on his cheek, the blood trickling down. Pressed against his neck, a wooden shaft with a feathered end was embedded in the beam behind him. His ruffled collar was stuck through by the shaft, held fast.

Galen wasn't huddled in the corner. He was pinned there, a crossbow bolt shot through his shirt.

CHAPTER 20

GALEN WOULDN'T CALM DOWN.
For a few minutes after we'd freed him, he stayed in the
corner, terrified, howling for no one to touch him. Once
we finally convinced him he was safe, his mood shifted.
He paced around the workshop in a rage, ranting about
thieves, assassins, and conspiracies.

Dr. Parrett managed to coax out of Galen what he'd
seen—which was mostly a crossbow bolt coming toward
him, fired from the open back door by a shabbily dressed
man. Beyond that, Galen was barely coherent. Dr. Parrett
finally quieted him a little by slipping some poppy into a
draft of medicinal wine.

Henry looked like he needed that wine himself. He wasn't just panicked about the attempt on Galen's life; he was worried about what the people of London would do if anyone found out about it. News that Galen had a working cure had already begun to spread through the city; the removal of the quarantine on Aldebourne's house had only added to the buzz. If the crowds heard of an assassin loose in the streets, there was no imagining what kind of chaos that would bring.

"You can't tell *anyone*," Henry insisted. Once we'd agreed, Henry ran for Guildhall's guards. He returned with ten of them. They whisked Galen away, along with Dr. Parrett, leaving Tom, Sally, and me staring at each other in shock. None of us could even speak.

Someone had tried to assassinate Galen. They'd tried to murder the man who'd *discovered the cure for the plague.*

The crossbow they'd used lay on the counter, the bolt Tom had pried from the wall beside it. Sally had found the weapon nose down in the dirt in the herb garden behind my house. The assassin had discarded it as he'd fled, no doubt to sneak away undetected after his attempt on Galen's life had failed.

It was odd how sinister the thing seemed. If Tom and I had got our hands on a crossbow before, we'd have spent the rest of the year punching holes in anything we could find. Now, neither of us wanted to touch it. This weapon had nearly killed Galen—and with him the thousands more who would suffer without his cure.

"It's madness," Tom said, dazed. "Who would do this? *Why* would they do this?"

Sally had been the first to spot a clue that might answer that question. Someone had etched a symbol into the wood near the trigger.

"But . . . that's just like Melchior's symbol," Tom said anxiously. "The one on the bronze talismans. The one painted on Melchior's chest."

"Actually," I said quietly, "it's precisely the opposite."

"What do you mean?"

I picked up the weapon. It was smaller than a standard crossbow, designed more for stealth than for war. Still, the weight of it pressed into my hands.

I held it as if I were going to shoot it. The symbol was carved so it lay directly beneath the palm of my trigger hand. It felt like my skin was burning.

I put the thing down. On a piece of scrap, I inked the symbol from Melchior's medallions and put it next to the one on the crossbow.

"Melchior's symbol is a combination of two separate glyphs," I said. "The triangle represents fire. The down-turned sword is the symbol of the Archangel Michael."

Tom stared at me, wide-eyed; he knew just what that might mean. I shook my head. "In this case, the symbols, with the words—*contra malignitatem protege nos*; protect us from malice—make this a shield; an amulet of protection.

"The other symbol, however, is just a single glyph. The triangle over the short cross represents sulphur. Sulphur can mean a lot of things, but in this case I'm pretty sure it stands for brimstone. So then that represents demons—

or fallen angels, like Samael. The inscription makes that clear."

"What does it say?" Sally asked.

"*Cadete ante iram suam.*" The words stung my lips. "It means: Fall before his wrath."

My skin still burned where I'd touched that crossbow. I wiped my hands on my breeches, as if that would somehow take the stain away. "This new symbol is not a shield. It's a sword. And it serves the angel of death."

Despite Henry's desperate desire to keep the attempt on Galen's life a secret, within hours the crowds were near rioting at Guildhall. The three of us locked ourselves in the shop, door bolted, shutters closed until dark. It wasn't safe in the streets.

We all froze when someone knocked on the door. We stayed quiet, listening, until Dr. Parrett's voice called through the wood. "It's me, Christopher."

Henry was with him, looking terribly shaken. A third man came, too, a city guard. I let them in, then quickly threw the bolt behind them.

"How did people find out?" I said.

"Galen," Henry said, exasperated. "After the calmative

John gave him wore off, he panicked again, started shouting about assassins. One of his guards must have told someone. This is a disaster. A *disaster*."

Dr. Parrett seemed rather wild-eyed himself. "It's all right. Galen is safe now."

"Fine enough for you to say." Henry pulled at his collar, stained with sweat. "An assassin! The Lord Mayor wants my head. Aldebourne might just give it to him."

Henry was right to be worried. It wasn't just his job he was talking about. If the people of London believed Henry was the one who'd failed to protect Galen, they'd tear him apart in the street. Nevertheless, it seemed to me that it was *Galen's* head he should really have been worried about. Two inches to the left, and the apothecary would have been finished—along with his cure for the plague. The assassin hadn't just tried to kill Galen. He'd attacked every one of us just the same.

Sally was curled up on the windowsill, watching silently as usual. Tom huddled next to her. I think he was still in shock.

"Did anyone see the assassin flee?" he said.

Henry threw his arms up in frustration. "No one! Not a thing."

I'd hoped otherwise, but I hadn't really expected it. Ordinarily, Galen's shrieks would have brought dozens of onlookers to the scene of the crime. But no one listened to cries for help anymore. And they wouldn't give a second glance to a shabbily dressed man; these days, that sight was all too common in our streets.

"What happens now?" I said.

"The attack has frightened the magistrates," Henry said. *They aren't the only ones,* I thought. "They offered Galen a thousand pounds if he'd tell them the recipe."

I was stunned. *A thousand pounds.* "Did he take it?"

Henry looked miserable. "It only made him angrier. You should have heard him. He said maybe the assassination was an attempt by the *magistrates* to frighten him so he'd give them the cure."

Considering someone had just tried to put a bolt through his head, it wasn't hard to understand Galen wasn't feeling particularly trusting. Still, that idea seemed a little far-fetched.

"I told you, he was ranting. It was only John's intervention that calmed him down again." Henry waved at Dr. Parrett, who was pacing back and forth in front of the shop's counter. "Anyway, the magistrates have instructed that we begin setting up Galen's workshop immediately. I've paid the merchants for the ingredients he needs, and ordered the equipment he wanted as well. I've also rented an empty warehouse near the river that should suffice to produce mass quantities of the cure."

"Does Master Galen want me to work there?" Tom said.

Henry shrugged. "I don't know. I'm not even permitted to tell you where his workshop will be. Galen's insisting it remain a secret; only the magistrates will know its location. But it should be ready soon, so if Galen wants you, he'll send for you. In the meantime, he's staying in one of the houses at Guildhall, surrounded by guards and refusing to come out."

Henry turned to Dr. Parrett. "Galen listens to you, John. You have to get him back to work *immediately*. He says he's only made one more pouchful of the cure. That's nothing. We need enough for the whole city, and fast. I've already spent the full complement of charity for the week. Until that cure's ready, the people of London will keep dying."

Dr. Parrett continued pacing.

"John," Henry said. "Are you listening?"

Dr. Parrett just stared into space. I exchanged a glance with Tom.

"Um . . . Dr. Parrett?" Tom said.

Dr. Parrett stopped. Slowly, he looked over at us. "Yes?" He shook his head, as if to clear his own thoughts. "Oh. Yes," he said, more forcefully. "I'll speak to him, of course."

"It'll still be a few days before everything is set up. Get Galen back here. Drag him in chains if you have to. The guards can come with him, watch over Blackthorn while he works." Henry turned. "In the meantime, I'll have to search you for a key."

It took a moment to realize he was talking to me. "What? Why?"

"That's why we're here. Galen's demanding to know how the back door got unlocked."

"But . . . I didn't do it!" I said. "You were looking right at me when it happened!"

Henry spread his hands in apology. "Galen insisted. So did Magistrate Aldebourne. Turn around, please."

I fumed while the guard Henry had brought prodded me in uncomfortable places. He did the same to Tom and Sally, finding nothing. My guts fluttered for a moment when Henry looked around the room for other places a key might be hidden, because I *did* have a key, secreted in one of the pockets of my apothecary sash, which hung from its hook behind the shop counter. Fortunately, Henry wasn't taking Galen's concern about me too seriously. As I'd already pointed out, he'd been with me when the assassin had unlocked the back door.

Of course, that led to a different question.

"How *did* the assassin open that door?" I said, after Henry and Dr. Parrett had left.

My first panicked thought was that *I'd* accidentally let the killer in, through the roof hatch I'd left unbolted. But Galen himself had confirmed the man had come through the back door. And he'd heard it unlock with a key.

"Could Galen have been mistaken?" I said. "What if someone tampered with that door, like Melchior's man did the front?"

Tom shook his head. "It was locked. Proper locked. I checked the bolt hole for wood and everything. Galen even ordered me to try and open it before he sent me out of the workshop."

"Then someone else must have a key," Sally said. "Can you think of who?"

There were only three keys that I knew of. Galen had mine. The spare key from behind the brick outside was in my sash. The third had been Master Benedict's. I explained that the Apothecaries' Guild Council had confiscated it last May, after his death.

"Did they give it back?" Sally asked.

"They were supposed to," I said. "But the Guild left with the plague." Along with the money they owed me.

"Then maybe that was the key the assassin used."

It almost had to be. But I didn't know how they'd got it. Apothecaries' Hall had been locked up months ago.

"What if someone there kept it?" Sally said.

Tom looked spooked. And I knew why. Some of the members of the Cult of the Archangel had been apothecaries. We'd broken that conspiracy, but as Lord Ashcombe had told me, we had no way of knowing if some secret members were still around.

"Is it possible your master had a fourth key?" Sally said.

I thought about it. "I suppose. But I don't know where it would be."

"What about here?"

"The shop?"

"Your house," she said. "What if there was a spare key hidden somewhere inside?"

Tom blinked. "Then the thief who broke in—"

"Could have taken it," I finished. Along with what-ever else they'd come for. "But it was *Melchior's* man who broke in."

"That would mean—" Tom began.

"*Melchior* tried to murder Galen?" I said.

Tom threw his hands up, frustrated. "None of this makes sense. Why would Melchior want to kill Galen? Why would *anyone* want to kill Galen? He's the only one who knows the cure."

"Unless someone else knows how to make it," Sally said.

"How could someone else know the recipe?" Tom said. "He won't even let *me* near him, and I don't know anything about apothecary ingredients."

"Well . . . Galen discovered it. Couldn't somebody else have found it, too?"

"If someone else had a cure," I said, "we'd surely already know about it. They'd make a fortune with it. And they'd have saved thousands of lives in this city."

Unless, I thought, *it wasn't about money. Unless they didn't* want *to save those lives.*

I stared at the crossbow, the symbol carved into the wood. My guts fluttered.

"Melchior," I said.

Tom and Sally looked at me.

"How does he know who's going to die?" I said.

"He's a prophet," Tom said.

"That's what everyone thinks. But what if he's not? What if Melchior knows who's going to die next because *he's the one making it happen*."

"He's *spreading* the plague?" Sally said.

"That can't be," Tom said. "The plague came over on a Dutch ship, in the spring. Melchior wasn't here then. He didn't come to London until a couple of months ago."

"How do you know?" I said.

"I'm pretty sure people would have noticed a man in a bird mask."

"What about without it?"

Tom made as if to respond. Then he stopped, his mouth hanging open.

"What does Melchior look like?" I said. "He's always wearing that costume. Has anyone ever seen his face? He could have passed us on the street—he could have been in this *shop*—and we wouldn't have looked twice. So how do we know how long he's actually been here? He could have brought the plague to the city."

"If that's true, how is he infecting people?" Sally said.

"I don't know. Maybe this business about Samael is true; maybe he's in league with dark forces. Maybe he just understands how the plague actually works. Either way, if Melchior's spreading the disease, then Galen is his biggest threat. His *only* threat. If Galen dies, no one else will know the cure. And there'll be no one left to stand in Melchior's way."

"But . . . *why* would Melchior be doing this?" Tom said. "Why would anyone want to infect a city with plague?"

"I don't know that, either," I said. "But I think we'd better find out."

CHAPTER
21

IT WAS TOO LATE TO DO ANYTHING
about it that day; we'd have to wait until tomorrow. That
led to another restless night.

Tom went home. Sally claimed she wasn't in much pain
anymore, but I knew she was just trying to get me to take
my palliasse back, so I made her keep it. Too tired to argue,
she hummed herself to sleep, her melody fading into the soft
sounds of her breathing, broken only by the crackling of the
fire. Finally my own sleeplessness finally caught up with me,
and I slipped away, too.

I dreamed of our birds. Master Benedict was there with
me. We fed them from our hands, watching as they swallowed

little scrolls of burnt parchment inked with jumbled letters.

"Will they give us the answer, Master?" I said. "I need to find your treasure."

"You already know where it is," he said. "You just don't believe it."

He offered me the scrolls. I pecked half of them out of his palm before I realized I'd turned into a pigeon.

The strangeness of the dream shook me awake. Bridget, nestled beside me, rustled her feathers and gave me a sleepy coo.

I was a little disappointed. I was pleased my master had visited me in my dreams, but in this one I'd been a pigeon and I hadn't even got to fly. Still, something about the dream nagged at me. It kept running through my head so that, exhausted as I was, my mind wouldn't drift back to sleep.

I tossed and turned a little before giving it up for good. I rose and tried to work on the fragments of Melchior's code, but with the tiredness of my mind, the sweet smoke from the fire, and the mesmerizing flicker of the flame in the lamp next to me, I just couldn't focus. It wasn't what I really wanted to be doing, anyway.

I wanted to search for my master's treasure. I'd planned

to wait for Tom to return, to do it together, but I didn't want to put it off any longer. So I picked up a drowsy Bridget, grabbed a lantern and a small spade from the workshop, and went up to the roof.

Bridget seemed pleased to be back in the coop again; she flapped from my shoulder to her old perch at the back and poked her beak into the straw. I took the spade and got to work, scooping away the dirt that lined the floor until the metal scraped the tiles underneath.

I pried with the tip of the spade at the cracks between the stones. I expected one to lift out, but they all stayed where they were, stuck fast. I crouched, running my fingers along the cracks.

As far as I could tell, the mortar between the tiles hadn't been touched. It looked decades old, as cracked and aged here as everywhere else on the roof. I thought about digging the tiles out anyway, but from what Isaac had told me, Master Benedict had hidden the treasure sometime after the Cult of the Archangel started hunting him earlier this year. So it couldn't be under the coop. My answer to the riddle was wrong.

And it had made so much sense, too. Downcast, I tossed the spade in the pile of dirt and left it there. Bridget flapped back onto my shoulder. I coaxed her to nestle in the crook of my arm and stroked her feathers.

"What do I do now?" I said.

She cooed.

"The dream's gone, Bridget. I don't remember how to speak pigeon."

But you already know where the treasure is. That's what my master had told me in my dream. His original message to me had said the same. *You won't find it until you realize something incredibly important.*

Not "discover," I thought. *"Realize."*

What was I supposed to realize? What did I already know?

I thought about it. Master Benedict left me this shop, this home. The treasure was somewhere inside, somewhere hidden. It had to do with birds, which he'd cared for.

Now Master Benedict had come to my dream. In it—

I was the bird.

I pulled my master's message from my waistband. I opened it, read it again.

The young bird finds its treasure when it settles in its place,
Hidden deep, beneath its feet; don't let it go to waste.

Its treasure, it said.

But that treasure was meant for me. It was *my* treasure.

So *I* was the bird.

I'd come up here to search because our birds' place was in the coop. But my place was . . .

In the shop.

As an orphan, I'd been lost, with no idea where I could go, what I could do, what would happen to me. I'd only found my place when Master Benedict had chosen me at the testing. Under his guiding hand, I'd become an apothecary's apprentice; *his* apprentice. Before I'd met him, I'd never known such a world existed. Now I didn't want anything else.

The shop; the workshop; my life here, at Blackthorn. That was my place.

So then the location of the treasure would be beneath *my* feet. Which would place it . . .

Under the floorboards?

I frowned. I'd spent every day of the last three years treading those worn old boards—and plenty of days scrubbing them, too. I knew every scratch, crease, and crack. If Master Benedict had pulled any up, I'd have noticed it. So how could he hide anything beneath my feet? He'd have to get under—

My heart began to thump.

Hidden deep, beneath its feet; don't let it go to waste.

The crawl space. The crawl space under the floor. The crawl space, which Master Benedict had planned to turn into a proper cellar but never got around to.

I ran downstairs. I placed Bridget on one of the almost-empty shelves in the pantry. Then I shoved the barrel of ale I'd bought at the market into the corner and pulled on the ring in the floor. The hatchway opened onto the darkened space below.

I took a lantern with me. There wasn't much room, even for that; the crawl space was less than three feet high. The ice vault had been dug just to the side of the hatchway, surrounded by clay bricks to seal in the chill. The rest of the space had indeed "gone to waste"; the ground only packed earth, smelling of must and stale air. Among the wide support beams and bricks were just a few items my master had placed down here, mostly old equipment he didn't want to throw away because of sentimental attachment: the apparatus he'd used as an apprentice, and the like.

It was cooler here, below ground, but even free of the summer heat, the dampness made the space uncomfortable. Sweating, I inched forward on hands and knees. I peered at the ground, wondering if my master had buried his treasure—hidden deep, like he'd said. If Master Benedict— or Melchior's thief—had dug something up, that would have left an obvious sign. Yet the earth here was untouched.

Stone supports were everywhere. I brought the lantern close, scanning the bricks for some mark, some symbol that would serve as a clue. Nothing jumped out at me. Growing frustrated, I swung the lantern around, looking for anything anywhere nearby.

A shadow shifted in the corner of my eye, an odd shape. There. On the other side of the support.

I scrambled back and around. The lantern illuminated a worn leather apothecary's satchel with a tarnished iron buckle, mostly lost to rust. The satchel was small, fit for carrying a sheaf of papers, a handful of ingredients, and not much else.

I pulled it open. The leather cracked in my hands as I searched the pockets inside.

Nothing.

I took the satchel with me, out of the crawl space. I brought it into the workshop, sat at the bench. Bridget fluttered over to pace beside me.

In the better light, I searched the satchel more closely. I scanned its pattern, its inner weave, its seams. I pulled it, shook it. The leather split at one end, and at that I nearly tore it open.

Still nothing.

I threw the satchel aside. If this was where Master Benedict had hidden his treasure, then the thief had taken it. If it wasn't, I was lost all over again.

My uncertainty made me wonder again what his treasure really was. Gold, like I'd originally thought? You could fit a lot of coins in that satchel.

But that's not what it had once been designed for. It was for notes and ingredients. Which made me think: if the treasure *wasn't* gold, how would I recognize it? It would have to stand out as something special.

That's what Isaac had said, I recalled. *Something special. Something Benedict wanted only you to have.*

And then a thief had broken in. Melchior's thief. He'd sent one of his men to take something in secret. Something they didn't want me—or anyone else—to know about.

Thoughts whirled around in my mind.

Melchior, predicting the spread of the plague, his prophecies always correct.

An assassin, hunting Galen, the only man who'd ever found a genuine plague cure.

And my master . . . who used to be a plague specialist.

Galen found the cure, Sally had said. *Couldn't somebody else have found it, too?*

Your master left you something special. A recipe, Lord Ashcombe had said.

My mind buzzed, nothing but questions. I couldn't know for sure what had been taken. But sitting there in my workshop, missing my master, and thinking of Melchior and Galen and plagues and cures, I knew one thing above all.

It was time to take it back.

WEDNESDAY, SEPTEMBER 2, 1665

Yesterday's plague deaths: 1,275

Total dead: 33,024

CHAPTER
22

THIS DAY, WE DIDN'T HAVE TO
hunt Melchior down to find him. We knew exactly where
he'd be.

To help fight the plague, King Charles had declared
the first Wednesday of every month a fast day, for all to
spend in prayer. It was a responsibility the city took seriously. Crowds packed the churches, unafraid of strangers,
relying on God's protection to keep them safe. And from
the crowd we'd seen following Melchior yesterday, I knew
no church would be quite as packed as Saint Andrew's, the
centuries-old chapel next to Cripplegate where the plague
doctor had made his home.

Still, I hadn't expected *this*. People squeezed in shoulder to shoulder; the din from a thousand conversations rang in my ears. When I was still at Cripplegate, we'd come to services here sometimes, where I'd count the cracks that lined its weathered stones and wonder how much longer the place could stand before the walls collapsed. The way this mob pressed into it made me worry this was the day the church would finally burst apart.

I sighed, and not just because I didn't relish shoving my way through the crowd. This place reminded me too much of my days in the orphanage. From where we stood, I could barely see the blockish towers of Cripplegate; the trees in the private garden behind the church shielded most of the building from view. I'd still rather have been anywhere else.

We aren't here for the past, I reminded myself. We'd come to see Melchior. That meant actually *seeing* him, and for that, we'd need to get inside. Fortunately, pushing through any crowd was a lot easier with Tom leading the way. I followed in his wake, Sally clinging to the back of my shirt.

"He would have been handy in Cripplegate," she shouted into my ear. I nodded; I'd already lost count of the number of times I'd wished I'd known him then.

Tom got us into the chapel all right, but we could forget

about getting a seat. I figured we'd just stand at the back when Tom pulled at my sleeve. "Look."

He nodded toward the western wall. Standing under a stained glass window was Dr. Parrett. The doctor gazed up at it, ignoring the jostling crowd, a dreamy sort of look on his face.

Tom squeezed us through. We pressed against the wall next to him. Dr. Parrett didn't appear to notice.

"Hello, Doctor," Tom shouted, loud enough to be heard over the crowd.

Slowly, Dr. Parrett brought his eyes down. Sweat beaded on his forehead. "Hello, Tom. And Christopher and Sally, too. Of course." He looked back up at the stained glass window. "Beautiful, isn't it?"

The window was bordered by an intricate pattern of colors. In the center was Christ resurrected, His opened tomb empty below. He rose from the Earth toward a dove with an olive branch in its beak.

A chill ran down my spine. The glass *was* beautiful. But I didn't think the window's craftsmanship was what he'd meant.

"James will be here soon." Dr. Parrett smiled. "Not long now."

Tom glanced at me, worried, and looking more than a little afraid.

"Dr. Parrett—" I began.

"Are you here to see Melchior, then?"

The change of subject threw me. "I—yes. Actually, I wanted to ask you about—"

"That's wise. He knows the truth."

"Dr. Parrett . . . I'm not so sure he's really—"

"I thought this day would never come." Sweat dripped from the doctor's chin, staining his doublet. "The omens are all present. The comet of last winter, the heat of the summer. The conjunctions of the planets. The war with the Dutch. All harbingers of the end times. Into this comes a prophet. And in his wake follows the cure. This is it, do you see? The innocent will be reborn, and we will be reunited with those we lost, those we love."

The crowd nearby burst into cheers. The call for Melchior spread throughout the church, shouting, pleading. Tom looked helpless. I felt the same. The death of children under Dr. Parrett's care, Melchior's predictions, Galen's cure . . . Dr. Parrett's mind had finally snapped. It was heartbreaking to watch.

Sally, who'd never really known Dr. Parrett, seemed more worried about what his speech had started. She pressed into me, holding her side as the crowd's chant became deafening. The mass shifted and swelled, like a living thing. For a moment, I really believed they'd bring the roof of old Saint Andrew's crumbling down.

Then Melchior appeared.

The crowd cheered once more, shouting his name. Voices lingered, then fell away, as the throng grew quiet. Melchior waited, shrouded in shadow cast by the archway where he stood, south of the chancel, until the chapel was completely silent.

Then he came forward. Smoke curled from his beak. The head of his plague doctor staff dragged across the ground. The sound of one gargoyle wing rang over the stone, his leather heels clicking an echo from the rafters.

At the lectern, he stopped. Melchior stared at the crowd. When his voice came, it started low, like the rumble of distant thunder.

"There is a sickness in this city," he said. "I walk among you, care for you, weep with you. I hear your words, your pleas. For there is a sickness in this city."

"Save us!" a man cried.

Others took up the call. "Save us! Save us!" Melchior waited until the shouts drifted away.

"You call for salvation," he said, "because you believe this sickness is special. Of course you do: It destroys your lives, your families, your homes. But I have walked in other places, other countries, and I tell you: It is not special. What plagues this city is a sickness of the *soul*. And it has lived in men's hearts since we first tasted that forbidden apple."

Slowly, Melchior raised his silver staff. His voice rose with it; the thunder rolling closer. "You hear tell of a cure. I have seen it work. Have you?"

The staff hovered over the crowd. The rows closest to Melchior stared at the gargoyle looming over them.

"The magistrates—and their children—have been cured. Have yours?"

A rumbling started, low and heavy, as the people shifted restlessly in their seats.

"Why have you not seen this cure? The magistrates do not know. What is the delay? The magistrates will not say."

The rumble grew louder, sharper. The crowd swelled, anger seeping from it like a rising heat.

A riot, I thought. *If he keeps this up, he's going to start a riot.*

And then I realized: *He* wants *to start a riot.*

Melchior swung his staff overhead.

"And so it is *you*, the common man, who suffers. It is *you*—" His voice cracked. "It is you . . ."

Melchior's words trailed away. He stood there, silently swaying back and forth.

Then he collapsed. His body shook. Great racking spasms seized his limbs.

The crowd gasped. It pressed backward, desperate to get away.

Suddenly, Melchior sat up. He stared through his mask at the crowd.

"The angel of death," he said.

He pointed at the far corner, at a stained glass window. A shadow dulled the colors.

Then it moved.

"He flies!" Melchior said. "Follow him!"

Melchior sprang from the ground, his staff banging against the lectern. He leaped into the crowd. The people pulled back, startled. Even his own bodyguards looked surprised.

He ran forward. With the press of people, I wouldn't have thought it possible, but the crowd somehow melted out of his way. No one wanted to touch him.

The mob crushed us against the wall as Melchior passed and ran outside. Then the crowd swirled behind him like flowing water. They chased after him, howling for his protection. His guards followed, shoving parishioners aside roughly in an attempt to get to their master.

I covered my head and pulled away from the stampeding crowd. A big arm grabbed me, held me close. When I peeked around my elbows, I saw Tom holding Sally, too, turned away from the crowd toward the center of the nave, so the rushing horde beat against his back instead of us.

After what seemed like forever, the crowd thinned. Tom let us go. I turned to see what had happened.

Almost no one was left behind. Near the back, an old woman knelt, her head bowed. On the other side, a family of five remained huddled, the children crying into their father's breeches. A few more lingered, stunned. Dr. Parrett had gone, too, following his newfound prophet.

Sally slid down the wall, breathing heavily. She'd gone pale, hands pressed against her side.

I knelt next to her. "Are you all right?"

"We should take her home," Tom said, but she waved us off.

"I'm fine." She pushed herself back up the wall, trying

to smile. It mostly came out as a grimace. "Really."

"That speech," Tom said, shaking his head.

He'd seen the same as I had. Melchior had inflamed the crowd deliberately, pitting them against the magistrates. If he hadn't stopped to chase the angel of death, I'd swear he'd have sent the crowd to Guildhall to burn it down.

"We should follow him," Sally said. "See what he's going to do next."

"We know exactly what he's going to do next," Tom said. "Predict more death. So we should absolutely *not* follow Melchior." He turned to me, as if daring me to disagree.

I didn't. "Tom's right."

"I am?" His eyes narrowed. "Why?"

"Look around. Everyone's gone. Even Melchior's guards."

"So?"

"So Melchior lives here," I said.

Tom frowned. "I don't see what that has to do with— oh no."

From where we stood in the aisle, I could just see the edge of the door from which Melchior had come before his speech. He'd left it open.

"We won't get this chance again," I said.

"We don't want this chance now!" Tom said. "Christopher!"

I ran through the pews, then darted down the aisle. The few remaining parishioners were too wrapped up in themselves to pay any attention to what I was doing. I slipped under the archway and through the door. Sally followed, then Tom, dragging his feet.

The room to the south of the altar was just a small enclosure. To the left was an equally small storage area holding a row of mops, brooms, and other cleaning supplies. Ahead was the door that led to the private garden behind the church. To the right was another door, with a small cross-barred window at eye height. Through it, I could see stone stairs spiraling downward, lamplight flickering on the steps.

I tried the door. "It's locked," I said. I suppose I should have expected that, but I was still disappointed.

Sally looked puzzled. "You don't want to use the keys?"

"What keys?"

"The church keys. For the door."

Now *I* was puzzled. "Why would I have the keys to this church?"

She gave me a curious look before squeezing into the storage closet. She reached behind a set of old, dried-out mops at the back. She returned, holding a ring of keys jingling on an iron loop.

I stared at them blankly. "How did you know those were there?"

"We used to come in here from Cripplegate sometimes. There's a hidden path through the garden in the back."

I knew about the hidden path; I'd used it myself when sneaking out of the orphanage at night. But that was to go somewhere more interesting, like down to the docks to run among the ships, or into the back of the playhouse. "Why would anyone want to break into a church?"

"To raid the pantry. On Tuesdays, when the sexton went to the tavern." Sally seemed surprised. "Didn't you boys ever do that?"

"We were too busy getting beaten on Tuesdays," I said indignantly.

She shrugged and turned the key in the lock. "See?" She opened the door and went down the steps.

Tom stared in horror, one hand on his cheek. "She's worse than you are."

"Yes," I said. "I rather like her."

CHAPTER
23

WE ALL WENT DOWN. TOM TUGGED at my sleeve the whole time.

"Stop it," I whispered. "You're going to tip me down the stairs."

"Maybe that would rattle some sense into you," Tom whispered back. "Remember what happened the last time we went creeping about underground?"

"You're not helping."

"I'm not trying to."

The spiral stairs opened into a narrow hallway, lit by four lamps hanging along the right wall. Across from each lamp was a door, with one more door opposite an alcove at the far end.

"What's behind all these?" I said to Sally, lifting a lamp from its hook.

She shrugged. "We never tried them. We only ever went into the pantry. I know one of these rooms was the sexton's quarters, though."

"Where is the sexton?" Tom said.

"Dead of the sickness. Melchior predicted that, too, I heard."

She showed us the pantry, which was behind the first door by the stairs. Inside were several bottles of sacramental wine, plus a few dozen jars of preserves. There were also numerous jars of common kitchen herbs and spices: mint, cloves, and the like. Most of the rest of the food had been removed. A wheel of hard cheese rested on the counter beneath the preserves, a knife stuck in the center, crumbs trailing to the floor from a missing wedge.

The next two rooms were filled with old church supplies: tarnished crosses, dusty furniture, painted saints peeling in broken frames. The room after that was empty, just a single iron hook hammered into the far wall.

We came to the last door at the end of the hall. The alcove across from it drew my attention first. I stood there, staring at it. Sally and Tom joined me, their breath quick.

"Dear God," Tom said.

Hung in the middle of the arch of the alcove was a painting, the tempera cracked with the passing of years. It depicted a man, surrounded by a crowd of onlookers, kneeling with his arms stretched upward in prayer. Lying across his knees was another man clad only in a loincloth, his pale skin covered in angry red boils. Behind them both stood a skeleton, a bony hand reaching toward the afflicted, his skull a mocking grin.

Around the painting, the stone arch of the alcove was carved with detailed figures. On the right was an angel, his wings folded behind him. He stood over a dozen praying men. In one hand he held a sword, its point just touching the ground. He gazed sternly at the figure opposite.

That figure was another angel, his beautiful features twisted into a sneer. He gripped his own sword, also point down, but shorter, narrower, sleeker than the sword of his opponent. He stood upon a pile of skulls.

From behind them both flowed a host of winged soldiers. They rose upward, like waves in the stone, until they met in the center with a clash of crossed swords.

These two main figures were the angels of death. On the right, Michael. On the left, Samael. Above them, their armies, fighting over the souls of the dead.

"Look," Sally whispered.

She pointed at the arch. Beside Michael's and Samael's heads were carved two symbols. We'd seen them before.

Tom shook his head, muttering. I didn't have to hear his words to know what he was thinking; I'd begun to think the same myself. But there was one more door behind us to try. Unlike the others, it was locked. Luckily, it opened with a key from the ring Sally had taken.

This had clearly been the sexton's quarters. A simple bed with a straw mattress was in the corner, a trunk at the foot of the bed, next to a small cupboard. On the night table beside the palliasse was an unlit candle and three bottles of the same sacramental wine we'd seen in the pantry. Two were empty, the third nearly there, only a couple of mouthfuls left inside.

Crammed next to the bed was a rudimentary clothes

cabinet, worn and beaten with age, tall enough to reach the ceiling. The only other furniture was a desk and a rickety chair, placed against the wall near the door. Papers were scattered across the desk, weighed down by an empty dinner plate, an oil lamp, and another unlit candle burned to a nub.

"Will you please explain what we're looking for?" Tom said.

"Anything that could have been taken from my home," I said.

"And that is?"

"I don't know. Gold, maybe. Or any notes with my master's handwriting." I almost didn't say it. "Maybe a recipe."

"For what?"

I didn't answer. I wasn't willing to tell them what I thought Melchior's men might have come for until I knew for sure that's what it was. But as I stood there, looking around, something didn't feel quite right. Melchior was so . . . well, *grand*, I guess. And this room was so plain. Even the walls were bare, just a single black spot among the water stains on the stone above the right edge of the desk.

"Why does Melchior live down here?" I said.

Tom looked around unhappily. "I think it rather suits him."

"Where should he live?" Sally said.

"The rectory," I said. "If Reverend Glennon fled, no one's living there. It would be a lot bigger—and a lot nicer—than these quarters. And where do Melchior's men sleep?"

"They don't. Sleep here, I mean. They go home."

"How do you know that?"

"We watched them," Sally said. "Before Cripplegate shut down. You can see the front of the church from the library. Melchior's men leave at night. Two of them stay to guard the main doors. The rest don't come back until morning."

"What about the side door, beside the stairs? You can't see that from the library."

"No, but the secret path in the garden goes right by it. There was never anyone there."

That was odd. If Melchior lived down here, the side door would be the place he should *most* want to guard. After all, with the path through the garden, anyone with a key could sneak in and out of the church without being seen.

"Maybe he doesn't live here after all," Tom said. He stepped back to show us the cabinet, which he'd opened while Sally and I were talking.

It was empty. So was the closet, it turned out. Sally opened the trunk at the foot of the bed. Except for a single set of undergarments, there was nothing in there, either.

"Where are all his clothes?" I said.

"Maybe he doesn't need any," Tom said. "He's always wearing that leather suit."

"You think he sleeps in it? There aren't even any bedclothes."

It seemed strange that there were no personal items anywhere. It was almost like Melchior wasn't an actual person. Except for the undergarments, the empty bottles, and the mess on the desk, you wouldn't even know anyone was living here.

I went over to the desk, looked at the papers. The candle was on top of some of them. I lifted it to look at the papers underneath, and that was when I noticed something about the black spot on the wall behind it.

It had an odd shape. On the left side, it was rounded. On the right, the outline was straight. I rubbed a finger over it. A faint gray smudged on my skin.

"What is it?" Sally asked.

"Smoke," I said.

The spot on the wall was the stain of smoke from a candle—hundreds of candles, really. But the outline was wrong. The cut-off line on the right meant—

"Something used to be here," I said, pointing at the empty space.

A painting, maybe? The one in the hall?

I stepped outside to look at its frame, but found no soot. I returned to the desk, following the smoke line upward. It faded, until I couldn't see it in the lamplight. But the stain was long enough to indicate that whatever had been against this wall had been big.

I ran my fingers along the wall. There were no nails, pegs, hooks, or anything else hammered into the stone. Not even a hole that had once held one. Yet something had definitely been here.

I looked around. There was only one thing in this room that fit that line. The cabinet, filled with nothing, crammed into the corner beside the bed.

I went over to it, looked at the side, at the height where the desk's surface would be. There was a dark splotch there; the rest of the smoke stain. It was clear: This cabinet used to be beside the desk.

I frowned. Why would Melchior move it here? There was barely any room for it. And he didn't appear to be using the wall he'd cleared.

Unless—

I grabbed the front of the cabinet. I pulled it outward, its legs scraping over the stone.

"Look," I said.

Behind the cabinet was an alcove. Inside the narrow space, hanging from a set of hooks, were Melchior's clothes, his shoes resting on top of a trunk crammed into the space underneath.

There were three different outfits. The first was a set of silks: breeches and hose, an embroidered waistcoat with a baize back for warmth, and a silk doublet and scarf. It was the wardrobe of a wealthy man, which made the outfit behind it all the more puzzling.

It was a bundle of rags, stained and threadbare: a pauper's togs. The tears in the jacket and breeches were patched with cuttings of cloth that didn't match. It reminded me of—

No. Not reminded. They were the same.

"Miles Gaspar," I said.

"Who?" Sally said.

"The beggar. The one who came to Blackthorn." Who'd

been there, begging for a job, for food for his children—while Melchior's men were waiting to buy Venice treacle. "These are his clothes."

But they weren't the last set hidden behind the cabinet. Beyond them was a plain ensemble: shirt, scarf, doublet, breeches, and hose. Ordinary, really, the kind of clothes a shopkeeper or merchant would wear. They fit the sort of man you'd pass in the street and not even notice. I wouldn't have given them a second thought, except for one thing.

They were all blue.

My heart pounded. I reached out, pushed the scarf away, and saw what I knew I'd find.

Underneath, sewn into the doublet over the heart, was a bronze medallion.

CHAPTER
24

MELCHIOR.

It was him. Not his men. It was Melchior *himself* who'd broken into my home.

Hands shaking, I pulled the shoes off the top of the trunk. There were three pairs: one was simple leather, stained blue; a second was smooth doeskin, so polished they shone; the third, a stained, ratty pair of boots with well-worn soles. One pair each, to match the outfits above.

Inside the trunk itself were wigs of several different styles and a single stack of hats. Underneath those was a wooden box. In it I found a set of thin brushes, some false beards, and several small ceramic containers filled with different color pastes: cosmetics. There was also a compartment full of false scars, scabs, even noses. Including one, rather bulbous, with a wart right near the tip. Just like Miles Gaspar's.

"Disguises," I said. "These are all *disguises*."

"Christopher."

I looked up. Tom pointed to the silks, the first outfit in the line. "I've seen that one before, too," he said.

"On the street?" I said.

"In your shop. The man wearing this came to Blackthorn."

I stared at the outfit, but I couldn't remember it.

"You were in the workshop," Tom said. "A man wearing this came in on Saturday. He asked to speak to Master Benedict."

"What did he say?"

"Nothing, really. He just asked for Benedict Blackthorn. I told him about what had happened with the Cult of the Archangel, and the man seemed surprised. He asked who'd replaced him as the apothecary, and I said nobody, the shop wasn't really open. Then he left."

"What did he look like?"

Tom flushed a little. "I . . . I didn't really look at him.

Just kind of ordinary, I guess. The thing is . . . I didn't recognize him as the beggar."

But he wouldn't have, just as Dorothy hadn't recognized the man in blue. They were all disguises. Different clothes, false nose, hunched over, limping. A transformation, from one role to another.

I stepped back, trying to piece together what Melchior had done.

He'd come to my shop on Saturday. *To speak to Master Benedict,* Tom had said. *He'd seemed surprised to hear he'd died.*

On Monday, Melchior had returned, costumed as a beggar. In advance, he'd sent his men to buy Venice treacle.

But Tom had already told Melchior the shop's master had died. He had to know I couldn't sell anything to his men. Yet they seemed genuinely annoyed I wouldn't, and from the way they'd reacted to the beggar, I didn't think they knew who he was.

Which meant *they* were the distraction; tricked by his disguise, just as we'd been. Melchior had used that distraction to put the wooden block in my door so it couldn't be locked. Then he'd watched my shop. When we left, he'd changed his clothes and returned. With us out of the way, he'd have plenty of time to search the house.

Except . . .

I'd thought Melchior might have come for my master's treasure because his men had overheard Isaac telling me about it on Monday. But Melchior had been in my shop, looking for my master, on *Saturday*. When he sent his men on Monday, he was already planning to break in.

Which meant whatever he'd come for, he'd known about it before Isaac had even returned to London. Before our conversation, before I'd got my master's letter. Before I'd even *found out* about the treasure. So either Melchior already knew about it . . . or he really was there for something else entirely.

Disguise after disguise—all something to do with my master.

No, I thought. *Not all.*

Someone had tried to murder Galen. He'd seen his would-be assassin: a shabbily dressed man. I was willing to bet that was Melchior once again, in his beggar's costume.

Which would mean Melchior had tried to kill Galen *himself.*

Beggar. Follower. Nobleman. Plague doctor.

An *actor.* That's what Melchior was. An actor, playing a set of roles. And his biggest role?

"The prophet," I said. "That's just a disguise, too."

"But his predictions always come true," Sally said. "He really does know where the plague is going to strike next."

"Then he's infecting them himself," I said. "Because everything else is a fake."

Even those bronze protection medallions, I realized. He'd taken the Archangel Michael's symbol, and the one for Samael on the crossbow, from the carvings around the alcove outside this room. More props the actor had put together as part of his play.

Tom began to edge toward the door. "We need to go."

"No." After what we'd just discovered, there was no way I was leaving now. "Try to leave everything as you found it. But search everywhere. Search everything. Search the whole room."

Sally got to it immediately, rooting through the trunk. Tom stood there for a moment, looking desperately unhappy, before turning out the pockets in Melchior's clothes.

The first thing I examined was the desk. I rifled through Melchior's papers. Most of them seemed to be the weekly Bills of Mortality. There was a quill and ink on the desktop, but I couldn't see anything Melchior had written himself.

There were two drawers on the right side of the desk. I opened the top one and found a collection of apothecary jars. There weren't any labels, but opening one wafted the smell of honey and herbs. A taste of the gooey mixture inside confirmed it. It was Venice treacle, though not my master's recipe. The rest of the jars held the same.

Suddenly, my heart began to thump. False prophet or not, Melchior *was* spreading the plague. It was possible it was his Venice treacle that was doing it.

And I'd just *tasted* it.

I nearly dropped the jar. I tried to spit out the flavor before I realized that probably wasn't how he was passing the plague on. After all, he'd given Sally the treacle back at Cripplegate.

That made me wonder. "Those children he infected at Cripplegate," I said to Sally. "Did he touch them? Or give them something special?"

"I don't think so. We all got the treacle." She cocked her head. "He did ask the magistrates to pray over them before he treated them. So we did. Pray, I mean."

"Where was Melchior?"

"I don't know. I wasn't looking at him. I was praying, too."

There. A distraction. Just like in my shop, like with the feathers in the street yesterday, Melchior had created a distraction. But knowing that wasn't much help. Without Sally looking at him, she wouldn't see how he'd given them the plague.

She couldn't remember anything else that seemed important, so I went back to the desk, pulling open the other drawer. There was a book inside. I flipped through its pages.

"Look at this," I said.

The book was about the Black Death of 1347, the most devastating sickness the world had ever known. Tom shuddered as he looked at the sketches inside: withered figures, marked all over with pustules and buboes, dying miserably under the scythe of an angel that dripped poison into the victim's mouths. Another image of Samael for Melchior to use. I wondered if that's where he'd first got the idea.

Underneath that book was another. I recognized it instantly: *The Complete Herbal*, by Nicholas Culpeper. My master owned a copy; it was the last book he'd ever bought.

I flipped through that book, too, but saw nothing out of the ordinary. As I moved to put it back, I spotted a small bag that had been sitting behind it. Inside was a mix of spices; some kind of incense. I recognized the smell: It was the same incense in Melchior's smoking beak.

That wasn't any help. I rooted deeper into the drawers, looking more carefully. And there, tucked away at the very back, I found a bundled-up sack.

My heart beat faster as I opened it, hoping to find a recipe. Instead, I found two small leather pouches. I undid the knots that tied them closed.

Inside both were more herbs, a single type in each pouch.

The first one contained clippings. There was still some freshness to them; I guessed they'd probably been trimmed four or five days ago. On the stems were whitish flowers, crowded together in whorls. The broad-bladed leaves were heavily wrinkled and covered with white, felted hairs. Though drying, they still retained a curious, musky smell.

"What is it?" Tom said.

"Horehound," I said. Master Benedict had used it all the time. It was an excellent remedy, with many medicinal properties to balance the humors: It was good for coughs and wheezing, helping expel phlegm; it caused sweating, when mixed in a hot infusion; and it fought croup and consumption, and assisted with women's troubles. In large enough doses, it could even act as a purgative.

The second pouch's herbs were completely dried out, cut a few months ago at least. The plants inside had long, slim shoots with little black hairs. Long, narrow leaves sprang from the stems, each one shaped like the blade of a spear.

"What's that one?" Tom said.

I turned the shoots over in my hand. "I don't know."

They didn't give off any smell. I nibbled a bite from the end of one of the leaves, then spat it out. It tasted woody, with a hint of corn flavor, but acrid. My tongue stung a bit.

I'd never seen this herb before. Then I wondered.

Had Master Benedict?

That apothecary's satchel, I thought. The one I'd found in the crawl space under Blackthorn, when I'd been hunting for my master's treasure. It wasn't just for notes. It was designed to hold *ingredients*.

Was this herb what Melchior had stolen? It was dried out enough to have been cut while my master was still alive. Still, I had a hard time thinking a plant was the "something special" my master had left me.

That is, unless it did something miraculous . . . like cure the plague.

I thought of the pouch Tom had seen Galen handling, when he didn't know Tom was looking. A secret ingredient for his remedy, I'd guessed. Now I wondered: Was this the same kind of herb? Was this what made his cure work?

I wanted to take the whole thing. But if I did that, Melchior would know someone had been in here. And if he'd stolen it from Blackthorn, that's probably the first place he'd come looking. So instead, I folded up one of the shoots and stuffed it into an empty vial in the apothecary sash under my shirt.

"All right, you found something," Tom said. "Can we go now?"

We probably should. Searching the room had taken a while. And just because no one had stayed behind when Melchior had run from the church didn't mean they weren't going to come back.

"Sally, did you—" I turned toward the closet, then stopped when I realized she wasn't standing there anymore. Instead, a pair of legs wriggled from under the bed.

Sally grunted and dragged herself out, rolling over. Her hair flopped over her face; she blew it from her lips, holding her side. If she kept this up, she'd finally break that rib.

"What on Earth were you doing?" I said.

"Getting this," she gasped.

She held out her hand. Inside it was another tiny scroll

of parchment, the same type as the fragments Melchior had thrown in the bonfire yesterday.

Except this time, the strip of parchment was intact.

PISODWOSTRGAITWNELSROERBOAORORNTDOWOMEAFAOAETBNKGACUD

I grabbed it and scanned the letters. "Are there any more?"

Sally shook her head. "I don't think Melchior meant to hide that down there. He probably just dropped it. But there's something behind the desk."

She pointed. I knelt next to her and spotted what she'd seen: an oversize piece of parchment. Tom and I pulled it out.

It was a map: London, rendered in full detail. A dozen locations had been marked with a red X, all within the city walls. One of them jumped out immediately.

The corner of Budge Row and Walbrook Street. Sally and I were there just yesterday.

"That's where Magistrate Eastwood lived," I said. "And look." I pointed to another cross. "There's the house of Magistrate Dench."

"Are all of these plague deaths?" Tom said.

I didn't know. We'd need to check the different locations and find out who lived there—

I froze.

Tom saw my face. "What is it? What's wrong?"

I pointed to the map, my finger shaking.

Tom looked where I'd indicated. There was a large red X over one of the houses. He frowned, examining the cross streets. Then his eyes went wide.

"But . . . that's . . ."

He didn't finish the sentence. He didn't have to.

Melchior had marked Blackthorn on the map.

CHAPTER
25

TOM LOOKED FRIGHTENED. "WHAT does this mean?" he said.

I studied the map some more. Were these all Melchior's predictions? Eastwood's and Dench's houses were. My home could have been, too, depending on how you took what he'd said to me at Guildhall. But he'd predicted deaths at Aldebourne's home, Cripplegate, and here in this church, too. None of those were marked on the map.

Sally motioned to the scroll she'd found. "Maybe those letters have something to do with it."

That was an interesting idea. I unfurled the scroll again, but I couldn't make any sense of it. There were too many letters, and I didn't know what most of those marked places on the map were.

"What are we going to do with all this?" Tom said.

I wasn't sure what we *could* do with it. Once again, our status as apprentices kept us shackled. Without standing in the city, we'd need the support of someone who mattered—and hard evidence that Melchior had done something wrong.

We didn't have anything close to that. The different clothes and cosmetics weren't evidence of anything; Melchior could say they'd been left behind in the church. The map he could explain as him marking down his "prophecies." And I didn't know what the herb I'd found was, nor did I know how to decipher the code on that strip of paper. In fact, if anything, breaking into Melchior's quarters would get *us* in trouble.

And who would believe us, anyway? Dr. Parrett knew us well enough that, under different circumstances, he would have been an ally, but his mind had broken entirely. Henry seemed fairly rational, but he also seemed to trust Melchior. Even if he thought this *was* worth investigating, he'd have to confront the plague doctor. Then Melchior would know we'd gone through his room. And that was the last thing we wanted.

The person I really needed to talk to was Lord Ashcombe. He'd believe us for sure. When we got out of here, I resolved to press Henry for an introduction to Magistrate Maycott. In the meantime, we had the herb to identify, and the code to decipher. And we had to figure out what all these marks on the map meant.

I grabbed an old Bill of Mortality from the pile on the desk. On the back, I wrote as best I could the locations of each of the points marked on the map. I'd have to hope Melchior wouldn't notice the bill was missing when he returned.

As I wrote, one more spot stood out. "Look at this one," I said.

The map was marked in a section just north of the Thames, not too far from the Tower. None of the other Xs were anywhere close to it.

"Who lives down there?" I said.

Tom frowned. "I don't know. That area's mostly warehouses for the docks."

Warehouses?

I remembered what Henry had said last night. *I've also rented an empty warehouse near the river. Galen's insisting it remain a secret; only the magistrates will know its location.*

I pointed that out to the others. Tom looked horrified. "But if Melchior's marked Galen's warehouse . . ."

I folded the Bill of Mortality and stuffed it under my master's apothecary sash. "We need to go see what's there."

Tom didn't even object; I think he was just happy to get out of the church. We locked Melchior's quarters and the door to the cellar behind us and hurried down to the docks. There we waited, peeking around a set of abandoned crates, watching the building Melchior had marked on his map.

At least I thought it was the right building. From the outside, it looked like nothing special, just another of the countless abandoned warehouses that lined the Thames. The windows were boarded up, like everything else around here, making it impossible to tell what, if anything, was going on inside.

It didn't take too long to find out we were right. After half an hour waiting, the front door opened.

It was Galen. He stuck his head out, looked around quickly, then slammed the door closed and threw the bolt. He did this twice more, ten minutes apart. The third time, he kept the door open. What he'd been waiting for had finally arrived.

Six carts trundled up in a train, each stocked with goods. Two workmen jumped from the back of each cart and began unloading. The first two carts contained heavy ceramic jars. The other four were laden with large burlap sacks, sealed and clamped at the top. From our position behind the crates, I had no way of seeing what they were, but I guessed this was Galen's first shipment of ingredients.

Galen beckoned the men inside, then disappeared into the darkness. The workmen began hauling the wares into the building.

Now was my chance. "Wait here," I said.

"Christopher!" Tom began. But I was already sprinting past the carts. I ran around the building, out of sight of the workmen, hoping to find somewhere I could look inside.

Unfortunately, whoever had boarded up these windows had done their job well. I couldn't see a thing. I ran from window to window, looking for an opening. Finally, I just poked out a tiny knot in one of the wooden planks and peered through it.

The window was in a long hallway with several doors along it. At the end, the corridor opened into what looked like a much larger room. Through that entrance, I could see the occasional workman pass by, directed by Galen, carrying his supplies. Behind them all, I saw three long work-benches. I could just make out a stack of beakers and retorts.

I stayed there for as long as I dared. Then I ran back to where Tom and Sally hid.

"This is it," I said. "It's Galen's secret workshop."

Sally frowned. "Then why aren't there any guards?"

That was a good question. I hadn't seen any city guards inside, either.

"Maybe the magistrates don't trust them to keep it secret," I said. "They blabbed quickly enough about the assassin."

"So they're just going to leave Galen exposed? That doesn't seem smart."

"It's safer if no one knows where the workshop is."

"Except Melchior *already* knows," Sally said.

The magistrates are afraid of him, I thought. *But they trust him, too. So if he asked what was happening with the cure . . .*

I shook my head. Any one of them could have told him this location, without ever realizing what the man was up to. In fact, the only thing Melchior *couldn't* get from the magistrates was Galen's cure, because the apothecary wouldn't tell them what was in it. I was starting to think Galen's suspicions weren't so crazy after all.

The workmen came back out. We ducked our heads behind the crates as they piled into the now-empty carts and trundled off. Galen didn't follow them.

"Where is he?" Tom said nervously.

"He still needs to set up the lab," I said. But the wait was making me nervous, too. All alone, with no guards, Galen was exposed. Melchior could arrive at any time to finish the job he'd started at my house.

Seconds turned into minutes. And the minutes dragged on and on.

I didn't know what to do. I couldn't just go warn Galen; he'd be apoplectic if he found out I knew where his secret workshop was. He'd think Henry and I were plotting against him for sure.

"We should spread out," I said. "Watch the building, make sure Melchior doesn't come."

"What will he look like?" Sally said.

Good point. "I guess we'll have to look for his costumes." And hope he hasn't found a new one. "Sally, you watch the door. Tom and I will—urk!"

Tom pulled me down. The door had opened. Galen peeked his head around it, looking everywhere. Then he locked the warehouse and hurried up an alley, going north.

"He might be going to Blackthorn," Tom said. "I have to get back."

Tom was right. It was already well into the afternoon. If Dr. Parrett had convinced Galen to return to work, he'd expect Tom to be waiting for him.

Besides, after what we'd found in Melchior's room, I had work to do.

THURSDAY, SEPTEMBER 3, 1665

Yesterday's plague deaths: 1,411

Total dead: 34,435

CHAPTER
26

NOTHING.

Sally and I spent the rest of Wednesday looking through my master's books and notes on remedies, trying to find the herb I'd discovered in Melchior's room. I was sure I'd never seen it before, but I searched, anyway. I couldn't afford to miss a single clue.

It was painstaking work. The most popular of the references, Culpeper's herbal, had about four hundred entries alone. I could skip some of the more obvious entries—I was pretty sure Melchior's plant wasn't a beet—but that still left a lot of slow going.

The herb wasn't in Culpeper, as I'd suspected. I sighed.

Now I only had about a hundred more books to search, plus Master Benedict's own notes on medicinal herbs. I went through his notes first. Helpfully, Master Benedict always drew detailed sketches of the plant he was describing, so I could tell at a glance whether the entry was worth reading. Tom would have helped us, but Galen returned to the shop not long after we got back, this time under the protection of heavily armed guards. Galen stationed the guards at both front and back, then pulled Tom into the workshop as usual.

There was no semblance of friendliness today; all he gave either Sally or me was a furtive glance of suspicion. Tom followed him, resigned. I felt just the same. Why did I always get blamed for everything?

Frustrated, I read my master's notes well into the night. After Galen left the workshop, Tom stumbled from the back and fell across the counter.

"Mmnnnuuugghh," he said.

He looked awful. "You need food," I said.

Sally stood. "I'll get it."

"'M'not hungry," Tom said.

I couldn't believe my ears. "What's he doing to you in there?"

"Hhnnrrghhllgg."

"Look, just stay here tonight. I'll . . ." I wasn't sure

where I was going to put him. I guessed I'd have to give him my blankets.

Tom pushed himself off the counter, already nearly asleep. "Mother wants me home."

"Are you sure?"

"Mmllrrrgghh," he said. Then he dragged himself out into the street.

Sally didn't last much longer herself. We went back to my master's notes, but when I looked up, she was sleeping on the stool, elbows on the table, chin cradled in her palms. I poked her.

She stirred, eyelids drooping. "Another book?"

"Sure." I pushed a sheaf of bound notes I'd already read toward her. "Why not read it on the palliasse?"

"That'll be fun." She took the binding with her, laid it under her head, and promptly fell asleep.

I stayed at the counter and kept at it until I realized I'd read the same page four times without remembering a word of it. Then I put my head on my arms, just to rest for a minute.

I dreamed of our birds again.

Master Benedict held the little scrolls with jumbled letters, feeding our pigeons out of his palm. Tom lay on his back, eyes closed, hands folded on his chest, in front of a massive bonfire that snapped and crackled in the heat. Sally skipped around him, singing.

> *lacrimosa dies illa*
> *qua resurget ex favilla*

Her voice echoed, returning in a broken stutter.

"What's wrong with Tom?" I said.

> *judicandus homo reus*
> *huic ergo parce Deus*

Bridget paced back and forth across my master's shoulder. He ignored her.

"You already know the answer."

"I don't, Master. I need your help."

> *pie Jesu Domine*
> *dona eis requiem*

"I've already helped you, Christopher," Master Benedict said. "I've given you the answer. Think about how."

"I don't understand," I said.

"You must," he said. "You're running out of time."

He cast his hand up. The coded scrolls flew into the air. But they weren't scrolls anymore. They were feathers. Fine, white goose-down feathers swirled in the air like a twister.

Master Benedict grabbed my collar, pulling me off balance.

Except it wasn't Master Benedict anymore, either. A leather glove, its fingers too long, bent like talons, circled my neck. Another glove held an apothecary's bottle. I looked up into a pair of glass lenses. Tendrils of smoke curled from the beak, wrapping around my head, choking me.

"Time's up," Melchior said.

I fell off my stool.

I sat there for a moment, breathing heavily in the darkness of the shop. I shook my head, trying to rattle away the remainder of the visions I'd had.

Then I climbed to my feet. Sunlight had already begun to stream through the cracks in the shutters. It was time to feed Bridget, then get back to work.

Sally rolled over, rubbing her eyes. "Have you been up all night?" she said.

The way I felt, I may as well have been. "I got a couple hours."

"Find anything?"

I shook my head and sat back down, leafing through

my master's notes again. A minute later, a plate of cheese clattered onto the counter beside me. A mug of ale plonked down next to it.

"Fnnks," I replied, my mouth already full.

Sally gave me a bleary-eyed smile and sat next to me, pulling open a book. I was as grateful for the help as the food, because I couldn't concentrate. That dream was still in my mind.

Dreams solve problems, Master Benedict had often said. I'd never really been sure what he meant. I didn't usually remember my dreams; when I did, they mostly just confused me. But now my master had come to visit me, twice in as many nights.

And both times, he'd held Melchior's scrolls.

I kept thinking about the scroll Sally had found in Melchior's room. I pulled the parchment from my sash. I'd spent so long yesterday trying to discover what the herb we'd found was that I hadn't even got to work on this code. And I needed to, because Melchior wouldn't code irrelevant messages. Whatever was in here had to be important.

The problem was, even with the full message laid out, I still didn't have any idea how to solve it.

PISODWOSTRGAITWNELSROERBOAORORNTDOWOMEAFAOAETBNKGACUD

I tried reversing it:

DUCAGKNBTEAOAFAEMOWODTNROROAOBREORSLENWTIAGRTSOWDOSIP

Shifting a letter:

QJTPEXPTUSHBJUXOFMTSPFSCPBPSPSOUEPXPNFBGBPBFUCOLHBDVE

Shifting two:

RKUQFYQUVTICKVYPGNUTQGTDQCQTQTPVFQYQOGCHCQCGVDPMICEWF

Skipping a letter:

PSDOTGIWESOROOONDWMAAATNGCDIOWSRATNLREBARRTOOEFOEBKAU

And two:

POORINSEORNOMFABGUIDSGTERRAOTWEAENADSWTAWLOBORDOAOTKC

Now, that was interesting. My last attempt revealed some curious words: *poor in* at the beginning, and *terra* in the middle—that was Latin for "earth." Had I discovered part of the solution?

I wasn't sure. The rest of the message was still gibberish.

And I'd learned from my master's many lessons on ciphers that if you shuffled letters around enough times, words would naturally appear just by coincidence like they had in the two-letter shift, with *tick*, *nut*, and *mice*.

I stared at the still-jumbled letters for a while and came up with nothing. Frustrated, I put my quill down. I couldn't keep going about this randomly. It would take me weeks to try all the possible different combinations I could think up, and I didn't have weeks. If I didn't stumble upon the answer, I'd end up with the same thing I had now: a giant nothing.

I needed to be smarter about this. I needed the key.

But how would I find it?

I didn't know anything about Melchior that would help. In fact, as much as we'd learned about Melchior—he was a cheat, a thief, and a murderer—I felt like we knew even less about him than when we'd started. Everything about him was a lie.

He'd had those books in his desk, I thought. That tome on the Black Death, and Culpeper's herbal.

Was it possible he'd hidden a message inside one of them? Something that would show me how to solve this cipher? I'd flipped through both books, but I hadn't seen anything that might help in solving codes. No hidden letters, no notes in the margins.

No notes, I thought.

I looked at the pages in front of me on the counter. Just these few simple attempts to solve Melchior's code, and I'd already covered several sheets with ink.

But there hadn't been notes of any kind in Melchior's room. We'd found the scroll there, but nothing indicating what Melchior had done to encipher the code, or how to work it out. Melchior had had another scroll with him outside Magistrate Eastwood's house, too, but there were no notes about that one, either, as far as I could tell. Or any other.

I've given you the answer, my master had said. *Think about how.*

I remembered a time with him, long ago. It was the same week I'd become Master Benedict's apprentice. On that Saturday, he'd sat me down and taught me the first code I'd ever seen. It was a simple letter shift: *A* became *B*, *B* became *C*, and so on.

As an exercise, he had me encipher my own name.

DISJTUPQIFS

"Isn't this code too easy?" I'd asked him. "Just shift one letter? Anyone could figure that out."

Master Benedict had raised an eyebrow. "Is that so? And what would you have said, if I'd given you that word and asked you what it meant?"

I'd flushed a little. It was my own name, but I knew I never would have guessed that.

"When you know the secret, anything is easy," Master Benedict had said. "What you must remember is that few could even *imagine* the secret. Most people cannot read. Among those who can, knowledge of the art of ciphers is extremely rare. Unless you suspect you will be dealing with master code breakers—the king's spies and the like—it will not be necessary to use overly complex ciphers. In fact, that's often the *last* thing you want."

That had puzzled me. "Why?"

"Because every code that is *en*ciphered is meant to eventually be *de*ciphered. Someone is intended to read the message, yes? The more complex the key, the harder it will be for that person to solve.

"There are other problems as well. A complex code takes time to work out. If speed is important, that is an issue.

Also, the chances of making an error—for both the code maker and breaker—are greater." He pointed to the page in front of me. "Sometimes, the simplest codes are the best. If you encounter one, it will serve you to remember that."

The simplest codes are the best.

I thought again about the fact I hadn't found any notes. If Melchior was passing secret messages to his followers . . . well, they didn't seem like the brightest fellows in town. Definitely not the type to be code breakers.

Simple enough that anyone could decipher it.

Anyone, apparently, except me. I crumpled my papers in disgust.

I returned to Master Benedict's notes, trying to find that herb again. Sally went outside. I thought she simply wanted a break, so I was surprised to see her return an hour later with a rolled-up paper in her hand.

"Where did you go?" I said.

She held the paper out. "To get the latest Bill of Mortality."

I scanned the entries. The bill listed all the recorded deaths in the city with their cause. These days, no one cared about any entry except one.

The Diseases and Casualties this Week.

Abortive	2	Jaundies	8
Aged	52	Imposthume	10
Apoplexie	1	Infants	36
Bleeding	1	Lethargy	1
Childbed	38	Livergrown	2
Chrisomes	28	Meagrome	1
Consumption	106	Pallie	2
Convulsion	81	Plague	6988
Cough	1	Purples	7
Dropsie	18	Quinsie	1
Drowned 2, one at St. Michael Queenhithe, and one at Stepney	2	Rickets	7
		Riling of the Lights	16
		Rupture	1
Feaver	364	Scowring	6
Flux	1	Small-Pox	2
Found dead in the street 3, one at St. Mary hill, and two at St. Botolph Bishopsgate	3	Spotted Feaver	157
		Stilborn	11
		Stone	2
Frighted	1	Stopping of the stomach	8
Gowt	1	Strangury	1
Grief	2	Surfeit	69
Griping in the Guts	43	Teeth	138
		Thrush	3
		Tissick	6
		Ulcer	5
		Vomiting	1
		Winde	3
		Wormes	15

Christned { Males — 79 / Females — 88 / In all — 167 }   Buried { Males — 4116 / Females — 4136 / In all — 8252 }   Plague — 6988

Increased in the Burials this Week ——————— 756

Parishes clear of the Plague ———— 12   Parishes Infected ———— 118

The Assize of Bread set forth by Order of the Lord Maior and Court of Aldermen. A penny Wheaten Loaf to contain Nine Ounces and a half, and three half-penny White Loaves the like weight.

6,988 dead of the plague this week.

My heart sank. This was the highest number yet. And everyone knew the entries for diseases like consumption, fever, and teeth were mostly misdiagnosed plague. Plus, this tally didn't even include the bodies of those who'd died unrecorded, alone in the fields around the city. If the bill said seven thousand, the true number was probably closer to ten. If only Galen had arrived earlier with his cure.

Speaking of which, where was Galen? "What time is it?" I said to Sally.

"Around ten, I think," she said.

I wondered if he'd already moved into his new workshop. I also wondered where Tom was. He should have been here ages ago—for breakfast, if nothing else. Tom never missed breakfast.

"Did Tom say anything to you about when he was starting this morning? Or about going to the new workshop?"

Sally shook her head. "Maybe Galen told him he wasn't needed anymore."

"He would have said something."

"Maybe he's just sleeping in, then. He didn't look well."

The dream came back to me. Tom, hands folded, eyes closed.

Now I was worried. "I'm going to check on him."

But I didn't have to go anywhere. The moment I got outside, I saw a dumpy figure clomping down the street, holding her dress up as she ran.

It was Tom's mother. She kept running even as she saw me, her face as red as a beet. Sweat ran from her like a river. She gasped so heavily, it sounded like she was drowning.

"Chris . . . Christopher . . . ," she panted.

My guts began to knot. "Mistress Bailey? What's wrong? Where's Tom?"

"We've . . . we've moved." She bent over, trying to catch her breath. "We've gone . . . to the river . . . to one of the boats."

One of the ways people had avoided the plague was to pay for a berth on ships that simply stayed moored on the Thames. There were hundreds of them lying in the offing, their own watery version of hiding away in Isaac's vault.

"Tom's with you?" I said.

She shook her head, still gasping. "No. You have . . . to help him."

"Help him? What do you mean? Where's Tom?"

"I know . . . we haven't . . . been good to you." In between gasps, she sobbed. "We're being punished. But

Tom . . . Tom loves you. He's innocent. Please. You have to help him."

Panic rose in my chest. "Tell me where he is!"

"He's at the house."

"Then why did you say you'd moved to a boat?"

"No," she sobbed. "Just me and Bill and the girls. Tom's at the house. No one knows yet. You have to help him."

I thought I might throw up. "Knows what?"

"Our family has been cursed, Christopher! Tom has the plague."

CHAPTER
27

I SPRINTED ALL THE WAY THERE.

Sally fell behind as I ran through empty streets, past sealed and abandoned houses, my heart pounding in my ears.

It couldn't be plague. She was wrong. Tom's mother was wrong. People overreacted all the time. The slightest cough, a sniffle, no one wanted to come near you; everyone's first thought was the sickness.

She had to be wrong. I'd seen Tom, what? Not even twelve hours ago. He'd been fine. I'd seen him; he was fine.

Except he hadn't looked good, a voice in my head said.

He was tired, I replied.

And he wasn't hungry.

I had no answer for that.

You saw him, in your dream. You saw him.

Shut up.

You were warned. You remember.

Someone you love is going to die.

Shut up, I said. Shut up, shut up, shut *up*.

Tom was run down. We all were. That didn't mean he had the sickness. He was fine.

He had to be fine.

I ran.

I didn't understand.

Tom's mother had said she hadn't told anyone. But boards covered the ground-floor windows of his family's bakery, nailed in place. A padlock secured the door. Beside it, a red cross was painted, three feet high, those terrible words above.

A guard slumped against the door, a broadsword slung from his belt. He picked at a tooth that jutted out of the side of his mouth.

Tom's house was sealed. How had it already been sealed?

I shook my head. What did it matter? The important thing was: We could save him. Of *all* the people in the city, we could save him.

Sally hobbled up behind me, holding her side and puffing.

"The cure," I said. "Henry said Galen made more of it. We have to find him."

Sally nodded, too sore to speak. She turned to start running again.

"Wait," I said. Tom was all by himself in there. He must be so scared. "I want to talk to him first. Tell him we're bringing him the cure." Let him know he wasn't really alone.

I ran up to the guard. I could smell the fish on his breath. *I've seen him before,* I thought, as Sally came huffing behind.

I motioned to the padlock. "Could you open this, please?"

The guard stopped picking at his snaggletooth and spat. "No."

"I need to get inside."

He jerked a thumb at the door. "Can't you see the cross?"

I wasn't looking at the cross. I was looking at the left side of his chest. When he'd moved his arm, I'd seen it, pinned to his chest, over his heart. A bronze medallion. It glinted and flashed in the sun.

That's where I'd seen him before. With Melchior. Snaggletooth was one of his bodyguards.

A knot twisted in my gut. In the back of my mind, I heard a voice: my master's. *Be cautious, Christopher.*

"When was this house sealed?"

"This morning," Snaggletooth said. "By order of Melchior."

"Melchior was *here*?"

"Didn't I just say that?"

Be cautious, *Christopher.*

"I'm . . . I'm the apothecary," I said. "I mean, I'm with the apothecary. Galen Widdowson. I'm his apprentice."

Snaggletooth snorted. "Sure you are. And who's this, the queen?" He bowed mockingly to Sally. "Pleasure, Your Majesty. Begging your pardon for the smell."

"What does this—" I started to lift my shirt and show him my apothecary sash. But I'd left it at home. In my panic, I hadn't even thought to bring it.

The guard looked at me, amused. I ignored him and

called up to the unboarded windows of the top floor. "Tom! *Tom!*"

He didn't come.

Why didn't he come?

"TOM!"

"Quit your shouting," Snaggletooth growled.

I bristled. The guard saw it. His eyes flashed, a tiger smelling fresh meat.

Sally placed a hand on my arm. "Please, sir," she said sweetly. "Our friend isn't answering. He might need help."

"That's what Melchior's for, isn't he?" Snaggletooth said.

"We're allowed to talk to him if we want," I said, my voice rising. In fact, we were allowed to go *in* if we wanted, even if we weren't with an apothecary. We just wouldn't be allowed back out.

Snaggletooth shrugged. "Not according to my orders. No one in or out except Melchior until the boy's better." He picked at his tooth again. "Or dead, I suppose."

My mind raced. *Melchior doesn't want anyone inside. He won't even let anyone* talk *to Tom.*

Why not?

I was too angry to think about it. "I *am* an apothecary's apprentice," I said hotly. "I was trained by Benedict Blackthorn, the greatest apothecary this city's ever seen."

"Oh?" Snaggletooth leaned in so close, I gagged on his breath. "Well, boy, I was in the New Model Army. And I was trained by Colonel Scrope, the greatest skull-cracker this country's ever seen." He laid a callused hand on the pommel of his broadsword. "So clear off. The both of you. Or I'll show you what I've learned."

I stayed where I was. He grinned. He began to pull his sword from its scabbard, iron sliding over leather.

Sally stepped in front of me. "Our apologies, sir," she said, with a little curtsy. She put her hand on my chest and shoved me back.

I grabbed her arms, ready to toss her out of the way. She held on and shook me in return.

"You can't help Tom," she said, "if you're dead."

I glared down at her. Snaggletooth was still grinning, sword half out.

Sally didn't let go. "We should tell Galen what they've done to his assistant. Don't you think?"

Of course.

My mind cleared. Galen. Of *course*. It wasn't just the cure I could get from him. He was an apothecary. No matter what Melchior said, Galen would have the authority to get me in.

We started for Guildhall. As we ran, I turned to look at Tom's empty windows. Snaggletooth watched us, sliding his sword back into its sheath. He seemed disappointed I hadn't stayed.

Henry had told us he'd installed Galen at the Guildhall complex after the assassination attempt, so that's where we went to look for him first. Fortunately, we wouldn't have to fight any crowds to get there, as the Guildhall tenements were separate from the government offices, accessed via Aldermanbury Street to the west. Though we still didn't know which place was Galen's.

"Let's ask Henry," Sally said.

But we didn't have to. "Look."

In front of one of the doors stood a pair of guards. I recognized one of them from yesterday. He'd accompanied Galen to Blackthorn and checked the workshop was secure before taking his post outside.

We ran up to the man. "Please, sir," I said. "We need to speak to Master Galen."

"No visitors," the other guard said.

But the first guard recognized me. "They're all right; they work with him," he said, and he pounded on the door.

A servant answered. "Yes?"

I rushed right past her.

"What the—"

A narrow hallway on the right opened into the parlor. On the left, a staircase led to the upper floor. A guard leaned over the railing above.

I pounded up the stairs. "Master Widdowson!" I shouted. "Master Widdowson!"

I didn't make it very far. I'd just reached the landing when a hand grabbed me from behind. It dragged me to the floorboards, face down.

I hit the wood hard. A man's weight held me there. A blade pressed against my throat, the point pricking my skin.

I tried to call for Galen. It came out a ragged croak. "Master! Master Widdowson!"

"What's going on?"

I turned my head, hoping the blade wouldn't slice through my neck. The guard on top of me grabbed my hair and pressed his short sword deeper. Sally was near the bottom of the steps, held by the scruff of her dress by the servant who'd let us in. Everyone looked rather cross.

Galen stood in the doorway to his bedroom, still wearing his nightshirt. He stared at us through narrowed eyes, considering whether to let the guards slit our throats. Fortunately, he wasn't that suspicious. Yet.

"Let them up," he said.

The guard didn't so much let me up as hoist me by my neck. The servant below marched Sally up the stairs, keeping a firm hold on her dress.

"Master," I gasped. "You have to help Tom. He has the plague."

At the mention of the sickness, the guard holding me let go. He wiped his hand frantically against his tabard. Galen's expression didn't change.

"I know that," he said.

He *knew*? And he was standing there in his bedclothes? "Then what are you—"

A quick poke from Sally helped me catch my temper. "We have to go to his home, Master," I said. "Tom needs the cure."

Galen regarded us for a moment. Then he waved a hand at the others. "Leave us."

The guard and servant let me and Sally go and went back downstairs. When they were out of earshot, Galen scolded me. "Don't talk about the cure in front of strangers. You never know who's listening."

My blood was boiling. I'd had more than enough of Galen's paranoia. *Don't yell at him, Christopher,* a little voice said. It was all I could do to comply.

"Master Widdowson—" I began.

But the apothecary cut me off. "I've already given Tom the cure," he said, as if that should have been obvious.

"You have?" Now I was completely confused. "When?"

"This morning, of course. Do you think I'd let my own assistant die of the plague?"

"You were at Tom's house?"

"Why on Earth would I go there? I gave the cure to the men who came to collect it."

I didn't understand. "What men?"

Galen sounded irritated. "Melchior's examiners, I assume. They had those silly little bronze things on their chests. They told me Melchior had diagnosed the boy with the sickness, and Henry Cole said to come to me for the cure."

Melchior's men came for the cure. "Do you have any more?" I said.

"No, they took the whole lot. Now, listen." Galen drew

himself up. "There's nothing to worry about. Your friend will have taken the cure. Tomorrow, he'll be fine."

Galen sounded perfectly confident. I didn't believe it for a second.

I practically flung myself into Henry's office. He looked up from behind his desk, startled.

"What—oh, Christopher," he said. "And the young lady as well. How are you?"

"Please, Mr. Cole," I said. "We need your help."

He eyed us cautiously. I imagined we looked quite a pair: me, red-faced and panting; Sally, huffing, her dress not sitting quite right, still rumpled at the shoulders from where the servant had grabbed her. "All right."

"We need to see Tom," I said.

"Tom?"

"My friend. The big one, who's working with Galen. We need your help to get into his house."

Henry looked from me to Sally and back again, confused. "I'm sorry, Christopher, I don't understand. What's wrong with your friend's house?"

I was just as confused. "It's been sealed."

Henry frowned. Then, suddenly, he leaped from his

desk. His spectacles clattered on the floor. "You mean—he has—is *Galen*—?"

"Galen's fine. We're fine. I—" I stopped. "You didn't know."

"No. Lord defend us." Henry made the sign of the cross.

My mind was churning. "Galen gave the last of the cure to Melchior's men," I said slowly. "They came for it. To give it to Tom."

In fact, Melchior's men told Galen you had *sent them. But you didn't even know Tom was sick.*

Which means you'd never sent them at all.

"Well," Henry said, "if Melchior's looking after your friend, then that's all right." Relieved, Henry picked up his spectacles and put them back on. "Tom will be better soon."

Maybe sooner than anyone thinks. "We need to see him," I said.

"Best to let the cure work first, don't you think?"

What could I tell him to get him to help me? "Tom's all alone, Mr. Cole. His family's on a ship in the offing. We'd like to go in and take care of him until he's better."

"Well . . . that's very good of you." His voice softened. "But you do realize I can't countermand the city ordinances? You'll be quarantined until the cure has done its work."

"I understand."

"All right, then. You may go in with one of the doctors. I believe Melchior is at Guildhall at the moment. I'm sure he'll be willing to—"

"I don't want Melchior!"

I hadn't meant it to come out so harshly. Henry looked puzzled. "Whyever not? Didn't you say he sealed the house?"

Sally tugged on the back of my shirt. I took a deep breath.

"Please, sir, I'd like Dr. Parrett. He . . . Dr. Parrett knows Tom; he cared for him when he was small. I think it would help Tom's spirits to see him. Is he here, too?"

"Out serving the city, I think. I haven't seen John since Tuesday." Henry looked concerned. "Speaking of which, is he all right? I know he's your friend, but he's been acting rather odd."

Odd wasn't even close to the right word. But that didn't matter right now. Dr. Parrett might be lost in his madness, but he'd helped save my life before, and I knew he'd help Tom, too.

"If Dr. Parrett comes back," I said, "will you please send him to me, at Blackthorn?"

"Of course," Henry said. "In the meantime, are you sure you don't want Melchior to—"

"Thank you, Mr. Cole." I pulled Sally into the hall and shut Henry's door.

Sally whirled to face me. "Henry didn't tell Melchior to go see Galen."

"No," I said.

"So Melchior lied to Galen—to get the cure!"

This must have been what he'd wanted all along. He'd not only stolen from me, he'd now taken Galen's cure as well.

Though I still felt confused. If Melchior had already stolen a potential plague cure from Blackthorn—or a key ingredient, if that's what the herb I'd found in his desk actually was—then why did he need to steal Galen's? Or was it only the ingredient he stole? So he still needed to work out the full recipe?

"I can't believe Melchior infected Tom to do it," Sally said.

"Actually," I said slowly, "I don't think he did."

"You think Tom caught the plague some other way?"

"I don't think Tom has the sickness at all."

Sally blinked. "Tom's mother said—"

"I know what she said. She's not a doctor. Everyone's so panicked; even a sniffle is taken for the plague."

"Yes, but—"

"Listen." I paced across the corridor, thinking aloud. "Tom's mother didn't tell anyone he was sick. Yet when we showed up at his house, Melchior had already been there. That could only mean one thing: He *knew* Tom was going to be sick that morning."

"Because Melchior infected him," she said.

"That's what I thought at first. I still would, if it weren't for that guard outside Tom's house. Why wouldn't he let us in?"

"Because Tom has the plague."

"We still should have been allowed to go in. But he wouldn't even let us *talk* to Tom. Why not, if Tom was really sick? Besides, that was no ordinary quarantine guard."

Sally had seen the medallion, too. "He was one of Melchior's men."

"If Melchior's placed one of his own men as a guard," I said, "that means he wants someone there who'll follow his orders unquestioningly. Melchior goes in; everyone else stays out. And no one talks to Tom."

I could see Sally thinking it through. "Why not?" she said.

"Well, if Melchior's plan was to steal Galen's cure, then

he's done that. But he still has to figure out what's in it, right? Depending on how complicated the recipe is, that might be impossible. Unless—"

"You find someone who knows what's inside it!" Sally finished. "But Tom doesn't know anything."

"Melchior doesn't know that." I began pacing again. "Tom works for Galen. It's not unreasonable for Melchior to believe Tom's seen Galen prepare the medicine. And if that's what he wants Tom for, then he can't *afford* to give him the plague. He needs him alive."

But just because Melchior needed Tom alive didn't mean he couldn't be hurt. In fact, if Melchior started asking Tom questions, and he couldn't answer them . . .

"We have to go home." I hurried down the hall. Sally jogged to keep up with me.

"Are we going to wait for Dr. Parrett, then?" she said.

"No," I said. "I just need to grab something from the shop. Then we're going back to Tom's."

"But that guard won't let us in."

Anger burned inside me. "We'll see about that."

CHAPTER
28

SNAGGLETOOTH WAS STILL THERE.
Sally and I watched from the corner at the end of the street
as the guard relieved himself against the front wall of
Tom's house, then went back to picking his teeth.

"How do we get past him?" Sally said.

"We don't," I said. "We go through the back."

A narrow alley between a butcher's shop and a gold-
smith's led to another alley behind Tom's house. As soon
as Snaggletooth turned his head, we ran forward and snuck
between the shops, heading toward the rear.

"Won't the back door be padlocked, too?" Sally said.

"That won't stop me." I patted the apothecary sash

underneath my shirt—containing, among other things, a vial filled with oil of vitriol. That iron-dissolving liquid was why I'd gone home before returning to Tom's. It would burn through that padlock in minutes—

I stopped so quickly that Sally ran into me.

"Back. Back!" I whispered.

I shoved her into the side passage that we'd just exited.

"What's the matter?" Sally whispered.

I peeked around the corner and pointed. Six houses down was the back door to Tom's place. In front of it stood a guard, leaning on a spear, looking bored. A bronze medallion was pinned to his chest.

Sally didn't understand why I was so surprised. "Aren't there supposed to be two guards per house?"

"Not at the same time," I said. "One's supposed to work the day shift. The other one does the night."

I cursed. I already knew Melchior didn't want anyone seeing what he was doing with Tom. I should have expected something like this.

"Do you think there's anything we could say to the guards so they'd let us in?" Sally said.

I doubted it. But since we were stuck, we might as well try one last thing. I pulled my shirt off over my head.

"Take this," I said. "Make it look neat." I slipped off my boots, and my breeches, too, until I was left wearing nothing but my undergarments. I gave her all my clothes.

Sally folded them, watching me curiously. "Are you going to play the madman?"

"Actually, you'll be the one who's playing." I pulled a vial of wine vinegar from my sash and poured it over my clothes. "Go tell the guard you're the Baileys' maidservant. Say Dr. Parrett ordered you to bring these to Tom; that he has to wear them to help fight the plague."

Sally crinkled her nose at the vinegar. "These would never fit him."

"I'd bet a half crown that man doesn't even know what Tom looks like. Just tell him you need to take those inside."

Sally seemed puzzled, but she bundled up my clothes and carried them through the alley toward Tom's house. The guard watched her without much interest until she walked up to him. I stayed hidden in the side passage, peeking around the corner.

Sally said something. The guard responded, shaking his head.

Sally spoke again. The guard answered.

Now she gestured at the upper floors, looking worried.

The guard looked apologetic, but he still shook his head.

Sally came back, looking frustrated. She joined me in the alley.

"What did you say to him?" I said.

"Everything I could think of," she said. "I asked to go in; he wouldn't let me. I said Dr. Parrett had ordered me to; it didn't make a difference. Then I asked if he'd go in for me, or at least unlock the door and put the clothes behind it. I even asked if I could just throw them through one of the windows. I told him I'd lose my job if I went back to his family without giving Tom his new clothes. He said he was very sorry, but those were Melchior's orders. Absolutely nothing in or out of the house."

That was all the confirmation I needed. This wasn't about Tom being sick. We had to get inside.

The only question was: How?

We went back to the street, hiding in one of the alleys opposite Tom's house. From the shadows, I studied his place, thinking of all possible ways inside. Everything I thought of ran into the same problem: the guards.

The padlocks on the doors weren't an issue; oil of vitriol could handle them well enough. But the shackles were made of thick iron, so they'd take several minutes to dissolve.

The ground-floor windows were boarded up. I could pry off the boards and break the glass underneath, but that would make a lot of noise. And it would take time to make a hole big enough to crawl through.

The windows on the upper floors *weren't* boarded. A ladder could get me to those. But, once again, for that to work, I'd need time.

And time was the one thing I didn't have. The guard at either door would have to be gone, and I doubted I could lure them away. Snaggletooth had already demonstrated rather vividly that he wouldn't move even to relieve himself. The man in the back wasn't nearly as unpleasant, but I'd bet he was serious all the same.

If they kept the same hours as the other quarantine guards, they'd switch shifts at ten, and a new pair would come. But there wasn't any reason to think those men would have different orders. And the more time passed . . .

Maybe I was thinking about this backward. No one had ever broken into a plague house before. But plenty of people had broken *out* of one. How had they done that?

The most common ways weren't an option for us. When the plague started, some quarantined families had kept a key hidden inside and snuck out the back; that's why the doors were now padlocked. Others had simply broken down the doors; again, we couldn't do that because of the guards. And bribing the guards was not an option; these were Melchior's men, through and through.

There had been families who had actually tunneled out of their homes. Since most houses were attached to their neighbors', it was simple enough to chop through a side wall and walk out someone else's front door to freedom. But for us, not only would we have to break into someone's house, the walls of the Bailey home were thick stone. It would take ages to chip our way through them.

Which brought us to the last option I knew of. The one I'd tried to avoid.

Killing the guards.

This was the worst way people had escaped. They'd beaten the guards with clubs, chopped them down with swords, shot them with pistols, even burned them to death. I remembered that poor man Tom and I had helped, wounded with gunpowder, crying so horribly in the street.

Attacking Snaggletooth with a club or a sword was right out. I was no soldier; he'd cut me down the instant I raised a weapon against him.

But we still had the assassin's crossbow.

And I knew how to make gunpowder.

I looked at Snaggletooth. He shifted, making a rude sound.

Did he really know what his master was doing? I didn't think so. All Melchior's men had the air of a zealot. And the way Melchior hid his secrets from everyone at Saint Andrew's made me certain his men were dupes, pawns in his game, like everyone else in the city. If that were true, then Snaggletooth—all of them—weren't true parties to Melchior's crimes.

So if the only way to get past the guards was to kill them . . . could I do that? Would I go that far to save Tom?

When the answer came, it scared me.

Because the answer was: I'd do anything I had to if it meant I'd set Tom free.

But I didn't *want* to kill *anybody*.

Please, Master, I implored. *Help me. I don't know what to do.*

Sally tugged at my sleeve. "What about the roof?" she whispered. "Could we get in there?"

I shook my head. Tom's roof was slanted; there wasn't a hatch like at Blackthorn.

But I *could* get to the top floor, I realized. Tom's house was a story higher than the neighboring houses on the left. If I could get up there, then through a window—

I cursed. There wasn't a window on that side of Tom's place.

"Could we tunnel through the wall?" Sally said.

"It's solid stone," I said. "It would take forever. You'd need—"

Gunpowder, I thought.

No, that wouldn't work. To blow through a wall as thick as that would take more gunpowder than I had ingredients left in the shop. I'd need—

Something stronger.

My heart thumped. I *could* do it. I could blow a hole into Tom's house through the side wall, up near the roof.

But the sound. The explosion would be deafening. The guards would come and check right away.

Unless they thought it was something else.

"Come on," I said to Sally.

"Where are we going?" she said.

"Back to the shop."

"Are we waiting for Dr. Parrett?"

I shook my head. "We don't have time. Besides, I'm

pretty sure those guards won't let even him in. No, we need to put together a few things."

"Like what?" Sally said.

"Fireworks," I said.

And something else I'd promised Tom I'd never make again.

CHAPTER
29

I PLACED THE THREE JARS ON THE table.

One of them was filled with black, rocklike chunks. Another had a clumpy yellow powder. The third was filled with spiky white crystals that looked like ordinary table salt. Charcoal, sulfur, and saltpeter. They'd saved me once before.

"Grind the charcoal and saltpeter," I said to Sally, pulling three mortars and pestles from the shelves. "Then mix all the ingredients together. One part charcoal, one part sulfur, five parts saltpeter. When you're done, don't hammer the powder, and definitely don't place it near the fire."

"All right," she said.

"After you've done that, make the fireworks." I showed her how, using the diagram of my Smoke-Your-Home as a model. "Take a piece of parchment and wrap it around several times to make a tube. Twist it at the bottom with a few inches of cannon fuse and pack it with an inch of gunpowder. On top of that, pack in two inches of an equal mix of gunpowder, flour, and these things here."

I pushed two more jars toward her. One contained a powdered kind of salt, alum. "This will make the flame green," I said. "And the other will make it stink." I gave her the jar filled with yellow crucifer. When crushed, it would smell like rotting meat on a hot summer day.

"Don't overdo it with the gunpowder," I said. "We don't want to burn anybody, and we don't want to set anyone's house on fire. All we need is a bright light, a big bang, and a *really* bad smell."

"What are you going to make?"

"Something . . . else," I said. "It's better if you don't even know what it is. All I can say is: Don't, under any circumstances, come into the workshop. No matter what you hear."

She seemed nervous. That was good; I wanted her to be nervous. What we were doing was not at all safe. I scooped up Bridget and went into the workshop. I planned to lock the bird upstairs, to make sure she was far away from danger.

"This will take a few hours," I said to Sally. "Don't worry; I'll be all right."

I'm not sure who I was trying to convince.

The truth was, I was scared. I'd made the Archangel's Fire only once before. I'd survived—obviously—but I'd been shaking the whole time, and that was when I'd had Master Benedict's recipe right beside me. I didn't have that recipe anymore. I'd originally hidden it in my master's secret laboratory under Mortimer House. Then, four weeks later, once everyone thought the recipe had been destroyed, I'd retrieved it, taken it to Isaac's, and asked him to hide it in his underground vault. He told me he'd placed it in one of his books, but he hadn't told me which one, so even *I* didn't know where the recipe was now.

And there was a very good reason for that. The Archangel's Fire's explosive power had never been intended for mortal men. The hunt for its secret had killed many, and its creation had killed many more.

I'd promised Tom I'd never make it again. I'd promised myself the same thing. But now I had a choice. I could leave

Tom in Melchior's cage; I could kill Melchior's men to get inside; or I could break that promise instead. That made the decision very easy.

The manufacture? Not so easy. That first time I'd made the Archangel's Fire, I'd read the recipe over and over again, burning it into my brain. But that was months ago. I hadn't tried to recall it since. I wasn't so sure I remembered it.

I closed my eyes. I tried to picture the secret laboratory, the apparatus, the recipe beside me. The smell of the parchment. The ink. My master's smooth handwriting.

There.

The Archangel's Fire

Fill beaker with fuming aqua fortis. Immerse beaker in ice bath. Add fuming oil of vitriol with the greatest caution. Add more ice to bath until near freezing. Add, in small drops only, the sweet syrup of olive oil and litharge. Stir with the utmost care for . . . for . . .

Oh no.

Come on, Christopher. Please. You read it so many times.

Stir with the utmost care for . . . one hour?

No. It wasn't that long. I was sure of it.

One half hour. It was one half hour.

Wasn't it?

I couldn't remember.

My guts fluttered. My heart thumped. There wasn't any air.

I couldn't *remember*.

What do I do? Oh, Master, what do I do?

He answered me.

I saw his face, looking at me so kindly. *Calm, Christopher,* he said. *The answer is hidden in your mind. How do you find it?*

The response came automatically. *I step out of the way,* I said. *And let my mind find it for me.*

And how do you do that?

Work on something else, I said. *Solve a different problem.*

And I dare say, my boy, you have many problems at the moment.

I thought about it. *I need to make the sweet syrup of olive oil and litharge.*

Well, then. Perhaps you should get on with that?

I set up the equipment. I pulled the ingredients from the shelves. My mind rebelled, kept trying to slip back to the recipe for the Archangel's Fire.

Christopher.

Sorry, Master.

I got back to work. We didn't have much olive oil left—Tom had used a lot of it for cooking—but there was plenty of litharge, a reddish-orange powder. I mixed them, heated them, dripped the liquid onto a plate. I watched it fall. Each drop rang against the metal. Words echoed back.

One.

Quarter.

Hour.

I stood. My stool clattered to the floor.

Stir with the utmost care for one quarter hour. Transfer to water, and mixture will settle at the bottom. Take mixture and, in small drops only, add to natron. Repeat three times. The final liquid will have the look and feel of olive oil.

And you'd better not forget the sawdust.

I clasped my hands and pressed them to my forehead.
Thank you, Master.

He smiled.

• • •

I opened the door to the shop. The windows were dark; night had already fallen.

Sally, curled up in the chair by the fire, looked up from her book. Four fireworks lay on the table, each with a trail of cannon fuse three inches longer than the previous one. All four had long wooden sticks attached as launchers.

I inspected them. "These are perfect."

She smiled, pleased. Her smile faded as she pointed to what was in my hand. "Is that it?"

It didn't look like much. Just a small cylinder of oiled parchment, three inches long, one inch thick, with its own length of cannon fuse stuck in the end.

"Believe me," I said. "This is more than enough."

"It looks like a candle."

"It's really not."

And that she would see soon enough.

CHAPTER
30

IT WASN'T EASY TO WAIT.

Sally and I stayed hidden in the darkness of a narrow side passage between Tom's street and the alley that led behind his house. Sally clutched the four fireworks to her chest. I held the Archangel's Fire, the oil sticking to my fingers. Both of us had a small hooded lantern, neither one yet lit.

Six doors down, Snaggletooth leaned against the front door of Tom's house. His partner paced at the back, whistling softly to relieve his boredom. Just as restless, I forced myself to stay crouched against the corner. We couldn't afford to bring attention our way.

So we waited. The city stayed quiet, the only sound the distant call of the dead-cart. Then the clock struck ten, and the bells rang their lonely echo through the streets.

Sally nudged me.

I peeked around the corner. The relief guards had arrived. A squat sort of man with wide shoulders took over from Snaggletooth. A second man went around to take the friendlier guard's place in the back. He and Snaggletooth spoke briefly to their compatriots, then walked away.

Time to go. I lit Sally's lantern with flint and tinder from my master's sash.

"Help me with the ladder," I said.

We'd swiped one from a row of houses two streets down, when the quarantine guard had wandered away in search of a drink. We propped the stolen ladder against the sidewall of the house we were next to. Unfortunately, it was only tall enough to reach the window on the third floor. I was trying to get to the roof. The top rung rested five feet from where I needed to go.

I'd told Tom a couple of days ago we should climb to the top of my house using the half timbers. Now that I was actually doing it, it appeared I owed him an apology: this was a terrible idea after all. Still I went. Sally held the ladder steady as I reached the top, then climbed farther up, using the half timbers on the outside of the house as handholds.

The ladder creaked, slipped an inch. I froze.

Don't look down, I thought.

I looked down. Sally had already thrown her weight against the ladder to stop it sliding. I couldn't help thinking if Tom was here, he'd have told me how stupid this was.

Regardless, I was committed now. I pressed myself against the wall and slid upward. I grabbed the edge of the eaves, swung a leg up, and dragged myself onto the roof.

The tiles did their own fair amount of creaking, but they held. Slowly, slowly, I crawled upward, the glass of my unlit lantern scraping over the slates. Each clink made me cringe, but there returned no cry of alarm.

I rolled over the apex of the roof, heart thumping in relief. Tom's house was six buildings over, so I still had a lot of ground to cover, but the houses between were joined. As long as I stayed away from the edges, the hard part was over.

Unless you fall through a roof, I reminded myself.

I sighed. It would be nice if, for once, I didn't have something to remind myself of.

Back to crawling I went.

• • •

I made it to the side of Tom's house without breaking either someone's roof or my neck. I rested with my feet against Tom's wall for a moment, breathing slowly. Then I lit my lantern.

Now was the really tricky part. I had only one chance at this. If the Archangel's Fire didn't blow a hole in the wall, Tom was finished—and so, very likely, were we. I pulled a chisel from my sash and got to work.

In the light of the lantern, I found a spot where the mortar between the stones was widest. As quietly as I could, I chiseled it away, digging a hole. I had to work quickly. I'd given Sally a count of nine hundred, which would give me about fifteen minutes in total to get the job done.

Suddenly, from out of nowhere, a blazing trail rocketed up from the alley behind me. It arced over Tom's house, then exploded with a bang and a glorious blaze of green light.

Apparently, nine hundred counted faster than I'd thought. I rammed the Archangel's Fire into the hole I'd made and held the lantern's flame near the cannon fuse.

Shouts rose from Tom's street. Doors creaked; shutters clacked open. The stink of the burning crucifer wafted over with the scent of gunpowder and burnt flour.

A second firework exploded. This one went awry, bursting in a shower of green over the row of houses opposite.

More cries.

Now.

I put the flame to the cannon fuse. It popped and fizzed, sparks rushing toward the end of the cylinder.

No time for stealth now. I scrambled up the side of the roof of Tom's neighbor's house and dived over the peak.

The third firework was better aimed. It shot through the alley behind Tom's house and exploded, three stories high, some twenty feet from the guard at Tom's back door.

"Aaahhh!" I heard the guard cry and the clomping of booted feet. His own cries joined the others, near hysterical. "We're under attack!"

"It's the Dutch!"

"It's the Devil!"

"Help!"

I huddled behind the apex of the neighboring roof as I heard the fourth and final firework shoot past. Sally had saved the best for last; it burst with perfect precision right in front of Tom's place.

"For God's sake, man, take cover!" came a call from a neighboring house. "In here, in here!"

Then the Archangel's Fire exploded.

It boomed like a dozen cannons. Chunks of stone and shattered tile blew everywhere, scattering over the houses nearby and the streets below. Fragments smashed off the chimney behind where I lay. They ricocheted into me, ceramic needles raking my skin.

I clawed my way back over the peak of the roof and looked at what I'd done.

For I *had* done it. There, in the side of Tom's house, was a hole big enough to fit two men, the roof above it blown off in the blast.

And there, on the other side of the wall, was Tom.

He stared at me in horror.

"You . . . you . . . ," he said.

He fell to his knees. For one terrible moment, I thought I'd caught him in the blast.

Then I saw his face. He was sweating, buckets pouring down his brow. His skin was pale, almost ashen. His eyes twitched, as if unable to focus.

I'd made a mistake.

Melchior hadn't merely locked him in. Tom *was* sick. He *was*.

Oh, God.

CHAPTER

I SLID DOWN WHAT REMAINED OF the roof of the house next door and tumbled into Tom's. I hit the floorboards, banging my knee against the wood, and nearly went all the way down the stairs. Only a quick hand on the remains of the splintered railing kept me from breaking my neck.

Tom knelt in the doorway to his bedroom, shivering, almost shaking. He wobbled, his hand against the frame.

"You blew up my house," he said.

Then he vomited.

There wasn't much in his stomach. A thin yellow

stream dribbled to the floor. He spat the remnants away.

I dragged myself over to him. He recoiled. "Don't touch me!" he said.

I was wrong, I thought. *He has the sickness.*

"I don't want you here!" Tom said. He slid back, hands held out. "Stay away!"

Touch him, and you'll get it, too.

"Stop being stupid," I muttered.

"I'm not being stupid," Tom said.

"I wasn't talking to you," I said. And I took his arms.

If he'd been well, Tom could have resisted. He could have tossed me out of the window if he wanted. But all he could do was slump against me.

The first thing to do was get him out of here. I tried to pull him to his feet. I may as well have tried to lift a horse. "Come on, Tom. Get up."

He stuck his legs under him and tried to rise. He wobbled, then fell, dragging me back to the floor.

I tried again, hauling him upward. "Why'd you—ugh—have to be so big?" I complained.

"I'm not big," he said, his eyes glassy. "You're all small."

"I'm not—urgh—small," I said. "I'm a normal-size

person. Just because you're—agh—a giant—"

"You're tiny. Like a little puppy." He reached out a massive hand and patted my head.

"Stop that."

"Woof, woof."

"Will you please—" I cut myself off. There was no point in arguing; the sickness had already addled his brain.

He stopped making dog sounds at me and began singing—at least I *think* it was singing—one of the same catches we'd heard from Sally. He replaced some of the lyrics with extremely rude words.

"Shh," I said, though the noise from the street more than drowned out his caterwauling. "Come on, we're going."

"What about the cure?" he said.

I limped him over to the hole the Archangel's Fire had made. "I'll get Galen to make you some after we've got you safe."

"What's wrong with the cure I already have?"

"What do you mean?"

"On the side table, in my room," he said. "In the pouch. That's a funny word. Pouch. Pouch."

I stopped. "Galen brought you the cure?"

"Not Galen. Melchior. Pouuuch."

Melchior brought the cure?

But . . . wasn't Melchior trying to steal the cure? Why would he bring it to Tom?

I leaned my friend against the broken wall and ran back into his room. The stench of vomit hung in the air. I covered my mouth with my sleeve, trying not to retch.

There it was. One of Galen's leather pouches lay on the night table beside the bed.

So Tom really was sick. And Melchior really did bring Tom the cure.

I didn't understand.

The noise from the street was getting louder. I risked a glance out the window. The few houses on Tom's street that hadn't been abandoned were lit up against the blackness. People stood at the doors, in the windows, watching. The guard at the front, chased away by our fireworks, had returned. He looked up.

I dove to the side, pressed against the wall.

Had he seen me?

No time to find out. I grabbed the pouch from the night table and shoved it under the apothecary sash. Then I ran back to Tom. He'd gone back to singing the ballad, staring off into the night.

"Hello, Christopher," he said. "Did you know there's a hole in my house?"

"Is there?" I put his arm around my shoulders. His sweat dripped onto my collar. "Let's see where it goes."

"I can't. I have to take the bread out. Father will be cross."

"I already took the bread out."

"The sweet buns, too?"

"Especially the sweet buns."

"That was kind."

We staggered toward the hole.

He crinkled his nose. "This smells funny."

"Does it?"

"I've smelled this before. It's like . . ." His eyes went wide. "You didn't!"

"I did. Sorry." And with that, I heaved him onto the roof.

He toppled over and rolled into the cool night air. I grabbed my lantern and crawled out after him.

"Come on now, Tom," I said. "We have to hurry."

"Oh, hello, Christopher," he said. "Did you know there's a hole in my house?"

He leaned over and retched. This time, only a thin trickle of bile and saliva.

"I want to lie down," he said.

Shouts rose from below. "Please, Tom," I said. "We have to go. Please. I need you to trust me."

"That sounds dangerous."

I couldn't argue with him there. We clawed our way back over the roofs. Sally waited for us at the bottom of the ladder, holding it steady.

Now we had another problem. I hadn't really thought Tom would be sick. I couldn't possibly carry him down. "I need you to climb, all right?" I said. "I'll hold on to you."

For all the good that would do. If he slipped, he'd take both of us with him. Tom stared, bleary-eyed, at the gap between the roof and the ladder. I held his arms as he slipped backward down the wall, searching for the top of the ladder with his feet.

"I told you this was a stupid idea," he said.

Good old Tom.

His feet found the ladder, and he began to climb down.

"Hey!"

The voice came from behind me. I looked over my shoulder.

Through the hole in Tom's house, I saw the silhouette of the guard. And he was holding what looked like a very large ax.

CHAPTER
32

"THEY'RE IN THE ALLEY!" HE shouted.

No more time. Tom was already climbing down. I threw caution to the wind and rolled off the roof to grab the ladder.

Thunk.

The sound came from above me. I looked up.

A long wooden shaft wobbled against the night sky. The blade at the end stuck deep into the timbers of the house behind me.

It was an ax. The guard had thrown his ax at me.

I slid down the ladder, landing on Tom's shoulders.

He fell backward and landed on Sally, squashing her into the dirt.

"Ack," she said.

I scrambled to my feet and pulled on Tom's arm. "Get up. Come on, Tom, get *up*."

He wavered a bit—he wavered a lot, actually—but up he got. I put one of his arms around me. Sally did the same.

"Stop!"

The guard's command came from right above us. I glanced up to see the man leaning over the roof. He grabbed the handle of his ax and pried it out of the timbers. Then he turned himself around, ready to climb down the ladder.

I kicked it at the base. The ladder teetered sideways, then, wood scraping on stone, it slid down the wall and thumped into the dirt. The guard cursed.

"Time to go," I said.

We half supported, half dragged Tom into the alley in the back. Sally yelped, and I heard something heavy clatter against the base of the house beside us. I glanced over to see what it was.

Metal glinted on the ground in the flame of Sally's lantern. Her dress at the shoulder had been torn open, a red welt underneath.

"Christopher," Tom said. "Can I please rest for a minute?"

"They're throwing axes at us, Tom," I said.

"I'll rest later, then."

"Good idea," I muttered.

He kept making strange comments, but Tom remained lucid enough to stay on his feet. That was good, because if he toppled over, I didn't think Sally and I could carry him.

We stuck to the alleys. Both of us had left our lanterns behind—mine on the roof where we'd climbed down, Sally's discarded in an attempt to throw off our pursuers—so we no longer had light. Fortunately, Tom and I had run through these alleys so often that I knew these passages blind. Which was good, because right now the darkness was the only thing protecting us from the men who followed, their shouts echoing off the walls.

The winding routes all seemed to blend together, but there was a particular alley I pushed us toward. I'd been there three months ago, when I'd been on the run before.

The house I wanted was easy to spot: It wasn't really a house anymore. It had burned down last summer, leaving just a husk of charred timbers with a teetering second floor above it. It was the house everyone hurried past, eyes averted, as if the sorrow might slough off the broken hull and seep into their blood if they stared.

To me, it was different: an oasis in the desert, a place where help was guaranteed. The home Dr. Parrett had offered me when I'd had nowhere else to go.

Sally and I carried Tom inside without knocking. "Dr. Parrett!" I called. "Dr. Parrett!"

"Where do we put him?" Sally said.

When I'd last been here, Dr. Parrett had put me in his son's old room. I nodded toward it. "Over there. Dr. Parrett!"

A footstep on the stairs. "Who's there?" Dr. Parrett said.

I was relieved to hear his voice. When he hadn't come to Blackthorn earlier today, I'd started to worry. "It's Christopher. I'm here with Tom."

"Go away," he said.

I stopped. "Doctor, it's me. It's Christopher." The stairs creaked. "Tom needs your help."

Dr. Parrett reached the bottom. His figure loomed in the shadow of the moonlight. He was holding something.

"You'll find no help here, Christopher. Go away."

I couldn't believe what I was hearing. "But . . . Dr. Parrett . . . I—"

He stepped forward. A shadow cast by one of the blackened timbers obscured his face, but enough light fell on his body for me to see what he carried.

It was a pistol.

Dr. Parrett raised it. He didn't quite point it at me.

"Dr. Parrett," I said, backing away. "It's Christopher. Don't you remember?"

"I know who you are."

If he were lost to madness, would madness help him find his way back? "Your . . . your son, James—" I began.

"James is dead."

He took one more step forward. Finally, I could see his face. And finally, I understood.

His eyes were sunken and hollow. His cheeks were flushed. His brow dripped with sweat. His shirt, so new, so fine, was open at the collar, so I could see his neck. And there, on the side, bulged a deep violet swelling, turned almost black.

Sally and I staggered back.

The plague. Dr. Parrett had the plague, too.

And where it had driven others mad, it had chased his madness away.

"Now you understand." Dr. Parrett lowered the pistol.

"I . . . I'm sorry. I didn't mean to . . . I'm sorry. But you have to go."

He turned.

"Wait," I said. "Dr. Parrett . . . please. Don't give up. We'll bring Galen here. We'll get you the cure."

Dr. Parrett stopped, halfway in the shadow. "I don't want the cure, Christopher," he said.

And he disappeared back up the stairs.

CHAPTER
33

THERE WAS ONE LAST PLACE TO GO.

It wasn't easy to get there, mainly because it wasn't close. Our twists and turns had confused the guards; we'd already lost them before we'd reached Dr. Parrett's house. Now our real problem became keeping poor Tom on his feet. He kept pleading with me to put him down. "Just a little farther," I'd say, and loyally, he'd trudge on.

But I could see every step was torture for him. He kept retching up bile so hard that his stomach cramped. Each time I prayed that he wouldn't collapse. Finally, crossing Throgmorton Street, he did.

"Tom," I pleaded. "Tom, please. Get up. You have to get up."

But he couldn't.

I didn't know what to do. We were totally exposed. I needed help carrying him, but I knew no one would come anywhere near us. And if someone decided to call for the guards . . .

Sally got us out of it. She darted behind a row of houses with private gardens and came back with a wheelbarrow.

Brilliant. We loaded Tom into it and pushed him on. I had a moment of panic when we ran into a pair of men walking down the street, but they weren't guards. When they saw the two of us, and the body lying still in the wheelbarrow, they just backed away and fled.

Sally and I moved faster now, running. We finally made it to the alley I'd been looking for. It led to a maze of ten-foot-high stone walls with spikes on the top. Sally was confused by its twists and turns, but I knew the path through it well.

"Why is this here?" she said.

"It's protecting a secret place," I said. "Or at least it used to."

The maze opened up to a wrought-iron gate. Behind it

was a garden, and a mansion beyond, one broken window boarded up. This place, Mortimer House, had once been beautiful. Now the topiary animals had grown into misshapen lumps; the grass, once cared for, wilted and burned in the summer heat.

In the center of the garden, a cracked slate path wound around a vine-covered mausoleum. Three months ago, a secret passage under that mausoleum would have been our sanctuary. But there wasn't anything there for us anymore. Not that it would have mattered; we'd never have been able to carry Tom down the ladder.

Instead, we pushed him through the unlocked back door into the mansion. In the parlor, we flopped him out of the wheelbarrow onto a velvet daybed near the fireplace, then both of us collapsed to the floor. The dust we kicked up made me cough.

Sally squealed as something ran across her feet. I saw them bolt through the open door, one after the other. Rabbits.

There was a lamp in the corner, a thumb's width of oil still in its base. I lit it with the flint and tinder from my master's sash. The flame illuminated the wreckage.

Most of the furniture had been piled against the far wall. A thin layer of stone dust covered everything, giving the room a chalky smell. The once-polished floorboards were covered with dried mud. Most of the footprints tracked out of the parlor to a large hole dug into the floor of the hallway. A ladder led down into darkness.

"What's down there?" Sally said.

I shook my head. "Nothing, anymore."

Tom moaned. I went to him. He turned fitfully on the bed, his collar soaked with sweat. "I'm thirsty, Christopher. Please, I'm so thirsty."

I glanced over at the grate. There was a dusty pile of wood stacked behind it. "Can you set a fire?" I asked Sally. "We have to give him this."

I pulled the pouch I'd taken from Tom's room from underneath the sash and handed it to her. Sally drew the strings and looked inside. "What is it?"

"The cure."

She frowned. "But I thought Melchior—"

"I don't understand it, either," I said. "Maybe Melchior had already got what he needed from Tom, so now he's willing to save his life. Or maybe since both Galen and Henry now know he was supposed to give Tom the cure, he can't let Tom die even if he wants to. Either way, we need to give it to him."

"All right," Sally said. "What do we mix it with?"

I had a vial of water in the sash, but that wouldn't be enough. "Set the fire. I'll see what I can find."

Once, there'd been plenty of water down the hole in the floor, along with countless other ingredients in my master's secret laboratory. The Archangel's Fire had destroyed them, along with almost everything else inside. What little had survived had been taken by Lord Ashcombe's men, searching the rubble fruitlessly for my master's secret recipe.

I skirted the hole and went through the kitchen to the pantry instead. In it were a few moldy supplies, some ale—which by the reek, had long spoiled—and half a crate of wine. I uncorked a bottle. It smelled a little vinegary, but hopefully it would do the job. I took the bottle back to the room, along with a pot and mug from the kitchen.

Sally had got the fire going. I poured some wine into the pot and placed it on the hearth. Then I gave Sally the mug and sat next to Tom while we waited. I placed my hand on his forehead. He was dripping with sweat, but his skin was cool. I didn't think he had a fever.

Sally held up the pouch. "How much of this should I use?"

"All of it, I guess. Tom?" He was mumbling to himself.

"Tom! What did Melchior say to you about the cure?"

Tom grimaced. "He asked me if I knew what was in it."

"What did you say?"

"I told him I didn't know. Then he said I'd be all right. He had me drink it. I didn't want to drink it. He made me."

"He made it for you?"

"Every six hours."

"Every . . . what?"

Tom turned fitfully. I shook him gently. "Tom. How many times was Melchior at your home?"

"I don't know," Tom mumbled. "He kept coming back to give me the cure."

He kept coming back?

"Give me that pouch," I said to Sally.

She handed it over. "What's the matter?"

"You don't have to give Galen's cure over and over," I said. "Only once."

I looked inside the pouch. My heart beat faster.

"You drank this?" I said. Tom didn't answer.

I tipped the pouch over. The contents spilled into my palm, ran through my fingers. It was a collection of herbs, roughly chopped. The scent of mint rose from my hand.

"What are you doing?" Sally said.

I stared at the mixture. "This isn't Galen's cure."

Sally was quiet for a moment. "How do you know?"

"Because I saw Galen give it to Aldebourne's daughter. The cure is a gray powder."

"Then what did Melchior bring him?"

I dumped the herbs in my palm in front of the fireplace and spread them out on the marble. One by one, I plucked different ones from the mixture. I smelled them, chewed them, spat them out.

The first herb smelled like mint, but also flowery, with a light bitter taste. Hyssop.

The next tasted earthy, with a hint of raw beans. Marshmallow root.

The next was also earthy, but with a sort of licorice taste. Horehound.

I stopped.

Horehound.

Like we'd found in Melchior's room.

I rooted through the mixture on the marble, looking for something specific now. I found it.

The cuttings were small, but familiar. I saw the shoots, the leaves. I knew what it was, but I tasted it anyway. Woody, with a slight flavor of corn. Acrid, stinging my tongue.

This was the other herb we'd found in Melchior's room. The one we didn't know.

"Take off Tom's shirt," I said.

Sally looked at me, puzzled. "What?"

"His shirt." I rose. "We need to get it off."

I made Tom sit up. He groaned, but we managed to get him upright and strip him to the waist.

I looked him over in the firelight. His chest, his back, under his arms. Nothing.

His chest wasn't the only place I had to check. "I need to look in his breeches."

Sally raised her eyebrows, but turned away. "Sorry, Tom," I said. Then I examined him.

Nothing.

"What are you looking for?" Sally said.

"The tokens." I stood, began to pace. "The tokens of the sickness. He doesn't have any. No rash. No swellings. No buboes, no abscesses, no blisters."

"But . . . he's so sick." She frowned. "If Tom has the plague this badly, shouldn't he be showing something?"

"Yes." I spoke to Tom. "When Melchior was giving you the cure, how did you feel afterward?"

"The same," he said.

"Always the same? The same as this morning? As last night?"

"No. I'm feeling worse."

I put my head in my hands. I was so *stupid*.

Sally shook her head. "I don't understand."

"You said it," I said. "If Tom's this sick with the plague, he should have the tokens somewhere. But he doesn't. Instead, he's getting sicker with every dose Melchior feeds him.

"He doesn't have the plague at all." I pulled the shoot we'd taken from Melchior's room from my master's sash. "He's been poisoned."

CHAPTER
34

SALLY'S EYES WENT WIDE. "POI-
soned?"

"It's the only thing that makes sense," I said. "It's what
this herb is for. It's why instead of giving Tom one dose,
Melchior made him take it over and over again."

"But . . . why would anyone want to poison Tom?"

I thought of the guards outside Tom's house. I thought
of the ax, thrown at my back.

Tom had dozed off. I shook him awake.

"Tom. Tom!" He opened his eyes. "What did Melchior
ask you about the cure?"

367

His words came out slurred. "Told you. He asked what I knew."

"What about the ingredients?"

"Don't know them."

"But we talked about some of them, in the shop. You told me what you'd seen Galen working on, and I told you what it was. Did you mention that to him?"

"Uh-uh." Tom began to snore.

Melchior tried to kill Galen first, I thought. *Now it's Tom he wants dead.*

I shook Tom back awake. "What did you see? Tell me what you've seen Galen do."

"Nothing. Leave me alone."

"You must have seen something. Some ingredient, some process. Something."

"I didn't."

"You must have." I shook him again. "Think, Tom. Think!"

"I don't know," he pleaded.

He *had* to know. I shook him harder.

"Christopher!" Sally put her hands over mine. "Stop."

I nearly swatted her away. Then I saw Tom's face.

What was I doing? Why was I blaming him? *I* was the

one who got him involved in this mess. It was *my* fault.

"I'm sorry." I put my hand on Tom's chest. "I'm sorry, Tom. Just go to sleep."

He nestled back into the blankets on the couch. I stood up.

Tom mumbled something.

I turned. "What?"

"Galen," he slurred. "He was writing on your room."

Tom dozed off again. I looked over at Sally. "Galen was writing on my room? What room?"

"Did he say 'room'?" Sally said. "I thought he said 'broom.'"

That made even less sense.

"Maybe he's delirious again," Sally said.

Maybe. It didn't matter. It simply didn't matter why Melchior had poisoned Tom. He needed help, and now.

But I didn't know what to do. "If he had the plague, we could at least get Galen's cure. I don't know what this stupid plant is. If it's poisoned him, I don't know how to find the antidote. I don't even know if there *is* an antidote."

"We could go back to your master's notes—"

"For what?" I felt like collapsing. "We've looked through every one of his remedies—"

I froze.

"What's the matter?" Sally said.

I was such a *fool*. "We've been looking in the wrong place," I said.

"But . . . we've been looking through your master's notes on remedies."

"Right. We've been looking for *remedies*. This is a *poison*." That was a whole different set of notes. I hadn't even *thought* to look there.

But I still could.

"We have to go back to Blackthorn," I said.

"Now?" Sally said. "Both of us? Shouldn't someone stay with Tom?"

I hated to leave him here. If he woke up alone, he'd be scared. Still, other than offering comfort, there wasn't really anything Sally could do for him. And a second pair of eyes on my master's notes would be a huge help.

Sally wondered how we planned to get there. "Isn't there a chance Melchior's men will be waiting for us?"

"I'm sure they'll be waiting for us," I said. "That's why we're not going through the door."

CHAPTER
35

A STOLEN LADDER HELPED US
again. Sally and I swiped it from a plague house one street
over and used it to get onto the rooftops near Blackthorn.
My home wasn't joined to the others like Tom's was, but
the gap between it and the house next door was only two
feet wide; we made the leap easily onto my roof.

As I went for the hatch, Sally tugged on my arm and
pointed. Across the street, a man waited in the shadow of
the awning of the Missing Finger. Another man walked
down the lane. The two of them studiously ignored each
other as the second man passed by. When he got to the end
of the road, he turned around and walked past again.

Melchior's men, as expected. There were probably others in the alley behind my home, too. I threw a quick prayer of thanks heavenward for Galen's paranoia, or I'd never have had a way in.

Quietly, we climbed through the hatch. Navigating by touch through the blackness, I crept into Master Benedict's bedroom and snuck a lantern from his side table. I covered it with a thin cloth from my master's drawers and took it into the hallway before I lit it. Hooded, it gave off only the faintest illumination. It wouldn't be easy to see with, but it should be enough.

"Just don't go near any windows," I whispered. "And let's try not to make any noise."

The books on poisons were in the workshop. We crept down slowly, cringing with every creak of the stairs. Once there, I made sure both doors were locked, then pulled four books from the shelf near where Galen had been working and piled them in Sally's arms. "This should be all of them," I said.

She carried them to the middle bench and spread them out. I glanced over at the corner where Galen worked.

What did you see, Tom? What was Melchior trying to learn?

Like before, Galen had left the workbench spotless. The cutting boards were clean and stacked neatly; the mortars and pestles looked untouched. Even the brushes and brooms revealed nothing.

I turned to join Sally. As I did, Tom's last words echoed in my skull.

He was writing on your room.

I turned back.

Sally had thought he'd said "broom."

My broom was propped up in the corner, right next to where Galen had been working.

I picked it up. I turned it over. I brought the lantern close, peered at it.

It was a broom. I felt foolish. Tom had been delirious. And I had a poison to look for. I went to put the broom back.

I caught it out of the corner of my eye. In the dim light, I almost thought it was a shadow. But I looked again and saw it.

There was a smudge on the broom's handle, near the top.

I licked my thumb and rubbed it against the wood. Some of the smudge came off, marking my skin. I tasted it. Bitter, metallic.

Ink.

He was writing on your broom.

I looked at it more closely. There were scratches along the wood, but I didn't notice any pattern to them. There'd always been scratches on the handle. I'd been using this banged-up broom for years.

"What is it?" Sally said.

I shook my head. "I don't know."

And I didn't have time to find out. Tom was dying. The only thing that mattered was finding out how to save him.

So we read. I pulled the plant I'd taken from Melchior's room from my sash and laid it on the table so we could both see it as we went. Then I flipped the pages of the books as fast as I dared.

As usual, Master Benedict had inked little sketches of the poisonous plants where the authors of the books hadn't, which helped us go faster. He'd also scribbled notes of his own, filling the margins, often spilling over the main text. But one, two, three of the books showed nothing.

And then Sally grabbed my wrist.

"Christopher."

I leaned over to look. Master Benedict had written all over the entry in front of her. I could barely make out the text.

Corncockle. Stem over three feet long, covered in fine white hairs. Few branches, tipped with a single, scentless, five-petaled flower in summer months, one to two inches in diameter. Flowers deep pink to purple. Petals have black lines—

I stopped reading. "Corncockle's everywhere," I whispered. "That's not what Melchior used—"

"No," Sally said. She pointed to the margin. "There."

In one small corner, Master Benedict had drawn a tiny sketch. It showed a tall plant, with long, pointed leaves like a spear.

Just like the plant on the workbench in front of us.

I took the book, brought it close. There hadn't been room for proper notes; there had barely been space for the drawing. Instead, beside the sketch, my master had left a single message.

Volohosy. V poisonous. Mdgsc only. Nil med value. See Paris jrnl 1652.

See Paris journal, 1652.

CHAPTER
36

MY HEART POUNDED.

Paris, 1652, when plague had struck the city. Where Dr. Parrett had first met my master.

His journals. I needed his journals.

They were upstairs, in the spare room filled with books. We went there. We searched. We opened the covers, looked at the dates, tossed them aside until we found the right one. The first date on the first page.

June 12, 1652

Sally huddled next to me as I flipped through the pages,

scanning for a sketch of the plant we'd seen below. It was something different that caught my eye first. A name.

John Parrett.

I read the entry. It was from October 12.

Another of Chastellain's infernal dinner parties. At least this one came to some purpose. I met a fellow Londoner today, a young physician by the name of John Parrett. A most decent man, with a child on the way, here to learn how to best treat the sickness. I didn't tell him about the volohosy. Until I have tested it properly, I must keep it a secret.

Volohosy. There was that word again.

I flipped back through the journal, reading more carefully now. I looked for anything about Master Benedict's discovery and a possible cure. I found it, on August 7.

Something extraordinary happened tonight. My old friend and host, Marin Chastellain, demanded that I stop avoiding his incessant dinner parties and attend the one he had prepared for that evening. I tried to beg off as usual, but this time he waved aside all my excuses. "Do not look so sour, Benedict," he said, a little smile on his face. "You will like this one. I have brought you something special."

The "something special" turned out to be Jehan Gaillart, the French explorer—and, dare I say, pirate. The man delighted Marin's guests with accounts of adventure, and his stories were indeed entertaining. But it was the tale of his latest trip that froze me in my chair.

Returning from Ceylon, Gaillart's ship came across a Dutch merchantman in the Indian Ocean with a hold full of nutmeg. In the process of relieving the unfortunate Dutch captain of his cargo, Gaillart's ship took some cannon shot. Rather than try to round the Cape of Good Hope with a damaged keel, Gaillart put in for repairs at Fort Dauphin, a French settlement on the southern coast of Madagascar.

On this island, one of Gaillart's sailors purchased, of all things, a monkey. Gaillart described it as an uncommon creature: smallish, but with remarkable golden fur—and the meanest disposition he'd ever seen in a beast. Though the creature tormented his new owner with screeches, scratches, and thrown handfuls of its own waste, the sailor adored the creature and brought it on board in a wicker cage. He also had to bring a crateful of a type of bamboo the natives called "volohosy," as this was the only thing the monkey would eat.

Gaillart pointed out to his crewman that the monkey would run out of food eventually, as this volohosy was nowhere to be found but in Madagascar. Still, Gaillart acquiesced to the sailor's pleas to keep his pet, mainly because he found the abuse the monkey hurled at the man to be amusing.

The ship was repaired and the voyage resumed. Along the way, disaster struck. Some of Gaillart's men fell deathly ill. The symptoms grew quickly: weakness, cramping, and confusion, followed by vomiting, delirium, and eventually loss of consciousness and death. As they died, their skin turned red, then went dark.

Gaillart and his men were terrified. They believed the ship had been stricken by the plague. The monkey was blamed as the source of the sickness and branded a demon, in service to Samael, the angel of death. They killed the poor creature and threw the body overboard. They would have done the same to the sailor, but he was already dead. The remaining men prayed for deliverance.

The ship's physician, however—a man of some experience treating the plague—noticed the symptoms on board the ship were not quite the same as the sickness. None of the patients had chills or sweats, and none showed any plague tokens other than the discoloration of the skin; in particular, there were no buboes or swellings. Puzzled, the physician investigated and found the true culprit.

It was in the plants the crewman had brought on board for his monkey. The ship's cook, having seen the creature eating them, stole some and, as a joke, was using the shoots to season the stew. Once the physician realized the sailors were not afflicted by the sickness, but had instead been poisoned, he tried various remedies on the crew until he found one that worked: heavy doses of charcoal, sweetened with equally high doses of sugar. The antidote was not infallible. Those poisoned the worst still died. Nonetheless, some of the men recovered, and their illness ended there.

I was stunned by the captain's story. Though not identical, the symptoms of volohosy poisoning were so similar to the plague that a thought leaped into my mind: Could the remedy for the poisoning work also for the sickness?

I was not the only one to wonder. As we moved from the table to the parlor, I sought out Gaillart—and found he was equally looking to speak to me. He explained that he had asked Chastellain if we could meet, and for the same reason I had hoped.

I asked him if he had any of the volohosy left. "Yes," he said. "I have sold some of it to another apothecary who heard my story and wondered the same as you. But Chastellain tells me you are the apothecary with the greatest skill and renown in understanding the plague. So I will throw my lot in with you."

He eyed me shrewdly. "I shall give you what I have left of the volohosy at no charge. In return, if you find this plant leads to a cure, then you and I will share the profits in equal amount. If you need more, I will return to Madagascar and bring you as much of the plant as you desire."

I took the deal, and gratefully. This is the greatest chance I have had in twenty years to develop a cure.

I turned the pages, faster and faster. The months that followed were less journal entries than they were notes on his experiments, things my master had tried, results. But the results were always the same.

Nothing.

His final entry on this was dated the twenty-sixth of November.

It is enough. I have put a stop to my experiments. The cure does not work.

I have tested the volohosy in every way I can imagine. The plant's poison can be eliminated by boiling it in water for at least an hour, but beyond this transformation it has no medicinal qualities whatsoever. There is no extract I can obtain from it that acts in any way as a counter to the plague. If anything, its application does only harm.

As for its own counteragent, that, too, does nothing. I have confirmed the discovery of Gaillart's physician: If the volohosy poisoning has not yet reached fatal levels, a large dose of powdered charcoal and sugar may work as an antidote. But in no quantities, with no additional ingredients, does charcoal or sugar affect the plague in the slightest.

I will not continue with my research. Isaac has written to me from London with news; he says he has acquired a scroll from Jerusalem that *may aid us in the search for the Prima Materia. Perhaps that may lead to a cure for the plague. Perhaps it will lead to something even greater. I do not know, and at the moment, I do not care. I have worked for years to try to stop the spread of the sickness, and have learned nothing. I am overwhelmed with despair.*

I have failed.

His words cut into me.

I have failed.

I'd felt the same, ever since he'd died. Not just about losing him, but the way I'd tried—and failed, just like him—to help.

Master Benedict had buried his failure, hid it from me, never told me why. But he'd also moved on, started working on finding the Prima Materia, which had led to the discovery of the Archangel's Fire.

I understood now why he'd kept that past from me. And with those words, I understood what Melchior had done, too.

He wasn't spreading the sickness at all. He was poisoning people with that plant he'd hidden in his desk, and making it look like they'd died of the plague. With the volohosy, he'd been able to recreate most of the plague symptoms. By adding horehound to the mixture, he also gave his victims the chills and sweats.

In combination, it appeared as if they had the sickness. He hadn't been able to create the swellings, but with the panic in the city, even a single token—the reddening of the skin, which happened as the patient died—was enough to mark them as if with plague. It was a scheme so wicked in its brilliance.

And now I finally realized why Melchior wanted Galen dead. I didn't know what secret ingredient Galen thought made his cure work, but he'd been wrong. The important ingredients were ones that even Tom knew: powdered charcoal and sugar. Though Galen didn't realize it, what he'd actually made was the antidote to Melchior's poison. I remembered Melchior staring at Galen's cure at Magistrate Aldebourne's house. He must have been stunned to see what Galen was doing.

What was truly horrifying was that Galen *hadn't* found a cure for the plague. All the money the city had spent on ingredients, setting up Galen's workshop . . . it was all for nothing.

CHAPTER
37

"WE HAVE TO TELL THE MAGIS-trates," Sally said.

Henry's heart would stop. If he even believed me. A few days ago, he'd have jumped at what I said to discredit Galen. Now, Magistrate Aldebourne himself might throttle Henry. The city *definitely* would, when they realized the truth.

I put that aside; it was a problem we could deal with later. Right now, I had something much more important to take care of: Tom's antidote.

Powdered charcoal and sugar. I had plenty of that here. I'd used up most of the charcoal in the stores for the gunpowder for today's fireworks, but I still had a big vial of it in my sash. We could save him.

Maybe. Master Benedict's words echoed in my mind.

If the volohosy poisoning has not yet reached fatal levels, a large dose of powdered charcoal and sugar may work as an antidote.

If.

I ran back down to the workshop, not worrying about the creaking steps. I filled another vial in my sash with the last of the charcoal, and put more sugar in as well, plus water for Tom to drink. As an afterthought, I grabbed my broom, with the ink smudge on the handle. The assassin's crossbow was still resting on the counter in the shop; I took that, and the bolt, too. Just in case.

The weapon reminded Sally what was waiting for us outside. "We'd better go," she said, and she was right. I just needed one more thing.

"Bridget," I whispered. "Bridget!"

I couldn't leave her here. I wasn't sure when—or if—I'd be able to come back. After tonight, Melchior would hunt us to the ends of the Earth. Without someone to care for her, Bridget would starve.

She didn't respond. "Bridget! Come here. Where are

you?" I'd left her cage open when we'd gone to Tom's, so by now she could be anywhere in the house.

I frowned. I'd already *been* all over the house. I hadn't spent much time on the middle floors, but Bridget wouldn't hide there. Really, she wouldn't hide from me at all. She should have come to find me as soon as Sally and I returned.

"Have you seen her?" I said to Sally. She shook her head.

Now I was starting to worry. I was sure she hadn't flown out of the house when we'd come through the hatch in the roof. So there was only one way she could have got out.

Someone else had been in here when we were gone.

It could have been Galen. He had a key.

But so did Galen's assassin.

"Come on," I said, and we ran up to the hatch.

I was halfway through when a shape caught my eye. Something moved out there, across the rooftops, a black presence against the stars.

The shape shifted. Then it froze.

It was a man. A man, waiting on the roof, between us and the ladder.

I inched back down. Slowly, slowly.

And then the figure started to move.

I jumped down and closed the hatch, slamming the bolt shut. I heard scuffing from the roof. Then the hatch rattled. A heavy thump. And then a voice.

"He's here! He's here! He's in the house!"

We went for the stairs. Halfway down, I heard more noises above the banging on the hatch. Someone pounded at the back door. From the front, there was no pounding, just the stomping of feet on the shop's floorboards. They were inside.

We ran back up, but there was nowhere to go. The hammering on the hatch had turned rhythmic, each blow a chopping sound, a blade into wood. An ax.

Through the chopping came a voice from downstairs. Rough, crude. I knew it. "Stay here," it said. "Guard the door. And watch the windows. Don't let him out."

I gripped the crossbow. One man. I could take one man with this, then we were finished.

I shoved it into Sally's hands. Startled, she took it, already holding the broom. Then I stripped off my master's sash and gave that to her, too.

I pointed to the vials in the sash. "That's the charcoal, and that's the sugar," I whispered. "Tom has to take those. Grind them into powder, mix them in water, then make him swallow it all. Do you understand?"

"What are you—" she began.

I clapped my hand over her mouth. "Go hide under Master Benedict's bed. Stay there until we're gone. The man on the roof only saw me. They don't know you're here. You can hide."

Her eyes went wide. "They'll kill you."

"And if they see you," I said, "we'll *all* be dead. You stay safe. Hide until they're gone. Then go back to Mortimer House. You can still save Tom." I heard footsteps coming up from below. "You have to save Tom."

"But—"

"Please," I said. "If you don't go, we all die."

She bit her lip. Then she nodded.

Thank you, I mouthed. She ran into Master Benedict's room.

The wooden hatch splintered, sending oak needles into my hair. I could see the blade of the ax through the tear. It pulled out, chopped back.

For a moment, Sally turned toward me. In the dim glow of my hooded lantern, I caught a glint of the light in her eyes. Then she rolled under the bed and faded into the darkness.

More splinters showered me. The footsteps clomped from below. No point in waiting. I met them going down the stairs.

Three men were there, bronze medallions pinned to their chests. Snaggletooth was at the front. He gave me a toothy grin, equal to the blade in his hand.

I didn't even bother to fight.

They used a leather belt to tie my hands behind my back. They trussed my legs, too, with a rope cut from a coil in the workshop. Then they gagged me and put a sack over my head.

One man hauled me away, draped over his shoulder like a suckling pig on the way to its slaughter. I bumped and banged along the streets, turning this way, then that.

I was so scared. The only thing I could cling to was the hope that Sally would make it back to Tom. I hadn't heard them mention her. I prayed she'd stayed hidden.

At some point we entered a building, a large one, by the echo. They carried me down a set of steps into a room that sounded small. Its floor was stone; I found that out when they dropped me.

The gag flopped out of my mouth. I groaned in pain.

A man knelt next to me. I smelled fish.

"Does it hurt?" Snaggletooth said. "Maybe you should just go to sleep."

Then a fist cracked into my jaw, my head slammed into the floor, and the whole world went dark.

FRIDAY, SEPTEMBER 4, 1665

Yesterday's plague deaths: 1,524

Total dead: 35,959

CHAPTER
38

VOICES.

The murmurs came from somewhere outside the room. I couldn't tell where.

I opened my eyes. A haze of soft yellow light filtered through the sack on my head. A smell, too: incense and herbs.

I shifted. I stopped. My *head*.

My jaw throbbed where Snaggletooth had hit me. The side of my skull pulsed achingly in time with it. The corners of my mouth burned, raw and painful. The gag had been put back in place while I was out.

I moaned.

The voices stopped. Footsteps came closer.

My stomach fluttered as I braced myself for a blow. Rough hands tore the sack from my head. The back of my skull bounced off the stone.

"Gently," a muffled voice said, disapproving.

I could see now, sort of. Though the light in the room came from only two torches, it was enough to make me squint and turn my head away. Still, now I knew where I was. And it made me shake.

They'd brought me to the empty room under Saint Andrew's, next to where Melchior had made his home.

The gag was untied. Feeling prickled back into my lips, making them throb and sting. The sides of my mouth burned hotter than ever.

Footsteps again, someone leaving. Then the rustle of leather. A hand lifted my back at the shoulder, helping me sit up. I tried to scramble away.

The hand on my shoulder held me in place, though not roughly. "Here," the muffled voice said. "It's all right; no one's going to hurt you. Drink."

I looked. Right in front of me was Melchior's beak. The flames from the torches reflected in his lenses like the man himself was on fire, a demon made flesh.

He was holding a goblet. Through the sweetness of the smoking herbs I smelled the flowery, sour scent of fermented grape. I pressed my lips together and turned my head away.

"It's only wine," Melchior said. "Go ahead. You must be thirsty."

I was, desperately. My throat seized with the craving to gulp the liquid down. Still, I kept my mouth closed. I knew what was in the drinks he offered.

I almost said it out loud. I caught myself just in time. I needed to watch my words in more ways than one. Master Benedict's voice came to me, again, a warning. *Be cautious, Christopher.*

I listened, using the sound of his voice to fight the panic rising in my chest. My master was right. I had only one advantage here: Melchior didn't yet realize I knew he was a fraud.

"Please, your worship." My voice cracked. "Let me go."

Melchior put the cup down. "You broke the law."

"I didn't do anything. Your men broke into my house."

"Let's not play games," Melchior said. "You were seen carrying Tom Bailey away on the roofs."

I took a deep breath, attempting to calm myself before I answered. It didn't really work. "That . . . that sounds crazy."

"Indeed it does." Was I mad, or did Melchior actually sound amused? "Especially considering the hole you left in your friend's house. Where did you get so much gunpowder?"

"I don't know what you're talking about."

"You're wasting time. Your friend is sick. He needs the cure. You do understand that he'll die without it, don't you?"

I knew he was trying to manipulate me, but my heart still sank. Tom *did* need a cure, even if it wasn't the one Melchior aimed to provide. I didn't know if Sally had got back to him, or if the antidote to the poison would work. Or even if Tom would still be alive when Sally returned.

"Did you leave him with the girl?" Melchior said. "Where did she go?"

Was he trying to trick me? Or was he really unaware? "I don't know," I said.

"Christopher."

"I'm not her master." Sweat dripped down my forehead, ran into my eyes. "She's just the maid. She comes and goes as she pleases."

Melchior sighed. "Things don't have to go this way. Please. Help Tom. And help yourself. Tell me where you've hidden him."

"Why do you care so much?" I said.

Even through his mask, I saw him go tense. "What do you mean?"

"I mean, Tom's not a noble, or a magistrate. He's just a baker's son. Why is he so important to you?"

My answer seemed to relax him. "I'm a physician. Every life is important."

"But Tom's already dead." I tried to sound crestfallen. It wasn't hard. "You killed him."

Melchior tilted his head, tense again. "Why would you say that?"

"I didn't. *You* did. You told me I was cursed by the angel of death. You said someone I loved would die."

He paused. "You can't blame me for that. I'm not responsible for the visions I see."

I didn't answer. My mind raced, trying to think of any way to free myself. I couldn't come up with anything.

Melchior stared at me as if his burning eyes could see into my soul. When he finally spoke, it was more a statement than a question. "You won't tell me, will you?"

"I *can't* tell you," I said. "I don't know where he is. Besides, what difference does it make how Tom dies?"

Melchior stood.

"There are many different ways to die, Christopher," he said. "Some much worse than others. In time, you may find that matters very much."

He spoke to the men waiting outside the room. "Take him."

Four of them carried me, still trussed up, one for each arm and leg. They put the sack back over my head, but I could tell from the fish smell that the one holding my right arm was Snaggletooth. The sound of creaking leather came from in front of us: Melchior, striding at the head of his men.

From the light that filtered through the sack, I could tell it was daytime. I heard the sounds of the people we passed, muttering at this strange procession, joining behind like a flock of pigeons following a man scattering bread. Melchior's men hadn't put the gag back on, but as scared as I was, I didn't bother crying for help. No one would even try.

They took me inside another building and dropped me on another stone floor. Then Snaggletooth ripped off the sack.

Oh no.

I was inside the main hall at Guildhall. Melchior's men ringed around me, the crowd beyond buzzing with curiosity.

There was only one reason Melchior would have brought me here. The crowd wouldn't help, I knew, but I still began to plead.

Melchior nodded to Snaggletooth. The man grabbed my jaw and held it shut. Then Melchior raised his plague doctor staff in his gloved hands, the gargoyle hovering above his head. The crowd went silent.

"Good people," Melchior said. "This boy has broken the law. In defiance of those who would protect this city, he has violated the quarantine on a plague house and released the infected inside to wander free."

The crowd muttered.

Melchior pointed a finger at me. The tip of his glove bent like a claw. "This boy has defied us. Now he remains silent, while his friend walks the streets, dying, and spreading the plague to innocent lives."

The crowd glowered at me, seething with fear and rage. Stomach tumbling, I twisted in Snaggletooth's hands. He held me in place.

Melchior pointed his staff at the crowd. "What punishment does this boy deserve? What penalty would fit his crime?"

Their cries made me shake.

"Flog him!" a woman shouted.

"Hang him!" a man said.

"Throw him into the Thames!"

"Throw him into the *graves*!"

I curled up, as small as I could, as if somehow that would help. Then a reedy voice cut through the crowd. "What is this? What's going on here?"

Henry squeezed through the mass, holding his spectacles. He saw Melchior, and his eyes went wide. Then he saw me kneeling before the prophet. "Christopher? What on Earth . . . Melchior! What's the meaning of this?"

"This boy has broken the quarantine on the Bailey house," Melchior said. "Now he must face retribution."

I tore my head away from Snaggletooth and pleaded. My voice was hoarse, trembling. "I didn't break the quarantine, Mr. Cole, I swear. I'm innocent. Please. Help me."

"I . . ." Henry's eyes darted from me to Melchior.

"Mr. Cole." Melchior turned his full gaze on the little man. Henry shrank back. "Has he not violated the law? Does he not deserve punishment?"

"*Please*," I begged, before Snaggletooth clamped my mouth shut again.

Henry seemed to feel the menace of the crowd pressing around him. "If he has, then there should be a trial," he said weakly.

The crowd yelled back in response. Henry shrank even further.

"I-It's the law," he stammered.

Melchior held up his hands. The crowd obeyed, going still.

"But you know very well, Mr. Cole, that the sickness has closed the courts."

"Y-yes." Henry mopped at his forehead. "But we can't just—"

"What?" Melchior's voice rumbled like thunder. "Serve justice? Are you saying we should let this boy go?"

"No!" a woman shouted from the crowd.

"No!" howled the rest. "No!"

Henry looked three inches tall. He glanced at me, met my pleading eyes.

Then his gaze fell to the stone.

"No," he mumbled.

And the crowd screamed with joy.

CHAPTER
39

IT WAS ONLY BY MELCHIOR'S COM-
mand that they didn't tear me apart right there in the hall.
The crowd surged forward. Melchior raised his staff, bringing the mob to a halt.

"This boy's crime is against all of us," Melchior said into
the silence. "So *all* must administer punishment."

He pointed the gargoyle at the open doors.

"Take him to the square."

The crowd roared their approval. Melchior's men
grabbed my arms and legs and dragged me out of Guildhall, the crowd screaming abuse all the way. I tried pleading with Henry for help again, but he wouldn't meet my

eyes. He was swallowed quickly by the throng.

Melchior led the procession. Snaggletooth and the other three carried me aloft, so the crowd could see my terror. They hauled me all the way across the city to the public square at the end of Rosemary Lane, just north of the Tower.

There were already two prisoners on display. Clamped in the pillory was a weeping woman, her straggly blond hair thick with dirt. A cursing sailor was chained beside her, his thick, tattooed neck so squeezed by the wood holding him that his face had gone red.

There were more empty pillories beside them, but those weren't for me. Instead, Melchior pointed his staff at the gibbet next to them. A rusted chain tied around the vertical beam led up and over the crossbar on top. A cage hung from the end, long and cylindrical, with two-inch-wide riveted bands.

Melchior's men dropped me. I struggled as one of them placed a boot on my neck and pressed me into the ground. Two of the others untied the knotted chain at the beam. The cage fell to the ground, its door screeching open. They cut my restraints and threw me inside. Snaggletooth snapped the padlock shut as another man moved to winch me up.

Melchior waved his men away. He stepped up to the

iron bars and spoke, his voice quiet so no one else could hear over the roar of the crowd.

"Tell me, Christopher," he said. "Tell me where Tom is. Tell me, and I promise you, this will all be over."

"You can't end this." I motioned to the crowd, trembling at their thirst. "They'll never let you."

"But they will. They'll do *exactly* as I say."

And even through my fear, I understood.

That was it.

Melchior controlled them. They *would* do as he said.

That's what he'd wanted all along.

But why? I'd discovered Melchior was a fraud, a liar, a killer. I'd even figured out how he'd fooled the entire city with his so-called prophecies, and how he'd pulled off that deception. Yet I still didn't understand *why*.

The question hung at the back of my skull. I shook it off. Understanding it now wouldn't make a difference. Not unless I gave up Tom.

"Last chance," Melchior said. "Talk, and I'll save you from them. Keep silent, and you'll hang in this gibbet until thirst shrivels you to a hollow shell. You'll beg for death. And once you're gone, your corpse will remain, rotting above the square until the sun bleaches your bones."

I couldn't think. I couldn't breathe. "Please," I said. "I don't know where Tom is. Please."

Melchior seemed genuinely disappointed. "I'll return tomorrow." He traced a gloved finger down one band of the gibbet. "Perhaps a night in here will change your mind."

He spun on his heel and walked away. His men hoisted the cage, hanging me ten feet up in the air.

Then it began.

A rotten apple hit the rusty bar in front of my face, spattering me with rancid juice. With it came much, much worse: wooden splinters, ceramic tiles, jagged stones; everything, anything the people had gathered along the streets as they'd followed. Onto me, London piled its anger, its fear, its helplessness. Me, the avatar of blame for the sickness that had destroyed their lives.

I curled up at the bottom of the cage as best I could. It didn't help. A stone caught me on the ankle, sending a spike of pain across my leg. I howled. Two more thudded against me, side and back.

I wasn't the only target. The pair in the pillories got a lot of it, too. Braver boys dashed up to kick them from behind, dodging stones with upraised arms as they returned, victorious, to the safety of their friends. The sailor hurled curses at them. The woman never made a sound, just let silent tears drip onto the ground below.

Through the screams and the hail of rocks, I saw a flash of feathery white. Above me, a pigeon landed on the crossbar. She marched along the beam.

My voice was a croak. "Bridget?"

She cooed. She stuck her head down toward me and desperately flapped her wings.

A stone clanged against the cage. I jerked back.

The grinning boy who'd thrown it scooped up another rock. It sailed wide. His friends taunted him, and he tried again. This one cracked me on the shoulder. I crumpled, paralyzed with pain.

More stones came. Most missed. A handful ricocheted off the iron. A terrible few hit their mark. They got their rewards; I cried with every blow.

Still Bridget ran back and forth, flustered. Then a rock hit her in the side. She tumbled to the ground. Feathers followed her down, twisting in the wind.

She flapped around on the ground, trying to get up. The boy who'd thrown the rock ran up to her. He raised his boot over her head.

I couldn't move. I couldn't speak. All I could do was plead. *No. Please, no.*

The boy brought his heel down.

He missed. Bridget shifted, scrambling on the stone. The boy tried stomping her again, but she righted herself, ran a few paces, then flapped her wings and frantically flew away.

They took her escape out on me.

The worst of the mob spent their hatred early. As the day waned, most of the crowd went home. The remainder who straggled past didn't do much more than yell a curse or two, with the occasional rock thrown for good measure.

When the sun dipped below the horizon, a man in livery let the woman out of the pillory. She gathered her tattered clothes and limped away, the few remaining gawkers standing back like she carried the sickness. The tattooed sailor, still locked up, dripped blood from his face onto the wood. His curses had finally been silenced.

I wasn't any better. Angry welts and purple splotches marked me, my skin a map of the city's wrath. Everything hurt. Through the pain, I was hungry, thirsty, so badly that

I pulled the soggy flesh of rancid fruit from the rusting bars looking for something to eat.

It was while I was searching for scraps that I saw her. I'd never been so happy to see anyone in my life.

Sally entered the square. Her hair was covered with a scarf, and she carried a wicker basket. She looked around, then came closer. She reached into the basket and brought out an orange.

I sat up.

She held it for a moment, made sure I saw it. Then she drew back and hurled it at me.

Her aim was perfect. The orange sailed between the bars and thumped against my chest, squirting a mist of juice onto my chin. A man watching her nodded his approval. "Well thrown, lass."

The orange tumbled downward. I scrambled to get it before it fell through the bars. I brought it up and hugged it to my stomach like a beggar finding a gold guinea. The peel had already torn, a slice near the top. More juice leaked out. I licked my grubby fingers, then tore at the rind.

I didn't get far. As soon as my thumb went inside the fruit, I felt something hard. I pulled the orange open and stared.

Wide-eyed, I looked back up, but Sally had already moved away. At the edge of the square, one of Melchior's men remained, lazily turning the butt of his halberd against his boot.

Sally gave a little curtsy and spoke to him. He looked interested in what she had in the basket. She lifted the cloth covering it, and the guard peered inside.

Sally spoke to him a little longer. Then she pulled a small jar of vinegar from the basket. The guard dropped a farthing in with a splash. Sally capped the jar, glanced back at me, then handed the basket to the guard and walked away with the rest of the thinning crowd.

I watched her go. Then I stuck my finger in the orange again, felt what was hidden inside. And locked in that miserable gibbet, hanging above the square, aching from the worst beating I'd ever known, I felt freer than any time since the plague had come.

Because now I knew Tom was still alive.

CHAPTER
40

WITH DARKNESS CAME THE COLD.

Four torches lit the corners of the square, too distant to provide any warmth. I shivered at the bottom of the cage, aching arms wrapped around throbbing knees, watching the flags on the Tower's turrets snap and curl in the wind. Seeing the king's emblem made me wish for Lord Ashcombe. If only he hadn't left the city.

The square was empty now, except for the sailor in the stocks, and the single guard Melchior had left to watch me. The man leaned against the tenement wall on the far end of the square, whistling softly.

He'd already eaten his snack, a half dozen sticky buns

from Sally's basket. Concealed in my breeches were the remains of my own meal, the orange Sally had thrown at me. I'd swallowed every bit of its flesh, so just the peel remained. That, and the glass vial from my master's sash that my friends had hidden inside it.

The guard picked at his fingernails with his knife. I watched him, making sure he wasn't paying attention. Then I reached into the scraps of rind and pulled out the vial.

The glass was sticky with dried orange juice. The ink on the label had smudged, but I knew what was inside from the way it was capped. The cork stopper was sealed with red wax and tied down with twine.

It was oil of vitriol, that magical—and dangerous—substance that could eat through almost anything. This was how I knew Tom was alive. I'd never told Sally about the oil of vitriol, let alone mentioned which vial it was in. Only Tom knew that.

I sent a prayer of thanks heavenward. Then I broke the seal. The sour stink of vitriol rose from the glass, a scent even more welcome than the orange. I took hold of the padlock and carefully dripped the thin oil on the metal.

The iron began to fizz. I let the drop stand for a few minutes until no more bubbles appeared, then wiped it away with the orange peel. Then I poured another drop.

Slowly, slowly. Patience was the key. The whole time, I kept one eye on the guard. He pushed himself from the wall. I hesitated, but he wasn't looking at me. As he stood there, he began to shift restlessly from foot to foot. His leather heels scuffed the ground; the only sound in the square besides the snapping flags on the Tower.

I looked up at them again, wishing once more the King's Warden were here. The swirling wind caught the nearest banner with the king's coat of arms and wrapped it around its flagpole. The way the banner fell, it folded around itself, melding the creatures supporting the shield together. The lion's head joined with the body of the unicorn, forming a chimera of legend. The letters of the motto beneath the shield—DIEU ET MON DROIT, God and my right—wrapped around with the figures, forming a block of jumbled letters, unreadable, like a code.

Seeing that made me think of Melchior. He'd blended himself just like those creatures, taking off one disguise and putting on another. Plague doctor, preacher, prophet, thief. Underneath it all, a murderer. What I couldn't understand was why.

The vitriol stopped bubbling. I wiped it away and looked at the padlock. The shackle that held it shut was beginning to corrode. I dripped more onto the lock and returned to my thoughts.

If all Melchior wanted to do was kill people, he could have done that secretly. Instead, he'd placed himself right in the center of things. It wasn't enough for Melchior to murder them; he'd had to predict their deaths first.

Why? Was it the deaths that mattered? Their predictions? Or both?

The orange peel I'd been using to wipe away the vitriol turned black and crumbled in my hand. I pulled another wedge from my breeches and poured more vitriol on the lock. It continued to work its magic; more than half of the bar was eaten away now.

I heard my master's voice in my head. *Start from the beginning, Christopher.*

All right. Melchior comes to the city. He takes a job as a plague doctor. He starts predicting people's deaths and then poisons them.

So his predictions come true. His reputation grows. People believe him. They fear him. But they also follow him.

And getting them to follow him was the point. He'd revealed that today, when he'd spoken in soft tones before that howling mob. *But they will follow my orders. They'll do* exactly *as I say.*

That was his purpose. The crowd was his power. He manipulated them to do what *he* wanted.

So what was he doing with that crowd?

Melchior is playing a role, I thought. *Everything he does is about playing that role.*

I recalled the speech Melchior had given on Wednesday, when he'd almost caused a riot. He'd cut that off with a new prediction. Before that, he'd been talking about—

The magistrates.

The *magistrates*. The ones who ran the city. Eastwood, then Aldebourne's daughter, then Dench. He'd started with ordinary people, got them frightened, put the crowd under his control. Then he'd moved on to the magistrates.

And got *them* frightened.

There, Christopher. The answer lies in there. What would frightened magistrates do to save their jobs? Their lives? Their children?

The clank of metal pulled me from my thoughts.

The padlock had broken. The oil of vitriol had worked its magic, the iron shackle eaten through. I twisted it. It opened, clanging against the gibbet.

Across the square, the guard looked at me, eyes narrowed.

I wrapped both hands around the lock, as if I was still

trapped. I made as if I was pulling on it, banging it against the cage. "Please, sir," I said. "Let me go. I'm innocent."

He sneered. "Shut up. Decent people are trying to sleep."

"But—"

He grabbed his halberd. "You want me to come over there?"

I slumped against the bars, looking cowed. After a lingering glare, he leaned the polearm back against the wall.

Now I wasn't sure what to do. The padlock was off, but the cage would squeak when it opened. Did Tom and Sally have a plan to get me out? Or was I supposed to just jump down and run? The guard was thirty feet away; under normal circumstances, I might be able to evade him. But the mob had banged me up badly, and I'd been curled up in this cage for hours. I wasn't exactly sure my legs would work.

The guard shifted restlessly. I knew just how he felt. Despite the broken padlock, I was still stuck in the gibbet, like Melchior had wanted. And thinking about that made me wonder: Why did he put me here at all?

He'd threatened to let me die in this cage, but I knew he didn't really want that. If he did, he could have slit my throat in the basement of Saint Andrew's. He just wanted me to tell him where Tom was.

That's what started all of this, I thought. It was Tom he wanted dead. Which didn't make any sense. What threat was Tom to Melchior? And again, why not just cut his throat in his house and be done with him? After all, Melchior hadn't poisoned Galen; he'd tried to shoot him with a crossbow. So what did Tom know? What had he seen?

Tom's words popped into my mind. *Galen was writing on your broom.*

I frowned. I'd thought Tom was delirious, but then I'd seen that smudge of ink on the handle. Still, there weren't any words, so how could Galen have been writing on—

I froze.

I stared at the banner, wrapped around the pole atop the Tower. The wind relaxed, and the flag unfurled. The chimera separated from one into two, lion and unicorn once more. The letters in the motto unjumbled, too, the code deciphered. DIEU ET MON DROIT.

My heart thumped in my chest.

He was writing on your broom.

The banner recurled around the pole. Chimera and code, again.

Backward. I'd had it all backward.

But I understood. I *understood.*

It was all I could do not to leap from my cage. I looked at the guard, willing him to turn away.

I was surprised to see I might get my wish. The guard had now given up all pretense of hiding his restlessness. He winced as he hopped from foot to foot, then began to walk back and forth.

The pacing didn't seem to help. If anything, he looked more uncomfortable than ever. He wiped his face with his sleeve and looked about the square. He pulled at his belt, trying to loosen it. His breathing got louder. Finally, he gave one last look to see if anyone was around. Then, unbuckling his belt, he ran into a nearby alley.

Time to go. Slowly, I pushed the cage open. It gave a long, faint creak. I dropped to the ground below.

I crumpled on the cobbles. Pain stabbed my battered legs. For a moment, I couldn't move, just lay there, forehead pressed to the ground.

Then the door of the cage swung shut. The clang of metal rang through the empty square.

My heart's pounding doubled. I scrambled to my feet. My knees screamed at me. I ignored them.

I ran.

CHAPTER
41

I COULDN'T SEE A THING.

The alley was so narrow that there was barely any moonlight. I thought maybe I should slow down before I ran face-first into a wall. I weighed it against ending up back in the gibbet.

I ran faster. Suddenly, at the end of the alley, a hulking figure appeared. I skidded to a stop, leaning back so far that I traveled the last yard and a half on my backside. I clawed at the dirt, trying to drag myself away.

"Christopher!" the hulk said.

I stopped.

Tom reached a giant hand down and pulled me from

the muck. I stared up at him. Then I threw my arms around him and held him so tightly I heard him squeak.

He hugged me back. "You saved my life," he said.

"You broke me out of prison," I said. And we laughed.

Sally stepped out from behind my friend. I grabbed that Cripplegate girl and pulled her into our hug.

"Thank you," I said, and I released her. "What did you give that guard?"

She stepped back, a little flustered. "Walnut buns. Tom made them."

"With castor oil," Tom said. "A *lot* of castor oil."

I grinned.

"Melchior's having a bad day," Tom said.

"It's about to get worse," I said. "Because now I know how to decipher his secret message."

We returned through darkened streets to Mortimer House. Back inside, I found my master's sash laid out on the velvet daybed. I buckled it around my waist, let it hold me for a moment.

Then I turned to Sally. "Where's my broom?"

She brought it over. "You gave me the answer," I said to Tom.

"I did?" he said.

"When you told me you saw Galen writing on my broom. That's how I figured it out. This is the key to Melchior's message."

Tom frowned. "Your broom is the key?"

"Yes. There's something special about it."

"You have a magic broom?"

"I—no. Here. Who do I look like when I do this?"

I held the broom in one hand and slowly pointed it at them.

Tom and Sally looked puzzled.

"You look like a man with a broom," Sally said.

"A madman?" Tom said.

I made a face. "All right, how about now?" I pulled a vial from the sash and placed it on the end of my nose, sticking out like a beak. I pointed the broom at them again. "The angel of death is coming for you," I intoned. "He will be here on Tuesday."

"Melchior?" Tom said. "But what's the broom for— Oh! That's Melchior's staff."

"There's no gargoyle, though," Sally said.

"The gargoyle doesn't matter," I said. "It's the staff itself that's important. In one particular way, it's exactly the same as my broom. Every broom, really. That's the key."

I took a piece of paper from a sheaf on Mortimer's desk and tore a long, narrow strip from the side. "Remember how I said Melchior's code needed to be easy to decipher? Watch what I do."

I took the strip of paper and wound it around the broom so that each loop just touched at the edges.

"Now I write my message." I pulled the quill and ink from my master's sash. "But I don't write it around the paper. Instead, I write it *downward*. Then I move one column over when I run out of space." I read the words out slowly as I wrote. "Hello, Tom. Good evening, Sally. How are you?"

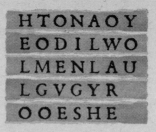

"When the strip is wrapped around the wood, you can easily read the message. But when you pull it away . . ."

HTONAOYEODILWOLMENLAULGVGYR OOESHE

"You get your code," Sally said.

"That's so easy," Tom said.

"And that's the point. You don't even have to work out what you're doing. All you need to grab is a staff that's the right thickness—anything like a broom will do—and the rod will decode it automatically."

"So what does Melchior's message say?" Sally said.

I pulled the piece of parchment from the sash.

PISODWOSTRGAITWNELSROERBOAORORNTDOWOMEAFAOAETBNKGACUD

I wound it around the handle of my broom. Melchior's message appeared, plain as day.

P I S O D W
O S T R G A
I T W N E L
S R O E R B
O A O R O R
N T D O W O
M E A F A O
A E T B N K
G A C U D

"Poison Magistrate Eastwood," Sally read. "At corner of Budge Row and Walbrook."

"Instructions," Tom said. Then he frowned. "They're instructions, for Melchior. But . . . I didn't see . . . I mean, *Galen* was writing on the broom."

"Yes," I said.

"But then . . . that means . . ."

I nodded. "Galen's the one sending orders to Melchior. They're working together. I know how. I know why." I wiped off my quill and slipped it back inside the sash. "And now I know the way to stop them, too."

. . .

I told them my plan. Sally took it in stride. Tom didn't.

"This sounds dangerous," he said.

It was. "It'll be fine," I said.

"But why do we have to go to Galen's warehouse? We already have the evidence." He held up Melchior's scroll.

"We can't prove Galen wrote that," I said. "We can't prove Melchior used it. If we want to show the magistrates we're right, we need to prove it in a way that can't be denied." I turned to Sally. "You go to Guildhall, as early as possible. Get Henry to bring as many guards as he can muster. Whatever you do, make sure Galen doesn't see you. And don't go anywhere near Melchior's men."

"All right," she said. "But Henry doesn't really know me."

"That's what this letter is for." I handed her the note I'd written. "It explains everything. It would be better for me to deliver it in person, but you'll have to do it. Tom and I can't go to Guildhall; we're already both marked for death."

Tom didn't seem pleased with the reminder. "Is that all the help we're bringing?"

"Who else is there?" I said.

"Well . . . what about Dr. Parrett?"

Of course, Tom didn't remember. He'd been delirious

when we'd gone to the doctor's home. I told him what had happened.

"But . . . couldn't his illness be from Melchior's poison, too?"

"He had the swellings," I said. "There's no question: Dr. Parrett has the plague."

Tom looked stricken. "We have to do something for him."

What could we do? Galen's cure was as much a fraud as Melchior's predictions. Only God could spare Dr. Parrett now. "We should leave him in peace."

Yet even as I said that, it occurred to me that if Henry didn't believe us, and things went wrong on our end . . . no one else would know what Melchior and Galen had done.

Would Dr. Parrett help us? I wasn't sure. He'd been despairing enough to wave a pistol at me. Then again, he'd been sorry for that immediately; he'd really only done it so we'd keep away from the infection.

I didn't know what he'd do. Even if he wanted to help us, by now he might be too sick to do so. But, either way, *I* could help *him*. He'd earned that, and more. I scribbled another note and handed it to Sally, along with the poppy and Venice treacle from my apothecary sash. The medicine wouldn't cure him, but it might bring him a little peace. And if we didn't make it, hopefully he'd be willing to pass that note to someone who could stop Melchior and Galen after we were gone.

"All right," I said to Sally. "Pass by Dr. Parrett's on the way and leave these for him. Just don't get too close. And remember, you have to get to Guildhall quickly. In the meantime, I'll go to Galen's warehouse."

"Why can't we just wait for the guards to come?" Tom said.

"Because with both you and me missing, if Melchior and Galen suspect we know what they're up to, they'll clean the warehouse of any evidence we might use against them. If we don't catch them now, we'll never be able to prove what they've done."

"But what if they're already *at* the warehouse?"

"Then I won't go in," I said. "I'm not an idiot."

He muttered something I couldn't quite hear. "So what am I supposed to do?" he said finally.

"You're coming with me. I need you in case things go wrong."

Tom looked desperately unhappy. "Can I just say again that this is a bad idea?"

"Sure," I said.

And as usual, he was absolutely right.

SATURDAY, SEPTEMBER 5, 1665

Yesterday's plague deaths: 1,703

Total dead: 37,662

CHAPTER
42

IT WAS STILL DARK WHEN I GOT to the warehouse. There were no lights in the windows or on the doorstep, no guards, no protective fires to ward away the plague. It looked like the place had been abandoned. *Exactly the way Galen wants it,* I thought. *And not because he doesn't want anyone to steal his "cure."*

There were three outside doors. I was relieved to see all of them were padlocked, since that meant neither Melchior nor Galen were here. I wondered if they'd decided to cut their losses, and had already fled the city. Part of me hoped they had—though if we let them get away, they could prey on another plague town the same as they had London.

Now I just had to decide how to get in. Oil of vitriol would have made short work of the padlocks, but I'd used up all I had getting out of the gibbet, and returning to Blackthorn for more would be madness. I'd taken a crowbar from the gardener's tools at Mortimer House, but I didn't want to pry away the padlock and warn an approaching Melchior or Galen with an easily spotted broken door.

It would have to be a window. I crept around the warehouse to the darkest one I could find. Like the others, it had been boarded up with thick oak planks. My aching body howled in protest as I wrestled with the crowbar, prying off enough wood to make an opening just large enough to squeeze through. Each creak and snap of the wood sounded like thunder in the quiet. I waited, cringing every time.

No one came to investigate. One last noise to make, then. I took off my shirt and used it to cover the window, hoping it would muffle the sound. Then I punched it with the crowbar, breaking a hole in the glass large enough to slip my arm through and undo the latch. I waited for a minute, blood rushing through my ears, but heard no approaching footsteps.

I crawled inside, headfirst. The room I fell into was pitch black. I'd brought a lantern, but I didn't want to light it until I was well inside the warehouse. So I stumbled around, banging my shins on invisible furniture until I found a doorway leading farther inside.

Safely away from the windows, I ignited the wick on my lamp, revealing a passage leading forward. I followed it, ignoring the side rooms until I got to a wide open space. The lantern filled it with dim light.

This was Galen's "workshop." There were three long workbenches, laden with apothecary tools and equipment. Three giant furnaces lay dormant against the far wall. Old tools lay in piles beside them—a glassblower's things, if I judged right—dumped to make room for Galen's new equipment.

The jars we'd seen the workmen deliver on Wednesday were arrayed on the shelves along the wall. They weren't labeled, but the number and size of them alone would correspond to hundreds of pounds' worth of ingredients.

And that, I knew, was where the proof of Galen's fraud would be. I took down a dozen, lugging them over to the workbench. One by one, I opened them.

And I didn't see what I'd expected.

The jars were filled with ingredients. Calamint. Juniper. Cinnamon. Crocus.

I opened more. Agaricus. Spignel. Hollowroot. Myrrh.

Myrrh? This much? A jar this size would cost forty pounds *alone*.

My heart pounded. I'd got it wrong.

I'd got it *wrong*.

I'd figured Galen was cheating the city. It would be easy for him to claim he was buying expensive ingredients, and then just buy something cheaper and pocket the gold. But this collection . . . this would cost exactly what Henry had given him. So if he wasn't siphoning money from the charity . . . I had no proof he was doing anything wrong.

My mouth had gone dry. I'd already sent Sally to collect Henry and his men. They'd be coming here soon—to the secret workshop I wasn't supposed to know about—and I'd have no evidence to show them. I'd already been condemned by Melchior. And worse, the people of London. If I got caught inside Galen's lab . . .

I needed to put everything away. Then I needed to get out of here. I needed to get out of the *city*. I began to heave the jars back onto the shelves. When I grabbed the crocus, the jar was much heavier than I'd thought it would be.

It slipped from my hands. I tried to catch it, but it bounced off my knuckles and fell.

The ceramic shattered on the floorboards. Dried crocus stamens scattered everywhere, along with a fine white powder. It burst over my shoes, sending a hazy mist into the air.

I fell back, coughing, trying to spit the powder from my mouth. It wasn't until it was mostly out that I realized it shouldn't have been there at all.

I blinked away the dust and stared at the pile of white among the yellow stamens and fragments of ceramic. I was pretty sure I knew what it was, but I dipped my finger in and tried it anyway. Tasteless, clumping dry in my mouth.

Flour.

Underneath the saffron, the jar had been filled with flour.

I opened the closest jar on the table. It smelled of cinnamon, and appeared to be filled with the reddish-brown powder. I stuck my hand in deep, swirled my fingers around. White streaks appeared in the mix.

I dumped the jar out on the surface and saw the same as I had before. A little brown powder, the rest mostly white. Flour here, too.

I tried the other jars. There were a dozen on the workbench, and dozens more still on the shelves, but I stopped after I'd turned over an additional three. They were all the same: a thin layer of some ingredient. And underneath that, underneath them all, was nothing but flour. Cheap, plentiful flour.

I was right, after all. This workshop was a sham. A veneer of an apothecary's tools and equipment, wood for the fire, ingredient jars everywhere, full of nothing but flour. This whole building was a stage; the tools, the painted scenery.

An illusion, like Melchior and Galen themselves. Actors, both, from the day they'd arrived to prey on the city.

This was it. I had the evidence I needed now. There was just one more thing that would put the final stake in their plans.

I moved deeper into the warehouse, checking the rooms that lined its corridors. Most of them were empty, filled with a season's worth of dust. But there was a door, far down one corridor from the main chamber, where a tread of dirt led.

It was locked. Of all the doors in the warehouse, this was the only one that had been locked. I hadn't seen a key, but I didn't need one. I wedged the crowbar between the door and the frame, splintered the lock, and brought my lantern inside.

The room had obviously been used for storage by the

glassblowers who had once owned this building. Tall, rickety shelves lined the walls; more shelves sat in the middle of the room, worn and sagging. Galen, it appeared, had also used the chamber for storage, as each shelf was stocked, four or five high, with plain burlap sacks. I tore one open, watched the white powder spill out. More flour; enough for a dozen bakeries.

What I couldn't find was money. I tried to estimate the cost of everything I'd seen in the workshop. It would take time for a full accounting, but with the equipment and the thin layers of actual ingredients, I'd guess at least a couple hundred pounds in expenses. Flour was cheap, so even the huge amounts in the jars and the untouched sacks in this storage room would be just a few more pounds. But I'd seen Henry's ledger; he'd said what Galen had asked for totaled a thousand pounds, just to start.

So where was the rest of the money?

I looked back at the splintered door. The lock had hidden Galen's secret, all this flour. Was that the *only* thing the lock had hidden?

Slowly, I walked around the room. I poked and prodded at the sacks. It was along the wall farthest from the door that I noticed something.

Whoever had brought the flour in had left tracks of dirt on the floor. Back here, mixed in with mud from the road, were little chunks of white. I figured it was flour that had spilled, but then I noticed the sacks at the bottom of the shelf had dirt on them, as well.

I plucked one of the chunks from the dirt. It was hard, crusty. I crumbled it between my nails.

Mortar.

The sacks here were sealed, like the others. I hauled them out and brought the lantern close. The wall behind was stone. The individual stones were laid on top of each other, like bricks. But in one area, there wasn't any mortar between them.

I tugged at one. It slid out easily, scraping against its neighbors, revealing a hole behind. I reached inside and felt wood. I groped around until my fingertips touched a metallic handle. I removed the rest of the stones, then grabbed the handle and dragged the thing out.

It was a cherrywood chest, the fittings brass. The chest was locked. I tried to use the crowbar on that, too, but I had trouble wedging its prongs between the lid and the case. Finally, I just bashed the thing open.

And out spilled a torrent of gold coins.

Trembling, I picked one up. It had an imprint of the king on it, and his coat of arms. It was a gold guinea, worth twenty-one shillings, slightly more than a pound.

Just one of these was a fortune. I was kneeling in a pile of them, bleeding out from the broken chest. There were hundreds of guineas here. *Hundreds.*

This was it. With the flour, and the coins, I had all the evidence I'd ever need.

And that's when I heard a sound.

CHAPTER

43

I SPUN AROUND. GOLD COINS scattered, sending jingling flashes of light dancing across the floor.

A man stood in the doorway. I couldn't quite see who he was; the lantern he'd hung on a hook in the hallway only cast his shape in silhouette. But his form looked familiar enough.

I leaped from the ground. "Uh . . . Master Galen . . . I—" Then I broke off.

It *wasn't* Galen. As I stood, my own lantern shone upon him. He was tall like Galen, but with a more slender frame. This man's eyes were narrower, his nose slightly crooked, his lips not as full—not nearly as attractive as the false apothecary. But the silhouette I'd seen came together with his features and jolted something loose in my mind. The final piece bumped into place.

"Brothers," I whispered.

The man raised an eyebrow. "You can tell? That's so interesting. I've never seen it, myself." He ran his hand across his not-quite-appealing features. "I certainly wouldn't tell my brother you saw a resemblance, if I were you."

He stepped into the storage room, leaving a gap between him and the doorway. He wasn't quite as big as Galen, but I didn't doubt he was stronger than me. I wondered if he was faster, too.

I took a step forward. My hand drifted toward my belt.

It didn't fool him. "No, no. Don't do that." He placed his fingers on the hilt of the blade at his side. "We may both have knives, but you'll find I'm quite a bit better with mine than you are."

I puffed out my chest. "I'm all right with testing that."

"Oh, stop." The man waved his hand dismissively. "Bravado is not in your character. You lack the inherent meanness to play that role."

He wasn't wrong. The last thing I wanted to do was get into any fight with him, knives or otherwise. Still, he didn't move. That was good. I needed to stall him, give Sally more time, wait for Tom to arrive.

"What do you want?" I said.

"I think you already know the answer to that."

"How would I?"

"Because it's written on every inch of you. The way you stare at me, then glance at the doorway. The tightness in your lips that screams of fear. Your hand, *still* creeping toward whatever you have hiding under your shirt. Even the way you're standing; not quite facing me, your body turned, ready to flee. I can read you, Christopher. That's my job. So I know you know who I am."

His description made me freeze. I realized I was doing all those things, just as he'd described.

My chest tightened. What else did he know? Either way, there wasn't any point in pretending. "You're Melchior."

He gave a little bow. "Walter, actually. But *Melchior* has such flavor, don't you think? That's critical, you know. A good name sets the character's stage."

Melchior—I couldn't see him as Walter—seemed happy to keep talking. All the better for me. "Melchior," I said, "was one of the three wise men who paid tribute to our Lord in His manger."

"Yes! What better name for a prophet of doom? Subject to God, but with an air of mystery. And menace, I think, in the sound of it. My brother thought I should go with Ezekiel, can you believe it? No imagination at all."

I caught myself looking toward the door again. I willed myself to stop. "Is that why he chose the name Galen? After the greatest physician in history?"

"Aha, you see? So heavy handed. You can't tell him anything."

"You sound like you think you're going to get away with this," I said.

Melchior motioned to the coins scattered around my feet. "I think we already have."

"I caught you. Others will, too."

"I doubt that. And really, Christopher, you haven't exactly *caught* us. You've just peeked behind the scenes of our little play." He rubbed the side of his nose. "I'm incredibly curious as to how you did that. I don't suppose you'd be willing to tell me."

His tone was so reasonable it caught me by surprise. "You're *asking* me?"

"Better than forcing you, isn't it? I could do that instead, if your pride demands it. But I'd rather not. I have to know where we went wrong, true—though I dare say we'll never be able to pull a job like this again—but I confess that I'm enjoying speaking to you."

I stared at him, dumbfounded.

"I've been stuck behind that infernal mask all summer," Melchior complained, "speaking of nothing but prophecies and plague. I'm beyond bored. I haven't had a real conversation in months." He shrugged. "Don't talk, if it pleases you. But you must realize we'll get the truth from you eventually. Why not spare yourself the hardship?"

I knew he was trying to manipulate me, that he needed to know what I'd found before he got rid of me. Even so, my fluttering guts agreed that he was right. He'd get the answers one way or another. And keeping him talking would give me more of what I really needed: time.

I caught myself looking at the door again. *Stop that,* I scolded. "All right."

I paused, as if collecting my thoughts. Melchior leaned against the splintered door frame, watching me with interest.

"The plague hits London," I said slowly. "You arrive early, before your brother. Or maybe you're already in town. Either way, you're the first on the scene.

"You enter wearing your costume: a plague doctor, here to help. It's not hard to get the job. Most of the city's physicians have already fled, and few remaining want the position; it's too dangerous. And maybe you do know a little about being a plague doctor; maybe you even try to treat people, here and there. But that's not what you're here for. You're here to set the stage."

Melchior smiled and nodded. "Go on."

I took a deep breath. "You begin by poisoning people. It's simple enough. All you have to do is offer them Venice treacle, say it'll help keep away the sickness. Then, whoever you want to poison, you slip it into their medicine. Since everyone thinks they're getting the same treacle, and most of them don't become ill, no one realizes what you're doing. And because you've chosen a poison with symptoms that look like the plague, when they *do* get sick, no one imagines it's anything else. You then keep giving them their 'remedy,' which makes them even worse. Eventually, they die, another casualty among thousands.

"But you're not doing this just to murder people. What you really want is to be seen as a prophet. So before you poison them, you make predictions. This man, that woman, those children will die. And, of course, your predictions come true—because *you're* the one making them sick.

"Initially, you just poison common people. Some of your choices have purpose; you poisoned the orphans at Cripplegate"—and here I had to take a deep breath, try not to throw myself against the man—"so you'd be able to sneak in and out of Saint Andrew's without anyone seeing you. But for the most part, who you poison doesn't matter. What you're really doing is building up your reputation. Then, when the city's taken notice of you and everyone is afraid, you move on to your real target: the magistrates.

"Magistrate Eastwood, you poison directly. But Magistrate Aldebourne, you *don't*, because you don't want him dead. Instead, you poison the people he cares about more than anything else in the world: his children. His youngest daughter dies. His older daughter, Annabelle, is also sick. Magistrate Aldebourne is devastated, and terrified for his little girl. And then onto the stage comes Galen.

"Like you, he's been playing a role of his own, fighting the quacks in the market and promising a cure for the people—and for free. Unlike the other cheats, however, Galen has something special: His cure works. He proves this to Aldebourne—and everyone else at Guildhall—by 'curing' a girl from the pest house. Of course, what Galen's cure *really* contains is the antidote to your poison. But Dr. Parrett, not realizing what you've done, confirms her miraculous recovery.

"Now your target is marked: Magistrate Aldebourne will do anything, *anything*, to spare Annabelle from the sickness. He gives Galen his chance, and of course, Galen succeeds. After this, Aldebourne is ready to fund Galen's workshop. Unfortunately for you, the only source of funds is the weekly charity the rest of the country has been sending to London to help manage the city and feed the poor; they can't spend it all on Galen, even for a cure. Yet since Galen's deception will eventually be discovered when his cure doesn't work on real plague victims, you need to grab as much money as you can before that happens. So you do two things to open the spigot.

"First, you poison another magistrate. Dench gets the cure in time; he's saved. Eastwood doesn't, and he dies. That convinces even the skeptics at Guildhall that Galen's cure is the real thing.

"And second, you rally the people behind Galen by

staging an assassination attempt on him." I shook my head. "That was what confused me the most. Why would anyone want to kill the discoverer of the plague cure? The answer, of course, was that they *wouldn't*. The 'assassin' was *you*. Galen sent Tom out of the room, then waited until Henry and Dr. Parrett arrived. Once everyone was there to hear it, Galen unlocked the back door to let you in. He stood against the wall. You stuck the crossbow in his collar and fired, then fled out the back, making sure to leave the weapon behind.

"Now the city went absolutely mad. Henry said the news of the attack got out because Galen was too angry to keep quiet about it. But he didn't *want* to keep quiet about it. Getting the people to scream for the cure—now, right *now*—was the whole point. The magistrates had no choice but to give Galen every penny he asked for.

"The fact that Galen doesn't really have a cure will still come out. But with him slowing the process as much as he can, how long will that discovery take? Weeks? In the meantime you'll steal thousands of pounds. Then, when it's about to come crashing down, you'll slip away into the night. Your brother will have to hide, but you? All you'll have to do is remove your costume. And no one will even know who you were."

Melchior applauded. "Fantastic. Really, Christopher, absolutely brilliant. You got a couple things wrong—some important things, actually—but close enough. I'm incredibly impressed. You still haven't told me how you figured all this out, though."

"That began when you broke into my house," I said.

It was the first time I'd seen Melchior look surprised. "You knew? How?"

"My apothecary jars had been moved. And you left that bit of wood in my lock."

Melchior made a face. "That silly girl, watching from the tavern. I couldn't get the block out with her there. But . . . the jars? You noticed that?"

"My master was very particular about how he kept his shop," I said.

"Fair enough. That still doesn't explain how you knew it was me."

"I didn't, in the beginning. I thought it was one of your men. You were spotted in your blue outfit. It had one of those medallions sewn into it."

"Ah." He shook his head ruefully. "That was a mistake. I'd have donned one of my other costumes, but I'd already worn both of those to your shop and I was worried someone might remember me. The truth is, I didn't expect anyone to put the two together."

He was right to think so; I wouldn't have, if Dorothy'd had anything to do with her time except sit in the window and knit.

Melchior tilted his head. "So you thought it was one of my men at first. How did you finally decide upon me?"

"It was your coded messages," I said. "I didn't really trust you from the beginning. I mean, I never suspected you were working with Galen, but I did think you were behind the attempt on his life. So I found one of your messages in your room."

He looked startled at that. "You were in my room?"

I decided to dig the knife in a little. "You're not the only one who knows how to break into a home."

He laughed. "How droll."

Melchior seemed content to talk forever. I was getting more worried every minute. How long was it going to take Sally to get here? And what had happened to Tom? Why hadn't he followed Melchior inside?

"I still don't understand everything you've done," I said.

Melchior spread his hands. "Ask what pleases you."

"*Why* did you break into my shop?"

"You already mentioned why. It was because of who used to own it."

"Master Benedict?" I said, surprised.

Melchior nodded. "We met him years ago in Paris, during another plague. We were working a different play then, on some rich old friend of your master's. Chastellain, I think his name was. He let slip that Blackthorn was supposedly close to discovering a cure.

"Naturally, we investigated, if for no other reason than a genuine plague cure would mean we'd have to find a different game to run. Anyway, we discovered your master's experiments were focused on investigating this particular poison. Nothing came of it, but it was his research that gave us the idea for a new, much better plan: a 'cure' we could fake that would actually seem genuine. But that presented a problem. The method of poisoning we used, Blackthorn knew very well. If anyone could have recognized what we were doing, it would have been him."

Melchior shook his head. "You can't imagine my panic when I heard someone mention your master's name. We

thought he still lived in Paris. I had to investigate him immediately. That's why I came to your shop last week, wearing this." He indicated his noble's costume. "I'd planned
to reintroduce myself to him, gain his confidence before
getting him out of the way. But Tom told me he'd already
been murdered. That was a relief, but I needed to be certain
your master hadn't kept anything from Paris that might
expose us. So I sent two of my idiot followers to distract
you, then came back disguised as Miles Gaspar to tamper
with your lock. That way, I could break in and look through
Blackthorn's things, see if he still had that old poison."

"You took it from my home?" I said.

"The poison? No, I brought my own stock with me to
London. Your master didn't have it. At least not that I could
find."

I blinked. "So then . . . what did you steal?"

"From you?" Melchior looked surprised. "Nothing. All
I cared about was that you didn't have any of the poison."
He waved at the gold scattered around my shoes. "We'll
have thousands of pounds by the time we're finished. Why
would I risk this to pocket a handful of pennies?"

My mind was racing. *He didn't take anything from*

Blackthorn. "But . . . if all you wanted to do was investigate my master, then why did you tell me someone I loved was going to die? And why did you go after Tom?"

"Ah." Melchior nodded. "To answer your first question, I made that prediction for the crowd, not you. You were the youngest person there, and so the most likely to arouse sympathy: an innocent boy, to be stripped of someone he loved. I hadn't actually intended to follow up on that; I had the magistrates to deal with, and once Galen was made to work in your shop—that was quite a surprise—I didn't think it wise to press the point.

"As for Tom, that was my brother's fault." Melchior sounded annoyed. "He was careless in writing our secret messages when the boy was around. He assumed he'd had your friend so cowed he wouldn't even look over at what he was doing. Nonetheless, once Philip—sorry, Galen— noticed Tom standing nearby, there wasn't much he could do. He couldn't just knife the boy in the workshop; with guards around Blackthorn, he couldn't reasonably claim an assassin got in a second time. Poisoning him was the only way to get rid of him.

"It was the better move, anyway. This way, when Tom

died, one more of my predictions could come true. Galen could then blame the magistrates, say they hadn't yet given him enough money to manufacture the cure. The plague savior's apprentice, dead of the sickness, because the city was too stingy! The coffers would have poured open like a waterfall."

Melchior looked at me curiously. "My brother's error would have turned to our advantage, in fact, if you hadn't freed Tom from his house. I still don't know where you got all that gunpowder."

I shrugged. Let him wonder.

"As you wish," he said. "It's not important. Still, your resourcefulness is magnificent. We should give you a job."

"You'd slit my throat the second my back was turned."

Now Melchior looked at me with interest. "We really *should* give you a job."

"I wouldn't take it." I pointed at the coins at my feet. "Not for every single one of these. This money was for the poor. They'll starve without it. How can you murder so many innocents? The people. The magistrates. Their *children*, who never hurt anyone. Isn't there enough suffering in this city? Don't you even care?"

Melchior laughed. "Why should I?"

I didn't know what to say to that. Melchior just looked amused. "These people you think so highly of, Christopher, were just yesterday ready to tear you apart in the street. I could have told them to rip your heart out and eat it, and they would have knifed each other in the back for the scraps." He shook his head. "That's what you'll never understand. *You* may care, but they don't. Not about you, or me, or anything except their own hides. You learn a lot as an actor: how men operate, their machinery, how their gears grind and tick. It's family first, Christopher—and the worst of them don't even care about that."

Melchior continued, smiling. But an edge had crept into his voice. "Look at what they do. Oh, they pack the churches well enough, make a grand show of giving charity, to be sure. But look at what they *do*. When a riot breaks out at the market, do they band together, protect each other? Or do they use the chaos to scrabble and steal what they can? When they're quarantined, do they stay sealed away, for the good of the city? Or do they kill the guards to escape, crowing 'better them than me'? When the city's children are in trouble, are there Miles Gaspars at every corner, starving themselves so their little ones can eat? Or are those children left alone in the streets, poor and hungry, abandoned as prey for the worst kind of men you can imagine?"

And that was it.

There, in his voice. The anger, the bitterness, the barely tempered rage.

"That was you," I said.

"What was?"

"Children, in the streets. Poor and hungry. That was you. Your parents . . . they abandoned you? In London's last plague? Left you and your brother to fend for your-selves?"

Melchior said nothing for a moment. When he finally spoke, it was with a strange blend of admiration and anger. "So very clever, you are."

"That *was* you," I said, amazed.

His eyes flashed. "Don't overdo it, Christopher. Yes, we lived on the streets. But not for long. A young actor took us in, taught us what we could become. He'd already learned from his own hard life that you'd never starve selling hope to the hopeless."

But now I saw the truth. "This isn't about money," I said. "This is *revenge*."

Melchior shrugged. "Pays well either way."

I thought of Sally, of me, of the children in Cripplegate. Of the children who had nowhere to live at all. The anger, the shame. Being alone, being unwanted. I understood it. Every orphan did.

And I wondered: If instead of Master Benedict, I'd met Melchior's young actor . . . would I have ended up the same?

I thought again of Sally. She'd lost everything, and soon she'd be on the streets, too. Yet she hadn't come to my home to steal; she'd come to help. I was no Master Benedict; I had no future to give her. Still she helped, for no other reason than because she could. She was nothing like them. She could never be.

"You're monsters," I said. "And you'll pay for what you've done."

"Oh, Christopher." Melchior laughed. "I'm going to regret killing you."

His voice was smooth again, pleasant again. He'd put that friendly mask back on. But for an instant, his composure had slipped.

Push him, I thought. *Push him further. Keep him off balance until everyone arrives. It's the best chance you have of staying alive.*

Then I heard a sound coming from the hall behind him. Footfalls.

My relief faded as I watched Melchior. He didn't appear troubled by who was approaching. I saw why as soon as the man came into view.

Melchior looked at me, amused. "Not who you were hoping for, I see."

It was Galen. He was wearing the same ingredient-stained clothes as always; he looked the same man. But I finally understood what Tom had seen, locked away with him in my workshop. Galen's mask had slipped, too, and behind it was something most cruel.

He looked at me as if I were a bug—one in dire need of being squashed. "What's he doing here?"

Melchior didn't like that. "Following clues *you* left."

"So why is he still breathing?"

Galen came toward me. I stepped back, bumping into the shelf in the center of the room. It creaked, trembled, and teetered, and for a second I thought it would topple and do Galen's job for him.

Melchior put a hand out. "Stop that. I still haven't learned everything he knows."

"What could he know?" Galen said.

"Quite a lot, it seems. What else did you let slip?"

"To this one? Nothing. I only ever spoke to that big, dumb ox he calls a friend."

Then, farther back in the hallway, I saw a different figure in the shadows.

"I wouldn't call Tom that, if I were you," I said.

Galen sneered. "Why not?"

"Because he's standing right behind you." I nodded toward the doorway. "And I'm pretty sure he's holding a crossbow."

CHAPTER
44

BOTH OF THEM STARED AT ME, AS if trying to read whether or not I was lying. Then, slowly, they turned.

I wasn't lying. Behind them, taking up half the width of the corridor with his bulk, stood Tom. He held the assassin's weapon—Melchior's weapon—cocked, loaded, and pointed directly at them.

"Yes," I said. "That's definitely a crossbow."

Melchior smiled. "Clever again. You left a lookout outside? In case anyone came before you got out?"

"That's right." I pointed at the corner farthest from the door. "Now get over there."

Melchior shrugged. He made as if to move.

Galen grabbed his arm. "No."

"Do I have to point out the crossbow again?" I said.

Galen ignored me. He spoke to his brother, keeping his eyes on Tom. "He won't shoot. He only looks big. Inside, he's just a little mouse."

Tom's hands tightened around the weapon. Sweat beaded his upper lip. He jerked his aim from brother to brother, hands shaking, fingers on the trigger. He sent a pleading glance toward me. I tried to will him a message. *Just hold them a little longer. Just a little longer.*

But my own worries were growing. Galen could read Tom as easily as Melchior had read me. And where on Earth was Sally? She should have been here already.

When we had been alone, Melchior had been entirely content to wait. Even now, with Tom holding a crossbow on them, Melchior didn't seem particularly concerned. Was that just the actor's mask? Or was it something else? His earlier words echoed in my skull. *You got a couple things wrong—some important things, actually—but close enough.*

What had I missed?

I needed to figure that out. In the meantime, I didn't like this situation at all. Tom was shaking like a leaf in the hallway, Melchior and Galen were blocking the door, and I was stuck in the middle of the storage room. Maybe boldness would work.

"Tom's saved my life twice already," I said. "You want to test him? Go ahead."

Melchior turned toward me, leaving the bolt pointing at his back. "There's only one crossbow."

"So?"

"So he can only shoot once. After that . . . as I told you, Christopher, we're rather good with our knives. If one of us dies, *both* of you will."

I tried to look casual. "Then I guess all you have to do is decide which one of you will take the bolt."

Melchior stared at me. Then he laughed. "Are you sure you won't take that job?" When I didn't answer, he folded his arms. "Then we wait. This should be interesting."

Galen didn't seem to agree. There was a coiled intensity to him, like a tiger who's just realized the door to his cage is open. Tom saw it, too. He stopped moving the crossbow between them and trained it squarely on Galen's chest.

Yet I didn't think Galen was the more dangerous of the two. The way Melchior watched me, amused, made me even more worried. Did he think Tom and I would come alone? Did he think we couldn't get help?

Or did he not care because help of his own was coming?

You got a couple things wrong. Important things.

I felt a flutter of panic. *His men,* I realized. But no, that couldn't be right. His men didn't know who he really was. He'd never bring them here to see this.

The more scared I got, the more Melchior's smile widened. *He's reading me again,* I thought. That made my guts squirm even worse. His smile got a little wider.

I've made a mistake. And that mistake makes Melchior feel safe.

What had I missed?

I didn't get any more time to think about it. From behind Tom, three other people appeared.

Sally stepped forward, into the light, panting, out of breath. Then came Henry, behind her. A third man, a city guard, looked a little puzzled at the scene before him.

My heart sank. One guard? That's all Sally could convince Henry to bring?

The little man blinked through his spectacles. He looked at the crossbow in Tom's hands, at Galen and Melchior in the doorway to the storeroom, at me by the shelf in the middle. Finally, his eyes fell on the gold coins scattered around my feet.

"Good Lord," he said. "If I hadn't seen it, I wouldn't have believed it."

Melchior hadn't stopped smiling. Why was he still smiling?

The guard remained puzzled. "I don't understand, Mr. Cole. What's going on here?"

"It appears that these three children—oh, never mind," Henry said.

Melchior winked at me.

And my guts dropped.

CHAPTER
45

"TOM—!" I BEGAN.

Henry twitched his wrist. A blade slipped from under his cuff into his left hand. The steel glinted as he slashed it upward, slicing through the string on the crossbow.

The string lashed back, whipping across Tom's neck. The crossbow sprang from his hands and cracked in two on the floor. Tom collapsed next to it, choking, his hand pressed against his throat.

Tom, was all I had time to think.

Henry whirled on the guard. The man didn't even move as Henry plunged the knife into him, three quick strikes to the heart. The guard simply crumpled to the floor, that puzzled expression never leaving his face.

I stood there, frozen in shock. Sally tried to back away, but Henry grabbed her hair. She squealed as he yanked her head back and pressed his blade to her throat.

The threat finally freed me from paralysis. "Wait!" I shouted.

I didn't get the chance to say more. Galen barreled into me, driving his fist into my gut. I crashed into the central shelf, making the wobbly supports groan and crack. Galen punched me again and I collapsed, doubled over, gasping for air.

Galen drew his blade from his belt. He pulled my ear, twisting it painfully. He brought my head up—my neck, exposed.

"No!" Melchior grabbed his arm. "I've not finished questioning him."

Back in the corridor, Tom lay huddled against the wall, fingers pressed against his neck. He stared dumbly at the floor, still stunned by the cord that had lashed his throat. I felt just the same.

The whole time. Henry was in on it the whole time.

Sally writhed in the little man's grasp. "Let me go!"

Henry shook her by her hair and pressed his blade to her lips. "Be quiet. Or I'll cut out your tongue."

She went silent. But her eyes smoldered. If only she'd had a knife of her own.

I glanced over at Tom. He was heaving, trying to catch his breath. The guard's body lay next to him.

Melchior crouched beside me. He pushed Galen's hand from my ear, helped me sit up against the teetering shelf.

"I did try to warn you," he said to me. "You did very well when you figured out that we'd poisoned Aldebourne's daughters. But you forgot: neither Galen nor I had ever been to the magistrate's house. So when you realized we'd poisoned the girls, you should have asked yourself *how*."

"Henry," I said, finally able to speak. Henry, Aldebourne's clerk. I remembered what he'd told us, the first day we met him. *I've been delivering him work at his home.* "Henry poisoned them. He was with you from the start."

"Quite literally. *He* was the actor who rescued us from the streets. He raised us, taught us how to read people. This whole plan was his. And we couldn't have pulled it off without him." Melchior waved his hand around the room. "After all, *someone* had to approve the false receipts, so it looked like real ingredients were being bought instead of all this flour."

"That's enough," Henry said.

Melchior stood. "Yes, Father."

Henry scowled at me. The kindly, fussy old man was gone, as much a mask as Melchior's plague doctor's beak. "Should have minded your own bloody business," he said.

Galen huffed. "Are we going to get rid of them or not?"

"If we disappear," I said, my voice tight, "there'll be questions."

Henry shook his head. "Not likely. There's no one left who cares about you."

"Tom has a family."

"And you took him from a plague house. Everyone will believe he died somewhere on the streets. As for you?" Henry shrugged. "You fled the city after you escaped the gibbet. And no one will even remember the girl. No, Christopher. Your time is up."

Henry nodded to his boys. "Kill him."

CHAPTER
46

GALEN GRABBED MY THROAT. HE
brought the blade up.

"Don't let them do this," I croaked to Melchior. "You
need me."

Melchior arched an eyebrow. "I can't say I'll be pleased
to see you go, Christopher, and I don't doubt you'd be useful. But that's hardly the same as needing you."

"Yet you still do," I said. Galen laid his knife against
my neck. I could feel its edge; sharp, cold, pressing with the
pulse of my arteries. "Kill me, and you'll never get out of
London alive."

Neither Henry nor Galen looked inclined to listen. But

Melchior stayed his brother's hand. "And why is that?"

"Because Henry wasn't the only one I told about you."

Now even Melchior looked skeptical. "Who else could you have told?"

"Someone a little more reliable," I said, speaking as fast as I could. "After the way Henry refused to stand up to you yesterday at Guildhall, I suspected his help might not be enough."

"He's obviously lying," Galen said.

Melchior studied me. "Yes, he is. A good try, Christopher, but I simply don't believe you."

"Then ask him." I nodded at Henry. "He knows."

"Knows what?" Henry said coldly.

"Who I went to. Who's coming for you now."

"This is a waste of—" Suddenly, Henry laughed. "Surely you don't mean Dr. Parrett?"

Sally stiffened and twisted in his hands. Henry shook her and pressed the knife against her throat, still laughing.

"Mad old John Parrett! Perhaps you haven't noticed, but Parrett has broken. He could stand atop Saint Paul's, surrounded by trumpeting angels, and still no one would listen to a word he says."

"I'm not talking about Dr. Parrett," I said. "Don't you

remember when I first came to you for help? Who I was there for?"

"Parrett brought you."

"No, Dr. Parrett brought me to *you*. But I was at Guildhall on someone else's orders."

Henry thought about it.

Then his grin faltered.

"You *do* remember," I said.

Henry's smile remained, but his eyes were no longer amused. "You're lying."

"Who's he talking about?" Galen said.

"No one. He's lying." Henry's smile had completely disappeared now. "Ashcombe's not even in the city."

Melchior blinked. Galen's eyes widened. "*Lord* Ashcombe?" he sputtered. "Father—"

"Quiet." Henry glared at me. "You're bluffing."

"Where do you think I hid last night?" I said. "The square was right next to the Tower."

"No one's left at the Tower."

"One guard is. Who has the authority to send a courier to Oxford."

"Lord Ashcombe's in Salisbury," Melchior said.

"He *was* in Salisbury," I said, "but the plague has struck

Wiltshire, so they're moving the Court to Oxford. Ashcombe's been there since Wednesday, preparing a new place for the king."

Melchior and Galen looked at Henry, alarmed. Henry seemed even more shaken that I knew the plans of the King's Warden. "No," he said. "No. The Tower's sealed at night."

"Not to friends of Lord Ashcombe. Go ask the guard. I'll wait." I made a show of ticking numbers off my fingers. "Let's see . . . five hours for the courier to ride to Oxford with the letter I wrote. Half an hour for Lord Ashcombe to gather the King's Men. Another five hours to return— maybe six, those men are armored . . ." I raised an eyebrow at Henry. "What time is it now?"

"Lies," Henry whispered.

"Is this possible?" Galen said.

Melchior stared at me. "What was in the letter?"

"Your names, your descriptions, and how you pulled off your plot," I said. "Your secret message about Magistrate Eastwood, with the code needed to break it. And the method you used to poison your victims so it looked like the plague."

"Ah." Melchior relaxed. "You *are* lying. You haven't the faintest idea how we poisoned them."

"You mean the volohosy?"

Henry turned white. "Wh-what did you say?"

"Volohosy," I said, as matter-of-factly as I could. "That bamboo from Madagascar. It produces the symptoms of the sickness. Except for the sweats, of course. Those you caused by mixing in a high dose of horehound."

Their eyes bulged.

"The antidote is simple," I said. "Just powdered charcoal and sugar. I'm curious: Did you go to Madagascar yourselves, or did you get the volohosy straight from Captain Gaillart?"

Suddenly, all three of them were shouting at one another.

"What did you tell him?" Henry screamed.

Melchior looked flustered. "Nothing. I never mentioned it. He must have got it from his master."

"You said he hadn't any volohosy!"

"He hadn't. I checked—I swear!"

Henry rounded on Galen. "Then what did *you* say?"

Galen screamed back. "Don't blame me for this! I've barely even spoken to him! *You* were the one who made me work at Blackthorn!"

I cleared my throat. "Sorry to interrupt, but you're

running out of time. I'll make you a deal. You let us go, give back the money you've stolen, then leave the city and never come back. I'll convince Lord Ashcombe not to follow you, kill you, and stick your heads on the pikes on London Bridge."

The brothers' expressions told me they were imagining precisely that scenario.

"This is over," Galen said. "The play is done. We take what we have and leave."

"No," Henry said.

"It's seven hundred pounds!"

"And we'll have ten times that in two weeks!"

"Father!"

"NO!" Henry pressed the knife into Sally's neck. She squirmed as a drop of blood swelled at the blade's tip. It trickled down her throat, staining her collar.

"Thirteen years," Henry said. "Plotting. Planning. *Waiting.* Thirteen *years* I waited for plague to finally strike this city. *And I will not be undone by a bloody child!*"

"But if Ashcombe is coming—" Melchior said.

"He is *not*! The boy is lying! He has to be!"

"We don't know that!" Galen said.

"Then wring the truth from his miserable little neck!"

Galen took the command literally. He grabbed me by the throat, hauling me up. He held me against the shelf in the center of the storeroom. It trembled, scattering flour dust into my eyes. He squeezed. I clawed at his hands, gasping.

"Put him down," Melchior said.

Galen gave a little extra squeeze before he dropped me. I wobbled and fell to my knees.

Melchior crouched next to me. "You've played a brilliant game, Christopher. Genuinely masterful. But now is the time for truth. And remember: I can read you."

That was the thing I was most afraid of. Because Henry was right.

I *was* lying.

I'd never called for Lord Ashcombe. The Tower *was* sealed at night, and I had no way inside. Even if I had, I doubted the guard even knew who I was. He'd certainly never arrange an overnight courier to Lord Ashcombe. Magistrate Maycott was my only link to the King's Warden, and Henry had never made the arrangements to introduce me.

I had one way out, and one way only. I had to convince them that keeping us alive might protect them from Ashcombe's wrath.

But I didn't know how to do that.

Melchior placed his finger under my chin and tilted my head toward him. "Tell me, Christopher. Is Lord Ashcombe on his way? Did you really write that letter?"

I didn't know what to say.

Oh, Master, what do I do?

And I heard his voice.

Calm, Christopher, he said. *The answer is in your mind. How do you find it?*

The response came automatically. *I step out of the way,* I said. *And let my mind find the answer for me.*

Let my *mind* find the answer.

That was it.

Melchior could read people, yes. But not because he was a prophet. He just understood human nature. If he could read me, it was because he could see the truth on my face.

But a man's expression only came from what he thought. What I needed to do was believe the lie.

So I imagined what I wanted to see.

I imagined Lord Ashcombe as I told him what these three had done to his city. I saw his black eye glow, his scar twist, his three-fingered hand wrap around the hilt of his sword. I watched him unleash the full measure of his wrath to rip them apart.

And I threw that back at Melchior.

"Wait and see," I said.

Melchior stared.

"Well?" Henry said. "Is he lying?"

I burned with revenge for my city. For the children of Cripplegate, for Aldebourne's daughter. For every soul they'd taken, every penny they'd stolen from the people who needed it the most. I sent those flames to Melchior. I incinerated him in the blaze.

And underneath, I prayed.

Please, Master. Help me.

Melchior sat back on his haunches, amazed. "I . . . I can't tell."

Henry looked from me to Melchior, uncertain what to do. For a moment, I thought he might order them to flee.

But Galen spoke. "Then we'll have to cut the truth out of him after all."

"No," Melchior said. "That won't work." He looked at me curiously. "Will it, Christopher? That's why I didn't torture you when I captured you the other night. There wasn't any point. I knew you wouldn't say where you'd hidden your friend." He smiled ruefully. "Of course, that doesn't mean I learned *nothing.*"

"I didn't tell you anything," I said.

"But you did. You forget, Christopher, we've spent our whole lives taking advantage of people. It's surprisingly simple. All you need to do is find their weakness. And when, despite your terror, you refused to tell me where Tom was, I learned yours."

He stood and pointed at my friends, back in the corridor.

"It's them," Melchior said. "Even if we cut you to make you talk—and we *would* make you talk—that might take too long. I know how to get the answer much quicker."

He nodded toward Tom and Sally. "We won't torture you, Christopher. We'll torture *them*. And we'll make you watch the whole thing."

CHAPTER
47

"TELL US WHAT WE WANT TO know," Melchior said softly. "Or they die. Slowly."

I didn't know what to do. I knew they'd kill us either way. I also knew they'd readily torture my friends.

Henry wasn't willing to wait to find out. "No?" he said. "Then which one will be first? The girl?" He pressed the knife farther into Sally's neck. More blood dripped down to stain her dress. "Would you prefer to hear her scream? Or shall I begin by carving up the ox?"

He waved the knife at Tom.

And that was his biggest mistake.

The instant the point was off Sally's neck, the Cripple-gate girl came out, like a snake shedding its skin. She grabbed the arm holding her and twisted her head, ripping her hair out by its roots. The pain didn't slow her. She just shrieked.

Then she bit him.

Her teeth sank deep into his wrist. Henry screamed, pure agony. Instinctively, he brought the knife back, drove it toward her neck.

It didn't make it. A heavy fist reached out and grabbed him. From the ground, Tom, bloodied and bowed, held Henry's arm, wouldn't let go.

Henry howled. Sally's teeth still in his flesh, she flailed at his face, raking her fingernails across his eyes like a cornered cat. Henry flailed back in response. He slammed her against the wall, shook the girl loose. Then a swinging palm caught her in the back of the head, driving her face forward into the stone.

Even from the center of the storeroom, I heard the crunch of bone. Blood flowed from her nose. She slumped to the ground, face against the wall, her head twisted to the side.

Sally! was the only despairing thought I could manage. Then I had no time for thought at all.

The girl down, Henry beat his free hand against Tom. Galen sprang forward, running into the hallway to help his father. Melchior whirled on me.

The blade in Melchior's belt was suddenly in his hand. The steel flashed in the lamplight, arcing toward my exposed neck. On pure instinct, I twisted and dropped to my knees. I felt a hot streak against my temple before I hit the floor.

There wasn't any pain. I remember thinking that was strange, because I knew I was cut. Blood dripped into my left eye. Blinking it away, I looked up to see Melchior launch himself at me. We went down together, his knee in my gut, his blade aimed at my heart.

I tried to slide out of the way. It wasn't enough. The blade missed my heart, sank into my left shoulder instead.

That, I felt. I howled. Melchior drew the knife out. He grabbed my collar, raised the blade again.

He was going to get me this time—I knew that. I tried to grope under my shirt, where my hidden apothecary sash held weapons aplenty, but Melchior's knee was in the way. So I used the only weapon I had left.

Gravity.

The shelf in the center of the storeroom had been threatening to fall since I'd entered. I granted its wish. I kicked at it, throwing every ounce of might behind my foot. The heel of my boot splintered the corner leg. The shelf shuddered and gave off a groan.

That groan saved me. For the briefest moment, Melchior halted, turned to look at what I'd done. He saw the old, worn wood teetering, then tipping, then toppling toward us. And with it came forty sacks of flour.

It crashed into the shelf against the wall. Under the weight of the flour, both shelves splintered into toothpicks. The sacks fell, hitting the ground with a thunderous *whump*.

And then the world was white.

I couldn't see. I couldn't breathe. The *air* was flour. It stung my eyes, like I'd been buried alive. It filled my lungs, as if I'd tried to inhale the desert. I choked and coughed, and each hacking breath brought more of the sweet scent inside, caking my nose, my tongue.

I spat it out, blinked it away. I could still barely see. The sacks had crushed my lantern, so the only light left in the storeroom came from the lamp in the corridor, glowing the faintest haze through the cloud of flour-air.

A form shifted, shivered, sat up. It must have been Melchior, because that's who'd been there before. I'd never have recognized him, even in better light. Like me, he was coated in flour. He looked like a living ghost.

In the midst of that white, I saw his own eyes blink, his own mouth open and cough. Three black circles in a mask of ivory, a thing of nightmares.

And there was his blade, a nightmare all its own. Melchior's eyes focused on the growing red stain on my shoulder, my blood seeping into the flour to form a bright pink paste. He swung the knife at me. I fell back, felt the blade cut my shoulder again.

This time, I had a different weapon to use in defense. I tangled my fingers in one of the half-spilled sacks of flour lying on top of me. Melchior brought his blade back to plunge into me once more.

I drove the sack into his face. I poured it into him. His eyes, his nose, his mouth filled with powder. He dropped the knife and clawed at my arms. I ignored his feeble beating and drowned him in flour; shoved it in until nothing was left. Let him choke on it.

Melchior fell backward, heaving. I scanned the flour on

the floor for his discarded knife, but I couldn't see it. I could barely see anything.

Melchior thrashed, hacked, started to clear his lungs. Never mind the knife, then. It was time to go.

I tried to stand. My heel slipped in the flour. I reached out for something, anything, grabbed one of the shelves nearby that was still standing, used it to haul myself up. I heard that wood creak and groan, too, and I waited for the second collapse.

It didn't come. Melchior, still lying on the ground, clutched at my feet. My hands found a sack on a shelf that hadn't fallen with the others. I flung it at him. I felt rather than saw the burst, adding more flour to the air, as if there were any more room in it for powder.

It worked. He let go. I stepped over him, tripping on broken sacks, slipping and sliding in the flour. I staggered toward the haze coming from the corridor, where everyone else had been when the world turned white.

Each step was like swimming through earth. The air choked me like it wanted me to die. My legs wobbled, and only one thought kept me upright. *I have to help my friends.*

I saw the doorframe too late in the haze, bumped my

nose into it. *No harm done,* I thought. It was my shoulder that was in real trouble. Me, too, if I didn't bandage it soon. The blood still pumped from underneath the flour. Idly, I wondered if the powder would cake the wound shut.

I stumbled into the corridor. The air was a haze here, too, though not nearly as bad. I spat out what I could from my lungs. I could see better, breathe better. And now I knew what had happened to everyone else.

Tom had recovered from the lashing from the crossbow string and had finally overpowered Henry, though not without injury. His shirt, sliced open at the waist, revealed a deep cut on his side, right over his liver. It looked terrible, but it didn't seem to be bothering him. He was holding the little man by his collar, dangling him half a foot above the ground. Henry kicked and cursed soundly at my friend, but there wasn't much he could do; his knife lay on the ground.

Under different circumstances, I might have thought this funny. But Tom wasn't the only one still on his feet. Galen, also covered in flour, had grabbed Sally. Once again, she had a knife to her throat. My heart leaped when I saw her twitch in his hands—Henry hadn't broken her neck, like I'd thought—but this time she wasn't going to free herself. Her movements were faint and feeble; she hung in the crook of his arm like a rag doll.

Galen spotted me coming from the storeroom behind him. He pressed against the wall. "Stay back!" Through his coughing and blinking away flour dust, he shouted at Tom. "Put my father down!"

"Let Sally go," Tom rumbled. He shook Henry. "I'll snap his neck if you don't."

Galen sneered. "I already know you're a mouse. You'll never do that. But I *will*."

Slowly, deliberately, Galen sliced his blade into Sally's forearm. Blood leaked from around the metal, dripping powdery pink bursts onto her shoes.

I coiled, ready to spring. Galen brought the knife back to Sally's throat.

"Don't even think about it," he said.

I did think about it. But I didn't move.

"I *will* kill her," Galen said to Tom. "You know I will. Now let my father go."

Tom looked at me, pleading.

I didn't know what to do. If he kept hold of Henry, Galen would definitely kill Sally. But if Tom let the man go they'd kill us all.

I heard scuffling behind me. Melchior, still alive, coming to join the fray.

I didn't know what to do.

"Fine," Galen said. "The girl dies."

And he began to thrust in the knife.

CHAPTER
48

VOICES.

Mine, shouting.

Tom's, bellowing.

Henry's, cursing.

And one more, echoing off the walls.

"STOP."

It came from beyond the haze. It seemed vaguely famil-iar, but I couldn't quite place it. When I saw the man, I realized it was because I'd never heard him speak so before.

Into the faint light stepped Dr. Parrett.

He looked even worse than we'd seen him last night. His clothes stuck to his body with sweat. His face was just as drenched, so wet that the flour in the air had already begun to clump in jagged white cracks over his skin. His whole body shook with a trembling fever.

But Galen *did* stop, for in Dr. Parrett's eyes was a murderous fury. And in his right hand was the flintlock pistol that could unleash it.

"Let Sally go," he said.

Galen hesitated.

Dr. Parrett lifted the pistol, placed the muzzle against Henry's temple. He sounded so calm. "Let. Sally. Go."

"John." Henry held out a hand, even as he dangled from Tom's grasp. "This isn't what you think—"

Dr. Parrett pressed the gun into Henry's head. "Sally brought me Christopher's note. And I know who I believe."

Henry looked just as murderous as Dr. Parrett. But he spoke to his son. "Let her go."

Galen released her, not kindly. She crumpled to the floor like an empty sack.

Dr. Parrett nodded at me. "Take her."

I did, scooping her up in my arms. I carried her past Dr. Parrett. He pressed against the wall, giving me room so I wouldn't have to touch him. All the while, he never took his eyes from the brothers.

Melchior stood with Galen now, still looking like a flour ghost. "This hasn't changed anything," he said to me. "Your side still has only one shot. And then you'll have to face *two* of us."

"I don't intend to fight you," Dr. Parrett said. "I only want you to let these children go. Then we can finish it all ourselves."

"No," I said. "You come with us."

Dr. Parrett shook his head. "I will not." He looked toward Henry. "Here's what's going to happen. The children will take you outside. Then they run away. After they've gone, you come back here, gather what you've already stolen, and all three of you flee the city forever. The children leave unharmed, and you have your gold." Dr. Parrett shuddered, his knees wobbled. He coughed fiercely and spat phlegm on the stone. "Do we have a deal?"

Henry eyed the doctor shrewdly. "This one," he said, jerking a thumb at Tom, "has to let me go first."

Dr. Parrett shook his head. "Not until they're outside."

Henry thought about it for a moment. "All right," he said. "But I walk out."

"Don't trust him," I said to Dr. Parrett.

But he just said, "Don't worry," and nodded at Tom.

After glancing at me, Tom let the little man down, keeping a hand on the back of his collar. Then he leaned in close. "We can't leave Dr. Parrett here," he whispered. "One shot won't be enough to stop them."

That wasn't half the problem. Dr. Parrett's sickness was weakening him by the second. He was slumped against the side of the corridor, shivering. If the wall hadn't been there, he would have hit the ground already.

The rest of them knew it, too. Melchior's eyes flicked from me to Tom to Dr. Parrett; I couldn't tell exactly what he was thinking. But Galen's expression was clear: The moment we were out of the way, they'd rush him. And pistol or not, he'd have no chance of fighting them off.

Still, they were hesitating. They knew as much about the plague as anyone, and Dr. Parrett clearly had the sickness, the *real* sickness. Would they actually try to grab him? I hoped not, because there was something far, far more dangerous they could unleash.

The air was full of flour. If Dr. Parrett pulled the trigger, the flintlock would spark. And with the flour dust in the air . . .

I glanced at the lantern on the wall. The only reason we hadn't blown up already was because the flame was shielded by glass. There'd be no such protection from the pistol.

I needed to warn my friends. And to do it without alerting the others.

"Campden's mill," I whispered back to Tom.

Tom looked puzzled.

"Last summer," I said. "Like in my Smoke-Your-Home."

His eyes went wide.

"Dr. Parrett—" I began.

And to my surprise, he said, "I know. Now listen. I've delivered your letter, the one Sally brought me. Take Henry outside. Then run. Run from this place, and don't look back."

Escape wasn't my only concern anymore. "You don't understand—"

"I do." Dr. Parrett nodded. "I heard what you said. Campden's mill."

I stared at him.

"I was still myself then," he said. He looked so small, slumped against that wall. "Before my James was killed. I went to Campden's mill. I helped treat the survivors. I know what will happen."

Henry was watching, listening, trying to make sense of

what we were saying. He'd told us he hadn't been in London last year. I prayed he hadn't lied about that, too.

"I'm sorry I didn't stand with you earlier," Dr. Parrett said. "When you came to my home, I should have helped you, and instead I turned you away. I am ashamed. Please forgive me."

"There's nothing to forgive," I said. " Dr. Parrett—"

He wouldn't look at me. "In case things don't go our way: Goodbye, Tom. Goodbye, Christopher. Since last summer, you've been my only true friends. I can't tell you how much that has comforted me. Thank you. For everything."

Dr. Parrett pushed himself off the wall, drew himself up, straightened his sweat-soaked doublet. "Now go. What happens from here is their choice." He waved his pistol toward them. "They can take their coins and leave you in peace. Or they can face the judgment of the Lord."

Galen looked furious. Melchior just gave me a half smile. "Farewell, Christopher," he said. I didn't wish him the same.

Melchior turned his eyes to Henry. "Father?"

"We have the money," Henry said with a shrug. "So

do as he says. We'll make for the copper city, under the statue."

Melchior nodded. Henry's face remained impassive.

That was not good. *Another code,* I thought. A secret phrase, appearing to say one thing but meaning another.

The problem was: What? Was it merely a location to escape to, like it sounded? Or something worse?

It didn't take long to find out.

My bleeding shoulder throbbed as I carried Sally's unconscious body. I walked backward out of the corridor, toward Galen's false workshop, keeping my eye on Melchior and Galen the whole time. Dr. Parrett had begun to slump again. His pistol wavered as he propped himself up against the wall.

We can't leave him there, I thought. *Melchior and Galen are going to jump him.*

Except I'd got it wrong again. I'd kept my eyes on the wrong person.

Tom was pushing Henry, prodding him forward in front of us. Suddenly, Henry stumbled. Off guard, Tom bumped into him, which knocked the man over farther. He fell to his knees.

Tom's response was automatic. "Sorry," he said, and reached out to help.

Henry's hand slipped inside his boot. He came up with another blade, sliced it backward.

Tom cried out. He pulled away, blood shining in a streak across his palm.

Henry drew back his arm. I couldn't react; I still carried Sally. Tom, off balance, was helpless.

But Tom wasn't Henry's target. He threw the knife past us. It tumbled through the haze.

Dr. Parrett had just started to turn toward the commotion. Henry's blade caught him in the back, halfway between his arm and his spine. He grunted in surprise and fell to his knees.

That was what Melchior had been waiting for. He rushed forward, grabbed the barrel of the pistol. He didn't struggle with it, or try to pull it out of Dr. Parrett's hand—worried, I assumed, about touching someone afflicted with the plague. Instead, Melchior just pushed the barrel of the pistol to the side and held it against the wall.

Melchior smiled. Galen grinned. Now the weapon was harmless.

Or so they thought.

Dr. Parrett sighed. Then he spoke. "Run, boys."

Holding Sally tight, I began to flee. Tom followed, pushing me forward.

When Dr. Parrett pulled the trigger, I didn't think Melchior understood. The hammer fell. The flint sparked. The gunpowder flared.

I turned the corner. I dived into the workshop.

I don't remember hitting the ground.

CHAPTER
49

I COULDN'T SEE.

Something was dragging me over rubble. It was big, and fearsome, with a shuffling gait, and for one groggy moment I thought I was back in Melchior's cell.

I flailed. Big hands steadied me. "It's all right," Tom said. "It's me."

I stopped struggling. My arm hurt. Everything hurt.

Tom dragged me a few feet more, until the sunlight finally fought through the haze. I lay in the street, catching my breath. When I raised my head, I saw what was left of the warehouse.

Almost nothing. The front of the building was still more or less standing, but the half where the storeroom had been had collapsed entirely into broken stones, a few scattered flames, and smoke. The windows of the warehouse opposite had shattered, chunks torn away from its painted face, crumbled at one corner where flying debris had left its mark.

We didn't look much better. Both Tom and I were covered with stone dust and dirt. His face was crusted with dried blood from a long gash on his forehead. His shirt was half gone, charred cloth burned away, the skin on his back red and blistered, another wound to add to the cut in his side. I could see he was favoring his right leg.

I didn't feel much better. My own blade wound in my shoulder throbbed mercilessly. The pain in my forearm was even worse, growing ever more steadily unbearable. I was pretty sure it was broken. The ache in my skull matched it. I hoped that wasn't broken, too.

"Where's Sally?" I said.

Tom pointed. She lay behind me, next to the wall of one of the nearby warehouses. Like the rest of us, she was covered in gray dust. Her nose, bent to the left, trickled blood. She rolled over and moaned, holding her side.

It was a stupid question, but I asked it anyway. "Dr. Parrett?"

Tom didn't answer. He didn't have to. Dr. Parrett—along with Melchior and Galen—had been at the center of the exploding flour. It would have taken a miracle for him to survive. And London had been painfully short on miracles this year.

I reached up and held Tom's arm. He clasped his hand over mine and bowed his head. We stayed there, together, for a quite a while.

The three of us weren't the only survivors. Though a little closer to the blast, Henry had made it out, too. He crawled from the rubble and slumped against the building opposite, one leg twisted awkwardly underneath him. He stared back at the wreckage, dazed, muttering. He seemed to be saying the same thing, over and over again, but he was too far away for me to hear.

I tried to climb to my feet. The world spun. Gently, Tom pushed me back down.

"You shouldn't move," he said.

I tried again. "We can't let Henry get away."

Tom sighed. Like me, he just wanted this to be over. Nonetheless, he started to limp toward the man. He only took a few steps before he stopped. From all directions, a crowd approached.

Of course. The explosion would have shaken the area. The people of London, hiding in their homes, had come out to see what had happened. They surrounded us, blinking their eyes at the dust and smoke like the first time they'd ever seen the sun. A few of them ran down to the Thames, collecting pails full of water to put out the dwindling fires. The rest of them just stood there and stared.

I was surprised to see a contingent of city guards among the crowd. I was even more surprised to see the man who pushed his way between them, holding an opened letter.

It was Magistrate Aldebourne. Like the rest of them, he stared at the rubble for a moment. Then he spotted me and came over. I recognized the paper he was carrying: It was the letter I'd given to Dr. Parrett, in the hope that he'd send it to Lord Ashcombe. It appeared that Aldebourne was the route Dr. Parrett had chosen.

Wordlessly, Magistrate Aldebourne held the letter out to me. I was too tired to speak, so I just nodded and motioned to the fallen warehouse.

Aldebourne spotted his clerk slumped nearby. "Henry. Henry!" he said, but the little man just kept muttering to himself.

I found my voice. "If you speak to him," I said to the magistrate, "he'll only tell you more lies."

Magistrate Aldebourne frowned. Again, he held out the letter. "And this is the truth?"

"Yes."

He shook his head. "It's too terrible. I won't believe it. It simply cannot be."

I pointed to the rubble. "If you clear away those stones, you'll find your proof."

"Which is?"

"Around seven hundred guineas," I said.

Magistrate Aldebourne blinked. Then he turned to the city guards. "Start digging."

They moved to obey him. After a moment, Aldebourne called two of them back. He motioned toward Henry. "Watch him."

They needn't have bothered. Henry wasn't going any-where. He just stared despondently at the guards clearing away the rubble, saying the same thing over and over. For a while, the sound of tumbling rocks and the buzzing of the crowd drowned him out. Then the wind shifted, and I could finally hear his words.

"My boys," he said. "My boys."

SEPTEMBER 6 TO
SEPTEMBER 10, 1665

Total dead: 46,394

CHAPTER 50

IT DIDN'T TAKE LONG FOR ALDE-bourne to confirm what I'd said. After spotting dusty gold coins in the remains of the warehouse, the magistrate told us we were free to go. The guards redoubled their efforts to uncover the stolen charity, minus the two men Aldebourne directed to haul Henry away.

I wished someone would haul *us* away. My forearm throbbed so badly that I couldn't feel anything else—which, judging from the growing bruises all over my body, was probably a mercy. Sally was in too much pain to walk at all. My broken arm and Tom's injured leg made it impossible to carry her. In a bit of turnaround, Tom found a wheelbarrow next to an abandoned house and put her inside, limping behind it all the way.

I walked beside him quietly, praying we'd get home before I passed out. Halfway there, Sally looked up at us and broke the silence, hooting through her mashed-up nose.

"You two look terrible," she said.

My chest spasmed. "Don't make me laugh," I said. "It hurts."

We took care of the damage at Blackthorn. Sally had got the worst of it. She'd finally broken those ribs, so a bandage went around her chest. Also, apart from the obvious problem of the cut on her arm and her broken nose, one of her cheekbones had cracked. After much poppy and even more yowling, I set her nose and bandaged her face, wrapping cloth around her head.

Her badly blackened eyes peeked out from inside the dressing. It made her look so much like one of my master's stuffed animals—a raccoon brought back from the New World—that as a joke, Tom started leaving the beast around the house so she'd come upon it as a surprise. In retribution, Sally cut the stitches in the back of his breeches while he slept, so now everywhere he went his drawers were exposed. I, of course, said nothing, though my occasional bursts of laughter made Tom increasingly suspicious.

Certainly, my body gave me nothing to smile about. I'd taken a beating almost as bad as Sally's. Tom splinted my broken forearm and helped me dress the knife wounds in my shoulder with spiderweb and honey. My whole left arm felt weak and numb, but being able to feel it at all was good—though for the next few days I wished otherwise. Still, if I managed to keep the wound clear of infection, I wouldn't have to lose the arm. I prayed every day for that.

Though Tom had been the closest to the blast, he'd fared the best of us all. He was badly bruised and burned—the entire back of his body was covered with yellow-purple splotches and blisters—and his right knee swelled like a bladder, but that was the extent of the damage from the explosion. Fortunately, the cuts he'd taken in the fight weren't too deep, though the gash on his neck from the crossbow string would leave quite a scar. The one I'd really been worried about, the knife wound over his liver, wasn't nearly as bad as it looked. The blade had gone into the flesh, but blessedly missed all of the vital organs beneath.

In the best shape of anyone, Tom took it upon himself to look after us, changing everyone's bandages and preparing our meals. Worried about what his family was thinking, he sent a message to their ship on the Thames, explaining he didn't have the plague after all. His mother wrote back a tearstained letter, telling him to join them on the boat right away. When her message came, Tom sat beside me in the workshop, reading it over and over.

"You can go if you want," I said, though my stomach twisted at the thought. "Sally and I can manage."

"They made the right choice, didn't they?" Tom said, still staring at the letter. "Leaving me behind, I mean. When they thought I was sick."

"There was no way they could have known the truth."

Tom nodded. "It was the right choice. I would never have forgiven myself if I'd given the sickness to my sisters." He glanced over at me. "You should have stayed away, too."

"And miss all this?" I waved at my wounded arm. "Never."

He looked at me again.

"Never," I said. "Ever."

Tom turned the letter facedown on the workbench. "Can I use your quill?"

His reply to his family was to the point.

I love you. I miss you all so much, and I pray for you every day. But I'm staying with Christopher.

                                                    Tom

We heard about Henry. The whole city learned of the con he, Melchior, and Galen had tried to pull. I worried that there would be riots, but surprisingly, nothing happened.

Well, almost nothing. Aldebourne announced that he planned to put his former clerk on trial. With the courts still closed, the people decided not to wait. They marched on Newgate Prison, broke into Henry's cell, and dragged him into the streets. I think they'd intended to put him in the gibbet, but they never made it that far.

It was over by the time they reached Cheapside. I heard some of them kept souvenirs of that day, to put in lockets, as talismans to fight the plague.

The following Thursday, a courier came by Blackthorn and summoned me to Guildhall. I went with bandaged shoulder and splinted arm in a sling, body aching all the way.

Magistrate Aldebourne took me into his office. He sat across from me, his desk between us covered with open letters.

"How are you feeling?" he asked.

"I think I'll get to keep the arm," I said. "Have you recovered the money Henry stole?"

"Most of it. Some of the coins were thrown across town when the warehouse exploded. I've been hearing rumors of people finding guineas in the streets." He smiled briefly. "That's not the only good news."

He pulled a paper from one of his desk drawers and pushed it toward me. It was the latest Bill of Mortality, just printed this morning. There was only one line I was interested in.

The Diseases and Casualties this Week.

		Grief	1
		Griping in the Guts	45
		Head-mould-shot	
		Jaundies	3
		Imposthume	6
		Infants	10
Abortive	23	Kingsevil	1
Aged	57	Lethargy	1
Bedridden	1	Meagrome	1
Bleeding	1	Plague	6544
Cancer	1	Plannet	1
Childbed	39	Quinsie	1
Chrisomes	20	Rickets	20
Collick	1	Rising of the Lights	15
Consumption	129	Rupture	4
Convulsion	71	Scowring	3
Dropsie	31	Scurvy	2
Drowned 3. one at Stepney, one at St. Katharine near the Tower, and one at St. Margaret Westminster	3	Spotted Feaver	97
		Stone	1
		Stopping of the stomach	5
		Strangury	2
Feaver	332	Surfeit	45
Flox and Small-pox	8	Teeth	128
Found dead in the street at St. Olave Southwark	1	Thrush	6
		Timpany	1
French-pox	1	Tissick	4
Frighted	1	Ulcer	1
Gangrene	1	Vomiting	2
		Wormes	15

Christned { Males — 90 ; Females — 78 ; In all — 168 } Buried { Males — 3783 ; Females — 3907 ; In all — 7696 } Plague — 6544

Decreased in the Burials this Week — 562
Parishes clear of the Plague — 11 Parishes Infected — 119

The Assize of Bread set forth by Order of the Lord Maior and Court of Aldermen; A penny Wheaten Loaf to contain Nine Ounces and a half, and three half-penny White Loaves the like weight.

6,544 dead of the plague this week. It remained a terrible number. And it still undercounted the true deaths quite a bit. Nonetheless . . .

"This week's count is lower," I said.

Magistrate Aldebourne nodded. "The sickness has started to ebb."

For the first time in months, I felt hope. There were hard days yet in front of us—hard months, really—but our prayers had finally been answered. Our city would survive after all.

Magistrate Aldebourne and I just sat there for a while. Neither of us really wanted to bring up why I was here. He spoke first, with a sigh, spreading his hands over the letters on his desk. "They fooled us all."

"What are those?" I said.

"Back in June," Aldebourne said, "Jonathan Wills, my longtime clerk and friend, died of the plague. Or so we thought. In retrospect, he'd probably been poisoned, because that very day Henry presented himself to me, sitting right in that chair, offering his help. He came with these." Aldebourne indicated the letters on the desk. "The most impeccable references, attesting to his ability and trustworthiness. All forged, no doubt. I didn't even bother to check them."

"Henry was counting on you being desperate," I said.

"He was right. At the time, I believed the man was a gift from God. For my foolishness, so many have paid. Including my own daughter."

He bowed his head. "We cannot return the dead to life. But we have rescued most of the charity. This is for you." He placed a leather pouch in front of me on the desk.

"What is it?" I said.

"A reward," he said. "For saving the city. It's thirty guineas, five percent of the funds recovered."

Thirty . . . *guineas*? I stared at the pouch. I took it, held it, felt its weight press into my hand.

Thirty guineas. This would erase all my financial worries. For years.

I laid the pouch back down. "I . . . I can't take it," I said.

Aldebourne's eyebrows shot up. "Why not?"

I felt sick. "It's . . . I want to. But it's blood money."

"I approved it with the Lord Mayor. He wants you to have it."

"It doesn't matter," I said, a hollow gnawing in my gut. "The only reason you're offering me this is because that money was stolen in the first place. It's supposed to help the city. I can't take it." What would Master Benedict think of me if I did?

Magistrate Aldebourne looked like he didn't know what to do with my response. "Well . . . is there anything you do want?"

When the answer came to me, I nearly leaped from my chair.

"Yes," I said, and I told him.

He seemed even more surprised. "Is that all?"

I shook my head. "Your men. Did they find Dr. Parrett's body?"

"Yes."

"Then I want him to have a funeral in Saint Paul's Cathedral. And I want him buried in the cemetery at Bunhill Fields, next to his wife and son."

"That's not possible," Aldebourne said. "The funeral, yes. But the plague ordinances forbid the burial of bodies in anything other than plague pits during the sickness."

"I know what the ordinances say. It doesn't matter."

"It does matter."

I pushed the leather pouch toward the magistrate. "When Dr. Parrett's house burned down," I said, "and he lost himself in grief, this city abandoned him. Yet he *still* gave his life for it. He didn't just save me and my friends in that warehouse. If it wasn't for him, that charity—and ten times more—would now be gone.

"You asked me what I want," I said. "This is what I want. He deserves to rest with his family."

For a moment, Magistrate Aldebourne was silent. Then he nodded. "All right. Is there anything else?"

"As a matter of fact," I said, "there is."

Tom grinned when I returned to the shop. "Look who's back."

"You figured Aldebourne was going to arrest me?" I said.

"I wasn't talking about you." He moved out of the way so I could see Sally. She was smiling, cradling in her arms a plump salt-and-pepper-speckled pigeon.

My heart leaped. "Bridget!"

She cooed at me. I took her from Sally and stroked her feathers, nestling her into the crook of my broken arm. The sling made a perfect place for her to rest.

"She showed up while you were gone," Tom said. "She's

missing a few feathers, and I think she hurt her wing, but otherwise she seems all right."

An injured wing, just like me. I held her to my face, where she nuzzled into my cheek. "I was worried about you."

"Now that that's settled," Tom said, "will you tell us what's going on?"

I recounted what had happened at Guildhall. Tom was hugely pleased that I'd got the city to take care of Dr. Parrett. I was worried he might think me mad for turning down the thirty guineas, but Tom understood right away.

"Good," he said. Then he looked worried. "Though I suppose we're back to being poor."

"Not quite," I said. I reached into my pocket and held out my hand. Sitting in my palm were six silver coins.

"You got us six shillings?"

"Six shillings a *week*. Two for each of us, until the plague has run its course."

Tom looked thrilled. So did Sally, raccoon eyes beaming over her bandage. We wouldn't live like kings—far from it—but at least now we wouldn't starve.

"I guess it's fair that we get some charity after all," Tom said. "It's not like we don't need it."

"Actually, it's only *technically* charity," I said. "In reality, I'm going to have to work for this. Besides the shillings, Magistrate Aldebourne's agreed to pay for whatever ingredients I need for the shop. In return, I'm to make Venice treacle for the city's new plague doctors."

It wouldn't cure the plague, of course. As my master had long ago discovered—and as the city had learned at such high cost—nothing we knew of could do that. But it could at least bring some comfort to the afflicted, and maybe, in some small way, help a few to survive.

"That's great!" Tom said. Then he frowned. "But won't the Apothecaries' Guild punish you? You're not allowed to make remedies."

"I'm not allowed to *sell* remedies. But I'm not selling them, see? I'm giving them away for free. The shillings, remember, are 'charity.'"

Tom scratched his cheek. "I'm not sure the Guild is going to accept that."

I wasn't sure, either. Though it was only six shillings a week—the barest fraction of what an apothecary should be paid—after the previous business with the Cult, I wasn't exactly in the Guild's favor. They could easily make trouble for me if they wanted to.

Sitting in Aldebourne's office, I'd considered that. I'd decided I didn't care. The Guild had fled London when the city needed them the most. Master Benedict never would have done that.

And in truth, I'd also wanted a little something for myself. "By the way," I said to Tom, "there's no limit on the ingredients the city's agreed to buy for me. So I can go back to experimenting again."

Tom looked horrified. "Oh *no*," he said. I couldn't tell if he was joking.

Sally clapped her hands in delight. Her cracked cheekbone made it painful for her to talk, so she had to mumble her words, barely moving her lips. "So what happens now?"

"I get to work," I said. "The new plague doctors have already demanded twelve jars of Venice treacle each. And, for a while, at least"—I lifted my broken arm—"I'm going to need a little help."

"All right," she said, and she stepped toward the workshop.

I stopped her. "Just a minute. I got something for you, too."

Sally looked puzzled. "Didn't you already get me a weekly pair of shillings?"

"This is better. The magistrate's agreed to contact Lord Ashcombe for me. I've already sent a letter asking if the King's Warden has found you a position. If he hasn't, the magistrate's agreed to give you a job at Guildhall."

Sally looked from me to Tom, as if we were playing a joke on her. "Are you . . . He said . . . Truly?"

I nodded. "Until then, I'd really like you to stay. We can—oof!"

Sally threw herself at me, arms around my neck, face pressed into my chest. I wouldn't have minded, except for my arm. My arm minded a *lot*.

"Ow," I said.

She pulled back, hand pressed to her bandaged nose. "Sorry." She flushed. But her eyes were glowing.

"All right. Well, before you go anywhere, I have to put all the equipment in the workshop back where it belongs. Since I've only got one arm, do you two mind taking care of that?"

"Of course we will," Tom said.

I showed them what needed to be done, then left them to it. "Thanks," I said. "I'll just be upstairs for a while."

I took Bridget with me. I heard the clinking of glassware as my friends returned my workshop to the way it should be. Unable to sing with a broken cheek, Sally hummed a merry tune. It lifted me up the stairs. Then, as I reached the top, I heard something else.

I called down to them. "Tom!"

"Yes?" he called back.

"I don't think you should sing anymore," I said.

There was a pause. Then he said, "You're probably right."

I perched Bridget on the windowsill in Master Benedict's bedroom. Then I began the painstaking process of moving the books from the storage room at the back of the house to here. Finding places to put them was a challenge; half the stacks in the bedroom already brushed the ceiling.

A broken arm made the work go very slowly; I had to slide book stacks through the corridor with my leg. I ended up making more work for myself by bumping my rump into a teetering pile in my master's room and getting rained on by paper. Sighing, I began cleaning that up, too.

From behind me, I heard a set of limping footsteps.

"You should be resting that knee," I said, "and staying off the stairs."

"You should be resting that shoulder," Tom said, "and not lifting things at all."

True enough. My arm was killing me.

Tom looked around the room. "What are you doing up here?"

"Making some space," I said. "It's a little cramped, us all sleeping in the shop. I don't know how much longer Sally will be here, but I figured she could stay in the room at the back."

Tom knelt, favoring his bad knee, and helped gather the papers I'd scattered. He nodded toward my master's goose-down bed. "Are you going to sleep here, then?"

"No, that's Master Benedict's bed. I'm going to sleep in the shop, same as you."

"Oh."

"Oh, what?"

"I thought maybe you'd come upstairs to look for your master's treasure," Tom said.

I shrugged.

"Don't you want to find it?" Tom asked. "Now that you know it wasn't stolen."

"I don't know it wasn't stolen," I said.

"Melchior said he didn't take anything. Do you think he was lying?"

"No. He wouldn't have had any reason to." I handed Tom the papers I'd gathered. He began stacking them. "But the Cult of the Archangel ransacked my shop, too, remember."

Tom made a face.

"What?" I said.

"What's going on with you?" he said.

"Nothing. What do you mean?"

"Well . . . I realize we're no longer desperate for money, but now that you know Melchior didn't take Master Benedict's treasure, I thought you'd tear this place apart to find it. Especially since he left something special, just for you. Don't you care anymore?"

"Of course I do."

"So then what's the problem?"

My frustration burst out of me. "I don't know how to find it," I said unhappily. I pulled the message we'd discovered in the book of birds from beneath my apothecary sash and threw it on the bed. It lay there, taunting me.

The young bird finds its treasure when it settles in its place,
Hidden deep, beneath its feet; don't let it go to waste.

"I realized that Master Benedict meant me," I said miserably. "That I'm the bird. So I looked beneath my feet, in the crawl space below the shop. There was nothing there. The treasure's gone."

"Maybe you misunderstood the message," Tom said.

"Then I don't know what to do anymore. I can't figure it out."

"You will," Tom said. "You always do."

I gave a bitter laugh. "Right. I can't make *anything* work."

"What does that mean?"

"Nothing." I began restacking the books.

"Are you talking about the Smoke-Your-Home?" Tom said.

"Yes. No. I don't know."

Tom studied me for a moment. Then he put a hand on my arm. "Wait a minute," he said. "You're talking about Henry."

"I'm not."

Tom was flabbergasted. "You are. You're blaming yourself for what they did."

I threw the book I was holding across the room. "I *am*

to blame!" I said. "I should have *seen* it. Galen, here in the house. Melchior's code. Henry. Tom, I sent the letter *to* Henry."

"There was no way for you to know. And we stopped them."

I snorted. "We got lucky. If it hadn't been for Dr. Parrett, we'd all be dead. Even keeping this shop going is an accident." I sat on the floor. "Some legacy I am for Master Benedict."

Tom looked down at me for a moment. Then he said, "Can I tell you a secret?"

"What?"

"You're the smartest person I've ever met," he said. "But sometimes you're kind of dumb."

"What's that supposed to mean?"

"Remember how Master Benedict thought it was important for you to work out this message on your own?"

It was always on my mind. *Understanding your nature, you probably haven't found it yet. You won't find it until you realize something incredibly important. Recognize exactly what that is.* "I can't even get that right."

Tom sighed. "I understand why he said that now. *You*

stopped the Cult of the Archangel. *You* stopped Henry and Galen and Melchior. Yes, we helped you: me, Sally, Dr. Parrett. Of course we did. That's what friends do. But all of it started with you.

"You were the only one to see Melchior for what he was. And it was you who realized Galen was part of his scheme. If it wasn't for you, all that charity would have been stolen, and tens of thousands more people would have starved to death. Yet you still don't realize how well you've done." He threw his hands up. "I can't even get you to sleep in your bed."

What was he talking about? "My bed is downstairs, in the shop."

"No, Christopher," Tom said patiently. "It's here." He pointed at my master's bed. "This is *your* house now. Master Benedict *gave* it to you. He could have done anything he wanted with it: He could have left it to Hugh, or to Isaac, or to King Charles's socks if he wished. But he wanted *you* to have it."

Tom spread his arms, almost knocking over another stack of books. "This room is where you belong. I see that, even if you don't. And I know, as much as I know anything, that Master Benedict is up in heaven, proud of you. Because I am, too. So be proud of *yourself* for once." He gave my backside a little kick. "And sleep in your own blasted bed."

I looked out of the window, where Bridget was perched, at the sunlight streaming through.

Is that true, Master?

I saw an image of him in my mind. He was smiling.

You are the bird, he said.

And finally, finally, finally, I understood.

The young bird finds its treasure when it settles in its place,
Hidden deep, beneath its feet; don't let it go to waste.

"What?" Tom said.

"My place," I said. "My place is *here*."

"That's what *I* said."

Hidden deep, beneath its feet.

I stood. I stepped over to the bed, pulled back the sheets. I looked at the mattress, pressed on it, felt its softness.

I grabbed one side of the mattress. "Help me flip this over."

With his swollen knee and my aching shoulder, we

made a hapless pair, but we eventually managed to flop the mattress on its front. I stared at the back of it, at the seams sewn into the canvas. Near the bottom—below where my feet would rest, if I was asleep—one stitch stood out. I wouldn't have noticed it, if I hadn't been looking; it was only slightly less worn than the others.

I held out my hand. Tom pulled his knife from his belt and gave it to me. Carefully, I sliced though the thread and pulled the mattress open. Soft white down spilled out. I reached in, felt around, my arm sliding in deep. My fingers brushed leather.

I came out with a large, heavy pouch. It was knotted shut with woolen strings. I untied it, opened it. I stared.

"What is it?" Tom said.

I handed him the pouch. He looked inside. For a moment, he just stared, like I had. Then he tipped the pouch over on the mattress.

A stream of coins fell out. They lay there, glinting in the sunlight.

Guineas. Gold guineas. We counted them. It took a long time.

There were seventy-two of them. Each guinea was a pound and a shilling. On my bed—*my bed,* I thought—was Master

Benedict's treasure. A little more than seventy-five pounds.

Tom tapped my arm. I looked over at him. He pointed back at the mattress.

When I'd removed the pouch, I'd pulled something else with it. Peeking out of the goose down was the corner of a folded sheaf of paper.

I picked it up. There were four pages here. Three were journal entries, written by my master. They'd been torn from their books, with specific passages specially marked. The first was dated May 12, 1662.

I made an unforgivable error today. When I rushed to Lord Bentley's home, I realized I had forgotten to make more Soothing Burn Cream. Bentley was furious, and rightly so. My carelessness has cost me a valued customer.

Hugh tells me it is no less than I deserve. For two years, he has been pressing me to get a new apprentice. With my private experiments, and the past trouble with Peter, I have been reluctant to do so. Finding someone with the necessary aptitude for the job is hard enough. Because of my own work, I must also choose someone who, when they are older, can be trusted.

And when faced with an unknown boy, how can one know what he will become? Hugh insists that Peter's descent into darkness was not my fault. But the boy was mine to shape, and I failed him. One more failure, of so many in this life.

Nonetheless, it has become clear that, on the matter of taking an apprentice, Hugh is correct. I feel my advancing age all too keenly. I can no longer continue my private experiments and run this shop on my own. There will be a testing at Apothecaries' Hall in June. I will go, though I do not hold out much hope for a selection.

The second page's entry had a date I knew well: June 15, 1662. It was the day that changed my life forever.

Today I surprised myself. I have come home with a new apprentice after all. His name is Christopher Rowe, an orphan by way of Cripplegate.

I am not entirely certain why I chose him. Partly, I suppose, it was because I found his examination impressive. Though it was clear the boy was terrified—Oswyn grilled him mercilessly, no doubt trying to prove to the Guild that this orphan could grow to best them all; he has always had a soft spot for those of poor upbringing like himself—Christopher's answers showed intelligence, curiosity, and a distinct sense of wit.

Still, that was not the prime reason why I selected him as my apprentice. Part of it was sympathy; despite his strong performance, no other apothecary seemed inclined to take an orphan, and I didn't want to see the lad crushed. But I really took him because I believed I saw something else.

I have heard stories of life in Cripplegate. Christopher's time there must have been terrible. Yet as he stood in the grandeur of the Great Hall, surrounded by all those powerful men, the boy seemed untainted by that cruelty. He was not cowed and defensive, broken of will; nor shrewd and calculating, seeking advantage; nor defiant in opposition, burning with anger. More than anything, he struck me as a resilient, and ultimately, kindhearted spirit—and one, I hope, that can be trusted.

Perhaps I am only projecting my own wishes onto him. But when we returned home today, I gave the boy a pair of lessons, and his innate understanding of the responsibility of our profession surprised me. It gives me hope that I have chosen well.

Time will tell. In the meantime, I did come back with an apprentice, so Hugh has won his wager. I owe him a shilling.

The third entry was dated nearly two years later: May 29, 1664. Oak Apple Day; a holiday, the king's birthday. And mine. It was the day I'd turned thirteen.

I hear the boys playing down in the workshop. I am trying not to listen too hard, for I am certain I just heard the word "trebuchet," God help us all.

The sound of their play leaves me in a reflective mood. I had wondered for years if I had not made an error in how I have lived my life. I have been so consumed with the discovery of nature's secrets that I chose never to burden myself with a family—nor them with me, for I did not think it fair to either wife or child to inflict upon them an absent husband and father like my own. And yet, as I grew older, I found myself filled with regret that I had no son or daughter with whom I might share the wonders of life.

No longer do I feel that emptiness. I did not understand, that day I took Christopher in, how greatly he would bless my home. For this gift, O Lord, I am deeply grateful.

I just heard the word "flaming." I am going downstairs.

The fourth page was no journal entry. It was just a few lines, inked with care on the paper. My master's final message to me.

Now you understand.

You were born Christopher Rowe. But you became Christopher Blackthorn.

I am with you always.

Benedict

Tom put a hand on my shoulder. He squeezed it, gently, for a moment. Then he left, following Sally's humming down the creaking stairs. I just stood there, the sun on my face, and held my master's message to my chest.

A FEW MATTERS OF HISTORICAL NOTE

Of all possible disasters, the one feared most by the people of Christopher's time was an epidemic of plague. Outbreaks terrified them not only because they were so deadly—the Great Plague of London would ultimately kill one in five of that city's residents: one hundred thousand victims in total—but because no one had any idea what caused them. It wouldn't be until 1676 that Antonie van Leeuwenhoek first spotted tiny "animalcules"—bacteria—in his brand-new microscope, and then another two hundred years afterward before people understood infections were caused by germs. (Plus a further seventy years to create penicillin, the first chemical antibiotic.)

To Christopher and his contemporaries, then, plagues were—quite literally—otherworldly. Various theories of disease were put forth to explain them, including the wrath of angels, the machinations of devils, and even the Earth's own terrestrial flatulence! ("The pestilence derives its natural origin from a Crisis of the Earth whereby it purges itself by expiring those Arsenical Fumes that have been retained so long in her bowels . . ."[1]) Smells, in particular, were believed to transmit the disease, hence Christopher's ill-conceived Smoke-Your-Home (don't try this, please) and the other odd preventatives he encounters in this adventure. The "cures" of the time were, as Master Benedict noted, all worthless, and in some cases, truly appalling.[2]

Plague held such a place in people's minds that it was often referred to simply as "The Sicknesse." We have detailed records of this particular outbreak, including one found in Samuel Pepys's famous diary. The best, however,

---

1. R. Saunders, *The English Apollo*, 1666; as quoted in L. Picard, *Restoration London*.

2. *Loimographia*, written by William Boghurst in 1665, gives a long list of apothecary cures and the recipes used to prepare them. I warn you: do not read that book too closely if you have a weak stomach. Or if you love puppies. I'm not kidding.

is *A Journal of the Plague Year*, written by Daniel Defoe (who also authored *Robinson Crusoe*). Defoe, who was five years old at the time of the Great Plague, wrote a harrowing account of life during that epidemic; readers interested further in the sorrow, hardship, and extraordinary courage of Christopher's contemporaries will find a rich and lively account in those (still eminently readable) pages.

And lest you think we are done with The Sicknesse, I will point out there has been an ongoing outbreak of plague in Madagascar since 2014. So stock up on that Venice treacle.

Two further notes: First, as in *The Blackthorn Key*, all places and names are given according to modern spelling. Second, I have once again retained the (modern) Gregorian calendar for all dates, instead of the Julian calendar in use in England at the time. This accounts for the discrepancy between the dates of the events as presented and those of the (actual!) Bills of Mortality printed in this book.

Oh, and one more thing: 3→.

ACKNOWLEDGMENTS

They say your second book is harder to write than your first. They are correct. Fortunately, I'm lucky to be surrounded by a lot of amazing folks who help guide my way. I'd like to say thank you to the following:

To Liesa Abrams, Ben Horslen, Emma Sector, Dan Lazar, and Suri Rosen, all of whom offered insights from beginning to end that made this story immeasurably better.

To Mara Anastas, Mary Marotta, Jon Anderson, Katherine Devendorf, Karin Paprocki, Julie Doebler, Jodie Hockensmith, Christina Pecorale, Lucille Rettino, Carolyn Swerdloff, Michelle Leo, Greg Stadnyk, Hilary Zarycky,

Laura Lyn DiSiena, Victor Iannone, Gary Urda, Michael Selleck, and Stephanie Voros at Aladdin.

To Francesca Dow, Amanda Punter, Wendy Shakespeare, Jacqui McDonough, Hannah Maloco, Sophia Rubie, and all at Puffin UK.

To Kevin Hanson, David Millar, Nancy Purcell, Felicia Quon, Adria Iwasutiak, Shara Alexa, Andrea Seto, and Rita Silva at Simon & Schuster Canada.

To Cecilia de la Campa, Angharad Kowal, Torie Doherty-Munro, and James Munro at Writers House.

To all the publishers around the world who have embraced the Blackthorn Key series.

To Julia Bruce, for her sleuthing prowess.

To Terry Bailey, and to Alma, for their assistance with Latin translation. Any errors remaining are my own.

And finally, once again, to you, dear reader: Thank you for joining Christopher on this adventure. You're the best friend a young apothecary could have.

READ ON FOR A GLIMPSE AT
CHRISTOPHER'S NEXT
HEART-POUNDING ADVENTURE IN
THE BLACKTHORN KEY, BOOK 3:

THE ASSASSIN'S CURSE

MONDAY, NOVEMBER 2, 1665

Matins

DO YOU BELIEVE IN FATE?

Once, after I'd become Master Benedict's apprentice, I'd brought the topic up. He'd stirred his soup, his spoon clunking against his bowl. "An interesting question. Why do you ask?"

"Well," I said, "the astronomy book you gave me says the universe is like a clock. That everything proceeds according to a grand design."

"It does."

"Yet we have free will, don't we? I mean, we're responsible for the things we do."

"Absolutely," he said.

"But . . . how can both of these be true?" I said. "If we have free will, how can there be a grand design? Couldn't you do something to change the universe's plan? And if the universe *is* just a giant clock, and we're only gears playing our part, then how can we be blamed for what we do? Isn't that just who we were born to be?"

My master regarded me sternly. "Is this about you breaking the Baileys' window?"

"Er . . . no." Though Tom and I wouldn't be playing Castle Siege at his house again anytime soon.

"Then wait here."

He went upstairs, where I heard him rooting through the library in the spare room. When he returned, he was carrying a stack of books so tall he had to peek his head around it to see where he was going. He dropped them on the table. I scrambled to stop the tower from spilling into my soup.

"Start with these," my master said. "Return when you're done."

With my regular duties, it took me several days to read them all. When I finally finished, I found him in the workshop, experimenting with a new recipe to cure gout.

"Well?" he said. "What do you think? Does fate rule, or free will?"

I scratched my head, embarrassed. "I have no idea."

He sighed. "Nor do I. I was rather hoping you'd find the answer."

Which is all to say that this is an incredibly difficult question. So as Tom and I bumped along in the carriage on the muddy road to Oxford, I tried to explain to him how history's greatest thinkers had pondered this exact query. How complicated the notion of blame really was.

To Tom, however, the answer was simple: This was all *my* fault.

CHAPTER
1

"THIS IS ALL YOUR FAULT," TOM SAID.

He folded his arms and turned away, gazing unhappily through the carriage window. Beyond the curtain, the lights of distant farmhouses dotted the darkness of the countryside.

"But I haven't *done* anything," I said.

"You think we're here because of me?"

"No, I—"

"*I'm* not the one setting fire to pear trees," Tom said.

"That was an accident."

"*I'm* not the one saying, 'Hey, let's blow up these pumpkins in the street.'"

"That was an experiment," I protested. "And it was *one* pumpkin. The rest were squash. What does that have to do with anything?"

"Maybe you destroyed an important pumpkin."

"How can a pumpkin be important?"

"Maybe it was a prize-winning pumpkin," Tom said. "Maybe it was England's pumpkin, to be entered into the International Pumpkin Fair. In Scotland."

"Now you're just stringing random words together."

"Oh? Then explain this." He grabbed the . . . invitation, I suppose you'd call it, that had fallen to the floor of the carriage and thrust it at me. "Explain it!"

That was the problem. I *couldn't* explain it. This whole business had come as a surprise.

Yesterday morning, Tom and I had been eating lunch in my apothecary shop when a heavy fist had hammered on the door. I'd opened it to find myself face-to-face with one of the King's Men, the royal coat of arms emblazoned on his tabard. Behind him was a carriage, a second soldier waiting beside it in the street.

"You Christopher Rowe?" the King's Man said. When I nodded, he handed me a letter. I stared at it, uncomprehending. When I read it, I understood even less.

Christopher:

Get Thomas Bailey and get in the carriage.

Ashcombe

Baron Richard Ashcombe, the King's Warden, was the Lord Protector of His Majesty, Charles II. I looked warily at the soldier. "Are we in trouble?"

He shrugged. "I was just ordered to bring you to Oxford."

Oxford? That's where the king's Court was staying. "Are we under arrest?"

The man tapped his foot impatiently. "Not yet."

And that was how Tom and I ended up bumping our way through the countryside in the back of this carriage. After a night under guard in an inn, Tom was convinced we were headed for doom.

"We're going to end up in the dungeon," he moaned.

"We're not going to end up in the dungeon," I said, though I was not entirely certain of that.

"Do you know what happens in a dungeon? There's no food. They *starve* you."

"We're not even in irons."

Tom's lower lip trembled. "All you get is a single piece

of bread, once a night. And not the good bread, either, with poppy seeds and maybe a bit of cinnamon. No. It's hard bread. Hard bread for a hard life."

Trust the baker's son to critique the dungeon's bread. Still, I wished he'd stop. The more he spoke, the more the prospect of wasting away behind bars loomed large in my mind. I tried to push his worry aside and think of why Lord Ashcombe would call for us.

I'd only had contact with the King's Warden twice since we'd stopped the plot against the city at the height of the plague. The first was after Magistrate Aldebourne had told Lord Ashcombe what had happened. He'd written to me separately, asking for my account. The second was when he'd found a job for Sally, as promised.

His note, characteristically brief, said he'd found her a position as chambermaid to the Lady Pemberton, and a horse would come to collect her. As the baroness was with the Court, which had fled London when the plague came, Sally had said a bittersweet goodbye to us back in September. Since she'd gone, I'd written her letters every week, but I hadn't heard back. That wasn't unexpected—her job wouldn't give her enough money to pay for post—but Lord

Ashcombe's summons made me wonder if she was in some kind of trouble.

The carriage slowed. Tom and I watched from the window as we turned north, off the road to Oxford. It appeared the city wouldn't be our destination after all. We skirted the town, the carriage lumbering through deep ruts in the mud, until our driver pulled us onto the grounds of a private estate.

Oaks lined the pathway, autumn-copper leaves stained rusty orange by the torches staked between them. Our horses, their breath puffing wispy clouds in the November chill, dragged us up the road to the mansion atop the slope. Lamps glowed through the windows, adding their light to the haze in the frosty air.

This place was no prison. And, whatever reason we were here, we wouldn't be alone. Dozens of other carriages lined the lawn, flattening the grass under their mud-caked wheels, while their drivers lounged about, waiting.

Our own transport pulled to a stop in front of the mansion, where a man in livery ushered us from the coach. The King's Men nudged us up the stairs, through a set of grand double doors. A coat of arms was carved into the stone above the entrance: crossed halberds over a shield emblazoned with antlers.

Wherever we were, this place was astounding. The entrance hall alone was as big as my entire house. A marble staircase curved upward from the center of the foyer to the upper floors. A pair of servants waited there, their livery matching the staff standing by the half dozen exits to the different wings of the estate. From somewhere beyond, I heard the sounds of a gathering and the faint strains of music.

"You're late."

Lord Ashcombe strode into the entryway, dressed in fine black silks. He wore a patch over his left eye and a glove on his three-fingered right hand—wounds from a battle with the men who'd murdered my master in May. There was no sword at his side, but his pearl-handled pistol was jammed into his belt.

"Sorry, General," the King's Man accompanying us said. "The rain's ruined the roads."

Lord Ashcombe grunted and looked us over. "We'll need to get you ready." He motioned to the servants on the stairs.

"My lord?" I glanced at Tom, who, by this point, was close to fainting. "Are we in trouble?"

Lord Ashcombe raised an eyebrow. "Should you be?"

"Uh . . . no?"

"Then I suppose it'll depend on how this evening goes."

"This evening?"

"Yes," Lord Ashcombe said. "The king wants to speak with you."

. . .

Wherever Christopher Rowe goes, adventure—and murder—follows. Even a chance to meet King Charles ends in a brush with an assassin.

All that's recovered from the killer is a coded message with an ominous sign-off: More attempts are coming. So when Christopher's code-breaking discovers the attack's true target, he and his friends are ordered to Paris to investigate a centuries-old curse on the French throne. And when they learn an ancient treasure is promised to any assassin who succeeds, they realize the entire royal family is at stake—as well as their own lives.

In the third heart-pounding installment of the award-winning Blackthorn Key series, Christopher, Tom, and Sally face new codes, puzzles, and traps as they race to find the hidden treasure before someone else is murdered.

Looking for another great book?
Find it
IN THE MIDDLE.

Fun, fantastic books for kids
in the in-be**TWEEN** age.

IntheMiddleBooks.com

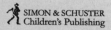